THREE

YOU SAY WHICH WAY

ADVENTURES

Between The Stars
Danger on Dolphin Island
Secrets of Glass Mountain

by
DM Potter & Blair Polly

Published by:
The Fairytale Factory Ltd.
Wellington, New Zealand.

ISBN-13: 978-1519771377
ISBN-10: 1519771371

How This Book Works

These stories depends on YOU.

YOU say which way the story goes.

What will YOU do?

At the end of each chapter, you get to make a decision. Turn to the page that matches your choice. **P62** means turn to page 62.

There are many paths to try. You can read them all over time. Right now, it's time to start the story. Good luck.

Oh ... and watch out for shape shifting plants, smugglers and those smelly morph rats!

Which book would you like to read first?

BETWEEN THE STARS

In the spaceship

You are in a sleep tank on the space ship *Victoria*. Your dreaming cap teaches you as you float.

You first put on a dreaming cap when you did the space sleep test. Although you thought it looked like you had an octopus on your head, you didn't joke about it. Nobody did. Everyone wanted to pass the test and go to the stars. Passing meant a chance to get out of overcrowded Londinium. If you didn't pass you'd likely be sent to a prison factory in Northern Europa. Nobody wanted to go there, even though Britannica hasn't been a good place lately, Europa was said to be worse.

When the judge sentenced you to transportation for stealing that food, you sighed inside with relief. You knew transportation was the chance of a better life on a faraway planet, but only if you passed the sleep test.

You lined up with other hopefuls and waded into a pool of warm sleep jelly. They were all young like you and they all looked determined.

"Stay calm," the robot instructed. "Breathe in slowly through your mouthpiece and relax."

Nearby, a young woman struggled from the pool. She pulled out her breathing plug and gasped for breath.

"Take her back," said a guard. You knew what that meant – back to prison and then the factories. An older convict sneered at the poor girl, the cruel look on his face magnified by a scar running down one cheek.

In your short time in prison, you had learned there were people who would have been criminals no matter what life they'd been born to. Something told you that he was one of them.

You put him out of your mind and concentrated on doing what the robot said. You thought of the warm porridge you'd had every morning in the orphanage growing up. The sleeping jelly didn't seem so strange then. When your head was submerged you breathed in slowly.

As the jelly filled your lungs you fought against thoughts of drowning. You'd listened at the demonstration and knew it was oxygenated. "This must be what it's like to be a fish," you thought as you moved forward through the thick fluid, "I only have to walk through to the other side."

Closing your eyes, you moved forward through the thick warm jelly. "Relax," you told yourself. "You can do this."

You opened your eyes just in time to see the scar-faced youth about to knock your breather off. Thankfully the jelly slowed his punch and you ducked out of the way just in time. Then a moment later, you were on the other side being handed a towel.

"This one's a yes," intoned a man in a white coat. He slapped a bracelet on your wrist and sent you down a corridor away from your old life. As you exited, you just had time to hear the fate of the scar-faced youth. "He'll do. Take him to the special room."

Days of training followed. You often joined other groups of third class passengers but you didn't see Scar-Face among them. You passed all the tests and then one day, you got into a sleep tank beside hundreds of others. Your dreaming cap would teach you everything you'd need to know in your new life.

You were asleep when the *Victoria* was launched into space. You slept as the *Victoria* lost sight of the Earth and then its star, the sun.

And here you are, years later, floating in sleep fluid and learning with your dreaming cap. Or you were. Because now you hear music. Oxygen hisses into your sleeping chamber and the fluid you have been immersed in starts to drain away. Next time you surface, you'll breathe real air, something that your lungs haven't done in a long time.

"Sleeper one two seven six do you accept this mission? Sleeper, please engage if you wish to awaken for this mission. Sleeper, there are other suitable travelers for this mission. Do you choose to wake?"

Passengers can sleep the entire journey if they want. They can arrive at the new planet without getting any older. First class passengers will own land and riches when they arrive but you are third class, you have nothing. Groggily, you listen to the voice. If you choose to take on a mission you can earn credit for the new planet – even freedom – but you could also arrive on the new planet too old to ever use your freedom.

"Sleeper, do you accept the mission?"

It is time to make your first decision.

Do you want to wake up and undertake a mission? **P4**

Or

Do you wait for another mission or to land on the new planet? **P84**

Wake up and undertake a mission.

Light filters into your sleeping tank from above, changing the fluid around you into a blurry rainbow. The breathing tube sends you chemicals to bring you fully awake.

You wonder how long you've slept and what you've been learning. Sleepers need new information to keep their brains alive. In your sleep you might have learned about medicine, robotics, farming, steam engineering, aviation or anything else the makers of the *Victoria* need third class passengers to know.

A pang of homesickness hits you, but you remind yourself how lucky you were to get a place on the *Victoria* instead of going to the prison factories. There was nothing for you on Earth.

The last phase of waking begins. Soon you will be using your own lungs and walking the halls of the spaceship. There is enough light now to see the shapes of other tanks around you with their sleepers inside. The ship must not have landed if they are only waking you.

"Sleeper, prepare to exit your chamber."

As the last of the fluid drains out of the tank, you feel air against your skin and you wonder what space will be like. You hope the electrodes attached to your body have been doing their job stimulating your muscles. If they have, you'll be strong and fit. If not, you'll move like some sort of space slug, with your muscles wasted away from lack of exercise.

Something stirs outside. It's a robot shaped like a person.

The hatch of your sleep tank opens with a hiss. There is almost no gravity and small globules of the last of the sleep jelly float up ahead of you. A small bird-shaped robot flies about collecting the excess fluid through its long beak. The hummingbot's wings are a blur as it sucks up each bubble-like blob. Large green eyes scan about for the next one.

You hold onto a ladder on the side of the tank and pull yourself up. Being almost weightless makes it easy.

"May I assist you?" purrs the helpful voice of the robot as it waits nearby. It is a butler robot. Rich people had them in their houses on Earth. You've read in history books that some people used to be butlers but that robots replaced them. They don't need to sleep or rest and they don't steal your valuables. They also don't need to be paid.

The butler hands you a thick toweling tunic. From your training you know you need to get cleaned up and find some proper clothes. Your legs are a little wobbly but you don't really need them yet. You push off in low gravity and float towards the exit. Your body rises and you look across a warehouse of hundreds of other sleepers all looking like specimens in a museum.

You drift past rows and rows of people frozen at about the age of fourteen. Some have their eyes open but they don't see you. They are deep in space sleep. Some are moving, with electrodes stimulating them to do exercises that keep their bodies healthy. Some seem to be working at invisible tasks. All are learning. Each mind is slowly becoming an encyclopedia of special information.

While you enjoy being weightless and the sense of flying, the butler wheels along below you on a magnetic strip set into the floor. When you reach the end of the room you pass your palm over a door sensor and head into a ready room.

This room has artificial gravity. After such a long period of weightlessness, your limbs feel heavy and you move slowly. You take a quick shower to remove the oily covering all sleepers are coated in to preserve their skin. Then, when you're clean, you put on the uniform that the butler has laid out for you.

You look at your reflection in the mirror. You still *look* young but you are now much, much older in Earth years, and much wiser because of all the learning you've done. Space-sleep preserves youth. Many years ago rich people would pay to be kept in sleep chambers in the hopes that their medical problems could be solved while they slept. Wealthy criminals sometimes paid to sleep away their sentences. Now it's the way to travel between the stars. One-way time travel, some people call it.

Again, you wonder why you've been woken. In theory, the journey to a new planet can be accomplished without waking anyone, the robots take care of most things. But there are times when travelers like you can be woken. If other life forms are detected, the robots will wake people to assess the situation. You could also be called on if the ship experiences some mechanical failure. The ship needs to consult with its passengers if a course change is required. You doubt you'd be woken for that sort of thing; you aren't anyone important enough to make that sort of decision.

"Hey! Are you in there? Sleeper one two seven six? Or whatever your number was."

The voice comes from a little intercom beside the next door and doesn't sound like a robot. It sounds like a real person, just like you.

You press the connecting button and identify yourself to whoever is on the other side: "Traveler one two seven six reporting for duty."

You sound very formal compared to the speaker, but this is what you're supposed to say. It seems a good idea to follow the rules.

"That's great one-two. My name is Trig. If you're feeling like I did when I woke up you'll be itching to know why you're awake. I've brought a 'sporter down to meet you. We can ride to the briefing."

The gravity in this room feels like treacle to move through – you know it's a reaction from the sleep chamber. You're grateful there's a transporter out there for you. You'll have to build up your strength before you can walk far on your own.

You glance in the mirror one last time before you leave the room. You have no personal items, just your memories of Earth and a future ahead of you. The face in the mirror is the same one that entered the space ship at the beginning of the voyage. You smooth down your uniform and rub your fingers through your close-cropped hair.

You feel nervous, but you're excited too – you're about to meet another human being for the first time on this journey. Together you'll share an adventure that the descendants of all the travelers on board might recount one day. With thoughts of glory on your mind, you turn the big brass wheel and open the air lock between the two rooms. The seal opens with a hiss and you step through the portal to find yourself face to face with your new ship mate.

Trig has red hair and freckles. He looks the sort of boy who, when back on Earth, would have darted between carriages carrying messages about town for a few coins. The sort who could have helped out by holding a horse's reins or, just as easily, picking pockets. That's probably how he ended up on the *Victoria*, you think.

He wears a space uniform just like your own but he seems to have gotten it rather grubby and to have made a few modifications – whether for comfort or artistry you can't be sure. Trig isn't quite what you expected but then, you remind yourself, your previous lives probably weren't all that different. You come from an orphanage, you ended up in trouble and you don't look very old either. You've been sleeping and learning just as he has.

Trig leaps astride the transporter and motions for you to join him. It's an electrified bicycle. It can be pedaled as you recall from your training, or it can draw from a reserve of stored power when needed.

Trig slaps the seat behind him and smiles. "Jump on!"

Trig pedals the 'sporter for a few yards and then flicks a switch. The bike leaps forward as the battery power kicks in.

You hold on tight, looking around the ship as the two of you zip along. The hallways are so wide that three horses could walk through them side by side. You see airlocks at intervals along the walls. Most have signs on them. They lead to storage warehouses, more sleepers, workshops and other facilities. The ship is carrying nearly one thousand men and women as well as animals. Everything needed to start a new colony is stowed on board and the ship itself is designed to be an initial shelter for settlers.

As Trig pulls up to a doorway, you see a butler wheeling along a magnetized strip on the floor. In the absence of gravity these strips keep the robots on track. Above your head a small flock of hummingbots fly by. They don't need the magnetic paths as their tiny clockwork motors can fly in any direction. They can even manage short excursions outside the ship.

"Where are we headed?" you ask, as Trig gets the 'sport moving even faster down a more ornate hall.

"To see the Captain." he says over his shoulder.

He doesn't need to yell, the ship is quiet and the 'sport whirrs along almost silently. The next corridor you enter seems more like something from a grand house than a spaceship. There are gleaming brass fittings around the doorways and inlaid designs on the walls and floors. Holographic frames display portraits of different people dressed in fine clothes. There are also scenic pictures of Earth – castles in Britannica, the Queen's palace in Londinium, mountains, lakes and other places you don't recognize. You wonder if the pictures are active when everyone is asleep or if they were just switched on for you and Trig.

The ship's port holes are normally closed while traveling at warp speed and its hull protected by layers of polymer metals shaped like feathers to withstand heat and cold.

Feathers! Wait, that's something *new* you've learned while sleeping. In your mind's eye you see pictures of a giant bird-like space ship covered in thousands of metallic feathers made from various metals that together, make a perfect shield against heat and cold.

Your thoughts are interrupted as the 'sporter pulls up to an important looking door. A brass sign reads 'BRIDGE'. The door has a carved border depicting the leaves of different trees. You recognize oak leaves but you aren't sure about the rest. You can't have learned any botany while you slept.

As Trig reaches towards the button he has a serious look on his face. "The Captain might not be what you're expecting

"What do you mean?" you say.

"You'll see."

A mental picture of what you think a Captain would be like flashes into your mind. He might be a tall man with a beard, perhaps someone from the military.

Trig busies himself turning the mechanism for the door. It swings open and you step through into the large operations room. Wide desks inset with navigation and monitoring equipment and several robots hum about the room. A special portal on the far wall displays a view of space outside. You can see stars and the never ending night. A young woman's voice interrupts your thoughts.

"I trust you woke well."

You turn to see a girl of about 15 or 16 standing in the centre of the room. She has long black braided hair arranged in a coil on top of her head. It is a simpler style than aristocrats wear on Earth, yet her hair tells you she is high born. You can't quite think why she is awake and not sleeping with the rest of the aristocracy. Then you realize what Trig was trying to tell you. This girl *is* the Captain.

"Ca—Captain, Sir. Reporting for du—duty," you stammer.

The Captain laughs at your nervousness and you feel yourself blushing. She crosses the room and extends her hand, smiling,

"Well, you took the idea of a female captain better than your crewmate there. My name is Helena Gillian Wells, and I've been sleeping for one hundred and seventy years, as have you. It seems the robots have picked me to lead this mission. Nobody programmed them to make a distinction about gender. It is the start of a brave new sort of world, after all. So here we are. A small crew gathered to undertake a big mission."

Captain Wells walks into the middle of the room and gives you and Trig a run-down of the problem you were awakened to solve.

"The magnetic field surrounding the ship has been compromised. We need to find out what is wrong and fix it."

"Why do we need a magnetic field?" asks Trig. He looks from you to the Captain. You find yourself answering him:

"Space is full of harmful radiation, Trig. On Earth, the planet's magnetic field protects it. But here on the ship we have to generate our own magnetic field to keep everyone inside safe."

As you talk about magnetic fields and spaceship design you realize this must be something you've learned while sleeping. It's exciting to find out you know about how the ship works. You hope you'll know enough to fix whatever has gone wrong. This is a serious problem.

It's also an urgent problem. You need more information quickly so you can decide what to do. You walk over to the instruments that will give you radiation readings and make a scan of the dials.

"How safe are we now?" asks the Captain.

"The sleepers are fine," you say. "The sleep chambers are deep inside the ship. It's a bit like being underground. The hydroponic garden systems might be at risk though. I need to take some readings."

You walk over to the engine monitor and sit down to scan the information it's giving you. The engines are behaving normally but they are using more power than usual. The ship's protective magnetic field is weaker than it should be. Something is interfering with it.

"Is there a way we can get a view of the ship from the outside?" you ask.

"We can send out some hummers to scan," replies the Captain, "but we'll need to slow right down."

"I was going to recommend we do that anyway," Trig says, "the amount of power we're using isn't sustainable."

The Captain glares at him.

"When were you going to tell me that?"

Trig looks a little embarrassed.

"I wanted another techie to talk with before I said anything, I didn't want to upset you."

"Let's get something straight," Captain Wells says with a seriousness that shows she really is older than she looks, "I'm your Captain and I need to know *anything* regarding the optimal running of this ship. Is that understood?"

You and Trig start swapping notes. While you're talking, you keep discovering that you know more and more. Trig is having the same experience. It's exciting for both of you.

The Captain heads to a big control panel and starts working too. She confidently manipulates dials that give her readings about the different power sources on the ship. You wonder if she'll also be able to access messages sent from Earth while you've been travelling.

Trig slows the ship down and sends an order for five hummers to assemble at an exit port ready to go and look outside. One of the hummers begins to act as your eyes. It transmits images of the robot crew to you on a section of the big screen in the Bridge. You also call up a spider-bot. If something needs fixing, the spider-bot will do the job. It can carry a large number of tools, has strength and agility, and its many arms enable it to hold on to the ship at the same time as carrying out repairs. The spider-bot is about the size of a small dog with a round central 'body' that holds tools. Its many arms allow you to perform remote mechanical work and its many eyes let you see all around it.

You and Trig go through a checklist of all the tools the spider-bot should carry. Trig calculates the flight path for each bird. Navigation is his specialty.

"Would you like me to check your calculations?" Captain Wells asks. Without waiting for Trig's reply she uploads the hummer's instructions to her display and looks them over. Trig bristles a bit. You suspect he doesn't like the idea of a high-born girl looking over his work.

You think things are a bit different now. Back on Earth, an aristocratic girl's job is to look good, make a good marriage, and then organize social events and run her grand house. On the new planet there won't be a lot of entertaining, and the marriage market might be a lot simpler. Captain Wells, and women like her, are going to face big changes on the new planet.

Judging by Trig's first reactions to having a girl in charge, there might be some resistance to changing some of the old ways.

Meanwhile the Captain has been surveying the plans. "How about you arc the flights out *here* and *here*," she says. "Your trajectories are well plotted but I think we'd do well to scan as much of the surrounding sector as we can. This is a part of space we don't know much about."

Trig nods. "You're absolutely right Captain. I was so focused on checking the externals of the ship I didn't think about looking over our shoulder."

You think about how you can improve the plan too. "I can place some scanners on top of the spider-bot," you say. "If there's anything we want to take a better look at, we can get the bot to move into position. It won't run out of fuel like the hummers."

"Great idea," says Trig.

The two of you head down to get the bots ready. You take your own transporter this time. You'll need extra room to collect the things you'll need. As you ride down a service corridor you feel a rush of exhilaration. On Earth your life was hard work and pretty dull. Now you are hurtling down a corridor to set up robots to go outside into a part of space nobody has explored before.

Waking up between the stars has risks. On this mission there's the threat of radiation poisoning for a start, but you'd rather be awake and dealing with it than sleeping through in ignorance. First class passengers don't want to get old. Space traveling takes a long time and they want to be able to get to a new planet and live there for a long time.

You round a corner and come to a long straight section of corridor. "Race?" asks Trig with a glint in his eye.

It is time to make a decision.

Do you want to race around the Victoria on the transporters? **P13**
Or
Get on with the mission? **P40**

'Sporter vs 'sporter – racing in space

"Let's do it," you say.

You're sure you won't jeopardize the mission with a bit of fun. The magnetic field is still holding up and you've slowed the ship down. What could go wrong?

The two of you work out a course that will take you the long way around to the equipment rooms to the exit port. You jump on your transporters and countdown:

"Five, four, three, two, one, go!"

You squeeze the transporter's throttle and accelerate smoothly. The corridor becomes a blur. You stare ahead, keeping the machine on a slight lean as you race down the giant circular path.

When a sharper corner comes up, Trig manages to pull ahead as you slow down, fearing you'll lose balance, but the magnetic strips keep you firmly glued to the floor. Watching Trig lean into the next corner, you do the same, opening up the transporter a little more.

As you come to a long straight, you draw level with him. You look at each other and grin wildly. Other corridors and rooms flash by.

When both transporters suddenly lose power and come to a halt, you realize you've used up all the stored energy and will have to pedal the rest of the way. Then the hummingbots catch up. You're sure they could have flown faster but they have been content to plod along. They are programmed not to waste power.

"How far have we come?" you ask some time later. It feels like you've been pedaling for an hour. Sweat drips off your forehead, despite the cool temperature inside the spaceship.

Trig groans, looking at the corridor names. Each is named for a different explorer.

"We've passed Columbus, Cook and Drake. That looks like Livingstone coming up. I think we're more than half way. The equipment room is in Magellan."

"It would have been easier if whoever designed this ship had given the corridors numbers," you grumble as you pump the transporter's pedals. "This is pretty good exercise though." You feel your body working strongly. You haven't lost your strength while you slept. In fact you might be stronger than when the *Victoria* took off.

As you pass different corridors you have time to look at pictures of different explorers. A small screen on your bike tells you about each one as you pass, and what lies behind some of the different doors.

All sorts of things have been stockpiled on the ship to help build the new settlement. There is mining equipment, steam engines and the components of dirigibles for airborne exploration. There are entire rooms holding seeds so you can grow crops and there are plant warehouses where plants are grown to help oxygenate the air of the space ship and recycle the waste. It must have taken The Inventor and his workers years of thinking and planning to ready this expedition – they knew there would never be any going back.

You get to Magellan just as the transporters are fully recharged. Captain Wells is standing there and she looks very angry.

"What took you so long? I finished everything I had to do and came down to see how you were going with the bots and you haven't even started!"

"Hold your horses -" begins Trig, but he's cut short by the spaceship rolling and lurching. Gravity cuts out and you find yourself floating off the floor. Thankfully the 'sport stays stuck to the magnetic strip so you grab its handles. You know you need to get to an oxygen supply in case that cuts out too.

"Into an emergency room!" shouts Captain Wells, pulling herself along to a doorway. You grab onto picture frames and door handles to follow her. It's extremely bumpy and you bang into light fixtures several times. You're going to have a few of bruises. The hummers shoot forward in spurts using a gas reserve for propulsion.

In short time you haul yourselves into a room with *EMERGENCY* stenciled in gold on the door. Inside you find a round room with padded walls covered in rich green velvet to protect you from the lurching motions of the ship. There is a circle of padded seats surrounding a central table. This looks like some sort of escape pod which could detach itself from the rest of the ship if necessary.

Captain Wells sits and reaches for belts tucked into the upholstery. She snaps the buckles closed to keep herself attached to the furniture. You do the same.

Whoever designed this ship made the emergency room just as beautifully as the rest of the ship. The table is intricately inlaid with command information and screens. The seats are comfortable and the ceiling is patterned.

The Captain sits at a smaller version of the controls on the bridge. You activate your own console and begin to monitor the *Victoria*'s engines.

You can hear rattling and banging outside the emergency room and you are grateful for the straps that keep you in your seat. You think about all the equipment you passed on your circuit of the ship. Will it be damaged? You check the readings for the cargo holds and see the gravity has been diverted to all the priority areas – sleeping passengers and heavy equipment. Captain Wells and Trig are both studying readouts too.

"The dials are showing a high speed – but *we* aren't the ones doing the moving," says Trig, "it's like we're being sucked into something. I'll do my best to keep track of our course, but at the moment we're flying blind down some sort of rabbit hole."

"I've tried to close all the portals," Captain Wells says, with steely determination. "But one won't shut. I'm going to bring it up on screen. We can at least take a look out of it."

An image appears in the centre of the table. You squint at the constellation you are viewing. It isn't familiar, but your knowledge of the stars is sketchy. Trig looks up from his navigation equipment:

"I've got good news, more good news and, depending on how you look at it, a spot of bad news."

Before you can offer an opinion about which news you'd like Trig to deliver first, Captain Wells thumps the table.

"Just make a full report and stop wasting time."

She looks at you both as she says it.

You blush, remembering you are partly at fault for this situation too. If you hadn't been racing around the ship instead of fixing it your ship might not have been sucked into this hole in space.

"Well Captain, we've stopped moving so fast and we're under our own power again such as it is, but we're completely lost. This area of space doesn't relate to any mapped constellations I know. I've tried steering us back toward the corridor we came through, but until we have more power, I wouldn't risk doing anything else."

You look at Trig. "And this is good news?"

Trig smiles "It's actually fantastic news. See that bright yellow star?" He stabs a finger onto his console leaving a bit of a smear on the glass. "That star has four planets circling it and at least two of them look to have the right conditions to support life!"

Captain Wells does a most un-captainly thing. She unbuckles her seatbelt, boosts herself over to Trig and kisses him. Then she turns and gives you a hug. "We've still got a porthole that won't close and a problem with our magnetic field. Get the robot crew together and sort it out. Okay? While you do that, Trig can figure out which of these planets is our best bet."

You leave them studying the new solar system and head to the Magellan room to ready up the spider-bot and hummers. As you enter, the spider-bot runs toward you and opens its tool case. Each tool inside has to be attached to the case in two places so they don't float away into space when the box is opened. You add everything you think will be needed and then get the hummers to fill themselves with methane. They will be able to manage short flights by burning the fuel but they won't be able to fly in space using their wings like they do in the ship.

As each bird takes in the gas it turns an iridescent blue. The little robots carry small optical relays which will give you an aerial view of the ship. You remember the Captain's idea of a larger optical relay and fit one of the hummers with one. The hummer is barely able to fly so you create a perch on the spider-bot where it can sit until it is outside the ship in zero gravity.

The robot menagerie follows you to an airlock. You open the first door and usher them in. They line up, ready to go outside, just like pet dogs and cats would do. You step out of the chamber and close the door. You feel a slight vibration as the air lock opens releasing the bots into space. The hummers fly with quick bursts from their methane powered jets. The spider bot uses suction cups and pincers to cling to the hull as it moves around.

Once you've closed the outer hatch you head back to meet Trig and carry out the inspection.

Trig and the Captain have made progress plotting a course to the first of the planets.

"The closest planet is really marginal," Trig says. "It's close enough that we can tell there isn't a lot of plant life. The ones that are further away look more promising. It's a big solar system though."

"Should we wake someone else up to help explore the planets?" you ask.

"They'll just want to pull rank on the Captain because she's a girl," says Trig. You remember all those corridors named after explorers. Were any named after a woman?

"That might be true," you say, "but we have protocols about waking up the aristocrats when a useful planet is found."

"But we don't really know that yet," Trig points out.

Captain Wells stands with her hands on her hips and looks at the screen which shows the robots outside.

"When you two have finished discussing the dangerous subject of mutiny, perhaps you should focus on fixing this ship. Besides, the robots will wake up The Inventor whether we choose to or not."

Trig blushes and you busy yourself sending the spider-bot instructions. The hummers orbit the *Victoria* and show you what is happening. One area of the ship seems to have suffered some minor damage – there is space dust, probably from the passing tail of a comet, embedded in the feather-like covering of the ship. The feathers shield the ship when entering a planet's atmosphere and generate an artificial magnetic field to protect from radiation. The dust has stopped some of them from working properly. You set the hummers to work, sucking up the dust while the spider makes any necessary adjustments.

"I've spent a hundred and seventy years in sleep school learning to be a cleaner and bird groomer," you say with a chuckle. "Hey Trig, how far out can the hummingbots go before we lose their signal?"

"Millions of miles. Why?"

"We could send some hummers out to scout the two planets. I think I can reconfigure them to get through the atmosphere and fly around the planets. That would give us an idea about which we should choose."

"Great idea," says Captain Wells. "That could save years of investigation. Tell me more when we've sorted this current problem. How is the magnetic field reading now?"

You check. "The magnetic field is almost back at 100 percent."

"Just as well," the Captain says. "We can't land without it."

"The feather protection is working perfectly again Captain," you report. "The bots also fixed the malfunctioning portal shutter. More space dust."

Captain Wells nods then stares out into space. You follow her eyes. This part of space is a deep purple, not the black you expected. It must be the effect of having a sun nearby.

"Let's follow through with this idea of some hummers taking an excursion to these new planets," the Captain says, looking at you and Trig. "Get the birds ready as soon as you can."

You and Trig head back to Magellan to pick up the spider-bot and the hummers. When they are back inside you carry out tests on the space dust.

"Blow me down," you say. "This dust is pure platinum."

"What's pla–tignum?" asks Trig.

"Platinum's a very precious metal, more precious than gold. It's very odd to think of a cloud of it floating through space. Maybe it wasn't from a comet after all. I think I can set up some sensors for this sort of thing – it played havoc with our magnetic field and could have caused us to get radiation poisoning."

"What are you going to do with the dust?" Trig asks. He hefts the box. It's surprisingly heavy, the little spider bot was weighed down by it once it entered the low gravity of the spacecraft.

"How about we store it somewhere with our names on it," you suggest. "Perhaps we could use it in the future?"

"Excellent suggestion." Trig gives you a big smile. "It might get us out of a few years' work." He takes the box off while you busy yourself checking over the robots and readying them to make a long journey. When Trig comes back he works out a route for the birds so they have the best chance of making it to their planets. A couple of birds are each packaged inside two small rockets. Each rocket will travel to a different planet. After the rocket enters a planet's atmosphere it will eject the hummers. The hummer will then navigate around the planet and send back information about what it finds.

You put the rockets into launching tubes as Trig does some last minute checks of his calculations. Then you each hold a finger over a firing button.

"Four, three, two, one, launch!" says Trig.

As you press your button down you hear a thunderous sound from the hatches below.

Then the two of you race up to a viewing platform so you can see your robotic explorers departing. A twin set of lights move off into the distance and then separate as they head off to different worlds. It might be that neither of the planets is suitable for living. They might have no water or no land or be too hot or too cold. Right now though, they are ripe with possibilities. When you can't see their lights anymore Trig turns back to you,

"We'll have a few years to wait. Reckon we should go back to sleep?"

You hadn't thought about this but he's quite right. You are at the outskirts of a promising solar system but it will be a few years before the birds report back. You probably shouldn't waste time awake.

You sigh. No point in being too old to enjoy exploring a new planet. It's time to go back to sleep. It's frustrating though – being awake and running the space ship is exciting. You've never been in a position to do such important work. When you next wake you'll probably be a lowly servant to some rich passenger or working on a settler's farm to pay off your passage.

"Hey," says Trig, a note of cunning in his voice, "think you can re-program the robots to wake *us* up when the hummers report back?"

All the schematics for the *Victoria's* robots come into your mind. What a great education you got while you were asleep. If you could get the robots to wake you when the hummers report back, you will be able to have more adventures. Trig watches you. The expression on his freckled face tells you he's trying to read your mind. He grins when he realizes you are thinking not about *if* you should do it but *how*.

Trig has gotten you into trouble before, though. It was his suggestion to race the hummers that ended up with the ship going through a hole in space.

It is time to make a decision.

Do you agree to reprogram the ship to wake you? **P24**
Or
Do you let the ship decide who to wake? **P21**

Let the ship decide who to wake

The robotics repair shop is always busy. All day settlers come in with malfunctioning robots used to break in the new planet. There are machines that take down trees, machines that dig for coal and machines that defend the colony from the native animals.

You weren't woken when the *Victoria* first landed here several hundred years ago. Some passengers were kept asleep while others made the first explorations and discoveries. Some became rich securing land and resources, others are spoken of in legends. Since you were woken, you've worked on the huge robots and the little ones too. Sometimes you travel out on the steam railways into the country to work on immense machines that can't be brought in. Your employer is Mr. Wells, the great, great grandson of a woman who once captained the *Victoria* for a short time. You have seen a picture of her when you visited his house. Sometimes you dream about her and a red-headed boy. Is it a dream? It was long ago. You have a very busy life and you don't think about it much.

An old man comes in from the bright sunshine and squints into the shop. "Is anyone here?"

He's dressed like a rich farmer. You recognize him as the same fellow who came in a few months ago wanting to get an irrigation snake serviced. The snake came over on the space ship and was an exciting robot to work on. Its internal mechanism crunched through rock and soil and filtered out water which it converted to steam to power it.

"I'm here Mr. Bower," you say. "How can I help you?"

"Ah I was hoping I'd find you here, I know you like old bots." the old man says. "Take a look at this. We recently drained a small lake and found it with a metal detector. What do you think?"

He holds out a box. You take it to a work bench and carefully open it up. Inside is a dirty and dented little hummingbot.

"They had these flying about in the *Victoria*," you say as you gently clean away dirt. You're not too sure how you know this. The little bird is dented and faded but still has all its parts. You detach a little solar panel, clean away the dirt and find it surprisingly intact. You set the panel under a solar magnifier then you turn back to the hummer.

"We may not get her working again, but let's give it a try," you say. "These little bots are things of beauty. They had time for fine craftsmanship back then."

You open the main mechanism and look inside. There are a couple of rusted springs which you replace and then add some methane to the flying cartridge. Some of the clockwork has rusted out too and you carefully slot in new parts. You delicately file and polish each part so it fits perfectly. When you snap the bird back together it starts to move and then surprises you both by taking off around the room.

You head off to get a net to bring it down. It's a delicate old specimen and you don't want it falling and getting more damaged. To your surprise the little bird follows you.

"That's interesting," the old man says. "Did you ever get woken up when you travelled out on the *Victoria*?"

You try to think back. "I can't remember. I don't think so."

"This little fellow seems to know you. People often forget waking moments in space travel. You go back to sleep and learn new things. Without any triggers your brain buries memories quite deeply. You should find out – a lot of the records of that time were lost but if you helped get us here well… The descendants of folks who worked on board are claiming compensation these days. If you woke and helped get us here you could end up being rich enough to own this shop."

"But how would I ever prove something like that?" you ask.

The hummingbot emits a high-pitched whistle and attaches itself to an input on the computer you use to diagnose robot problems in remote areas. Before long, images start to play of corridors and 'sports racing inside the *Victoria*. The images change, now there is a close up of Captain Wells.

"That's my great grandmother!" exclaims a voice behind you.

It's your boss, back from a meeting. The three of you keep watching. There's a scene where Captain Wells is in a padded room working on the controls. Something starts to tickle in your mind.

"This is amazing," Mr. Wells says, "this little hummingbot has footage of the famous moments when Captain Wells and a crew of two saved the entire ship after it was sucked through a black hole."

You keep watching. There are various scenes of the ship being fixed and then you see something extraordinary. A rocket is placed on the floor and the hummingbot moves towards it. Two hands come up and take the little bird and it is placed inside. The robot looks upward as the rocket is sealed shut. The last image it shows is a face frowning in concentration.

It is your face.

"That's you!" your customer shouts. "It's really you. This is amazing."

Your life is about to change. As a hero from the original crews of the *Victoria* you'll be a celebrity and you'll also be entitled to land and riches.

The little bird gets down from the screen and flies over to you. You hold it in your hand. Now you remember sending it off on its journey.

"Thank you for coming back to me," you whisper to the little bird. It's like a piece of the puzzle of your life is back in place.

This part of your story has finished but things could have turned out quite differently. Would you like to:

Go back to the beginning of the story? P1

Or

Go to the List of Choices and start reading from another part of the story? P380

Agree to reprogram the ship to wake you

You and Trig speak to Captain Wells about your plan. She agrees that it's a good idea to program the robots to wake the three of you when the hummingbots return.

"We make a good team and I think we should be able to see where our actions have taken us. If you don't need any help, Trig and I will go check the rest of the cargo. We should make sure there aren't any problems after that big shake up the ship had."

You ask a hummer to show you the way to the main robotics chamber. The hummer takes you to an elevator which leads you down a couple of floors where you find a wide doorway with a smaller door set inside it. The door is specially designed so something large or small can pass through depending on the need at the time. The door isn't locked so you open the smaller door and step through into a large warehouse. Lights come on and illuminate everywhere you walk. Your footsteps echo on metal flooring. There are few human conveniences because the robots are programmed to undertake routine maintenance on themselves.

In one corner, a couple of spider bots sit near a collection of tools. A hummer flies in, its movement through the air a little erratic. You watch as the spider bots quickly replace its wing. Then one of them gently tosses the hummer into the air and it starts to fly again completely restored. The spider bots track the little hummer for a few moments to make sure it is fixed and then freeze to wait patiently for the next robot in need of fixing.

It's great to see this part of the ship working, but you also remember something you once heard in the orphanage when you were growing up – people used to do all the work before robots took over. When robots started doing everything that's when some people couldn't afford to live honestly. You wonder why it had to be that way.

The middle of the room is taken up by high shelves with stores of robotic parts. You could make a vast variety of robots from them if you wanted – perhaps once on the new planet you will. More lights turn on and you gasp as you see a silent menagerie of different robots all along one wall. One is built like a giraffe, another like a snake. The snake is massively long and nearly the width of the ship's corridor. They must be here for some reason – the snake looks like it would be able to make big holes, perhaps the giraffe would make a good look out if you were traveling through a forest.

Near the row of robots is a desk with what looks to be a link to the central console from which you can make changes to the ship's programming. You start up the console and are soon engrossed in the task of programming a wake-up instruction for yourself and the others.

"Excuse me. Could I ask why you are making changes to the ship's instructions?" a polite but non-human voice enquires.

You spin around, eager to see who is speaking and are surprised to find that all the robots have moved closer to you. You nervously explain, sticking to the facts:

"Our team have found two planets in a new solar system and we're sending some hummers ahead to investigate. We need to sleep while we wait and we want the ship to wake us when there is more information."

You thought the idea was logical when Trig suggested it, but now you wonder if the robots will think you are overstepping your role. What will happen if they think you are not acting in the ship's best interests? There is quiet for a little while and then the giraffe's head looks back from the others and turns toward you.

"We have decided that your change of protocol is acceptable. Please continue. We'll review the new program and if it is what you have told us, we will accept the new instructions."

You are relieved that the robots are happy with your plans and you continue to make the changes. When you finish you see the robots have silently moved back to where they were when you first came in.

"I'm finished now," you say, but nobody answers back. Apparently they have said all they needed to say. As you leave the chamber, the lights go out behind you.

Back with Trig and Captain Helena, you explain about the group of robots you saw. "I think they were guardians."

Captain Helena listens carefully to you. "We need to be careful about what we do – the ship is programmed to protect everyone and we're lucky it agreed with our decision. We should get something to eat and enjoy a few hours of relaxation and then get to sleep."

She turns to a butler bot. "We'll take our meal in the hydroponic garden, thank you."

"Why do we want to go there?" you ask.

The Captain smiles, "You'll see."

You just hope she doesn't have you harvesting cabbages or something.

The butler heads off while the three of you run some final system checks.

Trig confirms the rockets are on track to make it to their respective planets. "It's all looking tickety-boo. They've covered thousands of miles already." He laughs. "We can wake up in a few years, look at the pictures they send back, and then decide to turn left or right."

The three of you race your 'sports down to the hydroponic gardens. The robotic control room was huge but the hydroponic chamber is even bigger. You expected some sort of garden factory so the beauty of the place surprises you.

You enter the garden through a little orchard of apple and pear trees so it's hard to see too far ahead. The fruit trees look deeply rooted and you wonder how far down the soil goes. It feels just like being outside on Earth. Springy moss carpets the ground. When you get out from between the fruit trees you see there are plants and vegetables everywhere. Vines run up the walls to high vaulted ceilings that remind you of a cathedral you once visited. Flying about through the garden are tiny butterfly robots that you suppose are used to pollinate the flowers. As you watch, a couple of hummingbots gently move a vine away from the lights that hang throughout the garden.

You walk to a small table sitting in a section of flower garden. The flowers don't seem to have any function except to be pretty. Captain Wells leans down and smells a rose and you do the same. The scent is heavenly.

Nearby you see a bushy shrub that has been trimmed into the shape of a large dog. It is so well done you can't see where the trunk is.

You are about to comment on the dog when a door opens in a far wall and a small car approaches you on a set of rails hidden in the dense moss. This miniature railway must be used to transport fruit and vegetables out of the garden.

Trig goes over and takes out a basket. He looks inside. "Lunch is served!"

"Or it could be dinner or breakfast," you say, "There's no day or night here, so we can't really say what sort of meal we're having."

"Whatever it is, it's a feast," Captain Wells declares, helping herself to baked potatoes.

You dive in too and soon you are all too busy eating to talk. In the quiet you hear a humming sound and realize there are some creatures in the garden with you - bees. As if to prove this, Trig pulls out a chunk of honeycomb from the basket and you all take a slice. It's deliciously sweet.

"That looks like fun," Trig says, pointing past the orchard where a number of strong vines are hanging from the ceiling. "Someone has woven them into swings."

"I think the seats are made from hemp," Helena says. "There's some growing over there. Hemp can be made into a fabric, like cotton. People used to use this to make clothes. Maybe they have a stock of it to make clothes for people once we arrive at a new planet."

Trig jumps on a swing and starts pumping his legs and leaning back. Before long his swing is covering a lot of ground. You both follow his lead and before long you are all soaring out over the garden

– you can see a lot from here.

Out of the corner of your eye you catch some movement. It's very quick and when you look again you don't see anything.

"Someone must have had a bit of time awake to be making picnic tables and swings," Captain Wells says, keeping her voice deliberately calm but you think she's probably on the alert too.

"Are they still awake?" Trig asks, glancing around.

Maybe it was what Trig said but suddenly the gardens seem creepy and you feel a shudder run down your spine. Are you being watched? You stop swinging and jump off, signaling the other two to keep talking to cover your movement. You circle around to the place where you thought you saw movement, hoping to catch whoever it is unawares.

As you tiptoe past a large avocado tree you see a bent figure with gray hair hiding from behind another tree. Just as you are about to say something, you step on a twig. The sound startles the watcher and he jumps and whirls around to face you. He has a frightened look on his face.

"It's Okay, Sir," you say, "I'm not going to hurt you."

The man looks old compared to the three of you. "Oh dear," he says. "I didn't want you youngsters finding me. This is very awkward."

There is a rustle of leaves as Captain Wells appears through the greenery. She sees that the old man is fearful. "Sir, we were woken up to undertake a mission. We hope you fared well when the ship was carried through that hole in space recently. Are you alright?"

The Captain ignores the fact that there are people awake on the spaceship - who perhaps aren't supposed to be.

"A hole in space?" the man mutters. "So that's what caused all that rumpus. I was in the library with Eva. We were picking up books for hours."

You hear footsteps to your right. "Who is Eva?" Trig asks, causing the old man to startle once again.

"Oh nothing, nobody! Don't listen to me, I'm old and confused."

Clearly he's hiding something, but you don't think he means any harm.

"Did you make the swings?" you ask, hoping to shift him to an easier topic, "and the picnic table?"

"Yes. Did you enjoy them?"

Captain Wells nods. "Very much, We might have learned a lot from our time asleep, but we're young and still love to play."

She leads the old man back to the picnic table and offers him tea. You join them looking around the chamber as they chat. You hadn't noticed the way some of the trees are shaped, or that there are decorative paths leading here and there, not to mention flowers and other plants and ornaments that just aren't essential at all. Someone has enjoyed living here.

"So," Captain Wells says, "I take it you were woken up at some stage and you didn't go back to sleep?"

"That's about it Captain."

The Captain sips her tea. "What did you wake up to do – topiary?"

"What's that?" Trig whispers to you.

The old man answers instead – it seems his hearing is perfectly alright. "Topiary is the art of shaping trees and bushes into interesting shapes young man." He pauses, "I'm sorry, I'm sure you're actually as old as I am, just better preserved."

You hadn't thought about age that way. But before you have a chance to comment the old man continues.

"I was woken up to take care of some issues here in the hydroponic garden – the bees were dying. I woke and found I knew about bees and plants and even the art of cultivating new hybrids."

"And after a while you were too old to go back to sleep?" asks the Captain.

"This is a pretty good life – I have a beautiful garden and all the fruit and vegetables I can eat. There is a wonderful library down the corridor and I'm always able to look at the stars. I'm sorry, I haven't introduced myself, my name is Amos."

As the Captain introduces the three of you and explains a bit about your mission, you notice one of the topiary bushes has changed its shape. Or are you imagining it? You're sure it was a dog shape, now it looks more like a rabbit. Or is it just the angle? You wander away from the others, aiming to look at the bush from another direction. Maybe you're confused and there is a dog somewhere else.

You jump on a swing and pump your legs to gain some height. You gaze over the rest of the garden. From above you see quite a few topiary bushes. There's one shaped like a lion and another like an elephant and there are sheep and other animals you don't know the names of. As you watch you notice something else – they are moving!

Three small rabbit-shaped bushes roll together and form a ball and from that appears the shape of a big cat. A lioness. It paces forward without a need for roots and it heads for Trig and the Captain.

You jump off the swing and run back toward them, but you're blocked by a green wall of leaves and twigs growing up in front of you!

You dodge off to the left, and a ball of green speeds ahead and reforms into another wall. You try and force your way through instead. At first you think you've outsmarted the plant when you feel the wall give way, but then the plant closes around you and you lose your balance as you're rolled up inside a new ball. You've been snared by a monster plant. Just as you're thinking you might throw up that picnic lunch you had earlier, the rolling ball of leaves comes to a stop. You're leaning a bit to one side, but it could be worse, you could be upside down. You can see through the branches that you're facing two other balls and the old man. You can just make out Trig and the Captain staring out of plant balls that encase them too.

"Alright Eva, let our guests sit down," says the old man. The foliage around you reforms to make a chair. You notice however that you seem to have some sort of vine seatbelt on.

"You owe us an explanation," the Captain says from her chair. "Your plant is currently undertaking an act of mutiny. I want an explanation!"

She still talks as if she is in charge even when she's strapped into a living plant. Trig is looking at her with complete faith that she'll get you out of this – he's changed since you first met when he couldn't believe a girl could be in charge of the ship.

The old man starts talking:

"Many years ago, I was woken to help with problems in the ship's garden and the bees. The plants were only just surviving. While I was sleeping I'd learned a lot about modern gardening techniques but I knew we needed new methods in space. I also knew that gardens need a gardener – this place is huge but it's too small to rely on robot monitoring. Some things really do need a human touch. I woke up a scientist and we experimented to develop plants that didn't need as much of a root system and other plants that could tell us about what was wrong with the garden. All of the plants here are hybrids of what was originally stocked on the *Victoria* – all except Eva here – she's very special: a combination of human and plant genetics. A whole new species.'

"Where's the other scientist you worked with?" Trig asks.

"Sleeping," says the old man. "We worked together for a number of years and then decided someone needed to stay awake with Eva and one of us should sleep. Eva will live a long time. She's very special, adaptable and intelligent. She's our baby – we want her to have a great life. When I'm near the end of my days I'll wake Eva's mother and sister and they can decide what to do next with her."

"Eva has a sister?" you say. You imagine a plant sleeping in a sleep pod.

"Her sister is human – like us. We decided to stay awake for a few years to see Eva settled into the garden. During that time we also had her sister, Esmeralda. When she turned twelve we decided it would be a good idea if Esmeralda went to sleep like everyone else so that she could live to see a new planet. My partner went to sleep beside her so that she will have her mother when she wakes. That was fifty five years ago."

Trig sighs, completely captivated by the story. "So you said goodbye to the woman you love so you could stay with one of your kids?"

Captain Wells isn't quite so fascinated by the romance of the story. "But the real question is, do we still need Eva to keep the hydroponic garden here working well?"

"No, she's managed to get it optimized. Her purpose is fulfilled."

"Hmm so if I've followed you correctly, you've created a plant that is intelligent and can make changes in an environment that will improve the chances of other plants growth?"

"That's right Captain, Eva would have been a great boon on Earth. She could have brought new life to places we'd destroyed with mining and pollution. You've seen what she can do – she can make herself into many plants or merge into one. She's very adaptive."

"Have you ever thought about Eva's potential to make a whole planet more habitable?"

The old man stared at her, his mind ticking over. "Well it's possible - there would need to be water and carbon dioxide – that's what she needs. And some heat. But Eva doesn't need the same conditions humans do."

"That's what I thought," Captain Wells says. "But awake here on her own she's a bit of a liability, and you, Amos, are in limbo unable to sleep for fear of what her 'adaptations' might do unchecked?"

Amos nods his head slowly as the Captain continues.

"We've just sent a couple of probes to two planets ahead of us. The ship will take a lot longer to get there and there are several other planets that don't have all the right conditions for us – but if Eva got there first she could make a closer planet ready for humans."

"I see what you mean!" The old man brightens, but then looks doubtful. "Well, it would be up to Eva naturally."

"Does she understand what we're saying?" asks Trig.

You are pretty sure the plant *does* understand everything that's being said. If Captain Wells doesn't come up with a good plan for Eva you suspect you could become fertilizer for this garden. Eva, like all other living things, will fight for her survival.

You need to help. "Captain," you say, "Permission to look at equipping a shuttle for Eva to make a journey between the stars."

"Permission granted," says the Captain, then she calmly speaks to the plant holding you all. "Eva, let my engineer and the navigator out of the garden so they can see about finding you a better home."

Has Eva been following your conversation? Is she going to let you go? You try and relax. If the plant picks up on emotions, your racing heart will let her know that you don't entirely trust her. In fact you've been wondering if the ship is carrying any chemicals to make a giant dose of weed killer. There's no way Amos could have left her alone on the ship. She's not like a robot, just following a program. She thinks for herself, and she might come up with something the people on the ship wouldn't like.

The vines and branches wrapping you onto the chair loosen; the cushion pushes you upward to a standing position. Eva seems to be in agreement with the plan. You walk toward the door with Trig beside you. You look back and find the Captain still seated – Eva hasn't let her go. Next to you, a little green doglike creature pads along. It seems like Eva is going to tag along. You wonder how well this little dog can communicate back to the main plant.

The Captain continues to act as if she's in control of the situation. "Go and investigate potential planets for Eva. It needs to be a place where we can be sure she'll survive and where her family can join her. Her job will be to prepare their new home. I'll stay here a while longer and make some preparations with Amos."

Outside the hydroponic garden you and Trig jump on transporters. The green dog paces alongside you when you take off. From time to time it forms a ball and rolls along before changing dog form again. You can't help thinking it would make a great pet.

Back on the bridge, Trig searches through nearby planetary systems he'd discounted earlier. You stare at the schematics for the various small shuttles on the *Victoria* and think about how they could be adapted to accommodate Eva. Your work takes hours and twice a robot comes in with a small meal. There is still no signal from the Captain and you assume Eva still holds her captive.

"This is an interesting one," Trig says at last.

The green dog has been lying on the floor as if asleep but it gets up and trots over with you to look at what Trig has found. You lean over Trigs shoulder and look at the planet he is pointing out. The green dog's tail coils up the desk and the rest of it unravels like a long strand of ivy. Once it has spooled onto the top of the desk it becomes a dog shape again.

"Excellent trick, Eva," you say. The green dog wags its tail then taps with its paw on the map. Trig tells you about what he's found.

"This is a volcanic planet with mountains of glass-like rock that form most of its land mass. There are also some plains and a big ocean. I discounted it earlier because the mountains looked uninhabitable, but Eva should be able to create adaptations that would make it quite pleasant. What do you think, Eva?"

The little dog looks at the information on the screen and seems to be reading. You recall Amos talking about picking up the books in the library so perhaps Eva can read. After a while the dog wags its tail and jumps off the desk and runs to the door. It looks back at you both, clearly telling you that it's time to go back to Amos and the Captain.

On the way back to the garden you have a sudden inspiration and stop your transporter. "I need to go and look at something – now I know what sort of planet Eva's going to, there might be something that will be really helpful. I just have to ask the robots if it's okay to use it."

You head back to the programming room. As before, all the robots are quiet. You sit down and start talking but can't tell if they are listening or not. You explain about Eva – about how the plant is so special but can't really be left on its own while everyone sleeps. You explain about the glass mountain planet and how Eva might make it a special place to live.

After you've finished your explanations, the giraffe takes a step forward and speaks. "Your logic is sound. You can take the supplies you want but with one condition. You must send 100 sleepers – male and female – along with Eva. Our trip is long and dangerous, we may not find an optimal planet for our cargo. It is logical to send some to this planet as a backup settlement in case ours is destroyed."

The giraffe-bot stops speaking and steps back. Its companion stirs. It fills the hallway perfectly as it follows you to the garden. When you get there you find Trig, Amos, and Captain Wells talking excitedly about the new planet. It appears Eva is keen to go. But there is stunned silence when the giant snake robot slithers into the garden.

"What's that for?" asks Amos.

"For making tunnels in the glass mountains. They'll be shelter and more. The ship has agreed to send it with Eva to help prepare for your family and 97 others."

Amos looks confused. "Others?"

You explain what the ship has decided, about investing 100 passengers on settling the planet.

"Then I guess we just need to decide something for ourselves," says Captain Wells.

"What's that?" says Trig.

"We need to decide if we get off at Glass Mountain or carry on."

Trig looks at you, suddenly excited – "I bet you could invent some great devices to slide down those mountains."

"And we'd own land and be our own bosses," you say.

He's right, the planet has all sorts of potential. Still, this will be a tough decision: There are many risks in putting so much hope on the abilities of a plant.

It is time to make a decision.

Do you, risk a less than perfect planet and go with Eva? **P38**

Or

Leave Eva and continue on between the stars? **P36**

Leaving Eva

The next few weeks are busy. You and the others are waking people and briefing them about the landing. There are three ships to get ready, including one with the huge mining snake. Eva makes herself very useful during the preparations, in particular, deciding on seeds and livestock to take to the new planet. On the third day you go with Amos and Eva's little dog to wake up Amos' daughter Esmeralda and her mother. There is a tearful reunion of the whole family. Esmeralda asks if her father might be able to take a sleep pod or two to the new planet. She thinks it might be nice for him to sleep for a few years while they set up their new home. Amos isn't too sure he wants to miss more time with his family but they agree the pods might come in useful.

Everywhere Esmeralda goes a little green dog pads after her – the two are inseparable. Some of the other passengers are a little bit wary of Eva. Eva senses this and tries to devise ways to get the settlers to know and trust her.

She splits herself up into lots of green balls that follow the settlers about. It becomes natural for the settlers to use their 'tumble weeds' as chairs and cushions. Before long people are very comfortable with Eva and you think that the ship will be missing a great asset when the landing parties have gone.

The day comes when the little ships are loaded and launched into space. Each passenger rests against a green pillow soaked in a natural herbs cultivated by Amos. Where once the settlers might have felt frightened or anxious, the pillow has a soothing effect.

"It smells like lavender," says one man.

"Mine smells like the old roses my grandmother used to grow," says another.

You watch from the bridge as the three ships leave the *Victoria* and head to the planet. Each of these vessels will make a temporary shelter for the settlers until the snake makes tunnels and caves for them to live in. They will not all land together as you don't want them to accidentally crash. Instead Trig has set them on courses to land on different parts of the planet. One will land in the mountains and another on the plains. They have plenty of equipment to build a new Britannia.

When the settlers have gone there is no more reason to stay awake. After a last meal you take a final tour of the *Victoria* on your transporters. You still haven't even been through half of it. A little hummingbot follows you through corridors. Behind you both, a small green ball rolls along as though attached by an invisible thread.

You know you shouldn't put it off much longer. It's time to head to your sleep pod and immerse yourself in warm jelly. You look forward to the sleeping cap teaching you wonderful new things. Just as you lose consciousness you look out through the glass. You must be dreaming already, for a moment you thought you saw a little green dog wagging its tail and chasing a green ball…

You have finished this part of your story. It is time for another decision. Would you like to:

Go back to the beginning and try another path? **P1**

Or

Go to the List of Choices and start reading from another part of the story? **P380**

On Eva's planet

Three landing ships set off from the *Victoria* to the glass planet. A part of Eva traveled on each ship.

The largest ship carried the robot snake. It was used by the settlers to make tunnels into the mountains. Eva adapted a local fungus to be highly nutritious. It could be grown hydroponically within these caverns. Over time the settlers adapted to mountain living. They discovered diamonds and used them for grip while traveling over the smooth glass surface.

The snake robot didn't get on with the new native fungus and burrowed deeper and deeper into the mountains. It returned to the highlands less and less often and eventually stopped coming altogether. But by then it had done its job and settlements we well established.

The second ship landed on the plains so the settlers started farming. There were many native plants and species which helped them have a good life. Sometimes these settlers glanced up at the mountains and wondered why anyone would want to make their homes there.

The plains dwellers, or Lowlanders as they became known, were often visited by the inhabitants of the third ship who explored the rest of the planet and developed a roving nature. Over time, members of this third group became the planet's traders – delivering goods and news between the different communities.

After a few hundred years with no written history, people forgot entirely where they came from. There were rumors that they had come from the stars and stories about metal creatures which dug tunnels and robots that did other useful things abounded, but nobody knew for sure. Many think the stories are only legend.

Sometimes a Highlander would take it into their head to develop new machines and start drilling and banging and thinking. They'd eat a bit of fungus and things would become clearer and their inventions more ingenious.

While the Highlanders were inventing machines, the Lowlanders enjoyed the many green tumbleweeds they found rolling around the planet (and which were so convenient as cushions and pillows). Settlers would snuggle into a tumble weed and before they knew it – more tumble weed would attach to the first and a cozy bed would form. Naps were common.

Other tumble weeds would roll off to make themselves useful as baby's cribs or settle under a roof being fixed in case a worker fell off.

People used to say. "It's like those tumbleweeds know what's going on."

The End

Psst! you can read more about the planet Eva went to when you read *Secrets of Glass Mountain*, but for now you might want to explore some more of *Between the Stars*:

Would you like to:

Go back to the beginning and try another path? **P1**

Or

Go to the list of choices and start reading from another part of the book? **P380** (The list of choices is also a good place to check to make sure you haven't missed any of the story.)

The mission

"Are you crazy Trig?"

You can't believe he wants to play with the equipment. "Let's get this radiation problem sorted."

"Nobody else is awake," says Trig, "We're in charge. Besides, we might get there faster."

You point to a floor plan of the spaceship attached to a nearby wall. "Look, there's an equipment room not far ahead. That's where we need to go."

You set off on your transporter and Trig paces next to you, looking disappointed so you cheer him up.

"Last one there's a rotten egg," you yell.

Trig lets out a whoop and opens up his transporter and surges ahead. You chuckle as he speeds right past the room and you get there first anyway.

The place is a treasure trove. Gathering things to equip the spider-bot is easy because things are so well organized. You pick up tools you never knew about back on Earth and confidently assess them. It's astonishing what you've learned.

When Trig joins you he calls a hummingbot over and starts to make adaptations to the little bird. After Trig's changes, the hummingbots fly up to a methane tank one by one and suck up a quantity of gas through their 'beaks'. Their wings won't work in the same way in space, they will need jet propulsion. As they take in the gas they change color to an iridescent blue.

You peer at a hummingbot's delicate metallic head. "If the Captain wants to see more, we need to give the hummers better optics."

You fit the hummingbot with a new eye piece, rather like a monocle. The robotic bird tries to fly but the extra weight is too much. You know that won't be a problem outside the ship though. In space it will be weightless. You add a little device that gives it a perch on the spider-bot.

"Nice," says Trig. "With that perch it can leave and re-enter the ship without flying at all."

Trig tucks the now flightless hummingbot into the pannier on his transport. Side by side you race to the airlock and set up the birds and spider-bot ready for their excursion.

The little hummers retract their wings and lie in a circle around the spider bot, while the one with the special long distance scope sits on its perch.

When the airlock opens, the birds will fire their jets and fly outside. Then, in formation, they will start their inspection.

The spider-bot will clamber outside, holding tight to the ship's hull, and go where you direct it from your console in the control room.

You and Trig step out of the airlock and close the hatch behind you. Once on the other side, you wind the mechanism that opens the outside hatch to let the bots out.

You watch the hummingbots float out and the spider, using its suction feet, walk out carrying the last bird, then head back to the bridge on your 'sports to follow them remotely and direct the repairs. You don't want to waste any time, so you both release all the power you stored on the ride down. The speed and low gravity mean you can hold on to the handle bars and let your body streak out behind you.

Trig is riding along beside you and you grin at each other as you race along. Abruptly Trig drops back and you look ahead just in time to avoid Captain Wells who is standing at the door of the bridge.

"That looks like so much fun," she says wistfully. "Come into the control room and let's get these repairs finished. We can all go for a race once the work is done."

You are relieved at the Captain's reaction. It seems bad to be enjoying the ride so much when the ship is in danger, but you couldn't help yourself.

At the console Trig starts monitoring the hummingbots. He's checking their flight plans and making little adjustments. "So far so good – there's a chance of collision so I'm mapping their progress. We should start getting some pictures about… now."

The monitor splits into several windows at once. The hummingbot with the high-powered telescope detaches from the spider bot and blasts away from the ship to start mapping this sector of deep space.

You are seeing the stars from a perspective no human eyes have ever seen before. "Wow look at all those galaxies!"

The hummingbots are starting their ship scan. You watch the golden-bronze exterior of the ship as they cover every inch. There are large circular port holes with their irises tightly shut to streamline the ship and protect it from meteors and heat loss.

A few portholes are open to allow light to filter into the hydroponic gardens. These gardens make oxygen for the ship and nutrients for the sleepers. Waste from the sleepers' is recycled back to the garden. You know that this system loses energy slowly and that the ship can't travel forever, but by gathering solar heat from the stars you pass the gardens can last a long time. But everything wears out eventually. And you know that in time, the gardens won't be able to function. You'll need to have found a new planet by then.

As you survey another porthole you see it twitching – not quite shutting and then opening again. It's jammed up somehow. This will be part of the reason the ship has been using more power than normal. It needs to be fixed before the ship can enter a new planet's atmosphere. The heat on entering a planet's atmosphere is tremendous. All the portholes must be closed for the space ship to land safely.

You signal to Trig and he gets a hummingbot to move closer to see what is happening. The surface of the ship isn't smooth – it is covered in several layers of metal feathers. As the hummingbot zooms in on the outside of the ship, you start to see some odd looking space debris clinging to the hull and coating the iris of the malfunctioning porthole.

"That's odd," says Trig, "Looks like a large cloud of some sort of dust has hit us. Maybe it's space poo."

"Space poo?" you say. "Is that a technical term?"

Trig blushes and looks at the Captain, but she's absorbed in what you are seeing on the screen and doesn't react.

"Let's get a sample," you say. "We're going to need to get that iris cleaned up so the porthole can close again before we enter a new atmosphere or we could roast the ship."

Trig directs one of the hummingbots to collect samples of dust as the spider bot starts cleaning the debris off the outside of the ship. The dust all moves in one direction as if there's a breeze out there. You wonder what could be causing it to move one way.

You keep watching the feeds that show the debris cleaning operation, making adjustments to the spider's progress.

The Captain taps her monitor like it's broken. "There's an awful lot of nothing showing in the starboard quadrant. Is my screen broken or is something strange going on?"

The special hummingbot has been feeding back a steady view of the stars, but when you look at what it is relaying now, you see only a vast blackness. As you watch, the trail of dust the spider-bot has disturbed moves into the blackness and disappears. "Something in the darkness is drawing it in," you say.

"Is it getting bigger, or are we getting closer?" asks the Captain, a touch of nerves showing in her voice.

Trig gets busy with his controls and looks up with a white face.

"We're drifting towards it Captain." Then Trig turns to you. "How much longer do you need? I don't want to get any closer to this thing whatever it is."

You check the bots. Thankfully they are nearly finished. You signal the spider-bot to get clear of the port hole and watch with satisfaction as the iris shuts smoothly. The hummingbots transmit images of a gleaming set of feathers all over the ship – the debris has been removed. You want to check the sample to see what that dust is made of so you order the bots to come back inside.

"Get the hummer to take a wider view of that empty patch, Trig?" The Captain says, obviously intrigued by the nothingness.

But before Trig has a chance to do anything, the little hummer has turned its scope toward the place with no stars. It breaks away from its orbit of the ship and starts drifting faster and faster out into space towards the darkness.

"Can you get it back Trig?" asks the Captain.

Trig tries to bring the hummer back but then shakes his head. "It's no good. Gravitational pull is too strong.

The three of you watch the little bird from the more limited scope of one of the other little hummers which Trig has turned to follow it's lost colleague's path.

You know the little robot isn't alive but you still feel sad as it disappears, knowing it hasn't a chance of getting back inside the ship.

"Speed it up crew, we need to get moving," says the Captain calmly. "Or we're the ones that will be space poo."

Once the bots are back inside, you switch off your monitor and head towards the door. "I'm going to analyze that dust."

The Captain nods as she works to reset the *Victoria's* course.

Then Trig pipes up, "The magnetic field is back at almost 100 percent."

Pleased that the problem has been fixed, you step outside and take a 'sport down to a lab room. The spider-bot is waiting for you when you arrive. The sample turns out to be almost pure platinum. No wonder the dust was interfering with the artificial polarity in the center of the ship. But how did it get there? Was it some sort of freak event? More importantly, is it likely to happen again?

The spider-bot follows you back to the bridge. When it falls behind, you put it on the 'sport and give it a ride.

"You were carrying a fortune, little spider," you tell it. "Platinum is even rarer than gold."

On a whim you stop at a storage room and find some room on a shelf. You write your name and number on a slip of paper and put it, and most of the platinum, in an empty box. Who knows, if you ever find yourself on a planet, that dust might be worth something.

One of the hummingbots flies along beside you – perhaps it has some relationship to the spider-bot, it seems to keep a constant distance from it. Maybe Trig programmed it to stay close and hadn't thought about changing the instructions once the hummer was back inside the ship.

You come to a fork in the corridor. The way to the Captain's quarters is smooth metal inlaid with the magnetic strips that stabilizes butlers and other bots that roam the ship, but to your right the corridor is carpeted in a deep green moss. You haven't seen anything like it elsewhere on the ship. You make a mental note to report this unexpected growth to Captain Wells.

The Captain smiles when you enter. Trig gives you a thumbs up.

"Now that the magnetic field is back to normal we've increased speed and moved away from that blackness," Trig says.

"But what caused the dust?" the Captain asks. "We can't go back to sleep and leave this unexplained."

"I think I know why the electromagnetic field was compromised," you say, as you take out the small sample of platinum powder.

"The precious metal interfered with the magnetic core of the ship and reduced the ship's artificial magnetic field and therefore its ability to withstand radiation," you say. "But I don't know where the platinum dust came from."

The spider-bot and the hummingbot move to a console and appear to be communicating with the ships main computer. The Captain inspects what they are up to and alerts you that the ship is taking evasive action to avoid a meteor shower.

"The *Victoria's* been instructed to move away from meteors so we don't take any damage. Strap yourselves in, we'll be…"

She doesn't have time to say any more. The ship lurches as it accelerates and swerves. Then once it's cleared the meteors it resumes a smooth quiet path through space.

"Let's see what we avoided," says Trig. He opens one of the viewing portals and magnifies the view. You look at the herd of meteors moving through space and wonder what explosion propelled them in your direction.

"What's that?" says Trig, wiggling dials to magnify a glinting speck tucked amongst the cluster of space rocks. As Trig zooms in, the speck grows larger.

You're amazed he even noticed it. "You've got sharp eyes."

When Trig goes on to full zoom, you see another spaceship, and it appears to be heading *towards* the meteor shower you just avoided. You are fascinated as the other ship draws a large boulder out of the whirling mass of space rocks with some kind of tractor beam.

"It's separating that one from the pack," says Captain Wells. "You've got to admire how they maneuver through those meteors without getting hit."

"They're a lot smaller than us," Trig points out.

"And nimbler too," muses the Captain.

The captured meteor glows and then contracts. In no time the meteor crumples like a wad of paper. Part of the once giant rock is sucked into the spaceship and the rest drifts away, pulverized in to microscopic particles.

"I think we know what caused our dust," Trig announces. "But why would they dump such a precious metal? It doesn't make sense."

"What would you do with precious metals out here? What could be more precious than that to them?" asks the Captain.

"Water!" you say. "It makes a crazy sort of sense. Everything contains a small amount of water, even rocks."

"Must take a lot of power to crumple a meteor just for a few buckets of water," muses the Captain. "I could see the value in capturing icy comets, but rock. They must be desperate?"

You and Trig look at each other, thinking the same thing.

Trig speaks it out loud, "Would they do the same thing to us?"

"Hopefully not," Says Captain Wells, "Still, I think it would be a good idea to get some more distance between the *Victoria* and that ship. We want to avoid getting another dust shower."

You consider what the Captain has said. If that ship was responsible for our first dusting, it had the opportunity to treat the *Victoria* like that meteorite before you were woken up. But it didn't. The strange space ship can't be an enemy. You explain your theory to the Captain and she agrees, but still thinks she should be cautious. You agree to use some reserve power and move out of the area.

That sorted, the Captain rubs her belly. "Let's have lunch. I might not know what that ship is doing out there, but I do know I haven't had a proper meal in 170 years."

A butler-bot appears and folds down a dining table from a wall. Dining chairs are set up and vegetables and a freshly roasted chicken are delivered to the table. There is a wine bottle and three elegant glasses. Trig picks up the bottle.

"Elderflower cordial – not what I was hoping for but I'm sure it's a great drop." He fills everyone's glass.

You all start eating. Your stomach growls as you savor your first mouthful.

The Captain puts down her fork. "While you were readying the bots I read through some of the messages the ship has received. Things have changed on Earth. More ships have been sent out, including mining ships. There are space stations reaching out across the universe and there are other peoples living in space.

"There were several messages for the *Victoria* asking if she'd found a new home. One informed us that the planets we were heading towards might be occupied before we get to them."

"How could that be?" Trig asks.

"Newer technology. Other ships have passed us even though they left after we did. That craft we saw harvesting the meteor could be one of those ships. There's no record of us being hailed though."

"Maybe we should try and communicate with it?" Trig suggests. "Maybe it can send us in the right direction."

"I don't like the look of that ship," says the Captain. "We were woken to deal with a technical problem and we've sorted it. If we're going to engage with that ship I think we need to change staff – we aren't diplomats and negotiators. If we make contact we need to wake people better suited to the task and go back to sleep ourselves."

You need to make a decision,

Get a new crew on the job and go back to sleep **P80**

Or

Avoid the other ship **P49**

You have chosen to avoid the other ship

Trig sets a course away from the mining ship. You are now running at full power, having fixed the problems you were woken up to sort out.

"We'll stay awake for a few more days so we can monitor that ship," says Captain Wells.

With the autopilot set and no more urgent tasks at hand, you all set about exploring the ship. You start by checking out the sleeping animals and wonder what species have been stocked on board. Perhaps the ship is like a Noah's ark in space.

Trig offers to help the Captain get through the news and messages. You're surprised about this, you thought he'd be off riding around on the 'sports to see how fast he could get them going.

You ask a hummingbot to guide you down into the livestock compartment.

The livestock bay holds horses and cattle and sheep and even birds in special sleep tanks, each engineered especially for them. There are dogs and pigs too. You wander around looking at the animals as they move in their sleep. In another area you find monkeys sleeping. They seem to have similar sleeping apparatus to your own. Are they learning too?

"What are the monkeys learning?" you ask the hummer.

The hummer flies over to a set of files on a shelf. You remember learning that it is important to stimulate the brain while sleeping. You expect that the material is geared specifically to animals, perhaps the monkeys are dreaming bananas. You chuckle. The dogs are receiving instruction too, and the horses. Several tanks at the back of the room are empty. They look like the one you slept in.

"Can I help you?" asks a voice.

A young man steps out of the shadows, he looks at you with his head tilted to one side.

"Hello," you say, and explain that you were exploring the ship while you wait for the next part of your mission.

"Know much about space sleeping do you?" asks the man. It's hard to tell if he's annoyed about your intrusion or not.

"I don't think so, Sir," you say. "I know something about robotics, and the engineering of the ship. That was why I was woken up. I didn't see much of the ship before I went to sleep so I just thought I'd look around. I hope you don't mind?"

"I'm naturally a little cautious," says the man. "You can call me Dr Ralph if you like. I take it you were a convict sentenced to transportation?"

"That's right, Dr Ralph, sir."

"What was the nature of your crime?"

You think back to that moment that seems only weeks ago but really it's whole lifetimes ago.

"I stole food Dr Ralph. Quite a lot of it."

"Tell me more."

You walk around the livestock compartment again, telling Dr Ralph about growing up in the orphanage and never knowing your parents. How you'd been apprenticed to a baker before your tenth birthday and worked long hours. You tell him about all the hungry people in the streets, including a few you'd grown up with in the orphanage. Over time, you worked out ways to siphon out stale bread to give to them. It wasn't much but you didn't think you were hurting anyone.

"Those poor people should have signed up for the factories," Dr Ralph mused.

"People don't come back from there," you tell him.

A serious looks crosses his face. He nods and you realize he knows this. "There are many I believe that make a better life and don't need to return but, I agree, there are tales of wrongdoing in the far reaches of Britannia."

"It is not easy to hire out your labor when there are robots who can work longer hours and make less mistakes. The cities of Londoninium were flooded with unemployed. That's why men like us decided on the transportation initiative. Unskilled people like yourselves can become highly skilled people while you sleep and we can build a better society in a land where there is room for us all."

Dr Ralph seems to have lost his distrust in you, although he isn't treating you as an equal like Captain Wells seems to do. You wonder how different a new society will be if people like him still think they are above commoners like you.

"Tell me," he says, changing tack, "have you ever played draughts or chess?"

"Yes Sir, and card games too," you tell him.

"Excellent!" He declares. "Desmond – step out and meet a new friend."

A huge monkey swings down from some pipes running along the high ceiling. When you look up you see several monkeys of different types up there. They must have been watching you ever since you came into the room.

"Desmond here is a chimpanzee," says Dr Ralph. "He's part of a breeding program started by my great-grandfather who pioneered the sleep method we use for space travel. "Desmond loves games of all sorts."

"Hello Desmond," you say, looking at the ape.

Desmond is almost as tall as you are and looks strong. The chimpanzee leans forward to sniff you. You doubt he's met many people before.

Desmond gestures for you to join him at a table and shows you various games. You start with snakes and ladders and then move on to something more complicated. You are surprised at how good Desmond is at chess, but he takes a long time to move, and enjoys swinging around from various pipes and brackets while he thinks about it.

Dr Ralph explains that his experimental program to improve the thinking abilities of animals was overlooked at the universities on Earth because everyone was interested in robotics. "Animals have only ever been interesting to men if they can eat them or get them to work," he says bitterly.

You can see he is passionate about his work and why he was so wary about you. Something puzzles you though. How long has Dr Ralph been awake?

"Dr Ralph I understand I've been asleep for nearly two hundred years. You seem to be one of the oldest people I've met on the ship but you can't have been asleep all this time?"

"You've caught me on one of my waking cycles," explains the scientist. "I didn't know how the animals would fare with the sleep jelly so I volunteered to wake every hundred years or so and run some tests. The animals have done well. I've made some adaptations to our research program. I've got them all learning as they sleep now. They will be even more useful when we get to a new planet."

Two more apes come down from the ceiling and start playing cards. Desmond beats you at chess and then brings out a game you haven't seen before. Patiently, he shows you the pieces as he pulls them out of a wooden box. There are hand carved animals and an intricate set of three boards that connect on rods. You see that the boards represent land, sea and sky. The game is beautiful and complex.

Each creature has a unique way of moving and each creature has both an enemy and a friend. Ingenious.

"Is this something the aristocrats play?" you ask.

Dr Ralph shakes his head. "It's a game the animals have devised."

The animals look at you expectantly. One of the chimps raises his eyebrows, tilts his head to one side and leans slightly forward.

"It's a fabulous game," you say. As you settle down to learn the rules, you help yourself to fruit that one of the monkeys brings around.

You take the role of a zebra and team up with a baboon to find water and food and escape a flood and a fire and an attack by lions. Eventually, you get the chance to join a herd or if you want to you can keep on with your baboon friend and a snake you've teamed up with.

As the game progresses, you wonder how things might have turned out if you'd made different alliances.

After a couple hours of game playing, you feel really tired and tell Desmond and the Doctor that you need some sleep. "Maybe there will be better treatment of animals on our new planet?"

Dr Ralph shrugs. "I'm not too hopeful. The rest of the cargo is filled with robots and new steam creations. We're just a backup."

On the next level you run into Trig and the Captain and ask them where your sleeping quarters might be. They take you to a section of the ship for passengers who are awake. There are just a few other people about, some are quite old.

"These are people who chose not to go back to sleep," whispers Trig. "They have jobs mostly in the hydroponic gardens. I spoke to a few of them earlier. I'm thinking about staying awake too."

"Welcome, travelers," says one of the men. "We hear you successfully sorted our engineering problem earlier. Thank you so much. You must be tired."

He shows you to a bunk room. It is big enough to sleep several people, but right now there is just you. There is no day or night in space so you figure people just set up their own sleep rhythms.

There's a spare set of clothing laid out at the foot of the bed and some snacks on a shelf nearby. Despite being bone tired you find it hard to go to sleep – you haven't slept in a bed for years and it all feels a bit odd. You lie there thinking through the events of the last hours. So much has happened and your life is so incredibly different to the one you had on planet Earth. You think about Trig wanting to stay awake and wonder if you should stay awake too? Space is very big and there may be no more excitement until you all reach a new planet. Would you want to miss that? Life is full of decisions; it would be so good if you could see how different choices played out. Eventually you nod off.

You wake with a feeling that you aren't alone in the bunk room. When you open your eyes you find Trig and Desmond quietly playing a game of cards.

"Someone taught this monkey how to play Wild Ladies," Trig says, when he notices you stirring. "I came in here to wake you up and he's sitting on the end of your bed telling me to be quiet. Next thing I know he brings out a deck of cards and I thought he might do something bad if I didn't play along. Turns out he's a proper card shark."

"He's good at all sorts of games," you say.

"You know him then?"

"Yeah, we met yesterday. I didn't know he was allowed to roam around the spaceship though. Where's Dr Ralph, Desmond?"

Desmond looks at you and mimes sleeping. Then he points to a large bag.

"What's inside Desmond?" The chimp passes you the bag. "It's his animal game," you tell Trig. "This is a really cool. Let's get some breakfast and play it."

When you sit down to a meal, Desmond sits with you. None of people who are awake seem surprised to see him so you figure he must be fairly well known.

You clear the table and are about to set up the game when the Captain comes in.

"We might have trouble," she says. Then she stops and looks at Desmond. "What's with the monkey?"

"He's a chimpanzee," you say. "What's up?"

"That spaceship is following us. The one that crunches meteorites. The holiday is over."

"Sorry Desmond," you say. "Duty calls."

Back at the bridge, you're not really sure what help you'll be – this isn't an engineering problem.

Captain Wells starts pulling up information. "I didn't want to worry you before, but I know something about the ship that's following us. Apparently it's run by a Chinese pirate called Ching Shee."

"A pirate!" Trig exclaims. He comes over to look at the dispatches.

"These are messages we've been sent since we left – there isn't much. Earth stopped transmitting to us more than one hundred years ago.

"Not long after we left, the Chinese Emperor sent some spaceships out too. The idea was to find new land just like Britannia. They had a terrible problem of overpopulation, just like us. The Emperor commissioned his best ship builders but a notorious pirate commandeered the space ship factory and sent out several ships herself.

"The pirate is called Ching Shee and her builders appear to have improved the technology the Chinese had originally. Our own science was kept a strict secret. They don't have our sleeping caps and sleep jelly for instance."

Trig interrupts: "Then Ching Shee must be long dead. Someone else must be commanding her ship."

Captain Wells shakes her head. "I said they didn't have sleep jelly, but they do have something else to manage years of space flight. Cloning."

"What do you mean?" you ask.

"The reports tell us Ching Shee has the ability to replace herself and her crew with exact copies. We've been sleeping for hundreds of years and they've been reproducing themselves. We're being tailed by the latest version of the original crew."

"How close is his ship?" you ask.

"*Her* ship. Ching Shee is a woman and captain of the *Orient Star.*" says Captain Wells. "Trig – can you check the ship and get any information you can on it, including how soon it will be here and anything you can pick up from radio transmissions that might help us understand what we're dealing with."

The Captains turns to you. "We might need to arm ourselves, so find out what we have that can be weaponized. I don't want to wake everyone up for a confrontation. I think we can deal with this robotically. Our ship isn't fast enough to outrun her. We have to be ready."

Trig springs to the console. "I'm on it."

You head off on a transporter to look at the robotic inventory. You remember passing a robot warehouse when you were looking for the animals earlier.

When you enter a small door set inside a larger one there is darkness, but lights start coming on as you move forward. A clanking behind you turns out to be a spider-bot. It's the one you programmed to go out and fix the ship. It's been a bit like your shadow lately.

There are hundreds of different robots standing facing the door. Some are shaped like humans and some like animals. On one side there is a huge snake which would almost fill the corridors of the spaceship. You know it is used for mining.

There is a workshop area in one corner. There is a flit of movement as a little hummingbot flies in buzzing as if it has a problem. The spider-bot moves to the worktable to see what is wrong.

The hummingbot has a wing bent out of shape and the spider-bot gets on to fixing it up. The hummer flies out. At another worktable there's a console where you hope to find an inventory. Again you sense movement behind you. You turn and find several of the robots have stepped forward and moved closer. They must be guarding the robotic system.

"There's another spaceship coming," you say, knowing some robots can understand simple human speech. "They might not be friendly. We may need to protect ourselves." You eye the big snake. Perhaps this would be the best machine to bring.

"Ye dinna need such a big brute to fight in close quarters," says a voice from the floor next to you.

It's your spider-bot, and it has a broad Scottish accent. You'd be tempted to laugh if it weren't for the stream of other spider bots appearing from among the bigger robots. Some are large like your spider bot and others are small and delicate like a ladies broach. They are arriving from everywhere, the warehouse, the ceiling, through the door and out of vents – perhaps they've been replicating themselves while everyone slept. They cover the floor and the walls and sit on every surface.

"We'll keep to the shadows and be ready should ye need us."

Wow! A whole Scottish spider army. This will be a great help if the pirates board the *Victoria*. You bow low to the spiders as they scurry off into the ceiling vents and passages.

Knowing you've got help if you need it, you take your transporter back to the Bridge and hurriedly explain the spider defense system to the others.

"And it has a Scottish accent?" asks Trig.

He seems more intrigued by this than your security plans. Just as he's about to ask more there's a clanging which heralds the arrival of the *Orient Star* docking below. You hurry down to meet it.

The dock is filled with most of the people you've already met, including the older people from the awake quarters and Dr Ralph. He has Desmond with him and another of the monkeys.

"This is Morris," he says to Trig.

You glance around the dock area – it has very high ceilings and you see some movement here and there – spiders at the ready.

One side of the *Orient Star* is moored to the open iris of the landing dock. The ship's is encased in smooth black lacquer with gold colored metalwork. A door slowly opens and a gang plank folds neatly out of the depths of the ship like a tongue. You hear marching feet and then a dozen armored soldiers come down the gang plank bearing long handled axes and wearing light metal armor that covers their body and head.

It is hard to tell if they are human or robots. They smoothly form a line either side of the door to the *Orient Star*. Next, a carpet rolls down the gangplank – it is a woolen carpet with patterns in dark blues and reds and deep green and gold. Your eye follows it unrolling and then back to the start where the tip of a golden shoe is just stepping onto it.

It is a very small shoe and belongs to a woman who manages to be both small and large all at once. She wears blue silk embroidered garments with deep sleeves, a little like an ornate dressing gown. The silk of her dress is embroidered at the edge with darker blue images of stars and comets and planets. It is as if part of the universe has come to visit you.

She holds her hands together, palms pressed, as she takes small steps down the carpet. Her hands are buried inside the long sleeves. Protruding from her back are the tips of a pair of curved knives. The glint and reflect the landing dock as if the air around her is being sliced up like a broken mirror. Her gown is cinched at the waist by an ornate gold belt. She wears a great deal of white make up and her eyes are colored in pinks and ruby colors. Her dark black hair sits on top of her head in a bun from which jewels glint and shimmer. She treads calmly down the gang plank like she is Queen Victoria herself and quite as though she met up with other space ships every day of the week.

Mesmerized by the person you assume to be Ching Shee you have failed to notice that Captain Wells has made her way to the bottom of the carpet and is bowing in welcome.

One of the visiting guards steps forward and announces: "The honorable explorer: Ching Shee the Ninth," then steps back into formation.

You can't tell from the way he (or she?) spoke, whether the guards are robots or people.

"Our pleasure to meet you. I am Captain Wells.". The Captain seems at ease and in charge. Although her uniform is drab in comparison to Ching Shee, it is also smart and practical and you admire the strong presence Captain Wells has.

Ching Shee eyes the Captain and the surrounds of the dock. You can't help feeling she is taking inventory of the *Victoria* as she begins to speak:

"I too am pleased to meet you," she says to the Captain imperiously, "There must have been some changes among the Britannian people to appoint someone so young and female to the task of commanding this large and most precious vessel."

Captain Wells smiles and offers her arm as if Ching Shee were a trusted friend.

"I am honored to be the first female captain of the *Victoria*. Perhaps you would like to accompany me to somewhere more comfortable where we can exchange news."

Ching Shee gives a regal nod and accepts the Captain's arm.

The Captain is the same height as the pirate as they walk side by side but when your visitor takes steps you see she is wearing high shoes. Ching Shee is about the size of kids you knew at the orphanage. Most of her guards fall in behind her, but two remain at the entrance to the *Orient Star*.

As you and Trig bring up the rear, you can't help wondering what the inside of Ching Shee's ship is like. You grab his arm, slowing him down so the others move ahead "Trig, can you distract the guards while I send a couple of spider-bots into the *Orient Star*?"

Trig doesn't need asking twice. He instantly understands what a huge advantage it would be to see what's in the visiting ship.

He boldly walks up the gang plank. One of the guards steps up and block his way. While Trig talks to the guard, you instruct two spider bots to get inside Ching Shee's vessel. This way if one gets caught, you'll have one in reserve.

While Trig continues his distraction, you see the first spider-bot lower itself from a beam above the doorway and slip in over the guards heads. The second bot walks up *underneath* the gangplank. When the guard standing closest to their ship's entrance steps forward to help his fellow deal with Trig, it flips up onto the gangplank and joins the other.

"Come on Trig," you say, satisfied your plan has worked, "they don't want visitors. Let's go check out what the captains are up to."

Trig jumps off the gangplank and joins you.

"How'd you go?" he whispers, as you rush down a corridor to catch up with the others.

"Two out of two," you say. "If we need spies we've got them."

The entourage moves to a large room where two chairs have been set up alongside a table with fruit and drinks. Ching Shee's guards stand to attention in a circle around the walls of the room. One guard steps forward and helps her remove the large and shiny knives from her back before she sits down.

"Just ceremonial of course, Captain Wells," she says with a smile.

The two leaders exchange pleasantries for a while. You study the guards, who barely move. Maybe they *are* robots. From time to time you look over to Trig. From something exciting and dangerous, this meeting has become quite boring. Now Captain Wells and the pirate are talking about trade.

"We have a good supply of water on board the *Orient Star*," Ching Shee says as the tea is poured.

"I am not aware that we are in need of water, but I'll ask my engineer to check," replies Captain Wells. "Should we want to trade, what type of goods are you interested in acquiring?"

"We want for very little, but we might identify some trinkets that may be of interest to others," Ching Shee replies. As she speaks she gazes about the room, her glance lands on a hummingbot which has just moved from a perch near the tea trolley to a table at the back.

"Can I ask Captain, how many generations old you are?"

"I'm sorry," says Captain Wells, "I don't understand your question."

Ching Shee looks at her curiously, "I am asking, of course, how many you are removed from your original. I myself relieved the former Ching Shee when she was 54 years old. I am Ching Shee the ninth. What about you?"

The captain is evasive in her answer – she has no reason to trust Ching Shee. It appears that although she has a faster ship she does not have the sleep technology you have.

"We've been travelling a long time – I'm not as aware of our history as you are." The ninth Ching Shee doesn't notice that the captain has avoided her question, she is looking at the corner of the room.

"What is that?" she asks, pointing into the corner.

Captain Wells follows Ching Shee's eyes and sees Desmond's game. "Oh that's just a game."

Ching Shee signals and one of her guards moves the table closer. "I don't know it. Demonstrate please."

Ching Shee's request makes you uneasy. It sounds a lot like an order.

The captain looks at you and shrugs, "Can you play?"

"Perhaps Her Eminence will be amused if we invite Desmond to play?" you suggest. He's actually the only other player you know. You sit at the game table and instruct a hummingbot to find Desmond. It doesn't have to go far — it turns out Desmond is in the very next room, presumably wanting to get the game back. When he strolls in, one of Ching Shee's guards takes a step back and gasps. So, you think, they aren't robots.

Desmond walks up to you and sits down at the game. You both begin to select your pieces. First your main piece — you select a dolphin. Because you've picked a water creature Desmond changes the boardscape so that a large portion is sea. He picks a killer whale. He gets to pick the partner — he thinks for a while and selects a white heron. A bird is a good idea, you start looking at birds as well.

"You need a bird too," says Ching Shee, agreeing with your strategy. She brings her chair closer and looks at the pieces. Her guards crowd around too. One takes off their helmet. You look at Ching Shee and you look at the guard — they could almost be twin sisters. Ching Shee sees you looking.

"She's one of the *nearly* Ching Shees — she is 'the same recipe'. She gets to be an honor guard and also to play games with me."

"How do you stop from getting mixed up?" The question comes from Trig, it seems like the ice is broken and everyone has stopped being so formal.

"She does not have this," says Ching Shee, rolling up her sleeve. Her arm is tattooed with a blue dragon. The head covers her wrist and the body coil up toward her elbow and beyond. "Only one of us wears the dragon. The seventh Ching Shee only wore the dragon for three days."

"What happened to her?" you ask.

"The eighth Ching Shee happened to her," purrs Ching Shee the ninth.

Desmond grunts and reminds you to pick your companion piece. You select an eagle and then the game begins. You start out by exploring territory and scoping out allies and enemies. A forest fire drives a bunch of animals your way and makes their living space smaller, there's a conflict and the monkeys start to take over all the spaces the birds nested in. If you can get some more territory you can sort out space for everyone and maybe if you could grow more trees… The game continues and is just as engrossing as the first time you played it.

"We have not seen a planet like this one in your game," says one of the guards, as you all munch on sandwiches an hour later.

"Like what?" Trig asks.

"A planet so full of life. Usually it's just water or just rocks."

"You've explored new planets?" The captain asks, leaning towards the guard.

Ching Shee shoots a glance at the guard then shrugs. "We've mapped a lot of new territory." Ching Shee says. "We get around, and we trade for information too. Perhaps we've found something you'd like to trade for: Information."

"And what would you like in return?" purrs the captain.

"I like this monkey and this game," Ching Shee states like a spoilt child. "That's what I want."

Desmond looks at Ching Shee. Does he understand? You think he does. Would the captain trade them for knowledge? Desmond taps you on the shoulder to remind you that you're in the middle of a game and it's your turn.

Desmond has joined up with a pod of killer whales and a flock of herons – he's playing to win and has your dolphins separated from the eagles. As you try to find another ally Desmond makes his final move. You are completely surrounded. The chimp has won. Behind you, Ching Shee's guards clap.

"My turn!" Ching Shee cries.

As she takes your place you leave the room with Trig. You want to see what the spiders in Ching Shee's ship have been up to. You duck into a service room and tap into the robotics system. With a bit of fiddling you manage to get a transmission from your spider-bots. One is on a wall looking down on row after row of what look like sleeping pods. Inside each pod is a girl at various stages of growth – this must be the cloning system. You tell the spider-bot to move on.

Next you find the feed from the other spider-bot. It is in a large library, filled with lacquered shelving, and on the walls are star charts. The bot is making copies of them all. The charts are covered in Chinese writing – you can't understand much of it but someone on board will have the skills to read the maps. A shiver of excitement runs through you. This information could help you figure out where the *Victoria* should head to find a planet to settle – or at least areas which are yet unexplored. You also feel a bit awful for stealing information.

Meanwhile, the second spider-bot has found its way deeper into the *Orient Star*. You see a long corridor with two guards at one end. A series of doors with barred windows make this look like some kind of jail. The guards are facing each other across a small table and are deeply engrossed in a game.

You instruct the spider to look inside the first door. It climbs stealthily across the ceiling and then lowers itself down to the bars. Because of the angle you are viewing everything from upside down.

Inside sits a man reading a book. He has brown skin. The man looks at the door and sees the spider-bot. He waves and gestures for the spider to come forward. You let the spider know it can approach.

"Who are you?" asks the man, he has a swirling tattoo on his face. "You don't look like *Orient Star* technology. Are you a spy?" He bustles around and writes a note. He holds it up to the spider-bot.

I am held captive by the pirate Ching Shee.

"Well little spider bot – perhaps if you're reporting back to someone you can tell them about me?"

The man in the cell doesn't realize you can hear what he's saying. You instruct your spider bot to open the door, but as it is about to do so, a commotion outside makes it pause.

You look through the bars cautiously through the spider-bot's eyes. It's Desmond. He's being marched down the corridor with both the game and his friend Morris. Ching Shee has kidnapped them!

You instruct the spider to stay put and check up on the one that is copying the maps. It's finishing up and sending the information back to the *Victoria*. You have nearly all the transmission when it cuts off. You jump on a transporter and head toward the Bridge hoping to find Captain Wells so you can tell her about Desmond. As you turn a corner you find her striding towards you.

"Engineer, do you have spider-bots on the *Orient Star*?" asks Captain Wells.

You're about to tell her what you've seen when Dr Ralph arrives on a transporter.

"Desmond and Morris have disappeared," Dr Ralph cries. "Morris is really shy – she hardly goes anywhere. I think the pirates might have her."

"They do," you say. Then you tell the two of them about the prisoner you found.

"I suspect they're planning to clone Desmond and Morris," says Dr Ralph, "but it won't work. Those chimps have years of learning using the sleep jelly. Clones will just be normal monkeys."

Trig arrives. "That woman and her clone army have just taken off!"

"The Bridge. Quickly!" says the captain. "Fill us in while we move."

"It's hopeless," Trig says, "she's a much faster ship and she knows where she's going."

"Desmond and Morris are just babies!" Dr Ralph moans. "They'll be confused and scared. I don't know what they'll do."

Once on the Bridge, you check that the *Orient Star*'s maps have been copied to the *Victoria*'s library.

You grab Trig's sleeve. "Hey take a look at this data we got from Ching Shee's ship. If we overlay it on what we mapped earlier can you decode the rest?"

Trig boots up another console and scours the maps.

"This is brilliant. Thankfully, quite a lot of it isn't Chinese, just standard nautical mapping signals. The pirates must have adapted a mixture of old sea faring mapping notation and newer mapping."

"Really?" you say. "Does that work?"

"It sort of does – ancient seafaring used the stars you know. Modern space mapping just adds a 3rd dimension. Basically, these Chinese mappers were just expanding the known universe like they were a sailing ship in the sky."

"Never mind that," Dr Ralph cuts in. "Do you have any idea where they're going? Desmond and Morris are like my own children, we need to get them back."

"What's this supposed to be?" you ask.

Drawn amidst the technical notes and figures is a picture of a dragon's head and a long tail.

"It's a comet," Trig says, "See, the observation dates written along the tail. They'd use those to figure out when the comet was due again. Then they could make sure they were out of its path."

You stare at the tiny mathematical notations as Trig continues to compare your own ship's maps and the new ones. You idly make calculations to figure the frequency of the comet's path.

Trig stabs his finger on Ching Shee's maps. "OK. We're here and Ching Shee took off that way. There's a planet in this sector here that's been well mapped. It's not very far away. I think this mark represents a space station of some sort. She might be heading there."

As Trig expands on his theory, an idea forms in your mind. It has to do with the comet you found marked on Ching Shee's map.

Your thoughts are interrupted by the Captain. "Dr Ralph, I'm dreadfully sorry but even though we know the direction Ching Shee's gone, we'll never be able to catch her ship."

"What if we could?" you ask.

All eyes turn to you.

You touch Ching Shee's map, tracing your finger along the dragon's tail. "This comet is due in about two days and it's going in the right direction. What if we hitched a ride? If my calculations are correct, we'll get there before her and have time to check out the space station and perhaps the planet. There's something else too."

You pause for effect, feeling quite proud of your clever plan, and wanting everyone to realize how brilliant you are.

"Well, spit it out Engineer!" says Captain Wells.

"If we get close to her ship, I could get the spiders to create a bit of mayhem."

The sense of despair on the bridge is gone. Everyone gets to work immediately. You set off to make a huge harpoon. Your plan is to hook the comet, get dragged along at high speed, and then cut yourself loose and slingshot the *Victoria* ahead of the *Orient Star*.

Three hours later you have a full complement of robots working on the harpoon and Trig has made several sets of calculations for the initial strike and the release. When you're dragged into the comet's tail you might lose control of the ship so you've designed a manual system that will allow you to release the *Victoria* when the time is right.

At the heart of the harpoon is an exploding pin with a cooling system to keep it in place.

"What's that for?" Dr Ralph asks as he puts a cup of hot chocolate and a plate of biscuits on the desk beside you.

"Most comets are big chunks of ice. If that's the case, we'll hook it and then fuse the harpoon onto it," you tell him.

"Thanks for trying to get Desmond and Morris back," says Dr Ralph.

"Are you kidding? Desmond has beaten me twice at that game – I want to get my own back." You laugh. "Besides, we can't have Ching

Shee out there taking whatever she wants. If we keep traveling on, who's to say she wouldn't be back for something else. If she ever found out about the sleep jelly she'd want that too. Who knows what havoc she'd make then."

Dr Ralph nods gravely. "If we catch her, what do you think we should do with her?"

"That's for the captain to decide," you say. You haven't really had time to think about that part of the operation. As the two of you eat, you stare into space. Somewhere out there, in the calm blue tranquility, a moon–sized comet is hurtling towards you at tremendous speed. Snaring the comet has absorbed your mind for hours. You suddenly realize how tired you are and yawn.

"I'll keep watch," Dr Ralph says. "Go get some sleep."

Seven hours later a spider-bot comes to wake you. You go to check that everything is ready for launch.

A big net is positioned across the comet's path. When the comet hits, the net will wrap around it and set off the harpoon.

You check your console. "Everything is ready, Captain."

"Let's do this," Captain Wells says.

A team of twelve hummers escort the net outside and stretch it out. When they get back inside you don't have long to wait.

"Comet ahoy!" shouts Trig, as his sensors pick up something approaching.

You look out a porthole but can only see a small bright dot.

A robot comes onto the bridge along with Dr Ralph. Everyone tucks into a meal as the bright light goes from a pin prick to the size of a tennis ball. It almost doubles in size by the time you finish your meal. The next job is to batten down the ship. It will be a bumpy ride when you catch the comet.

You close down the irises, leaving only the super reinforced window of the Bridge open. It has a dark screen installed to act like a giant pair of sunglasses. You've just strapped yourself into flight chairs when you hear the comet coming. It reminds you of a glass chandelier outside being tinkled in the wind. The noise increases to the sort of rattling and clanging you'd hear in a storm. The comet hits the net. Presumably the harpoon digs in because there is a lurching tug and you are suddenly streaming through space in the comet's ice storm of a tail. You've done it! You are racing faster than anyone has ever gone before.

"Start the count," you tell Trig, but you can see he's already on it.

You've got to withstand the tow for four minutes and then cut loose. Time has never gone as slowly. There's a tooth rattling vibration through your chair. It will be the same everywhere on the *Victoria*.

"I hope this crazy idea doesn't get us all killed." you say.

"Three minutes left," yells Trig.

"Really? We're not even a third of the way?" Your fingernails are cutting into the leather upholstery of the chair.

Then Trig calls out, "One minute."

OK nearly there. The ship has held up so far. There are no lights going red on the consoles. In fact the electrics are all still alive, you aren't flying blind at all.

"Thirty seconds, twenty nine, twenty eight…" Trig counts down.

It's nearly time to release from the comet.

"Release," you say calmly enough when the count hits zero but inside you are a mess of emotions. At first nothing happens but then the noise abates and the vibrating slows and eventually stops altogether – you are free from the comet.

"Full power!" the Captain says. "Engage all thrusters."

The ship's engines are almost silent compared to the racket of being towed by the comet. The quiet is like velvet to your ears. All over the ship robots will be checking for damage, including your army of spiders. You unbuckle from your chair and raise the main window. Outside is a new section of the universe.

Trig has added Ching Shee's maps to the *Victoria's* own and he's checking where you are.

"We've come further than we thought. I reckon we have a few days lead on the pirates," Trig says. "That space station is close by and beyond that is the new planet."

"How long to the station?" asks the Captain.

Trig checks his calculations. "Two hours, twelve minutes and sixteen seconds."

The Captain nods. "We don't know if they're friends or foe, Trig. If we can communicate with them from here let's do it. I'd like to keep a respectful distance until we know more."

All the exhilaration you felt at jaunting across the universe fades. You've still got to prepare to face the pirates.

"We've got a radio signal coming from the space station," Trig says.

While preparing for the comet ride, a number of new people were woken up. Some were ready to help with any damage to the ship and others were to be part of exploration and communication parties. One of the communicators comes onto the bridge now. Like you and Trig she wears the ship's uniform and she's managed to make it look quite smart. You look down at yourself, you're distinctly rumpled after a few days action.

She salutes Trig, assuming he must be the captain. He shakes his head a little and points at Captain Wells. The newcomer blushes and curtsies to the Captain.

"Pardon me ma'am, language specialist reporting for duty. I'm Flora ma'am."

"Good timing," says Captain Wells. The Captain introduces herself and the rest of you to the newcomer. "We've just had a transmission from that object over there."

Everyone goes silent as Trig tunes in to the message. The language is one you don't know. The others, apart from Flora, seem just as confused as you are by the strange sounding message.

Flora face is one of concentration as she listens "They're saying the planet below has terrible monsters ma'am. They want to know if we're planning on settling there. They've had a bit of bad luck it seems."

"What language are they speaking Flora?"

"It's Maori ma'am. From New Zealand."

The Captain frowns. "Isn't it because of those upstarts that we're colonizing way out here?"

You must have learned some history while sleeping. "That's right Captain. The Maori took their revolution from New Zealand to Australia and then on to the Americas. They own half of planet Earth."

"And now they're out here too," the Captain says. "Ask them why, if the planet is no good, they haven't moved on. Oh and check if they've come across Ching Shee."

Flora steps up to the microphone and begins talking. You are amused to see she flutters her hands about as she does so – although the recipients won't see any of the actions she's making. There's a good break as the people on the other side digest what she's said. When the reply comes there is a brief song and then a woman's voice continues. This time the speech is in English:

"Greetings people of the *Victoria* from Britannia. We are of the tribe Ngati Kahungunu from Aotearoa and we have travelled to these stars that herald Matariki - the beginning of new growth each year.

"Your speaker tells us that you met the warrior Ching Shee and she has taken something of yours. We are sorry about that. Ching Shee has taken something of ours too – our chief. She has also dismantled our craft. "

The travelers explain they were setting up a mission to populate the planet below when Ching Shee stole their chief and sabotaged their space station.

"Now Ching Shee says she will only help us colonize the planet only if we agree to her terms. We are to be her slaves. We do not even know if our chief is still alive."

"Tell them he's alive!" you interrupt. "They must be talking about the man I saw in the cell." You bring up a recording of what the spider-bot recorded and send the clip over to the space station.

There are exclamations from the other vessel. Things become a lot friendlier. You arrange to dock and work on a plan together. You must hurry. The Maori explorers are expecting Ching Shee to return soon.

On board the space station you find an efficient little set up with hydroponic gardens in every room. The floors are clear and you can see fish swimming under your feet. It is like being in a huge glass bottomed boat. The walls are covered in moss and there are plants everywhere. Unlike the opulence of the *Victoria*, this ship, with its forests and fern and gardens everywhere is practical and beautiful at the same time.

"We traded for water with Ching Shee several times – but then she double crossed us," explains Aroha, the woman you had been speaking with by radio. "She has taken parts of our engine to prevent us from taking the space station down to the planet. Without it, and all the equipment aboard, we won't survive against the creatures down there."

After some discussion, there is a decision to use the element of surprise seeing Ching Shee doesn't know you are here.

The *Victoria* offloads a lot of spider-bots onto the Maori space station. A number of them cling to the hull outside as well.

If your plan works there will be no harm to any people and, hopefully, no harm to your robots. There is still time to wait, everyone is eager to learn about the planet you are orbiting.

Aroha shows you the maps they have made of the planet's surface. There are many volcanic islands. On the continents there are huge animals. Some are herbivores and eat the massive trees that form a canopy across this world, but there are predators too.

"And I wouldn't want to meet one of them down a dark alley," says Trig.

"Tell me about it," you say. "But I reckon some of the robots we have on the *Victoria*, would be a match for these monsters."

Maybe settlers from the *Victoria* could carve out some territory where they could be safe and learn to get along with these huge land animals.

As you consider the possibilities, you get to work fixing the space station. Once again you thank your lucky stars that you have been given the training to be an engineer while you slept. The *Victoria* might be old technology but you've essentially cracked time travel and the problem of passing on knowledge, something neither Ching Shee nor the Maori explorers have done. Your new companions were all born in space.

The Maori space station is high tech but you are able to figure it out. With parts from the *Victoria* the *Takitimu* is soon mobile again.

"But we won't move the ship yet. We want it to be a surprise," smiles Kupe, their navigator. "I'm looking forward to getting the upper hand with Ching Shee."

You find yourself alone with Captain Wells and broach the subject of trying to settle the planet below. "It might have big monsters but it also has water and plant life. I wonder, if we pooled our resources with these settlers, could we make a go of it?"

Captain Wells nods, "That's certainly worth considering. We can't stay between the stars forever. Even if we put down some of our passengers we'll be spreading our risk."

At the end of the day the crew working on the space station re-join the *Victoria* and the ship takes off to the other side of the planet leaving you and your spider bot army to wait for the *Orient Star*. You fill in the time checking the position and programming the spiders, too excited to sleep.

"Will yee get some rest?" says your favorite spider. "We cannae have yee fallin' asleep in what is to come." It jumps on your bunk and scuttles up to your pillow, tapping it with two legs. You get in the bunk and your robot starts a story:

"Once upon a time there was a veeery intelligent robot shaped like a spider, and it had a lot of wee friends…"

Your eyes grow heavy and you start to nod off even though you are trying to follow the robot's tale. How on Earth did it get programmed to tell bedtime stories?

Aroha and Kupe wake you up with hot food and drink. You have noticed they mostly eat vegetables and fish. For breakfast you have hot potato cakes with salmon. "Delicious."

After a quick shower you put on the uniform of the Maori passengers to be as unobtrusive as possible. Then you wait as Ching Shee's ship nears. When it is within hailing distance Aroha opens up a frequency and speaks out to the pirate.

"Greetings *Orient Star.*"

"Hello most unfortunate stranded travelers," chimes Ching Shee's voice. "Are you ready to be rescued by my most generous self and live your lives in gratitude of my benevolence?"

Aroha keeps her voice steady and calm as she replies to the pirate. This part is critical to your plan.

"We have given your offer much thought as we've floated around this planet and have decided defeat is almost inevitable. However, we know Your Eminence enjoys games. Therefore, we challenge you to a game of your choice – chess, backgammon, cards – you choose. The victor will rule the planet and the loser will obey them in all things. What do you say?"

There is silence for a few seconds. Clearly the pirate had not expected such an offer but you know her ego will tempt her to take up the challenge.

Sure enough, her voice comes back to you, this time with a note of cunning in it. "I am a benevolent ruler and a wise one. We will begin the glorious history of our settlement of this planet with a game as you suggest. Let it always be said that I, Ching Shee the ninth, was reasonable and clever in all things. Prepare for boarding. I will challenge you in one Earth hour."

The pirate has given you time you don't want to waste. Quickly you contact your spiders aboard the *Orient Star*. They begin broadcasting the ship's schematics to the *Victoria* and you send over their final instructions. When all the information required for your plan has been transmitted, you ask the two spy spider-bots to locate Desmond, Morris and the Maori chief.

The Chief's voice comes through a few minutes later. "Aroha? Is that you? Kupe?"

You explain how have joined forces with his people to rescue him and let him know what to expect.

When Desmond appears on your monitor he doesn't seem too distressed and is just finishing a game with one of the Ching Shee's body guards. Morris is playing nearby. She glances at the spider-bot on the ceiling then gets up and walks over to the window and gestures to the space station outside.

Desmond doesn't appear to have noticed the bot.

The spider bot moves closer to the table where Desmond and the guard are playing. You can hear what the guard is saying.

"With her new slaves, Ching Shee is going to set up a mining operation on the planet. First she'll kill the large animals and then she'll gather the riches under its surface."

The guard speaks of this with such certainty that you know Ching Shee must have done this before. What a terrible thing to do – a good planet is hard to find and she would plunder it and ruin it!

More guards come into the room just as Desmond is claims victory. One of them has a big plate of fruit. They take away Desmond's game, but he's distracted by the food and another guard setting up a game of chess. At least Desmond doesn't look desperately unhappy.

Things are happening exactly as you expected.

There is a loss of picture quality as the spider moves into a small duct. The bot has work to do.

Meanwhile on the space station, a gang plank is lowered for Ching Shee and her guards. From your perch at the scanners you see the pirate captain make a similar entrance to the one she made on the *Victoria*.

Aroha and Kupe meet her at the end of the carpet. They start an interesting welcoming ceremony which you wish you could watch more closely, but you are busy deploying the spiders. The two spiders on the Chinese ship will open an airlock to let them in.

"Ah! There they are now," you say to yourself as you watch the progress on the monitor.

The spiders move carefully – metal on metal can make quite a clang and you want to surprise the pirates.

Aroha and Kupe talk with Ching Shee. She grandly gestures at Desmond's game which is being carried from the *Orient Star*.

Aroha and Kupe look dismayed, as if they had not expected this game. But in fact, you have told them all about it and coached them as much as you could on how it is played. They need to play the game long enough for the spiders to do their job if your plan is to work.

Kupe and Aroha offer a meal to Ching Shee but she declines – it would have been nice if she'd had time to socialize before enslaving these people but you hope you'll have enough time to do what you need to while the game is going on. Time is at a premium. Already Ching Shee's guards are setting up the board and arranging the pieces.

The last of the spiders are now aboard the *Orient Star* and the airlocks are shut. As the bots make their way into the depths of the ship you monitor their progress.

In the ceiling of the bridge a massive rewiring operation is going on. The spiders are establishing their own control center. The controls that the pirates use will be useless. Meanwhile several spiders have entered the cloning facility. They lock the doors and sit on top of the tanks. Two can play the hostage game.

Speaking of games, the game aboard the Maori vessel is well underway. Kupe is playing Ching Shee and he looks anxious. Never mind that he is supposedly playing for the freedom of his people, the game is complex and Ching Shee is winning. She has the benefit of having played every day against Desmond. The two opponents play with grim determination.

You tell the spiders to open the Chief's cell and watch through one of your spider eyes as he gingerly steps out into a corridor. There are no guards – everyone is either over on the Maori vessel or up in the games room watching the game from a live feed.

Desmond and Morris are in the games room. Desmond is interested but Morris is looking round. She knows something is going on. She notices when a door opens and a spider waves a leg for her to follow.

Morris takes Desmond's hand and the two saunter out. In the deserted corridor Morris points to a spider-bot and Desmond understands something is happening. The spiders take them to meet the other captive. The chief looks completely confused when he meets up with Desmond and Morris. Morris points to the spider and then at a passing pirate. She puts her finger to her lips.

That seems to be enough for him to know she is on his side. They head towards the open airlock between the *Orient Star* and the Maori vessel but the entry is blocked by guards who point them back the way they came. They sit a little way off and wait patiently.

"I've won!" Ching Shee says with a smile. "Now your children will say how Ching Shee the ninth won their loyalty. Now we will raze the planet below of its large and useless inhabitants and set up a profitable mining business to expand our empire into the next galaxy."

This is your moment, you step out from the control room where you have been concealed.

"I'm sorry, but you won't be taking these people as your loyal servants today."

Ching Shee squints at you. "Don't I know you?"

"Engineer of the *Victoria* ma'am, at these people's service. I'm sorry to inform you that your ship is suffering an infestation of spiders. They've rewired your ship and they have your cloning room under their control. I'm willing to help you get rid of them but first I need you to release all your hostages."

Just then a guard from Ching Shee's ship stumbles into the room and makes a signal. Ching Shee stands and starts barking orders. One of the guards draws a sword. Faster than the guard can step toward you, a spider drops from the ceiling and administers a swift jab to the guard's neck. The guard crumples to the floor. Another guard puts her hand on her sword and the same thing happens. Ching Shee and her entourage look up warily. The ceiling is alive with spiders!

"Back to the ship!" she cries.

"I'm sorry ma'am I'm going to have to ask you to listen to me," you say, walking forward and standing next to Aroha and Kupe. "The spiders in your ship have disabled your bridge, you have no power and you can't go anywhere. That's not all, you'll find a spider sitting above every cloning tank on the ship. If you don't start listening there may be no Ching Shee the tenth."

At this the pirate captain starts to fume and spit orders.

"Kill that engineer now!" she shrieks, stamping her foot. None of the guards move to follow her command, they all saw what happened to their fellows.

Ching Shee turns to you. "What do you want?" she hisses, cold as ice.

"For starters I'd like the safe return of the chief and my friends Desmond and Morris. Order your guards to return to your ship and send them over. Then we'll talk."

"I'm not handing them over. I won dominion over these people fairly. I won this game!" she points at the board. "You are bound by your British honor to give me these people and their ship. I will give you your monkeys in return."

"I think you're confusing me with someone who didn't grow up in an orphanage and wasn't caught stealing bread and sent to prison. There's no honor when you are hungry, Ching Shee. Hand over your prisoners. I'm not asking again."

"Ahh, so you are a pirate at heart," the pirate tries one last time, "You have humble beginnings like the first Ching Shee. You should join me. Together we could own the universe and take the Earth. We can replicate ourselves over and over until it is done. What do you say?"

"I asked nicely," you say, tiring of her antics, "put her to sleep, thank you."

Ching Shee screams like a banshee and dives toward a sword but the spiders are fast. Two jump on her and strike. She crumples to the floor. She looks like a child who fell asleep after a tantrum.

There is a clatter of swords as one by one each of the guards drops their weapon. Helmets are taken off and the Maori crew gasp as they see that face after face is the same – all copies of Ching Shee. One of the Chinese crew steps cautiously forward.

"Noble warrior, ah engineer. We have heard what you said. It is time for a new leader and new ways – would you consider leading our crew?"

As you are digesting this request you see the *Victoria* arrive from where she has been hidden behind the planet. There is a burst of static and then you hear the vessel being hailed. The crew scrambles to pick up Ching Shee and take her to a cell. Then they take the swords and weapons from her surrendering crew and lock them in a storage unit.

When Desmond and Morris arrive there's chaos as the two of them recognize you and rush over. When Dr Ralph arrives he weeps openly when he sees Desmond and Morris again.

Everyone moves on to the bigger *Victoria* for a feast and to swap stories. Captain Wells hints at some interesting developments. Has she more information about the planet below?

There is laughter and chatter all over the *Victoria*. It takes you a while before you find Trig zooming about the lower corridors on a transporter.

"Well done!" he yells as he hurtles toward you and leaps off. "Did the Captain tell you we've scouted the planet? We've found large islands without big animals. Did she tell you we might be settling here?"

"No," you say, "She said we'd swap stories over a feast. I've been looking for you. Let's go eat."

"Right," says Trig. "Try and look surprised when she tells you alright?"

Sounds like you have some decisions ahead of you. Do you take off as the leader of the pirate ship or settle down on the new planet? You've made some great friends and had adventures that will be told for generations to come.

You jump on the transporter behind Trig and practice your surprised face as you head to the landing bay where the feast will be served. It's the only place big enough for so many people. You slide open the door a crack hoping to make a quiet entrance but one of Ching Shee's ex-guards sees you and springs up to salute. Soon all the guards rise and bow and you're waved up to the main table. Trig settles into a spot right next to you and the captain.

The Captain starts telling you, Aroha and Kupe about the land the *Victoria* has found. "Why don't you look surprised Engineer?"

This part of the story is over but there are many other paths you can take. Do you:

Go back to the beginning? **P1**

Or

Go to the list of choices **P380**

Go back to sleep again

You have chosen to sleep again, sleep is so wonderful. Who would want to be awake when you can stay in blissful sleep? In your dreams your sleep chamber is moved to a new location and you dream of having the option to work on a new planet or to stay sleeping. Sleep is so good. So comfortable.

In your dreams you are working in a mine. You are always tired. It seems odd that you keep dreaming of mining. Shouldn't you be learning new things while you sleep? Next to you is another miner. He's very old. It's odd you are dreaming of older people when sleeping chambers preserves you in sleep.

Next to you the old miner staggers and sways with fatigue. "Rest," you say, but he doesn't hear you.

You put out your hand to steady him as he sways again and look around. You are deep in a mineshaft surrounded by other miners. They are all old like the miner next to you. There are old men and old women chipping away at a large seam of coal.

The old man sits down, he's had it. A robot comes down a railway line with a cart. It gently lifts the miner into the cart and starts to take him away.

"Where are you taking him?" you ask.

The robot pauses and turns to scan you. Did you do the right thing asking the robot about the old man?

"Are you awake?" the robot asks.

You think about the robot's question. Surely this is a dream, but then maybe it isn't. It seems very odd that someone in a dream would ask you if you were awake. How do you answer a question you're not sure of?

You have a couple of choices. Do you:

Tell the robot you are awake? **P82**

Or

Tell the robot you are asleep? **P81**

You tell the robot you are asleep

"That's right sleeper, you're dreaming. You never wanted to wake and do any work and you never will have to wake. I am authorized to send you back into a deep sleep. If at any time you want to wake up, you have only to tell me. We treat everyone with kindness on the new planet, sleepers and non-sleepers alike. Go back to seep now."

You are feeling very drowsy and your mind struggles to think about what you've just heard. You remember there were times when you have been asked if you want to wake and you chose sleep. Why wake when you can travel between the stars and never age? Sleepily you wonder what will happen at the end of the journey. What will the settlers do with people who don't want to wake...

That's the end of this part of the story. What would you like to do now?

Go back to the beginning **P1**

Or

Go to the list of choices and start reading from another part of the story? **P380**

You decide to tell the robot you are awake

"Yes, I'm awake," you say, stepping forward and staring into the robot's scanner. It pauses and relays information back to the central computer.

"Sleeper, do you want to be awake?" asks the robot.

You think about all the time you might have spent sleeping, the times you have had opportunities to wake and didn't. It's time to get on with your life.

"Yes," you say. "I want to be awake."

The robot sprays you in the face with a sharp smelling vapor. Your knees buckle and you fall backwards into another cart. You follow behind the old miner being carted up the railway tracks to the surface. On the way up you see old miners sitting in carts as they are wheeled down. They have a vacant expression on their faces. They don't seem unhappy, more like they're dreaming.

The walls begin to appear as natural light filters down from above. Tracks lead up towards a round circle of light. The increased light hurts your eyes.

You come out squinting to an alien landscape. The sky is a funny sort of purple and large red bats glide across the sky. As the smell of coal and grease and steam from the tunnel fade, you start to smell other things. The air is very different to the air on Earth and to the sterile air of the space ship.

Your little cart is still being pushed along by the robot. You enter a building and a man in a suit with a top hat greets you. He has a handle bar moustache and, at about 40, is the youngest person you've seen today.

"You must be the sleeper who has decided to wake up!" he cries and shakes your hand. "Welcome to Victorious. Welcome to our utopia. I am one of the great grandchildren of the original settlers. They broke in the land here and started the coal mines."

He babbles on, enthusiastically talking of the settlement of the planet, but you aren't listening. You have caught sight of your reflection in the window. You see an old face and gray hair. Slowly you look down to your wrinkled and liver-spotted hands. Old hands. He is still talking:

"…and then many of the sleepers said they didn't want to wake up. It seemed you got used to sleeping and preferred it. At first we let people sleep on in the cryo-chambers but then my grandfather had the bright idea to get some labor in exchange for the sleep. Unfortunately when you're sleep-working your body ages. But you'll be pleased to know that while you've been mining here you've cleared your debt, worked off your sentence AND made some savings. We've saved your money prudently. You now have enough set aside to retire!"

You look out the window. There's a new world beyond the mining works. Huge birds circle mountains carpeted in strange plants. There will be rivers nobody has ever traveled, and new animals, and so much more to explore. You don't have much time left but you want to see as much of it as you can.

You've reached the end of this branch of the story but that's not a problem – there's plenty more story left: Do you want to:

Go Back to the beginning and try another path? **P1**

Or

Go to the list of choices and start reading from somewhere else? **P380**

Wait for another mission or to land on the new planet

You don't know if months or many years have passed before you hear another voice asking you to wake.

"Sleeper. Do you want to wake up?"

You don't have to wake. You can keep sleeping. You are such a good sleeper. You vaguely remember something about a space ship. About travelling somewhere. That's it, you are on the space ship *Victoria*. You're travelling a long way away on an adventure. One day you'll get to a new planet. Maybe you're already there?

"Sleeper. Do you want to wake up?"

That's right. You can choose to wake up on the way. You can have adventures. But if you stay awake too long you'll be old when you get to the new plant or never get there at all. You won't get to spend your life exploring it. You need to choose. Do you:

Wake up? **P85**
Or
Stay asleep? **P80**

Wake up for an adventure

You are swimming in a large tank. Something is following you like a shadow but you aren't worried. You sense that your tank mate is a large fish-like creature, just like you.

You know you used to be human, but being like this feels ... wonderful. You just wish you had more water to swim in.

You beat your fluke and send your sleek body surging up to the surface. As you leap above the water you expel air from your blowhole and take in a fresh supply. Several humans are sitting on a platform at the top of your tank.

"Sleeper, I'm Dr Alan. Can you understand me?"

The speaker is a young man in a white coat. He's very tall. You click once for yes. It's something you learned in your sleep. Sitting next to Dr Alan is someone you know very well.

It is you. Human-you.

Human—you is standing next to a girl with tight black curls and a mischievous grin and they both look pretty excited.

You remember waking up and being asked about undertaking a mission. You agreed to have your mind copied into the body of a dolphin so you can explore a new planet. It's strange to see your old self there. The girl next to you must have shared her mind with a dolphin too.

Dolphin-you shoots a stream of water at human-you. Human-you and the curly haired girl try and duck away but end up wet and laughing.

Dolphin-you lets out a laugh that sounds like a high pitched spluttering whistle.

The man in the white coat frowns. "Yes, very funny. But we're not here to lark about. This is quite serious."

You and the other dolphin stop and listen.

"Your human bodies are still safe here on the spaceship as you can see. We have shared your minds with a dolphin. The dolphin mind is asleep and we are just drawing from its instincts. All its memories and thinking processes have been completely suppressed."

As you listen to the scientist explain why you are now in the body of a dolphin, you look at your old self on the platform yet feel perfectly normal as a dolphin.

Your human self leaves with the girl. Then Dr Alan explains how the human-you and the girl will wait on the ship to find out how the mission goes.

The Doctor throws you a fish which you snap up greedily. "I'm calling the planet Atlantica – partly because of the lost city of Atlantis and partly because of our beloved Britannia."

Another person climbs onto the platform and joins Dr Alan. You recognize him too, but it isn't a pleasant memory. It's the scar-faced youth you met when you were trying out for space transportation that first time. He very nearly ruined your chances for no reason at all.

You try to say something about it, but all you can do is make whistles and clicks.

"Sleeper, are you asking about the Inventor?" asks the white coated Dr Alan. He gestures towards scar-face. Surely, you think, he isn't the Inventor? The Inventor is an old man who designed the space ship you are travelling in and many of the wonders on board. His own father invented sleep jelly.

Dr Alan explains. "This is the body of the criminal Moriarty but I can assure you Moriarty's mind does not rule this body any more. Moriarty paid that price for his crimes. His body now carries the mind of the great man who made our journey possible. The Inventor was too old to sleep in space so his mind was transferred into this body. Do you understand?"

You click to say yes.

As Dr Alan tells you more about your mission you keep looking at the face of Moriarty – it is difficult to trust that face despite what you've heard.

"The ship has come very close to a new planet," Dr Alan says. "It is mostly covered in water. We've decided a dolphin is the best scout for this largely aquatic environment. There are other planets in this solar system, but for the mission to be successful we need to pick the best one to settle on. You are going to be the first explorers."

"Lucky us," whistles your tank companion in the language of dolphins.

Her clicking is very pleasing to your ears. You've never noticed how gruff and unmelodic humans sound when they talk.

"Hello?" you whistle back.

"Hello Proudfin," says the dolphin next to you.

"Proudfin?"

"That's what I'm calling you. Any objection?"

"That's fine ... Longtail," you say.

From the quick series of clicks she makes, you know she likes the name you just gave her. It has two meanings. Not only does the other dolphin have a long tail but the tales of your adventures will be carried a long way.

"Listen up you two," Dr Alan continues. "A small space ship, an 'explorer', is to be sent to the planet below. The explorer will also carry robots. They will build a radio station for you to broadcast back to the *Victoria*. You and Longtail will be placed in special tubes of sleep jelly. The jelly will help cushion you in space and also provide oxygen in the same way it does when you sleep. Once you land on the new planet you'll explore and report back via a radio station."

The Inventor steps closer to the edge of your tank. "We appreciate what you are doing. Your exploration will help us decide if we can settle down there on Atlantica. You are sentinels for all of us. Travel safely."

His voice lacks the sneering tone of the prisoner you met on Earth. Maybe you should just relax about him. Besides, you're heading off on a major journey.

In quick order, you are transferred to special capsules filled with sleep jelly. Then your capsules are sealed and placed in the explorer. It isn't long before you feel a lurch. Your journey has begun.

As you blast out of the *Victoria* you think about swimming in a large ocean on a new world. You drift and imagine – dolphins can't dream, but they can imagine. Strong images of the sea run through your head, you can almost taste salt water and the silver fish that school within it. These must be memories from your dolphin self. They are soothing things to think about as you hurtle through space toward the water planet.

Abruptly, there is a change in the way the flight feels. The explorer vessel shudders and you can hear a rushing, drumming sound. You've entered the atmosphere of the planet. The hull of the explorer is heating up outside and the metallic feathers that line it will be repelling the heat and keeping you safe inside. There will only be seconds for the robotic control to sense deep water and point the probe towards it.

Insulated in your pod, you don't hear the splash as the explorer drops into the ocean, but you are aware of a change in pressure as you hit the water. The pressure increases as the explorer is propelled into deep water. Then, the little space probe begins to rise again.

"Landing achieved," a robotic voice chirps. Your dolphin sonar tells you it's one of those little bird robots with a long narrow beak. It is taking off the straps that have held it safe on the journey. In the corner a spider-bot detaches itself from the wall too.

"We are scanning the water," a spider-bot tells you. "Please wait for the hatch to release. A location beacon will start shortly. You can follow the sound to come back to make your reports."

The spider-bot turns a valve, opens the hatch and moves upward to avoid the water.

There is a hissing noise as sea water flows into your section of the space ship. A mechanism unzips a hole in the outer casing of the jelly and you swim outside to explore the new world.

The cool water is deliciously full of life. You send out your sonar and it bounces off the sea bottom. You can tell when the water is incredibly deep and where it rises up to form a land mass above the sea. All through the water you feel the creatures of this ocean thriving and swimming about.

You flick your tail and head to the surface, expelling the last of the sleep jelly, ready to take your first breath. As you burst out of the water you inhale the sweet air, flip and dive sideways to circle the explorer. Longtail circles the explorer too. She looks as frisky as you feel. Your instincts are strongly urging you to take off and explore.

The robots have launched a floatation device. It bobs up to the surface. From there they will erect the transmitter. One of the bird-like robots flies into the air and shoots off in the direction of land to get information you won't be able to discover.

It is time to make a decision:

Do you want to find out what is happening back on the Victoria? **P90**

Or

Head off with your dolphin friend to explore this world? **P100**

Meanwhile back on the *Victoria*

Nobody tells you to go to sleep again after the dolphins leave the *Victoria*. You are left to yourself and you have fun exploring the ship. You jump on transporters and whizz around the different floors. Little robot birds – hummingbots – follow you around.

The hummingbots show you things by flying ahead after you've asked them a question. That was how you found a galley kitchen and some regular sleep quarters.

It was strange, and even a bit uncomfortable, sleeping in a normal bunk rather than a sleep tank filled with jelly. When you did get to sleep you dreamed you were swimming in a vast ocean. There were strange creatures in the depths and fearsome birds in the air above.

The spaceship is even bigger than you imagined. You haven't even explored half of it when you find a large room filled with sleep tanks like the one you slept in all those years. You expected to find it full of passengers but all the tanks are empty.

"Where are all the people?" you ask a passing service robot.

"One hundred went to a new planet twenty-seven years ago," it says.

That just raises more questions.

"Why didn't everyone get off at the same place?"

"The planet wasn't optimal. It needed help developing the ecology for human life. A decision was made to send some, not all."

You have one more question. "But why wouldn't everyone wait for a perfect planet to live on?"

"The *Victoria* will not last forever," the service bot answers matter-of-factly. "If some leave for a less suitable planet there are more resources aboard for the rest. It is possible the *Victoria* won't find a suitable planet before the ship is unable to sustain life on-board."

This is a sobering thought. What if you never find a home?

You decide to take more of an interest in the watery planet and stop larking about. You head off to find Dr Alan to get an update.

First you try the dolphin tanks but they are empty and nobody is around. As you are about to leave, a curly-haired kid scoots up and waves cheerily to you.

"Any news about how the dolphins are doing?" she asks.

"I'm looking for Dr Alan to find that out," you say. "Any idea where he is?"

The kid shakes her head. "No, sorry. I'm Grace by the way."

You tell her what you've just found out. "Did you know there have already been settlers sent off the ship?"

"Why would I know anything?" replies your new friend. "Wait, I do know a few things. I seem to know about geology and also the rudiments of thermal energy. Oh, and I know about radio too. I found myself down in an engineering store room the past few days constructing a transmitter just for fun. I suppose I learned all this when I was sleeping. Jolly useful those dreaming caps don't you think? And I can still remember the things I used to know too."

"Like what?" you say. You're not sure you learned anything from the dreaming caps.

"I managed to grow a crop of spuds up on a roof top once. Great things spuds – we're growing there here too you know."

"We are? Where are we doing that?"

"In the hydroponic gardens – haven't you found them? Well, I suppose it's a big place. I asked the hummingbirds to take me to where they grow the food. I've been interested in gardens all my life."

When you tell her that you've even been dreaming about the ocean on the planet below, she looks interested.

"Really? That's a bit of a coincidence then, I've been dreaming about the world down there too. It's like I'm swimming around in the sea. Last time I slept I dreamed about some rough looking fish with sharp teeth and arms. Pretty scary actually."

"That's more than odd then," you say. "I dreamed about the same things. What else did you dream about?"

When Grace talks about using sonar to map the new world you

both agree the two of you must be connected to the dolphins in some way when you sleep.

You look at the nearest hummingbot. "Take me to Dr Alan or The Inventor," you say.

The hummingbot flits off down the corridor. You jump on your transporter and get ready to follow. "Oh there's another thing," you say. "The Inventor's mind is in a criminal named Moriarty's body."

She pulls her transporter alongside yours: "Really? That's sinister. Thanks for telling me."

As the two of you zip along after the hummingbot, the corridor changes. Gold ornamentation and fancy scrolling starts to appear around the doorways. The walls are hung with beautiful paintings and there are dazzling lights set into the ceiling.

You pass an alcove with soft padded chairs and a chess board. The alcove looks out to space through a porthole with a large brass frame around it. The doors also have brass labels on them. You pull up outside a door with carvings of different trees and leaves on it. In the middle is the word 'BRIDGE'.

"What would we need a bridge for?" you ask Grace.

She knocks on the door. "It's the word they use for the control room on a spaceship."

This kid has learned everything there is to learn in the sleep jelly by the sound of it. What did you learn you wonder? You don't seem to have any special skills. Your thoughts are interrupted as the door swings open.

The Bridge is a large room. Monitors, keyboards, dials and switches are everywhere. Various instruments beep, and lights flicker across screens tracking space outside and things inside the ship.

The far wall is taken up by a window that looks out into space. Through it you see the blue planet.

You never saw Earth from space, when you blasted off, but from the maps you've seen you are fairly sure that the large continents like Europa, Australia and the Americas are much bigger than the islands you can see dotted about on this planet's surface.

"Beautiful isn't it?" says Dr Alan, coming over to greet you. "I'm calling it Atlantica. Unfortunately there isn't much land. The Inventor thinks it's promising though and who knows, perhaps he can devise a way to drain some of it."

"How are the dolphins?" Grace asks.

Dr Alan's eyes move to a receiving station built into one of the consoles. "We know they landed safely and we've had one transmission from the radio station. I'm monitoring them constantly."

He gestures for you to join him at a table in the corner of the room. It is set up with delicate tea cups and a plate of sandwiches. You and Grace fall on the food at once – it's been a while since you ate. Dr Alan eats at a more refined pace. He's probably never eaten with a horde of orphans you think.

"Mmmm, is this fish?" asks Grace.

"Yes," replies the Doctor. "The ship has several tanks, they provide excellent protein and also help with the filtration system by eating little scraps."

"I love fish," you say without thinking. Then you try to remember when you last ate fish. You can't. You've got a memory of chasing after a silver school quite recently but that can't be *your* memory.

You are about to say something when you feel a kick from Grace who must have thought something similar and is telling you to shut up about it.

"Where's the Inventor?" you ask Dr Alan, changing the subject "I expected to find you two working together."

"He's readying supplies and a landing crew should we need it. I've just woken up from a nap. Funny thing, I slept really solidly, you'd think I wouldn't sleep much after all those years in the sleep tank."

That's quite different to you and Grace, you'd had a lot of trouble sleeping. Grace takes a sip of the tea Dr Alan has poured and makes a face as if it tasted awful. When the doctor isn't looking, she spits the tea back into the cup. You decide not to try any.

"If we don't settle on this planet, are there any more nearby?" Grace asks innocently. You watch the Doctor carefully as he answers. He seems fairly relaxed.

"There's another star system about 300 light years away. We want to be sure about this one before we push on."

A buzzing noise and a faint voice distracts Dr Alan from your conversation. He leaps up and starts tweaking dials. "Hmmm," he says, "Transmission has cut out completely. It could be a problem at either end. The Inventor has the main radio receiver set up in his private rooms. Let's go take a look. Perhaps he got a message from our scouts. There's nothing coming through here."

The three of you head off to find the Inventor. Dr Alan sits on the back of your transporter.

"Jolly useful things these aren't they?" he says. "I say you two, I'm awfully tired. Must be the effects of space travel and waking up. Would you mind dropping me off for a sleep? I'll join you youngsters a bit later."

You find a bunk room and leave Dr Alan to rest. When you get back on your transports Grace directs you to a pump station room. Inside there's the steady noise of water being flushed through pipes.

Grace whispers in your ear through cupped hands. "I don't like this. I think Dr Alan might have been drugged. He didn't seem to know what's going on."

"Yes, very odd." Then you have an idea. "Didn't you say you'd built a radio? Maybe we should check it out."

Grace nods, "It's not far away."

You stop the next service robot that glides into view. Something has been worrying you. "Can you tell me who has the most authority on the ship?"

"The Inventor," the robot states.

"Is there any sort of safety override? What if the Inventor gave you a command that put people in danger?"

"The Inventor is the final authority," the robot says with simple logic.

After a few turns and a trip down a service lift, you find yourself in a maintenance room full of tools, wires, spare parts and pieces of robotics.

Grace bounds into the room, "Isn't this great?" she enthuses. "When I found all this I spent two days here. Until I got hungry. I'll just flip this switch."

A speaker in the far corner of the room starts making a noise, Grace walks to her radio and starts moving a dial. With less static you figure out you are hearing water – the transmission is coming from under the ocean. Then you hear a few squeals. Oddly you think they mean "Watch out! Crabs."

"Hmm," says Grace, "did you hear that? I mean, did it make sense to you?"

"Crabs," you say, marveling that you understand the language of the dolphins, "Have you heard anything else like that?"

"No, this is the first thing I've heard from the radio, but I've dreamed these voices and I listened for … oh!"

Another burst of static heralds a change of voice, this time it is a robot voice.

"This is the explorer. The dolphins have detected hostile creatures both on land and sea. The land masses are inhabited by large aggressive carnivorous birds. These birds would pose an ongoing threat to human habitation. Ocean life is very diverse. Some titanium deposits detected. Volcanic activity has potential for geothermal power. The dolphins are hooking the explorer up to a thermal power source now. Current conclusion: Planet not well suited to human habitation due to aggressive native species and limited land for settlement."

You turn to Grace, "Well that's not promising."

A dolphin interrupts the report, their broadcasts must have priority: You get a feeling something is wrong.

The message is faint but you hear the dolphin's words clearly "Do not trust the Inventor."

Your feeling of unease is confirmed. Grace picks up a microphone ready to answer the dolphins but you put a finger to your lips.

Grace hands you a piece of paper and a pencil.

You write: *Careful, The Inventor could be listening.*

Grace writes: *Need to confirm if the Inventor is a danger to ship.*

You write: *Let's investigate.*

Grace picks up the paper and stuffs it in her pocket. The two of you jump on to your 'sporters. Half way down the corridor you come across a hummingbot.

Grace hails the little robot, "Can you tell us where the Inventor is?"

The little machine spends a few seconds communicating with all the other robots. "Sleep Room 4."

"What is he doing?" you ask.

"Imprinting."

"What's that?" Grace asks.

"Transferring the thoughts and memories of one individual to another," the bird reports.

"To make more explorer dolphins?"

"No."

Grace frowns. "What then?"

There is a pause. After half a minute, the little bird says, "Classified," then flies off down the hall.

Grace gives you a confused look. "What is he up to?"

"I'm not sure. What's he copying?"

You ride slowly down the hallway. As you do, you think about what you'd copy if you were Moriarty … then it hits you.

"Himself! He's making copies of himself!"

"Why?"

"Elementary, Grace. He wants to take over. He wants to survive I suppose. He knows what the Inventor knows."

"If only we knew that too."

"Wait," you say, a brainwave hitting you, "maybe we can."

You explain your plan to Grace. As she catches on, her grin grows wider and wider and her head starts nodding.

"Yes, I can get the equipment together," she says. "And I can make the transfer – there's just one problem."

"Leave that to me," you say.

The two of you split up. Grace heads back to her radio room and you go looking for another robot to question.

It isn't long before you find another robot going about its business.

"Where is the Inventor?" you ask.

"In sleep room 4," it answers.

"Not that Inventor, the original, the original record of the Inventor."

"In the library," the robot intones.

"Great!" you say. "Can you show me the way?"

It turns out the library isn't far from the Bridge. The room is lined with book-filled shelves from the floor up to the ceiling. There are shelves in the middle of the room too. You haven't seen so many books before, but surely the Inventor's record isn't contained in a book? It must be something else you are looking for.

On one wall you find racks of learning disks, like the ones you've seen attached to sleeping caps. These disks contain lessons on robotics, engineering, agriculture, and all the other skills people need to learn to establish themselves on a new planet. There are languages too, what use will that be you wonder? Then you come to a shelf inscribed with people's names. There are hundreds. Out of curiosity you look for your name and find it in a group labeled 'indentured personnel'. Then another section catches your attention- 'criminal minds'. There are only a few files here and a gap exists where Moriarty's file should be. You shudder at the idea of hundreds of Moriarty's.

You quickly scan and find the Inventor's file. You scoop it up and walk as normally as you can to your 'sporter. You can't help feeling a bit guilty even though you're really sure you are doing the right thing.

Grace has totally reorganized her collection of wires, capacitors, transistors and other electrical components. A bath with a sleeping cap dangling into it, sits in the middle of the room . Grace is pouring sleeping fluid into the bath.

She looks up as you enter. "Good timing! Are you ready for your bath?"

"Do I need one?"

"You need to sleep. That's the only way to overwrite your consciousness."

"I'd better get ready then."

"Are you sure about this?" Grace asks. "There are dangers you know."

"The game's afoot! Besides, what other choice do we have?" you say as you strip down to your underwear and lower yourself into cold sleep jelly. Cold jelly is not as pleasant as warm jelly. You feel a little chill run through you as you go under but when you suck on the breathing apparatus the chill goes and, you are feeling sleepy....

...and then you are coming out of the bath and Grace is there waiting for you with a big grin on her face.

But something is wrong, it's just you. Why can't you feel The Inventor's thoughts? "I don't think it worked Grace, we'll have to try again."

To your surprise Grace laughs and waves a few people over. There's Dr Alan and someone dressed in a captain's uniform.

"We did it," Grace explains. After you came out of the sleep jelly your subconscious completely accepted the Inventor's mind. You overrode Moriarty's commands and had him sent, with some supplies, to an island on the watery planet.

"Atlantica," interrupts Dr Alan.

"Yes, Atlantica. Anyway he's down there now. It's not that great a place for humans but he should survive. He was going to send a lot of us down there. We've moved on – we're travelling further afield and about to go back to sleep ourselves. The Inventor wanted to give you back your body. And there's more. We've both been promoted. We're no longer indentured. We're toffs!"

Dr Alan interrupts, "Come on you two, let's have a last look at these stars before we go to sleep between them again. I look forward to working with you again in a few hundred years when we reach our next destination."

You look at Atlantica getting smaller. Dr Alan sees an inhospitable planet where the criminal Moriarty is marooned for the rest of his life. You see a planet where an alternate you, in the body of a dolphin, has found a sort of paradise.

Strangely, you and Grace have achieved the thing Moriarty was trying to do. You are both living more than one life. Seeing there is a part of you swimming below, you wonder if you'll dream of swimming again. You're pretty sure you will.

This part of the story is over. But there are many paths to take.

Would you like to:

Go to the List of Choices? **P380**

Or

Go back to the beginning? **P1**

Exploring Atlantica

You have decided to explore while the robots set up the transmitter. That way you'll have information to communicate back to the spaceship sooner.

"Let's head south for a while," you trill to Longtail. "We won't be long."

Using your sonar, you scan the seabed below the explorer. There's a pointy crag down there with warm vibrations coming from it – that should be easy to find again. You can almost smell the forest of seaweed growing around it. Hundreds of little fish and crabs are sheltering from bigger creatures within the seaweed fronds. You'll be able to make a meal from them if you need to, but first you're bursting to explore.

As you swim off you also feel the steady throb of the beacon through the water. You're pretty confident you won't need it but it's an extra way to find your way back.

You and Longtail skim the surface and bounce along the waves. You swim faster and faster enjoying your sleek speedy body. This is better than running, it is more like flying. The contours of the ocean floor are mapped in your head as your sonar bounces off things close and far away. You detect big and small creatures.

Never did you imagine how far a dolphin can 'see'. In the distance you pick up some creatures of a similar size to you.

There is land to one side. It sends nutrients down the rivers and into the water. These nutrients feed the sea. You can taste the difference in the water. This sense of taste is a little like your human sense of smell but much more specific.

With a burst of speed you arch your back and explode out of the water. Longtail leaps out of the sea right next to you. You hang in the air for a few seconds and look out on the bright sunny day and see birds in the sky. Huge dark birds with wings like bats and long triangular beaks.

"Did you see those birds?" Longtail clicks.

You take another jump out of the water to see what the birds are doing. They are a lot closer.

"Their beaks have teeth," you whistle and click back to Longtail. "Perhaps we shouldn't have drawn attention to ourselves."

You start to panic. The large birds are coming right towards you. You and Longtail dive deep and change direction. It's clear the birds think the two of you will make a good meal. What should you do?

"That's good," says a voice deep in your mind. "Keep scanning for them. You can't sense through the air as well as water, but you should be able to make out something that large."

You don't have time to think about whose the helpful voice is. You just know you want to get away from those big birds.

"Slow down," the voice says, "You can stay under water longer if you use less energy, just stay deep."

Longtail follows as you do what the voice says. The mammoth birds continue circling above. They know you are around somewhere. Diving deeper you disturb a shoal of small fish. The little fish flit and dart and disturb a school of bigger fish. All the movement makes it impossible to sense where the birds are. You start to panic again.

"You're fine," says a voice. "Swim away from the fish. The air creatures will make a meal from the small ones instead."

The voice is right, you've created a distraction by disturbing the shoal. You head further away from land, into the open sea. Behind you the giant birds dive into the water and feast on the fish.

A small blast of sonar finds Longtail swimming in the same direction directly ahead. You risk a quick trip up from the depths to take in some air barely breaking the surface with your blowhole before you dive down again. Sending out a blast of sonar, you look to see if you've been detected. You are safe. No birds in the area.

Then you remember your mission, explore the world. With a strong kick of your tail, you swim forward, only pausing to taste some delicious small fish those 'air creatures' sent scurrying in your direction.

"Delicious," Longtail clicks as she circles a small school to keep them from darting off into deeper water.

After lunch the two of you head further away from land. Here you start to detect larger life forms. You also pick up on the creatures you sensed before, the ones that were about your size.

"Be cautious, don't enter their territory," the voice warns.

"Who *are* you," you ask. The voice has been quiet since you escaped from the birds. Now that you are out of danger you want some answers.

"I'm the one who was there before you came."

"What?"

"You joined my mind on the great travelling ship."

Now you understand. You're talking to the dolphin, the original inhabitant of the mind you were copied into. It's a reassuring feeling to have this wise soul with you, though you feel like a bit of a trespasser.

"Sorry for invading your mind."

"Don't worry, little one. Together we are exploring this beautiful clean sea. It's a pleasure to have you along. I've enjoyed learning your thoughts."

"What shall I call you?" you ask.

"My pod called me Seeker, because I always sought to find new waters."

"You're living up to your name then," you say.

You and Seeker journey on for a while taking note of the planet and its different creatures.

"We should turn back," Longtail calls.

You start to circle back while reading the map of the sea floor with your sonar. Every time you send out a sonar signal you collect more details, it is like painting a picture in your mind of the undersea landscape. You can sense some of what must be on the land by the taste of the water and by which plant life grows near river mouths. In an area rich with tall strong kelp you recognize the last tugs of a strong river as cool fresh water pours off the land.

"You'll be able to tell them there is fresh water for their steam engines," says Seeker.

Seeker has read your thoughts.

His tone is one of disappointment. "Coal mining makes the sea taste horrible." Seeker says. "Your machines belch smoke and bleed oil and tar. They choke the fish and the creatures of the air."

You suddenly feel sad. This place is so clean, so untouched.

Sensing your distress at the idea of hurting this world, Seeker changes the subject and talks of the long distances he travelled on Earth. Of the many places he visited.

As you swim on, making maps of the ocean, you listen to tales of the southern ocean where men paddling large canoes had driven out the Europeans.

"I know about the Maori savages," you say. "They caused an uprising in the new lands. Britannia used to send prisoners to Australia but the Maori came over and told the Aborigines not to accept any more. After they kicked us out, Maori went on and found coal and gold and other minerals. They became rich. That's why we've had to go out into space."

"The Maori did not seem savage to me," Seeker says. "They kept the sea around them very clean. Britannia fouled the water with all manner of things."

With the giant birds no longer a threat, you think about what Seeker has said. As you do so you drift into a sleepy state. Beside you Longtail does the same. It's a different experience to human sleep. You're semi-conscious and feel part of your brain drift, yet you're never unaware of what is going on around you. Dolphins, you discover, don't really dream but do replay memories. Some of the memories are your own and some belong to Seeker. The memories aren't just sonar pictures but sound and taste too. You find yourself learning about Earth's ocean and how different it is from the sea you are in now. For one thing, this place is cleaner.

You become alert when your sonar picks up two creatures about your size. They are far off but they have abruptly changed course and are coming closer.

You take a breath, remembering how you escaped the big birds by diving, and begin to move away, not too fast to look like you are retreating, just steadily. Mentally you whistle a little tune, like you did back in Londinium when there were street thugs about. An image of walking down cobbled streets flashes into your mind.

"Much as I like to look at your memories, now is not the time to daydream." says Seeker, distracted by your attempt to keep calm.

You feel him checking the creatures with your shared sonar. There is no question now that they are swimming toward you. And they are swimming fast!

It is time to make a decision. Do you:

Swim back to the explorer for shelter **P110**

Or

Swim further out to sea to seek cover **P105**

Swim further out to sea to seek cover

You have decided to swim further out to sea. If the creatures mean you harm it would be better to go out to open water rather than risk damaging the space probe.

"I'm heading out into open water," you click to Longtail. "Keep tracking those two large creatures."

"They're following," Longtail clicks in reply.

You send out a burst of sonar to track where you are going. You don't want to lose the location of the space probe. "Just keep moving Longtail."

The ocean beneath you gets deeper and deeper but there are mountains and distinctive currents that make understanding this area in your dolphin mind as easy as if you were gazing at city streets from a high tower. Far below you sense a huge life form moving along with a steady pumping and spurting motion.

"Squid," says Seeker. "It won't bother us. They don't usually come to the surface. Just don't dive too deep for a while."

You come to a large reef and sense another land mass further behind it, perhaps an island. Seeker suggests the reef as a place to hide if needed and suggests you map out some routes through the coral.

You and Longtail take particular note of tunnels through the sharp coral. Toward the centre of the reef your sonar picks up a confusing mass of life forms.

Your followers are close. They may not know there are two of you. You might be able to use that to confuse them. You signal to Longtail to hide in a nearby tunnel. It has a break to the surface where she can breathe.

You swim out of the reef and take another big breath as the creatures come into view.

Their bodies are long and sleek apart from an appendage hanging from each side. The front third of the creature is all mouth and teeth. They look like sharks with arms, and they don't look friendly.

The two creatures split up. For a second you think they are leaving but then you realize it's the way they hunt. They are closing in from two sides like a crab's pincer. When the hunters start moving, you feel your own mind being pushed back and Seeker's taking over.

Seeker speeds toward one of the creatures who opens its toothy mouth ready to take an easy bite. But Seeker deftly swerves, pounds the attacker in the gills with the side of your body and keeps moving towards the reef where he and dives into one of the natural tunnels - narrowly avoiding the sharp coral.

Hopefully your pursuer isn't so lucky.

Seeker takes a sharp turn at a fork in the tunnel, blasts a whistle to Longtail and comes back out again. With Seeker's mind in control, you feel like a passenger in a speeding submarine.

Longtail and Seeker surprise the creature you pounded earlier with another blow to the gills. It's clear this creature is out of the fight. Now it's just you and the other one, but you need a breath.

Seeker shoots to the surface spreading sonar widely to detect the other creature's location. It isn't far behind but breathing is the most important thing. Seeker propels you out of the water. Your body twists as you change direction and then dives once more. You're clear of the cover of the reef now. Will you be able to outrun the second shark-like creature?

"It's still following you!"Longtail clicks as she streaks up beside you.

Without warning Seeker slows down. You fight your way into his mind in an effort to speed up again.

"More creatures are arriving!" Longtail says.

Oh no - this is it, the hunters are closing in. Why don't they come in for the kill? Perhaps Longtail will still be able to get back to the ship if they attack you.

"Save yourself Longtail!" you whistle. "I'll try to hold them back. Swim for it!"

"You're brave but a bit stupid," says Longtail. "Pay attention."

"Slow down," Seeker says, "Friends have come."

And it's true. Newcomers are swimming with you. Your pursuer flees, chased away by some of these new dolphins. You slow, take a fresh breath, and try to get your heart to stop pounding.

The newcomers take turns to swim close. You study them too. They are very much like your dolphin-self, air breathing mammals that use sonar and are able to sing the high pitched noises that form a basic language.

They are singing you a welcoming song. You listen and join in when you recognize a part that repeats. Pretty soon you and Longtail are singing in unison with the other dolphins. The song has connected you and you start to understand each other.

"Where did you come from?" you ask one of the pod.

"Inside the reef," she says.

You remember that mass of life you detected. The pod must have been clustered inside a cavern in the reef. When they heard you call to Longtail they came to your rescue.

You travel with the others for many days. You map and explore great tracts of the ocean. You find that the huge birds that you met on your first day nest along every rocky outcrop and feed upon sea creatures. They do not fly far out to sea and they can't fly in bad weather. You doubt they'd get on well with humans.

Your new pod have a very wide territory. Whenever it is your turn to lead the pod you lead them back towards the explorer. Before long the others realize there is somewhere you want to go and are content to go along.

Eventually you return to the explorer with its robot escort.

As you approach the floating vessel, Seeker speaks to you directly. For the last few days the two of you have acted as one and you had almost forgotten you were two separate minds.

"Are you going to tell the humans that this is a good place to come to, or say it is a bad place for them?"

You hadn't really thought about it like that. You just know that you need to make a report so they can decide. You remember the time you passed the river mouth and Seeker noted how clean and fresh the water was. You think back to the river Thames in Londinium – its waters would be fouled and polluted when they reached the ocean. If the *Victoria* lands here there will be changes everywhere. The sea will be a major source of food for the new settlers and they will want to get rid of anything that threatens them. You don't like those big birds on the cliff but now you know not to make yourself a target, they can't harm you. You aren't fond of the shark creatures but you are safe from them in your pod. You know they have a role to play in the ocean.

Seeker has been following your thoughts. "You must tell the humans what you think is best for them to know."

It is night. The big birds don't fly at night so the pod comes close to shore to sing. Phosphorescence covers their bodies and they shine in the water along with hundreds of other creatures. Out of the water comes a mammoth animal. The dolphins have sung it up from the depths as the moon hangs low over the planet and the tide pulls toward it. On the cliffs the birds raise their heads and sing too. By day they are fierce, but now, on this moonlit night, their humming choir makes an operatic contribution as it echoes off the cliffs.

You swim inside the space ship where two robots sit waiting to help you with the transmitter. You nudge the 'transmit' button with your nose and send your report.

Planet not suitable for human habitation.

Outside the explorer, you hear your friends and the great ocean singing. Beyond the moon twinkle millions of stars. One of those will surely make a suitable home for those on the *Victoria*.

Moments later, the *Victoria* fires its engines and, like a comet, streak off across the sky returning to it quest of finding a home.

You on the other hand, are home. You exit the explorer, swim at top speed, then leap from the water, twirling in the air before you splash down. Then you raise your voice and sing.

You have come to the end of this part of the story. Do you:

Go back to the beginning? **P1**

Or

Go to the list of choices and read from another part of the book? **P380**

Swim back to the space probe for shelter

You don't know what those creatures were, so it seems safest to get back to the explorer and check on the transmitter. You have things to report now. You know a little about the waters, you've discovered giant birds, but most importantly, you need to warn the crew on the *Victoria* that the Inventor might not be safe from the criminal whose mind he took over.

"My mind was dormant, until a moment of great stress," says Seeker, reading your thoughts. "If this bad person is the same, he may return to consciousness too and not want to share his body."

Seeker has a good point, but as you swim back you notice that the creatures are still coming your way. You don't have time to worry about the Inventor right now.

If these creatures mean you harm, you can swim inside the explorer and close the hatch. Longtail chirps in agreement about the direction you've taken. She's picked up the creatures with her sonar too and you know she'd prefer not to take a risk.

Soon you sense the warm mountain on the sea floor, and not long after that, you hear the *ping* of the beacon. Are the creatures attracted to the beacon too?

The top half of the explorer is bobbing above the surface, but the tunnel you exited from is submerged and ready for you to enter. You both speed inside. Longtail activates the door closer with her nose just as you catch a glimpse of two long shapes speeding toward the opening. You hit the LOCK button and then relax when you hear a satisfying *clunk*.

You swim up a level and look out through a porthole. Two black fish are now circling the pod. They have the huge eyes of creatures that spend a lot of time in deep water. They also have arms.

One of them takes a run at the porthole and attempts to smash it open. When it fails the second one tries biting at the window and ripping at the outer coverings with webbed fingers. You stare into a large open mouth spread over the porthole. Several sets of jagged teeth, one behind the next, glisten in the light emitted from the explorer.

You and Longtail watch in horror as webbed hands scrape and grasp as the porthole.

Longtail sends you a long series of frightened clicks and whistles.

You send back strong blasts of reassurance. "If the explorer kept us safe through space it will withstand this."

You're almost positive, but then you don't really know what these creatures are capable of. Around you, the explorer clanks and clangs as the predators try to break into it. Thankfully the feathered hull repels the attack but you can't stay inside forever and for the first time since landing on the water planet you wish you hadn't accepted the crazy adventure you're undertaking.

You swim to another porthole and watch the creatures outside. They stop bashing at the hull and swim in lazy circles around your vessel. You swim upward to take a breath. Thank goodness the explorer is set up to house the robots above, and there's a pocket of air where you can breathe safely. When you look up, you see a large clear ring set into the top of the small craft. You can see the sky.

A robot opens the roof and sends out a hummingbot. It must be going to scan the creatures swimming around your craft.

You haven't seen the dry area of the explorer before – the robots have been very busy. You knew they were going to erect a radio transceiver but it looks like a lot more is going on. Beyond the wet area where you surfaced, you see sparks from welding and building.

Several flying robots approach when they see you. One carries a radio microphone. It wants you to make a report.

The other makes an announcement to you both: "You left the explorer without armor and tracking equipment. You must put on your armor in case of hostile native activity. You must wear your tracking device to gather information about the planet."

You wonder if the robots have realized you've brought some

hostile natives back to the explorer with you and whether armor will be enough to help you defend yourself against them.

"Please come out of the water and onto the dock," says the bird. You submerge and swim back down the way you came. When you are almost back to the locked sea door you set off with speed so you can propel yourself out of the water and onto the dock mounted just above water level.

The creatures outside pick up your movements and become more alert as they see you swimming about inside the explorer.

With a splash and a flop, you land on the dock. Then you hear banging and tapping on the hull again. The creatures are not giving up.

The nice thing about robots is they aren't emotional. Humans would have given you a lecture about how bad it is to leave without being fully equipped, but the robots are all business. You can't help feeling a little guilty though. If you hadn't made it back here the mission would have failed and you also wouldn't be able to report about the consciousness of your host animal.

The microphone is slung over a rafter and hangs in front of you.

"Please report. We know the explorer has landed safely. What can you tell us about the planet? Over."

Longtail begins to make a report – she squeaks and trills into the microphone. Her human counterpart should be able to interpret what she says. She explains about the large birds. She talks about the warm water and something under the ground. You didn't really put it together but Longtail understands there's some kind of underwater volcano – there might be earthquakes she tells them. She's noticed all sorts of things.

"This is Seeker," you say, and pause in case anyone answers you. There is no answer though – it must take some time for your transmission to reach the *Victoria*. You describe everything you have discovered so far.

Every so often there is a clang from the creatures outside. You tell the people on the space ship far above you what the creatures are like.

Then you tell them about your experience with your dolphin mind, how it's awake and just as much in control of its body as you are.

"I can speak with the dolphin mind, but sometimes it takes over – for instance when the bird predators attacked us. We may share this body but the host's mind is not dormant like you told me. Repeat. The host is not asleep and it can take control. Did you hear me?"

There is a sudden click and the transmitter is silent. Without the noises of the transmission you hear water lapping on the dock and the occasional clang of the creatures outside.

Three robots set to work trying to re-connect it, but after a while they stop. One of them perches on the microphone looking down on you.

"What is the problem?" Longtail asks.

"The problem is not at this end. We must wait until the *Victoria* is receiving again," one hummingbot chirps.

"What could have caused the disconnection?" you ask.

"Sunspots or solar flares possibly, or mechanical failure."

"Longtail," you say, "is your human brain the only mind operating in there – or is your dolphin mind awake too?"

"We're both here, Seeker."

"Let's leave another message for the *Victoria*. We need to make sure they understand the significance of the host's mind being active Then we need to get rid of the monsters outside."

"I'm frightened," trills Longtail.

"Don't worry. The bots will sort something out," you say.

And perhaps you are right because the robots bring a fine chainmail sheath toward you and slip it over most of your body. You can feel little electrodes activating against your skin. It is surprisingly lightweight, like the fine leather gloves rich ladies had back in Londinium. You once got tipped half a crown when you returned a glove that had been dropped on the street. It felt soft and warm in your hand as you raced after the carriage.

"Won't I rust in this?" you ask, imagining yourself rusted up at the bottom of the ocean.

"No, your armor is a titanium alloy," the hummer above you reports, "It won't rust."

Woven inside the armor is something not unlike the sleeping cap you wore on the ship.

"Why do I need a sleeping cap?"

"It won't send you to sleep, it will read your brain impulses and help you. You can make broadcasts back to the explorer."

You ease back into the water and swim around, trying out the armor like a new pair of shoes. You feel a little heavier but also stronger. You pause at a porthole looking for the mean toothed fish. All you can see is the light filtering down from above, so you send out a blast of sonar. You get crystal clear images this time – it must be something to do with the armor, a built-in antenna perhaps.

When your sonar bounces back, you see that the predators are swimming away from the explorer at speed. Has something else caught their attention?

You look at Longtail and she gives a nod. The nod strikes you as a very human response but you know she's suggesting you head back outside.

Once in the ocean you make a few quick turns, ready to head back inside if you feel encumbered by the armor. To your surprise it fits very well and doesn't slow you down. With a burst of speed, you venture out further.

Another blast of sonar tells you there's no danger about. The amplifying effect of your suit means you can read things in the air. You pick up a small gull wheeling in the sky above.

This means you'll be able to spot the large birds too! A small fish scoots by and you put on a burst of speed to catch it. Your suit gives you a boost of power and you shoot past the startled fish. Longtail surges past you too and for a while you're both racing about showing off your new powers. This is great, you'll be able to out run those horrible creatures if, or when, they return. Suddenly you're incredibly hungry and you feast on fish and small squid.

After the meal you try some jumps. You surge out of the water and find Longtail jumping over you. In the distance one of those large birds is cruising in the sky and moves toward you. Now you are so fast you decide you won't run. You jump again teasing it, but it doesn't come much closer and you wonder why.

"They might not want to be too far from the cliffs," speculates Longtail.

She might be right, but before you can experiment with what distance the big birds are willing to go out to sea you get a message from the explorer.

"Please survey the volcanic activity below."

You and Longtail take another huge leap out of the water and make a teasing flip at the faraway birds then dive.

You soon realize the suit lets you to go much deeper than normal. It is protecting you against the water pressure and helping boost your oxygen levels.

"These gadgets are wonderful," says Seeker. "I've never been this deep before."

You're glad Seeker feels that way. He might have felt horribly used, but his adventurous spirit means that he sees the enhancements the robots have given you as a way to do more exploring. You've learned more about space and other animals on this journey than you ever expected. Until now, you never realized how intelligent another creature could be.

You dive into deeper and darker shades of blue until the water around you is the color of midnight. Mountainous shapes below glow red and orange as lava oozes from their vents.

"Please describe what ye be seeing," instructs a voice in your cap. It must be the Scottish spider-bot.

Beside you Longtail makes her report. She tells the robots on the explorer that the water is getting warmer, which it is, and that there is a glow from the lava in the depths. She says there are 'multiple fissures' and you wonder what those might be, probably the little volcanoes. It seems the human part of Longtail has knowledge of geology that you don't have.

You circle the volcanic area. There are craggy looking fish everywhere and the bottom is alive with crabs and the long tendrils of swaying seaweed. You see a crab nimbly step away from some hot lava but unfortunately it moves into the path of a creature with tentacles the same color as the seabed. The crab is gobbled up in seconds.

"Return to the explorer. Your next task is to hook a cable to the steam vents. We can generate some power for the explorer."

Longtail swishes upward to go get the cable. You turn and follow her, passing by a tall lava formation that towers up higher than the rest.

Just as you pass the lava tower there's a sharp jolt and you feel yourself held back. Something has hold of your tail.

You twist around and see that the tower wasn't a rock at all. It's actually a rock creature. You beat your tail, but can't break free.

Are you going to be its next meal?

You beat your tail once more and stare toward the surface. Longtail is a disappearing shadow in the glimmer of the world far above. The grip on your tail grows tighter as you thrash about in panic. You'll need more air very soon. If you don't do something to get free you'll die.

Then you hear the spider-bot. "Use the laser."

Laser? What laser?

Seeker's voice comes through, as it always does in moments of stress, "Let's try out some human gadgets!"

There is a sudden hum and a beam of white light comes out of your helmet. Wherever you look, the beam follows. You direct the laser toward the rock creature. It cuts through the tentacle holding you. and, the creature lets go.

You shoot upward with your lungs pounding for fresh air.

Longtail meets you on the surface and brushes her body up against yours. She feels smooth and warm and reassuring.

"Your tail!" she exclaims.

Glancing back you see ragged cuts along its length. You shudder as you think about what might have happened if you'd been permanently injured. Any more damage to your tail would mean you couldn't swim.

You explain about the rock creatures to Longtail and how you used the laser to free yourself.

"It will be a great deterrent against those big fish," you say. "They won't want to mess with us."

Longtail agrees but says we also need to learn to get along. "I love it here and I've been worried about the big fish, but we need to find a way to live alongside them. If we only use strength and power we won't ever be friends. Perhaps they are intelligent too and we need to find a way to speak with them."

The robots insist you return to the explorer to get your tail looked at.

Longtail will make another report to the *Victoria*. You re-enter the explorer and go up to the deck. The spider-bots gently take off your armor. You feel a little lighter with it off and are surprised to find yourself looking forward to wearing it again – its proved itself very useful. Soon you're getting a full medical from the spider-bots who treat your wounds and check for infection.

They say you won't have any natural immunity to any microbes the rock creature might have passed on through your cuts. Despite the bots patching you up, you have mixed feelings about them.

Robots displaced a lot of workers on Earth and led to hunger and crime. They could have led to a better life for everyone, but they were taken over by the rich. Perhaps in a new world people will use robots to make things better for everyone.

The robots finish checking you over and say you should both rest before taking the cable down to hook up to the volcano.

"I can do it on my own," Longtail says.

"Don't you dare!" you say. "There are too many dangers out there.

Even with our new armor I think we need to stick together."

"That's right," says Seeker. "Always act as a pod."

The next day a hummingbot flies through the port in the top of the explorer. The spider-bots check the bird over for damage. They apply oil to its joints so it can keep working in the harsh sea air. Once its maintenance is taken care of it reports that it has found several islands but they are all quite small.

"There might be a way to build bridges between some of the islands over time. Settlers will have a tough time here though," Longtail muses.

It's a pity everyone can't become a dolphin you think, this place is pretty good if you are a good swimmer.

The next day you and Longtail take the power cable down to the underwater volcano. You take care not to swim close to the rock crabs now you know what they are. Just as the pair of you have finished connecting the cable you notice shadows above you. It's the vicious fish who chased you … and there are lots of them!

Longtail blasts some sonar to check where they are. They are close but they don't seem to be coming any nearer. Something else has their attention. You pick up a faint sonic cry. It sounds like a distress call from a youngster.

Dozens of sharky voices answer. One croons softly and sounds just as distressed. Something tells you that it is the mother whose baby is in trouble.

The shark fish don't seem to be able to help the baby – they are circling above but unwilling to dive down.

"The baby must be caught by one of the rock crabs," says Longtail.

You were thinking the same thing.

"Let's help," Longtail says.

With your new armor you might be able to help, but you can't help thinking these creatures wanted to kill you not long ago. The baby gives another cry, fainter this time.

Longtail doesn't wait, she takes off toward the noise.

"Let's help," says Seeker.

So you follow. At least you can look out for Longtail. You come to a shelf in the ocean where it suddenly gets very deep. A forest of crab spires pokes out of the deep. Near the top of one of these you can see a small shark fish weakly pulling to try to free itself. You know just what that feels like.

Well above the crabs the shark people swim. Occasionally one of them swims overhead with a rock in its hands and tries to aim at the crab arms. It is trying to hit them. Other crab limbs have formed a sort of net above the baby though and the rocks aren't getting through.

The shark people have noticed you now. You don't know what they are thinking. There are perhaps twenty of them. If you don't rescue their baby you don't like to think what they'll do.

Longtail gets as close as she can to the baby and carefully activates her laser. You circle around above her, vulnerable now to an attack by the shark folk. You hope they realize you are there to help. You activate your own laser and one by one the smaller crabs over the top of the baby pull away. Now Longtail goes closer and works on the arm holding the baby.

The baby is barely moving now. Perhaps it is almost out of air.

A rock crab claw moves toward Longtail and you give it a blast. It recoils back into the crevice. With a *crack!* the arm holding the baby breaks and the little one drifts upward then stops, too weak to swim.

Longtail dives underneath braving the rock crabs and nudges the baby up toward the surface. You give short laser blasts to the area beneath her and then as she comes level with you join her in nursing the baby upwards. As you clear the danger area, all the shark people race toward you and you brace yourself for a fight.

The mother of the baby gets there first. She is crooning and joins you to bring her baby to the surface. The others swim nearby, focused on the little one. When the baby takes a breath it starts to wriggle and then swim. It comes back to Longtail and nudges at her, making little chirruping noises and then swims to its mother who repeats the noises.

Silently, the rest of the shark people swim past and then move off. The mother and baby are the last to go.

"I don't think we'll have any more problems from them," you say to Longtail.

"I hope they'll be kind to our children," she says.

"What?" you say. It's true that Longtail has been getting pudgier by the day but you just thought it was all that fish she was eating. You haven't felt lonely for a second on this adventure but the thought of having a new member of your pod makes you launch yourself out of the water and twirl in the air. How lucky you are to be a dolphin.

"What should we call the baby, do you think?" asks Longtail.

"How about Victoria if it's a girl?" you say. "Victoria Oceanborn."

"Perhaps," says Longtail. "In that case perhaps Victor for a boy?"

You swim back to the explorer and get the bots to turn on the radio.

"Come in *Victoria*. I have exciting news."

You have reached the end of this section of the story. Do you:

Find out what happened back on The Victoria? **P90**

Or

Find out what would have happened if you had not swum back to the explorer? **P110**

Or

Go to the List of Choices? **P380**

DANGER ON DOLPHIN ISLAND

Lagoon Landing

From the float plane's window, you can see how Dolphin Island got its name.

The island's shape looks like a dolphin leaping out of the water. A sparkling lagoon forms the curve of the dolphin's belly, two headlands to the east form its tail and to the west another headland forms the dolphin's nose. As the plane banks around, losing altitude in preparation for its lagoon landing, the island's volcanic cone resembles a dorsal fin on the dolphins back.

Soon every camera and cell phone is trained on the fiery mountain.

"Wow look at that volcano," shouts a kid in the seat in front of you. "There's steam coming from the crater."

The plane's pontoons kick up a rooster-tail of spray as they touch down on the lagoon's clear water. As the plane slows, the pilot revs the engine and motors towards a wooden wharf where a group of smiling locals await your arrival.

"Welcome to Dolphin Island," they say as they secure the plane, unload your bags, and assist you across the narrow gap to the safety of a small timber wharf.

Coconut palms fringe the lagoon's white-sand beach. Palm-thatched huts poke out of the surrounding jungle. The resort's main building is just beyond the beach opposite the wharf.

Between the wharf's rustic planks you can see brightly colored fish dart back and forth amongst the coral. You stop and gaze down at the world beneath your feet.

You hear a soft squeak behind you and step aside as a young man in cut-off shorts trundles past pushing a trolley with luggage on it. He whistles a song as he passes, heading towards the main resort building. You and your family follow.

"Welcome to Dolphin Island Resort," a young woman with a bright smile and a pink flower tucked behind her ear says from behind the counter as you enter the lobby. "Here is the key to your quarters. Enjoy your stay."

Once your family is settled into their beachfront bungalow, you're eager to explore the island. You pack a flashlight, compass, water bottle, pocket knife, matches, mask, snorkel and flippers as well as energy bars and binoculars in your daypack and head out the door.

Once you hit the sand, you sit down and open the guidebook you bought before coming on vacation. Which way should you go first? You're still a little tired from the early morning flight, but you're also keen to get exploring.

As you study the map, you hear a couple of kids coming towards you down the beach.

"Hi, I'm Adam," a blond haired boy says as he draws near.

"And I'm Jane."

The boy and girl are about your age and dressed in swimming shorts and brightly colored t-shirts, red for him and yellow for her. They look like twins. The only difference is that the girl's hair is tied in a long ponytail while the boy's hair is cropped short. Both are brown and have peeling noses. By their suntans you suspect they've been at the resort a few days already.

"What are you reading?" Adam asks.

"It's a guide book. It tells all about the wildlife and the volcano. It also says there might be pirate treasure hidden here somewhere. I'm just trying to figure out where to look first."

Jane clasps her hands in front of her chest and does a little hop. "Pirate treasure, really?"

Adam looks a little more skeptical, his brow creases as he squints down at you. "You sure they just don't say that to get the tourists to come here?"

"No, I've read up on it. They reckon a pirate ship named the *Port-au-Prince* went down around here in the early 1800s. I thought I might go exploring and see what I can find."

"Oh can we help?" Jane says. "There aren't many kids our age staying at the moment and lying by the pool all day gets a bit boring."

"Yeah," Adam agrees. "I'm sure we could be of some help if you tell us what to do. I've got a video camera on my new phone. I could do some filming."

There is safety in numbers when exploring, and three sets of eyes are better than one. But if you do find treasure, do you want to share it with two other people?

It is time to make your first decision. Do you:

Agree to take Adam and Jane along? **P124**

Or

Say no and go hunting for treasure on your own? **P127**

You have agreed to take Adam and Jane along.

You have a good feeling about the friendly twins. "Sure why not," you say. "It will be nice to have some company."

"Arrr me hearties," Jane cries out, getting into the spirit. "So where do we go first to find these pieces of eight?"

Adam glances at his sister and shakes his head. "Don't mind her. She does amateur dramatics at school. She always acts like this."

Jane frowns at her brother, closes one eye and growls out of the side of her mouth."You'd better watch it you lily-livered land lubber or I'll shave yer belly with a rusty razor then make you walk the plank!"

You can't help chuckling at Jane's pirate imitation. Even Adam cracks a smile.

Pleased to have made friends so quickly, you point to the map of the island in the guide book. "I've read that cyclones —that's what they call hurricanes in this part of the South Pacific — usually sweep down from the north. So I'm thinking we should start on the northern part of the island. I reckon that's the most likely place for a ship to hit."

Adam nods. "As good a theory as any."

"North is on the rocky side of the island," Jane says. "I know because I was talking about stars to one of the staff the other night. They showed me how to tell which way is south by using the Southern Cross." Jane points to the sky out over the reef that protects the lagoon from the ocean swells. "South is that way, so north is the opposite."

You pull out your compass. "Yep, you're dead right. I guess it's time for us to trek to the other side of the island."

"Better get some gear then," Adam says. "We'll meet you by the pool in five minutes."

While Adam and Jane go to get their stuff, you wander through reception and to the paved courtyard where your family and other tourists are sprawled on loungers around the pool.

"I'm off to the far side of the island with some friends," you tell your family. "I've packed myself some things for lunch so don't worry about me."

Your family waves you off. Their noses dive back into their books before you've taken a step.

When Jane and Adam arrive, the three of you follow a sandy path between the buildings, past more bungalows tucked in amongst the lush garden and head inland.

Before long the path narrows as it weaves its way between broad-leafed shrubs, ferns and palms. Many plants are covered in beautiful flowers of red, blue and yellow.

When you hear a loud squawk you stop and look up into the canopy. Adam and Jane look up too.

"There it is," says the sharp-eyed Jane. "See, on that branch near the top. It's got a green body, yellow wings and red head."

The parrot squawks again before swooping down and sitting on a branch not far away.

"Wow, so pretty," Jane says.

Adam pulls his cell phone and takes a few shots of the bird.

You look at Adam's phone. "Nice. I bet it's got GPS. That could come in handy if we find treasure."

"Unfortunately there's no signal on the island," Adam says, zipping the phone back into his pocket.

"That's a shame," you say. "Just as well I've got my compass then."

For about half an hour the three of you follow the main path. The ground slowly rises and the soft ferns give way to taller trees as you work your way inland around the lower slopes of the volcano.

Jane hums softly behind you.

When you come to a fork in the path you're not sure which way to go. Then Adam spots an old sign covered in vines. He pulls the greenery aside and reads the faded writing. "It says there's a waterfall ten minutes' walk to the right and a place called Smuggler's Cove straight ahead."

You pull out your guide book. "Smuggler's Cove is a small bay on the far side of the island. It's here on the map. Might be some good treasure hunting there."

"Let's go and check out the waterfall first," Jane says. "I feel like a swim."

Adam shakes his head, "I think we should go on to Smuggler's Cove and start looking for treasure."

The twins look at you. You have the deciding vote. What should you do? It's only 10am but it's already hot and a swim would be nice. But then treasure is the main reason you've come to this side of the island.

What should you do? Do you:

Go to the waterfall and have a swim? **P132**

Or

Go on to Smuggler's Cove? **P136**

Say no and hunt for treasure on your own.

Adam and Jane look friendly enough, but you've always preferred doing things on your own.

"Thanks," you say, "but I'm a bit of a loner. I think I'll check a few things out on my own first. Maybe another time, okay?"

When their smiles disappear, you feel a little sorry for them, but you've been planning this expedition for ages and you don't want to be distracted.

"Okay," Jane says, looking down at her feet and kicking the ground. "If you change your mind let us know."

Adam shrugs and wanders a short distance down the beach where he sits in the sand and starts digging a hole with his toes. Jane joins him.

Trying to forget the look of disappointment on the twin's faces you study your guidebook. There are a couple of options you can take. The first is to head across the island to Smuggler's Cove, a sheltered inlet and only safe anchorage on the rocky, northern side of the island. The northern side, without a protective reef, is pounded constantly by ocean waves which makes it a treacherous place for ships.

The path to Smuggler's Cove runs from the resort, through the jungle, clockwise around the lower slopes of the volcano, and then winds back down to the sea. Marked on the map are a number of scenic lookout points and another path that branches off to a waterfall.

As well as maps, the guide book has numerous pictures of the native wildlife, mainly birds, insects and the various sea creatures that inhabit the lagoon. Luckily for the island's birdlife, rats and other predators like stoats, ferrets and snakes have never gained a foothold here. Nonetheless, thanks to man, a number of bird species, including three species of lorikeets are listed as endangered.

Your other option is to head along the beach to the westernmost end of the island where the rocky point protrudes out to sea. This is the point that looked like the dolphin's nose when you were in the plane and is another prime spot for ships to run aground.

A hundred yards beyond the nose-shaped point, and submerged, except at low tide, are a jagged cluster of rocks. These rocks are marked on the map as a serious hazard to navigation. The guidebook explains how three boats have fallen victim to these rocks in recent years, two of them while sailing from New Caledonia to the Cook Islands, the other a small inter-island freighter whose skipper cut the corner too sharp in an effort to outrun a fast approaching storm.

If modern sailors have had problems navigating these waters, maybe the pirates of old did too. Could this be where the *Port-au-Prince* ran aground and floundered as it tried to find shelter from the storm?

You look across the lagoon. The point is way off in the distance where the western end of the reef meets the shore. Maybe snorkeling off the point would be the best way to find treasure.

After brief consideration, you decide to go overland to Smuggler's Cove. The day has barely begun and the temperature is already climbing. As the sun rises in the sky it will only get hotter. Walking under the jungle canopy will be much cooler. Maybe you'll even spot a lorikeet or two on the way.

Tucking your guidebook into a side pocket of your daypack, you brush the sand off your shorts and turn inland. Weaving your way through the cluster of bungalows and resort outbuildings you find a shell-covered path and enter the jungle. Within minutes you are in a different world.

Under the canopy there is a faint but constant hum of insects. Swarms of midges fly in mini-tornadoes this way and that. A bright blue butterfly flits past followed by a red-winged dragonfly. You hear lots of birdsong but so far have only seen mynas with their brown bodies, yellow eye patches and flashes of white on their wings. These bold bird are common in the South Pacific and you've seen quite a few around the resort already.

Leaves and twigs scrunch underfoot as you work your way uphill onto the lower slopes of the volcano. Flowering shrubs, vines and ferns crowd the path. Sturdy vines hang in tangles from trees.

When you see a flash of green above your head you stop and crane your neck upward hoping to see the bird again. You suspect it's a lorikeet. Then you see it swoop down onto a bush covered in pink flowers. The bird hops along a stem and sips nectar from the flower with its long tongue. As it drinks you admire its beautiful colors. Its body is bright green. On its chest is a patch of red and there is a tuff of blue on top its head. It is a startling contrast to the more subdued colors of the birds back home.

As you watch the blue-crowned lorikeet move from flower to flower, you hear whispers and the snap of twigs on the path behind you. Turning your eyes in the direction of the sound you see a brief flash of color through the foliage, first red, then yellow. Crouching down, you ease yourself back into a large fern, pulling one of the fronds down in front of your body to act as a shield.

"Where's he gone?" Jane mumbles as she approaches your hiding spot.

"He can't be too far in front," Adam replies. "I caught a glimpse of him a few minutes ago."

You pull the fern fond down a little more and keep as still as possible. A few seconds later you hear the footsteps pass your position and head further along the path.

Once the footsteps have disappeared, you ease yourself out of the fern. Walking as quietly as possible, you take off in pursuit, keeping a sharp lookout for flashes of color ahead of you.

Should you give them a fright for following you? Maybe you could pretend to be a dangerous animal and scare them away. You wonder if they've done much reading about the island's wildlife. Do they know that the most dangerous animal on the island is the wild pig … or is it the mosquito? You can't quite remember.

You are walking fast trying to close the gap between you and the twins when you see a flash of red in the distance you cup your hands around your mouth and growl as loud as you can. You've been to the zoo plenty of times, and you're not sure your lion impression is that realistic, but you give it your best attempt.

When you hear a frightened squeal and then see the twins rise above the surrounding shrubs as they scurry up a tree you smile.

"That seemed to work," you say to yourself.

You hide behind a tree trunk and try monkey sounds this time. "Oooh, oooh oooh!" you howl doing your best to sound like a chimpanzee. Surely they must know there aren't monkeys here on the island. "Oooh, oooh, oooh!"

The twins are still climbing. Then you see Jane stop and tilt her head. She says something to her brother then braces herself in the crook of the tree and starts scanning the area below her.

"Okay who's making monkey sounds!" she yells. "Come on, I know you're out there!"

Sprung.

You come out from behind the tree and walk along the path. Thirty seconds later you are standing at the foot of the tree looking up at the twins.

"Why are you following me?" you ask.

Their faces are tinged with red as they start to climb down.

Jane is first to reach the ground. "Sorry. We just want some excitement."

"Yeah the resort is boring," Adam says. "Besides, we can go wherever we want. You can't stop us."

You look from one twin to the other and think. Maybe you've been a little harsh. Maybe it would be fun to have some friends to go exploring with.

"Okay. You can come along on one condition."

Suddenly the twins are smiling again.

"What's that?" Adam asks.

"I get to be expedition leader. After all I'm the one who's done the research."

The twins nod eagerly, grins spreading across their faces.

"Okay well let's get moving, we've got a bit of ground to cover before we get to Smuggler's Cove."

The three of you follow the path in single file, with you in the lead. You can hear Jane humming softly behind you.

When you come to a fork in the path you're not sure which way to go. Then Adam spots an old sign covered in vines. He pulls the greenery aside and reads the faded writing. "It says there's a waterfall off to the right. Smuggler's Cove is straight ahead."

"Let's go and check out the waterfall," Jane says. "I feel like a swim."

Adam shakes his head. "I think we should keep going and start hunting for treasure."

The twins look at you. You have the deciding vote. What should you do? It's hot and a swim would be nice. But then treasure is the reason you're here.

It is time to make a decision. Do you:

Go to the waterfall and have a swim? **P132**

Or

Go on to Smuggler's Cove? **P136**

Go to the waterfall and have a swim.

"I like the idea of a swim too," you say. "The treasure's been around for 150 years. I don't think it's going anywhere."

Jane picks up her pack. "I bet I can hold my breath under water longer than you!"

You like Jane. She's so enthusiastic about everything.

"Okay, well let's get going," Adam says in a grump as he moves down the path. "We'll have a quick swim and then get back to the treasure hunt okay?"

You nod and follow Adam. The path narrows and winds its way higher up the hillside. After a couple of zigzags you can see over the trees back towards the coast where waves crash white with foam on the reef. Tiny triangles of color, from the resort's fleet of sailing boats and wind surfers, dot the aqua water on the far side of the lagoon.

Before long you see a swing bridge in the distance. The swing bridge is made from woven vines. Its deck is laid with arm-thick branches chopped from the jungle. The bridge crosses a swiftly moving creek that has cut a deep channel into the side of the hillside as it races to the sea.

Adam stops when he reaches the bridge and turns around. "Do you think this is safe?"

You have a closer look. "It looks pretty sturdy so it should be safe."

About ten vines have been woven together to form the main cables. You grab hold of the bridge's handrails, also made of woven vines, and take a step.

"It feels okay," you say to the other. "Look!" You jump up and down a couple times. "It's hardly moving."

Despite your confidence, the other two wait until you've reached the far side before venturing across. Jane is first. She comes across with no problems, but when Adam is half way across, Jane grabs one of the handrails and starts shaking.

Adams face goes white. "Stop it, Jane!" he yells in a voice a little higher pitched than normal."I swear I'll hit you!"

"Don't be such a baby," Jane says. "I'm just having a bit of fun. You're not going to fall."

Jane steps back and lets Adam wobble his way across. You can see the relief on his face when he reaches solid ground again.

"That wasn't funny. You know I hate heights."

Jane turns her back on Adam to head up the path, but not before you see a little grin cross her face.

Jane is trouble.

You hear the waterfall up ahead. It sounds like someone is running a bath only louder. Then you feel moisture in the air as the wind-blown spray drifts into the jungle.

Jane is the first to see the tumbling mass of white water as she comes around the corner. "Wow! Look at that!"

You nearly bump into her as you take in the scene.

The waterfall is about fifteen feet wide and thirty feet high. It pours over a lip of rock straight out of the jungle into a shimmering pool below. Ferns and palms crowd the stream on both sides. Grey stones cover the bottom of the pool and waves of bright green weed dance in the current.

"Last one in is a monkey's bum!" Jane yells as she runs down the path towards the pool.

Before you know it, Adam has scooted past you and is in hot pursuit of his sister. At the pool's edge Jane throws off her t-shirt and makes a running dive. Adam tosses his phone onto the pile and follows.

Adam is first to surface about half way across the expanse of water. Jane continues to swim underwater, the bright yellow of her swimsuit glowing under the water, until she is nearly under the cascade. When she surfaces her teeth gleam white and her long hair plasters itself to her neck and shoulders.

"I win!" she yells as her fist pumps the air in triumph.

Not bothering to remove your t-shirt, you dive into the pool. The water is cool and refreshing. After paddling to where Jane and Adam are treading water you look down into the depths. "Amazing how clear the water is," you say.

You dive down to see if you can touch the bottom but you're forced to surface again before you get there.

"The water's a lot deeper than it looks," you tell the others when you surface. "I can't reach the bottom."

"Let me have a go," Jane says before flipping over and kicking towards the bottom.

You and Adam watch as she pulls herself deeper and deeper. Before you know it she's holding on to a clump of weed and looking around. After 20 seconds or so, slowly releasing air bubbles as she goes, she rises to the surface.

"Wow you *are* good," you say when her head finally breaks the surface. "You were down there for ages."

Jane has a grin from ear to ear. "And look what I found."

Glinting in the palm of her hand is a small metal cross, like one you'd wear around your neck.

The three of you swim to the pond's edge and sit on a rock.

"Looks like silver," you say, taking the cross and peering at it closely. At the end of each arm is a small hollow. You suspect these would have held precious stones at one time.

On the other side of the cross you see some tiny scratches, but then realize as you inspect them closer they are words etched into the metal. You tilt the cross so the light hits the surface and you can read the words.

"CAROL IIII D.G. 1805," you read. "That sounds vaguely familiar." You're sure you've read seem something similar in one of your treasure hunting books. You hand the cross back to Jane and try to remember what you've read.

You grab a towel from your daypack and dry your hair, still thinking hard as you do so. "Right, CAROL. If I remember correctly that's Spanish for Charles."

Adam seems interested. "Do you think it came from the treasure ship that went down?"

"It's certainly the right time," you say. "The pirate ship we're looking for was raiding the French and Spanish colonies along the South American coast and then came to this part of the Pacific chasing whales to restock their supply of oil. I wonder if some the treasure was salvaged from the wreck after all."

"We could get some scuba gear from the resort and come back. Maybe there is more stuff at the bottom of the pool," Jane says. "I got my dive ticket last summer in Hawaii."

"That's a good idea. I have my ticket too. The two of us could team up for safety."

You've got to admit that the bottom of a deep pool under a waterfall would be a great place to hide treasure.

"Or we could check out this Smuggler's Cove place first and then decide," Adam said. "It's almost an hour back to the resort."

Once again the twins look for you for a decision. The cross was a good find, and the date is certainly from the right era.

Should you check out Smuggler's Cove before going all the way back for scuba gear? Or is the cross an indication that there is more treasure to be found?

It is time to make another decision. Do you:

Carry on to Smuggler's Cove? **P136**

Or

Go back to resort for scuba gear? **P140**

You have decided to carry on to Smuggler's Cove.

As the three of you make your way along the jungle path to Smuggler's Cove, the path twists and turns so much it's hard to know which direction you're heading. The canopy overhead is so dense that in places it feels like evening has come even though your rumbling stomach tells you it is probably closer to lunchtime.

When you come to a large tree that's fallen across the path you stop. "Anyone hungry?" you ask. "Maybe we should have lunch."

Jane and Adam nod their agreement, sit on the tree trunk and rummage through their daypacks.

"I've got a couple of apples and a chocolate energy bar," says Jane.

"Snap," you say, holding up a couple bars of your own. "I love chocolate."

Adam pulls out a bottle of water and packets of cheese and crackers. "I've got heaps of nuts too," he says waving a bulging zip-lock bag. "Sing out if you want some."

As the three of you have lunch you discover that Adam and Jane's parents are both dentists. Jane tells you they're only happy when they're on vacation.

Adam nods. "Nobody is ever happy to see them at work. Their clients are either in pain or unhappy about how much it's going to cost. It's no wonder Mom and Dad are happy to get away from all the grumbling."

You'd never really thought much about the life of dentists. "Still they can afford to buy you the latest phone and take you to nice places so I bet you're not complaining."

Adam shrugs. "I'd rather they were happier sometimes. What's the use of money if you're miserable?"

Jane jumps up and starts closing her bag up. "Let's make them really happy and find some treasure. Then they can retire and be on vacation all the time."

"I'll go along with that," you say as you stand up and get ready to move off.

You and the twins have only gone on a hundred yards or so when a waist-high pile of stones appears about ten paces off the path.

"I wonder who made that cairn?" you say, pushing back fern fronds and making your way through the undergrowth.

The stones have been stacked with care and fit together snugly. On top of the pile is large flat rock overgrown with lichen and moss. The moss is growing in a funny pattern.

You pull your pocket knife out and start scraping the growth off the stone. As you do so, letters are revealed.

"Wow, come look at this," you call out to the others.

Adam and Jane work their way through the greenery and peer down at the characters you've uncovered.

"Does that say 1806?" Jane asks.

The grooves in the rock are shallow. Wind, rain and plant life have pitted the surface over the years but you can still make them out.

"That's the year the ship went down!" you say.

Adams eyes widen. "So the rumors are true."

You can't believe what you're seeing. "It looks that way."

Jane steps back and gives the pile of rocks a quick once-over. "Do you think something is buried here? Treasure maybe?"

You shake your head. "Too obvious I would have thought." Then you have a thought. "Hey, Adam, help me lift the top stone, maybe the cairn is hollow."

You and Adam grab a side of the rock each and hoist it off the pile, flipping it onto the ground as you do so.

"Nope, not hollow," you say. Then you notice more writing on the underside of the rock.

"What's this?" you say, bending down and running your fingers over the surface. "Letters, but they're upside..."

Jane does an excited little hop and says, "*Port-au-Prince*! It says *Port-au-Prince*. Isn't that the ship you told us about?"

"The one and only," you say unable to stop your face from twisting up into a grin.

Adam bends down to stroke the rock. "So it did run aground here on the island."

"Crikey! We're going to be rich!" Jane squeals.

"Not so fast," you say. "The treasure may be here on the island, but we still have to find it."

Adam scratches his head. "So what now?"

You're not quite sure what to do. Why would shipwrecked sailors build a cairn here in the jungle? And why would they put the date on one side and the name of their ship on the other? Could it be a hint as to where the treasure is hidden, or is it a memorial to those lost when the ship sank?

"I think we should carry on to Smuggler's Cove," you say.

With the cairn penciled onto your map, you rejoin the path. You've only walked another mile or so when you hear the faint sound of waves breaking. Minutes later you come upon the rocky shore. To the east, about two hundred yards down the coast, is a small cove protected from the sea by a rocky arm that protrudes out into the ocean. To your surprise, there is a yacht anchored about thirty yards off shore. Sitting on the boat's deck are two men wearing straw hats and floral shirts.

Pulled up on the beach is a small rowboat.

"Get down," you whisper. "Someone's rowed their dinghy ashore, they must be nearby."

Jane's hand rests on your shoulder as she crouches down beside you. "Do you think they're looking for treasure too?" she whispers.

"Let's hope not. But if they are, we don't want them to know they have competition."

"So what do we do?" Adam asks quietly. "What if they're dangerous?"

"We could pretend we're tourists who've come for a swim," Jane says. "I doubt they'd hurt a bunch of kids."

"We *are* tourists silly," Adam says with a hint of sarcasm in his voice. "We don't need to pretend."

"They won't know we're looking for treasure," Jane says. "And if they are, we might be able to get some valuable information from them."

Suddenly the twins are both looking at you to make a decision. You're not sure what would be the best plan of action. The men on the yacht could be innocent tourists or they could be up to something fishy.

What should you do? Do you:

Watch the yacht from the jungle? **P146**

Or

Pretend you're tourists going for a swim? **P149**

Go back to the resort for scuba gear.

After finding the cross in the pool at the foot of the falls, you want to see if there is more treasure sitting on the bottom. Only Jane is a good enough swimmer to get to the bottom without scuba gear, and even she will tire quickly once she's swum to the bottom a few times.

"Okay, let's get back to the resort and get some gear," you say. "We'll be able to search the whole pool thoroughly that way. Where there's one artifact there might be others."

Everyone has a bounce in their step and talks of what they'll spend their bounty on as the three of you head back to the resort.

The dive shop is tucked around the back and in the basement of the main building. You hire a small tank, regulator, and weight belt, divide the equipment between you, and within fifteen minutes you're trudging back into the jungle towards the waterfall.

The day is heating up and the jungle is humid. Sweat drips down your back. Half an hour later, just as you turn off the main path and head up towards the waterfall, a sudden flurry of wings and bright red bodies flash through the canopy overhead.

"Something's spooked the lorikeets," you say.

You are only a short way up the waterfall track when you hear heavy footsteps crashing through the undergrowth off to your left.

"Quiet, someone's coming," you whisper. "Quick, hide in the ferns. We don't want anyone to know we're here."

The three of you burrow into a mass of fronds beside the path and wait. The footsteps get closer and louder. Someone is breathing hard, like they've been running.

Then, through a gap in the ferns, you see a man carrying a wire cage full of lorikeets.

"Don't move," you whisper to the others.

When the sound of the man's footsteps has passed, you climb out of your hiding spot.

"Did you see the cage full of birds?" you ask Adam and Jane.

"He's been trapping. That'll be what scared the lorikeets a few moments ago."

Adam's face twists into a frown. "Surely that's illegal."

You leaf through your guidebook. "You're right, the book says the birds are protected."

"We need to do something," Jane says.

"But what?" you say. "This island's miles from anywhere."

Adam pulls out his cell phone. "We may not have a signal, but my phone still works as a camera. I should take some video so we have something to show the authorities."

Jane nods her agreement. "Let's leave the scuba gear here and follow him. If we get some pictures the police on the mainland might be able to identify them."

Their plan sounds dangerous, especially if the poachers see you taking photos. But you agree with the twins. You can't let some greedy idiot get away with poaching protected birds.

"Okay," you say. "But we'll need to be careful. Bird smuggling is big business and poachers are dangerous. Who knows what he'll do if he catches us spying. He might even be armed so keep quiet and no talking."

That said, you push the scuba gear under a fern and break one of the fronds so you'll know where it is when you come back. Then you pick up your daypack and start moving down the track.

You are confident of catching up with the man carrying the heavy cage so you don't rush. Instead you walk quietly and hope that you see him before he sees you.

When you get back to the junction where the waterfall track meets the main path you stop.

"Which way?" Jane asks.

You think a moment. "I can't imagine him going towards the resort."

"I agree," Adam says. "He must be heading towards the cove."

It isn't long before you see a flash of color ahead of you.

You signal to the others and come to a stop. "There he is," you whisper. "Let's keep pace with him and see where he goes."

Fifteen minutes later Jane tilts her head and cups a hand around an ear. "I think I hear the ocean. Maybe he has a boat."

"Okay, easy now," you say. "We don't want him to spot us."

As you move along the path, the sound of the waves gets louder. Coconut palms start to appear amongst the ferns and other broad-leafed plants, and after another fifty yards you see the ocean through a gap in the trees.

When you reach the edge of the jungle you stop. The man is walking along the shore towards a dinghy pulled up onto the rocky beach a hundred yards away. In the sparkling blue water of the cove, a single-masted yacht rocks gently at anchor. Two men sit on deck drinking beer.

"Welcome to Smuggler's Cove," you say.

"So what now?" Adam asks.

"Follow me," you say. "And keep low."

You step back into the jungle. Jane and Adam follow as you walk parallel to the beach in the direction of the yacht. The ground is sandy here and the shrubs and ferns less dense so the going is relatively easy while still giving you cover from the men on the boat.

When you think you've gone far enough, you creep back towards the beach along what looks like a natural watercourse. The twins follow close behind.

But just as the clear waters of Smuggler's Cove appear before you, your feet are whipped out from under you and you're hoisted into the air.

"Yow!" Jane yelps in surprise.

"Ouch," Adam says. "Someone's squashing my legs."

The more you squirm, the tighter the net pulls around you, squashing the three of you together. Your arms are pressed to your body and Adam's weight pins you against the mesh.

"What now?" Adam grunts. "Any other bright ideas from our

expedition leader?"

Jane's foot is pressed against the side of your face. You can see the ground about three feet below you. The net rocks back and forth like a hammock.

"I've got a knife in the side pouch of my daypack. Can anyone reach it?" you say.

"I think ... I think I can," Jane says, contorting limbs.

You hear Jane breathing hard with effort and then feel a tugging on your pack.

"Can you move to your right?" she asks.

"I'll try," you say, pressing hard with your elbows while rotating your body at the same time.

"Okay, that should do it."

With your face pressed hard to the mesh you roll your eyes and try to see what is happening on the beach. Did the men on the boat hear the *twang* as the trap went off? Are they coming?

"Got it!" Jane says.

"Well, start cutting," you urge her. "Quickly, in case the men heard us."

"Watch it with that knife Sis," Adam says. "You nearly got my leg there."

"Sorry," Jane says, hacking a little more carefully.

You can feel the net stretch as Jane cuts at it and you sink closer and closer to the ground as each minute goes by. Then, like a zipper opening, the net splits apart in a rush and dumps you on the ground.

"Oooof!" you grunt as Adam lands on top of you.

Adam rolls away and you get onto your knees and look around. Two men in flora shirts are moving up the beach towards your position.

"They've seen us!" you say. "We need to get out of here."

"I'm still caught up!" Jane says, kicking her foot like she's trying to shake off her shoe.

You hear panic in her voice. When you look over, you see that a section of net has become entangled around her foot.

"Quick, give me the knife! Stay still." You start hacking at the strands holding her foot. "Get ready to run the moment you're free."

Adam has his camera out and is taking shots of the men coming towards you.

"Hey you!" one of the men shouts. "What are you doing with that camera?"

"Hurry up!" Adam says. "They're nearly here."

"Go," Jane says. "Save yourselves."

With one final slice of the net, Jane pulls her foot free and scrabbles to her feet.

"Split up and run," you say, taking off back the way you came. "Meet you where we left the scuba gear."

With that, the three of you plunge into the jungle running for all you're worth. You duck and weave around trees and shrubs, barging through clumps of fern and eventually come to rest at the base of a large tree. Breathing hard, you stop to catch your breath and listen for footsteps.

Then you hear Adam's voice. "Let me go!"

As you suck in air, your heart pounds. The men must have gone for Adam because he had the camera. You wonder if Jane got away or has suffered the same fate?

"If you kids tell anyone, your friend is toast!" of the men yells into the jungle.

They sound so angry, but what can you do? Luckily the contour of the land gives you a hint as to where you are. You head down a slight slope hoping to cross the waterfall track, pulling the greenery back as you go. Every few minutes you stop, duck down and listen for footsteps. Finally you find the track you're looking for and a couple hundred meters up the trail you see the broken fern frond.

You tuck yourself deep into the ferns and wait to see if Jane turns up. As you wait you inspect the underside of the nearest frond. Two rows of little brown dots run in down each side of the leaf's finger-sized offshoots. These are the spores that will be blown into the wind and grow into more ferns when the conditions are right. You must remember to tell Adam all about them when you see him next. If you see him again, that is.

Fifteen minutes later you hear the crunch of footsteps. You lean back deeper into the greenery and hope that it's Jane and not one of the men. Then you hear a voice.

"Helloooo. Anyone here?" It's Jane looking for the spot where you stashed the scuba gear.

You crawl out from your hiding place and stand up, looking around as you do so. When you catch Jane's eye your put one finger to your lips and wave her over."Shush… The poachers might still be around."

Jane comes over and the two of you duck back under cover.

"Did you see them get Adam?" you whisper.

Jane shakes her head. "I heard him yell, but kept going. I didn't see any point in both of us getting caught."

"So what do we do now? Do we try and save Adam ourselves or go for help?"

"I don't know. I'm afraid they might hurt him."

"Don't worry, we'll work something out," you say.

You think hard. What should you do? Going back for help will take time. Do you have that luxury? What if the poachers take off with Adam in their boat? You may never see him again. But how will two kids be able to handle evil poachers?

It is time to make an important decision. Do you:

Try to help Adam? **P166**

Or

Go back to the resort for help **P178**

You have decided to watch the yacht from the jungle.

The three of you sneak back to the cover of the jungle and creep silently towards the cove.

"Stay in single file," you whisper, "and watch where you step so we don't make too much noise."

Jane suppresses a giggle and falls in behind. "It's like we're ninja spies."

You carefully pull the shrubbery aside so it doesn't snap back in Jane's face and work your way closer to the yacht.

"I hope you know what you're doing," Adam whispers, bringing up the rear. "What if they catch us spying on them?"

You put your index finger up to your lip. "Quiet… If you guys keep talking they'll hear us for sure."

The ground is sandy underfoot. Flowering shrubs crowd one another and the going is slow. Bees hum from flower to flower collecting nectar. After a few minutes, you've worked your way to a spot just inland from where the yacht is anchored. The beach slopes steeply towards the water and unlike the white sand, made from ground shells, on the lagoon side of the island, the sand here is course, dark and volcanic in origin. The men's voices can be heard talking and laughing over the slap of the waves.

You signal the others to get down and crawl towards the beach on hands and knees. From under a bush, you get a better view of what the men are doing. Jane and Adam follow your lead.

The three of you peer carefully through the lower branches. The men are close. The two on deck keep looking towards shore, obviously waiting for whoever is on shore to return.

"What are they doing?" Jane whispers close to your ear.

You look at her sternly and move your hand across your lips in a zipping motion. The last thing you want is for the men to hear you.

Black lettering graces the side of the boat's hull. *Moneymaker* it says. That sounds like the name of a treasure hunter's ship if ever you've heard one.

A moment later there is whistling in the jungle behind you. You drop flat and hope whoever it is doesn't see you. The sound is ten yards to your right and moving towards the beach.

When you sneak a glance, you see a man with a cage full of brightly colored bird walking towards the dingy.

Holding the cage in one hand, the man drags the small boat into water. He stows the cage in the front of the boat, climbs aboard and slots the oars into the rowlocks. The man's rowing technique is good. It doesn't take him long to cross the short distance to the yacht.

"Traps are working well," he calls up to the men on deck. "Here grab this rope and get ready, I'll pass the cage up."

With a heave, the man raises the metal cage above his head where it is grabbed by one of the men. The man on deck swings the cage over the railing and is about to lower it, when he screams out and drops the cage with a thump.

"Ouch! Filthy bird just took a hunk out of my hand!" he howls waving his hand in the air.

The other men laugh at their companion's misfortune. "I've told you before to watch out. Their beaks can take your finger right off if they get hold of it properly."

The hurt man tucks his injured hand under his armpit and paces around the deck for a moment, grumbling and cursing under his breath before coming back to kick the cage. "Watch it you horrible birds. Next time I'll drop you overboard!"

"Horrible birds," a parrot mimics. "Horrible birds. Horrible birds."

The two men laugh again. "Those birds are smarter than you are Jimmy. Maybe we should drop *you* overboard."

The man in the dinghy chuckles again and then grabs the railing and slides the dinghy through the water to the stern of the yacht. He climbs up a short ladder and secures the dinghy's painter to a cleat on deck.

"Another day, another dollar," one of the men says. "It always amazes me what people will pay for exotic birds."

As the men start preparing the yacht for departure, the man with the sore hand moves to the cockpit. He turns the key to start the diesel engine and with a puff of smoke the engine rumbles into life. The man checks that water is coming from the exhaust port in the transom and then waits by the wheel. The other two go to the bow ready to pull up the anchor. The man behind the wheel inches the yacht forward.

The men on the bow are talking, but the throb of the yacht's motor drowns out their voices.

"Poachers," you say to the twins. "The lowest of the low."

"Poor birds. What will happen to them?" Jane asks.

"Life in cages." Adam looks angry and starts to say something else, but then clamps his jaw closed and growls like a dog protecting his territory. His face is red and his clenched fists shake.

"Don't blow a foo-foo valve little brother," Jane says. "Adam works at the animal shelter as a volunteer," she says to you. "He gets so angry when he sees animals being mistreated."

"With good reason," you say. "But what do we do about it?"

"We need to tell the authorities," Adam says. "That's what we do."

"But we're already here, we may as well have a look around," Jane says. "The poachers are leaving. It will be a wasted trip otherwise."

The twins look to you. You could go back to the resort, but would the resort's management do anything? And Jane has a point about your trek being wasted if you go straight back to the resort.

It is time to make a decision. Do you:

Go back to resort and report the poachers? **P154**

Or

Have a look around Smugglers Cove? **P160**

Pretend you are tourists going for a swim.

"If we're going to do this," you say, "we've got to get our story straight."

Jane smiles at your decision. "I read somewhere that it's best to tell as much of the truth as possible when undercover, there's less things to remember that way."

"Okay, let's go for a swim and see if they approach us. If the men are tourists they'll most likely say hello."

"And if not," Adam buts in, "they'll try to scare us off."

"Exactly!" Jane says.

"Whatever you do, don't mention treasure," you say. "If we ask too many questions they'll get suspicious."

With that, Jane pulls her towel out of her pack and walks calmly out of hiding and on to the stony beach. You and Adam, now committed to the plan, follow her lead.

You keep your head down, as if watching your step as you walk, but your eyes dart up every few seconds to see what the men's reaction is to your arrival. One of the men sees you and nudges the other with his foot. The other man is less subtle and stares a little too long, his smile turning down a little too quickly.

"They don't look pleased to see us," you whisper. "Keep moving, but get ready to scarper in a hurry."

Jane's acting skills are quite convincing. She skips on to the beach and, a short distance from the dingy, lays out her towel. "I'm going for a swim," she announces loud enough to carry to the men onboard the yacht."

You bend down to lay out your towel and whisper to Adam, "One of us should stay on the beach and keep an eye out for the shore party."

"I'm not a great swimmer," Adam says. "I don't mind staying."

"I might go for a quick snorkel and have a look around then," you say.

Jane hits the water then turns and calls out, "The water's so warm!"

With your mask and flippers in your hand you walk to the water's edge. After rinsing your mask you slip the rubber strap over your head and sit in the coarse sand to put on your flippers. Then lifting your feet high, you walk backwards into the water.

Jane is right, the water is warm. You've only just started snorkeling when you hear Adam yell.

"Hey! What do you think you're doing?"

Jane has heard him too and is staring past you towards the beach.

You turn around to see what has got Adam so excited.

A man, carrying a cage of brightly colored birds has come out of the jungle and is making his way along the beach towards the dinghy.

By now, Jane is swimming back to shore. When she reaches your position she says, "These guys are trapping birds. Adam's a fanatic when it comes to animal welfare. I hope he doesn't do something stupid."

"Me too."

By now, Adam is up off his towel and marching towards the man carrying the cage. The men on the yacht have seen him too.

"Quick," Jane says. "He's going to nut-off at this guy. We need to stop him."

"And fast," you say. "That man could get violent."

As the two of you race back to shore you watch Adam. He's marching towards the man with the cages like a zealot on a mission, his vision focused straight ahead, his arms pumping.

The man sees Adam coming at him and is not happy that he and his friends are not alone. He sets the cage down, and puts his hands on his hips, seemingly unconcerned about the angry boy striding towards him.

You can't help admire Adam's courage as you hit the beach.

When Adam speaks, you can hear every word.

"These birds are protected you brain-dead imbecile!" he yells. "Let them go or I'll report you to the authorities!"

"Subtle, your brother," you say to Jane.

Adam, although brave, is being guided by his heart and not his head. You're not quite sure what he expects to achieve. Does Adam really think this criminal is going to take any notice of a kid?

"Who are you to tell me what to do?" the man says. "You tourists think you run things now?"

But Adam isn't listening. He's had a rush of blood to his head, his face has gone scarlet in rage and he's not thinking straight.

"I'll see you in jail!" Adam yells, spittle flying. Then he looks over at the men on the yacht. "I'll see you all in jail!" Without warning, Adam runs at the man on the beach and pushes him hard in the chest.

The man, standing with feet spread in front of the cage, loses his balance and tumbles back, trips over the cage and falls awkwardly on the ground.

In a flash, Adam reaches down and unhooks the top of the cage. In a blur of color the dozen or so lorikeets fly off into the jungle.

"Why you little brat," the man growls from the ground. "Those birds were worth hundreds of dollars."

Thankfully, you and Jane have reached the scene.

"Adam, let's go." You grab Adam's arm but he stands fast. "Adam, I said it's time to go."

The man snarls like a wounded animal and lurches to his feet.

"Run Adam!" Jane yells.

Adam sees the man coming at him with fists clenched and finally realizes how furious he is.

You hear splashes and cast a glance towards the boat. The two other men are swimming strongly towards the shore. They will be here in a moment.

But Adam is too slow and the man's meaty hand clamps around his forearm.

"I'll teach you a lesson you little rat bag!"

Jane takes a couple steps forward and kicks the man in the kneecap.

"Ouch!"

It's not a crippling blow, but it's enough of a distraction for Adam to break the man's grip.

"Run!" Jane yells again.

The other men have reached the beach and are sprinting towards you.

"Now!" you scream once more, tugging at Adam's arm.

Jane needs no prompting. In a flash she heads back toward the pile of gear on the sand, scoops up her daypack and scurries into the jungle. You and Adam are twenty yards behind her.

As you hit the track leading inland there is a thud and a grunt behind you. Without even turning, you know Adam has fallen. When you spin around for confirmation, you see one of the men from the yacht is nearly upon him."Go!" Adam says, his eyes pleading. "Go get help!"

You want to help, but it's too late. Adam is right. There is nothing to be gained by both of you being captured. You take off, casting a quick glance over your shoulder as you enter the jungle.

The man has hold of Adam's arm and is dragging him back towards the beach. Once you're twenty yards along the path and out of their view, you duck into some ferns and watch through the fronds. The second man from the boat is out of shape. The swim and the run have sapped his energy. When he sees that his friend has captured Adam, he bends over, puts his hands on his knees and gasps for air.

The man that Jane kicked in the knee is last to arrive. He hobbles over and glares at Adam, then yells into the jungle. "Hey brats, if you don't want your friend hurt you'd better keep you're your mouths shut!"

And with that, two of the men force Adam into the dinghy and start rowing back towards their boat. The other picks up the empty cage and heads a hundred yards or so further down the beach and then turns and walks back into the jungle.

"Jane?" you call out. "Can you hear me?"

You climb out of your hiding spot and start down the path towards the resort, hoping to come across Jane. It isn't long before you hear a rustle of leaves in the canopy.

"Jane?"

Chimpanzee noises come from a tree branch above you and you catch a flash of yellow. "Jane, come down. They've got Adam."

Within 30 seconds, Jane is back on the ground. "Is he okay?"

"I don't know. Did you hear them yell out that we'd better keep quiet?"

Jane shakes her head. "What do we do?"

"We either try to help Adam, or go back to the resort I suppose." But you're not sure. What should you do?

It is time to make a decision. Do you:

Try to help Adam? **P166**

Or

Go back to the resort for help? **P178**

Go back to the resort and report the poachers.

You can't help agreeing with Adam. Unless you report the poachers right away they could disappear before the authorities have a chance to locate them. There are so many yachts cruising the South Pacific islands this time of year, a few hours could make all the difference.

"We'd better get back to the resort pronto," you say, doing some quick calculations in your head. "If we move fast, we'll be back in an hour. If that yacht is traveling at 8 knots, every hour that goes by the authorities will have another um … 250 square miles to search."

Jane looks surprised."How did you figure that out so quickly?"

[Want to find out how the math works? **P216.** If not continue reading.]

You start down the path back towards the resort. You hear the twin's footsteps behind you. Jane mumbles numbers as you half walk, half jog through the jungle.

You've hardly had time to build up a sweat when you see something that looks like a huge spider's web off to your left. You signal a halt and point at whatever it is hanging in the trees. "What's that?"

Adam takes a step forward. "A bird net, I think. Those poachers must plan on coming back for more. I bet they anchor in the safety of the lagoon tonight and come back tomorrow."

You shrug. "It's possible I suppose."

The net is positioned in such a way that that you hadn't noticed it before. The fine mesh, barely visible in the shade of the jungle canopy, stretches between two trees. The net hangs loose and there is already a parrot struggling in its mesh.

The trapped parrot squawks and flaps uselessly.

Adam is first to rush forward. "Have you got a knife?"

You think about Adam's comment about the poachers 'coming

back as you fish your pocket knife out of your daypack.

"Careful with the pressure you put on the net," Adam warns. "The fine bones in their wings are extremely fragile."

Adam holds the frightened bird still as you cut the strands of nylon holding it. The mesh, though fine, is as strong as fishing line. After a few minutes the last of the net falls away. Adam holds the bird in his outstretched arms and lets it go. With a squawk and a series of rapid wing beats the bird darts off to join his flock in the jungle.

"We should take the net back as evidence," Jane says. "The authorities may not believe us otherwise."

"Jane's right," you say. "I'll cut it down."

Five minutes later the net is bundled up in your daypack and the three of you are back on the path towards the resort.

"I wonder how many more of those awful nets they have strung up around the island," Adam says. "And how many poor birds they've captured."

"Don't worry, Adam," Jane says. "Once we report them, I'm sure the authorities will put an end to their operation."

"They'd better," Adam says. "Otherwise I'll sink their boat."

"How will you do that?" you ask. "Got a torpedo hidden in your luggage?"

"No, but I bet I can find a drill at the resort," Adam says, his voice sounding serious. "It doesn't take a very big leak to fill a boat with water."

Jane looks at her brother. "Let's hope it doesn't come to that."

"Enough talk about sinking boats," you say. "Save your breath for the trip back."

With that you start jogging. Within minutes sweat is dripping from your forehead and down your back. The twins puff along behind you.

When the first of the resort's outbuildings appear, you slow to a walk and pull the water bottle out of your pack. Its contents are warm, but at least they're wet.

"So who do we report the poachers to?" Jane asks.

You turn your palms upward and shrug. "That's the problem isn't it? Who can we trust?"

Jane gives you a curious look. "You don't trust the resort management? Do you think they're in on it?"

"They could be," Adam says. "It's hard to believe nobody's noticed nets before, but what choice do we have?"

"Adam's right," you say. "There aren't any police on the island, so management's the closest thing to authority there is around here."

"Unless we can contact the police directly," Jane says.

"How would we do that?" Adam says.

Jane gives her brother a cheeky grin. "Sneak into the office and use their phone. Who needs to know?"

Jane has a point. If someone at the resort is involved, telling them what you've discovered would only give the poachers time to retrieve their nets and flee. It could also be dangerous for you and the twins. Criminals don't like it when people interfere with their cash flow.

You're not sure Jane's plan is a good one. Adam's not looking too convinced either.

"Oh come on you two," Jane says. "Embrace your inner ninja!"

"Let's check the office before we make a decision," you say. "See if it's even possible."

Adam reluctantly agrees.

"Yippee, it's ninja spy time." Jane announces gleefully, about to set off.

"Wait," you say, grabbing her arm. "We need a plan, Miss Ninja."

After some discussion, the three of you decide that Jane, using her acting skills, will distract whoever is on the main desk, while you and Adam scope out the phone situation in the office next door.

"Right, can I go now?" Jane asks, keen to begin her role.

You look toward Adam, who nods his agreement. "Right," you say. "Let's do this."

Jane skips towards the main entrance and the reception desk beyond, while you and Adam walk around to the side door.

"Let's give Jane a minute before we go in," you say. "If we keep near the back wall of the lobby and walk quietly, we should be able to make it to the office without anyone at the main desk seeing us."

When you reach the side door, you can already hear Jane's voice. She's speaking to a middle-aged man in a floral shirt behind the desk.

"So what fishing charters do you offer?"

As the man lays a number of brochures on the counter and explains the times and costs of each option, Jane continues her act.

It's time for you and Adam to make your move.

When Jane sees you enter, she moves along the counter a little more so that, as the man follows her, his back is turned towards you and Adam.

It's only twenty paces to the office and you cover the ground quickly. Thankfully, the office door is open. You cross your fingers and hope it is empty, but unfortunately, as you get closer, you hear a man's voice.

"How many birds?" the voice in the office says. "Forty? Great."

You and Adam freeze, your backs to the wall next to the office door. You hear the crackle of a VHF radio and a male voice, but can't quite make out the words.

Then the man in the office speaks again. "Great ... Yeah ... I've got the buyer lined up."

"He must be talking to the poachers," you whisper in Adam's ear.

"Bring the yacht into the lagoon. Just make sure you keep the cages below deck so the tourists don't get a look."

Adam's jaw is clenched, his face turning red. You're afraid he's about to storm into the office so you grab his arm and drag him back to the side door and out into the garden.

Once outside, you guide him onto a bench and sit down beside him. "Easy does it. You can't rush in there and confront the guy. You've got no proof, and no backup. What are you going to do, lock him in your family's bungalow until the police arrive? Duh, I don't think so."

"But…"

"Think," you say softly, hoping to calm Adam down."We need a plan if we're going to stop these guys. You *do* want to stop them don't you?"

"Well sure but…"

"Right then let's use our heads and do this right. Too many crooks have gotten off because someone's gone off half cocked and blown the investigation."

You can see the tension leaving Adam's face as he realizes you're on his side.

"Yeah okay," he says. "I suppose you're right."

Moments later Jane arrives. "Why'd you come outside?"

You explain about the conversation you've overheard.

"So they *are* in on it," Jane says. "What now?"

"There are phones in the rooms," Adam says. "Let's use those."

You shake your head. "We can't. You've got to get reception to put you through to the number you want. They'll want to know why you're asking to be connected to the police or wildlife rangers. There must be another way."

Adam stands and places his hands on his hips. "Well if they're bringing their boat to the lagoon, I say we find a way to free the birds and sink it. That'll teach them a lesson."

"Yeah, let's sink their boat!" Jane says hopping up and down eagerly. "Underwater attack of the ninjas!"

"Are you serious?" you say, wondering what has gotten into these two. "Do you have any idea what would happen if we got caught?"

But Adam's eyes have glazed over. In his mind he's already planning his assault.

You shake his arm. "Are you listening to me?"

Adam comes out of his trance and glares at you. "Well I'm going to do it with or without your help. I don't care if I get caught!"

"What do you suggest?" Jane asks, staring at you. "Got a better plan?"

There is nothing you'd like more than seeing the poachers yacht on the bottom of the lagoon. It would certainly put a halt to their operation. But if you get caught, who knows what the poachers will do.

It's not an easy decision to make, but time is running out. Do you:

Try to sink the poacher's boat? **P203**

Or

Try to find some other way to contact the authorities? **P211**

Have a look around Smuggler's Cove.

You've come this far so you don't see any harm in having a look around Smuggler's Cove while you're here. "A quick snorkel to see if it's worth coming back, then we'll go report the poachers. What do you say?"

The twins seem happy with this compromise.

The beach on this side of the island is steep and the sand is dark from the island's many volcanic eruptions over the centuries, unlike the white sand of the lagoon beach. No reef means this part of the coast is open to whatever the Pacific throws at it. If it weren't for the cove being sheltered by a rocky point, snorkeling would be difficult except in the best of weather.

As the smuggler's yacht disappears around the point, the three of you come out of the jungle and make your way down to the water's edge. You stick in a toe. The water is warm and inviting.

You pull out your mask and flippers. "I'm going in."

The twins are quick to get their flippers on.

Within minutes the three of you are floating on the surface looking down into a wonderland of gently swaying aquatic plants and interesting sea creatures.

You veer left to inspect the western side of the cove. This side is a little more exposed to the wind. You figure if something was to wash ashore, it's more likely to end up on this side of the cove.

At first the water in the cove is reasonably shallow. You can see the bottom as clear as if you were in a swimming pool. Blue fish dart left and right. Anemones, their tentacles waving, do their dance in the current.

You wonder if there are giant squid in these waters. Probably not you figure, they tend to hang around where waters are colder and deeper.

You are pleased the weather is calm and the waves slight. This coast would be treacherous in a storm. It's easy to imagine how a sailing ship could run aground in a spot like this.

As you kick your flippers, you glide along the surface and your head sweeps back and forth scanning the bottom for any sign of wreckage. Various corals, orange and purple starfish, sponges and crabs cover the rocky bottom along with a multitude of empty shells. Brightly colored fish dart this way and that.

When a large moray eel poke its head out of a crack in the rocks and stares up at you, his sharp teeth glistening in his partly open mouth, you kick a little harder. Morays are not a creature you want to tangle with and this one looks hungry.

After about 15 minutes you stick your head out of the water. Where have the twins gone? At first you can't see them. Then there is a splash as Jane's head breaks the surface. Adam surfaces a split second later.

You pull off your mask and spit out your snorkel. "See anything?"

Both of them shake their heads.

"Okay well let's give it another few minutes and then head back."

The twins give you a thumbs-up and resume their search.

As you move further from shore, the water gets deeper and a sheer wall of rock plunges into the blue. On this wall grows an underwater jungle of marine life.

You feel the ocean swell lift you gently as you stare at the beauty below. When a big flash of silver appears out of nowhere, you jerk with fright thinking it's a shark, but then the mass breaks up into thousands of smaller units and you realize it's only a school of fish.

Where did they come from? The rock wall looks solid all the way down, but there must be a passage or something you can't see from the surface. Once you heart rate returns to normal you take a deep breath and dive.

As you descend you see the wall has an overhang. Below this protrusion, hidden from the surface, the dark mouth of a cave beckons. Thriving in the cracks around the entrance, are a number of red lobsters, their eyes moving back and forth at the end of spindly stalks as they watch your every move.

You grab the flashlight strapped to your leg and shine its narrow beam into the opening. The light only reaches about ten yards into the cave but it's enough for you to see an old anchor covered in barnacles up against one wall. Could this anchor be from the pirate ship that ran aground all those years ago?

In desperate need of air, you kick for the surface, angling out from under the overhand as you rise. When your head breaks the surface you spit out your snorkel and suck in a deep breath of warm tropical air. Your heart jumps around in your chest. If there's an anchor here, maybe treasure isn't that far away.

You pull off your mask and look around for the others. When you see them off to your right you wave and yell out. "Quick! Come over here!"

Jane reaches you first."What is it?" she asks as she treads water beside you.

"There's an old anchor in a cave about 10 feet down."

Adam's heard you too. "Could it be from the pirate ship?"

"It's looks about the right size and shape."

"We really need scuba gear if we're going to be exploring caves," Jane says.

"But how will we find the right place again?" Adam asks.

You look towards the beach and then out towards the point near the entrance to Smugglers Cove. "We need to find reference points and line them up," you say. "See that palm with the crooked trunk on the beach? We're in line with that and the top of the volcano behind it." You spin around and point towards the rocky coastline to the west. "And we're about thirty yards from shore. See that unusual rock with the narrow pointy top?"

"So," Jane says, "when we come back, we line up the funny palm tree, the volcano, and that pointy rock, and we'll be in the right spot?"

"Near enough," you say. "Shall we go get some tanks?"

"In a minute," Jane says. "I want to have a quick look first."

You pass your flashlight to Jane. "Here take this and be careful. I wouldn't recommend going inside. The currents are strong and unpredictable around here."

Jane takes a couple deep breaths, flips her feet into the air and dives headlong into the blue. You hold your mask to your face so you can watch as she kicks her way down.

Then with a big kick, the rest of her body disappears.

You lift you head out of the water and look towards Adam. "I hope that crazy sister of yours doesn't go inside."

Adam shrugs. "What can I say? She thinks she's bulletproof."

With a splash your mask hits the water again. There is still no sign of Jane and it already feels like she's been down there for ages. Has she got stuck? Should you dive down to help?

You start taking a series of deep breaths in preparation to dive when a mop of blonde hair floats out from under the overhang. It's Jane and she's kicking hard for the surface.

Moments later she spits out her mouthpiece and takes a breath. You are about to tell her how reckless she's been when she holds out her hand. On her palm is a triangular wedge of silver.

You carefully pick up the piece and hold it closer to your face. "It's part of a coin," you tell the twins.

"Part of a coin?" Adam asks. "What happened to the rest of it?"

"In the old days, when they didn't have the right change, they'd chop coins into smaller pieces." You turn the piece over. Along one edge are three letters, a C, an A and an R. "I bet this once said Carolus. That's Charles in English. King Carolus the fourth ruled Spain in the late 1700 and early 1800s."

Jane's grin gets even bigger. "That date fits with your wreck doesn't it?"

You nod. "Historians think the *Port-au-Prince* went down in the early 1800s but coins last hundreds of years so this certainly could have come from the ship we're after. Fingers crossed we can find some more."

"I didn't go in very far," Jane says, "so I couldn't see much. But how could treasure have ended up in the cave?"

"Storms on an exposed coast like this can really toss things around."

Adam is listening intently to your exchange. "Well let's go get some scuba gear so we can check it out."

The three of you are deep in thought as you make your way back to the beach. Within ten minutes your gear has dried in the sun and you pack up and start back along the track to the resort.

By the time the first of the resort buildings comes into view, you've been walking for over an hour and your legs are tired.

The three of you sit on a low stone wall by the pool and discuss what to do next.

"I'm for getting back to the cove," Jane says. "I need treasure!"

"We *need* to report the poachers first," Adam says.

"But who can we trust?" Jane says. "What if the poachers are working with someone from the resort?"

Jane has a point. What if reporting the poachers to the management ends up warning them?

Maybe you should gather more evidence before you do anything. And, if you do decide to report them, what happens if the authorities stake out the cove? How will you secretly investigate the cave and find treasure with people lurking about?

Adam stands up. "I've been thinking on the walk back and I reckon there's a good chance the poachers will sail in to the lagoon and anchor overnight. It's the only real anchorage on the island. When they do, I'm going to find some way to sink their boat."

"Brilliant," Jane says. "My brother the eco-warrior against three hardened criminals. Good luck with that, sport."

"But what if they don't come here?" you ask.

"I bet they do," Adam says with a serious look on his face. "In fact I'll bet you ice cream for a week they do."

"Well if they do, and that's a big if," Jane says. "I think we should report them and then get back to treasure hunting. We're not even citizens of this country."

You're not quite sure what you think. You'd love to sink the poacher's boat and put them out of action. But Jane has a point. Is it even your fight? And besides, what can three kids do against dangerous men?

Then you have an idea. "Maybe we can bypass the resort management and contact the authorities directly."

Adam frowns. "Well I'm waiting for the boat. I'll sink them even if I have to do it alone."

It's time to make a decision. Do you:

Agree with Adam and try to sink the poacher's boat if they turn up?
P203

Or

Try to contact the authorities? **P211**

You have decided to try and help Adam.

"Okay, let's see if we can find Adam," you say to Jane. "I don't think we have enough time to go all the way back to the resort for help."

Jane climbs out of the ferns. "So what do we do?"

"We'll have to be stealthy as ninjas, sneak up on them, free Adam, and then get away." You give Jane a big smile. "What could go wrong?"

Jane grins back. "I can think of a few things, but let's not worry about that now. Let's go get my brother."

"First, we'll need camouflage," you say. "Break off some fronds and tie them around your waist with vines. Have them pointing up like a real ferns, that way when we stand still, we'll blend right in with the jungle."

"I've seen movies where commandos rub dirt on their faces," Jane says. "Maybe we should do that too?"

"Good idea," you say. You dig your fingers under the leaf litter at your feet. "The ground is damp under the leaves. Should smear just fine."

Despite the seriousness of the mission you are about to undertake, the two of you can't help laughing a little as you cover your arms, hair and faces. When the two of you have finished, you can barely recognize Jane. She looks half plant, half wild animal.

"Perfect," you say. "Let's go."

You take it slowly in case the poachers have posted a lookout. Every twenty yards or so you stop, stand perfectly still and listen for footsteps. When you see a flash of color, you stop so abruptly. Jane bumps into your back.

"Shhh… I see one of them."

"Where?" Jane whispers back.

You lift your arm and point to a spot 100 yards or so ahead. The man is leaning against a tree. He has a cigarette in one hand and a walkie-talkie in the other. As you stand there pretending to be a fern, you think about what should be your next step.

The man is too big. How can the two of you possibly subdue him?

You look around at your feet. "No rocks, the soil's soft here," you say."We need a weapon of some sort."

Jane digs a hand into her pocket. "I have something that might help."

"What's that?"

She removes a small bundle of nylon netting. All scrunched up, it looks quite small, but as she spreads the net out, your see it's bigger than you first thought. You stand on one side and give the net a sharp tug. The thin, clear filament is deceptively strong.

"I saw it lying just off the path a while ago and picked it up so some poor animal didn't get tangled up in it." Jane says.

"Good thing you did. At least now we've got something to work with."

After thinking for another few moments, you come up with a plan. "If we secure this piece of net between two trees, we might be able to get the man to run into it and tangle himself him up. Then we can pounce on him, tie him up with vines, and he'll be our prisoner."

"But how do we get him to run into the net?" Jane asks.

"Bait. Once we rig it up, you attract the poacher's attention and then lead him to our trap. Then we pounce."

Jane tilts her head to one side and then back to the other, considering what you've said. "Might work. But what then?"

"Prisoner exchange. We use his walkie-talkie to negotiate with the guys on the boat."

You know the plan has risks, but it's the only one you can think of. If Jane agrees, you'll need to set the trap fast. If the man leaves the jungle and goes back to the boat, your opportunity will be gone.

"Dealing with one man at a time is our only chance, Jane."

She exhales a long sigh, looks around the jungle as if she's trying to come up with an alternative, then turns back to you. "Okay, let's do it."

Thankfully there are vines everywhere and your pocket knife is sharp. You and Jane move back along the path a bit and then work quickly cutting lengths of vine and weaving them through the sides of the net.

Then the net is tied to saplings on either side of the track. These small trees should give way when the man's weight hits, bend inward and add to the tangle. Extra lassos of vine are piled up near the trap for quick use. As an added measure, another length of vine is strung across the path at ankle level, a yard or so before the net, to trip the man up and send him flying headlong into your trap. When you stand back to survey your handiwork, the trap is almost invisible.

"Okay," you say. "We've only got one chance at this. If the man looks like he's getting free, run for it. We'll meet back at the resort."

Jane gulps. You can see her hands are a little shaky. But then so are yours.

"Right, now we need to attract his attention. Take off your camouflage and stand on the far side of the net. Here, use some water from my drink bottle to wash some of that mud off you. Otherwise he'll think you're a member of some long lost tribe."

Jane takes your bottle and squirts water over her face and hair.

"Remember, keep the net between you and him at all times."

Jane wipes her face on her t-shirt. "Okay got it."

As Jane stands in position, ready to act as decoy, you walk closer to where the man is standing and move a few steps off the path. Your camouflage gives you a view through its fronds. When you're near enough that you think the man will hear, you grab a dry branch and snap it sharply in two. The crack is like a rifle shot in the stillness of the jungle. When a flock of lorikeets takes off from the canopy above you, you duck down, hoping your camouflage is up to the task.

It isn't long before you hear footsteps. The man is coming to investigate. Then the footsteps speed up. He must have seen Jane further along.

You hear a yelp from Jane as she takes off, and then a yell from the man chasing her.

As soon as the man passes your position, you rip off your camouflage and race down the path after him.

A shout of alarm followed by a loud thump tells you the trap has worked. Around the next bend, you find the poacher lying on the path cursing and struggling in the net. The more he struggles, the more the nylon snags his feet and arms.

You grab a couple of loops from the pile you prepared earlier and slip the sturdy vines over his shoulders pulling them tight around his torso and tying knots to hold them in place.

Moments later Jane arrives back on the scene. She leaps into the air and body slams the man on the ground like she's a big time wrestler.

"Oomph!" the man grunts as the air is forced from his lungs.

Jane jumps up and grabs some more vines and between the two of you the man is trussed up tight within minutes.

You pick up the walkie-talkie, and look down at him. "Well, well, what have we here?"

"You'd better let me—"

Jane kicks the man in the stomach. "You'd better hope my brother is okay mister!"

This is a side of Jane you didn't expect. It's like she's taken the whole ninja thing to heart.

"Stop it girly, or you'll be sorry."

Without hesitation, Jane kicks him even harder.

"Oomph!" the man grunts.

Jane glares down at him. "And don't call me girly old man!"

As Jane and the man lock eyes, you hear the crackle of the walkie-talkie.

"Jimmy, are you there?" More static, then a click. "Come in, Jimmy. Can you hear me?"

You look at Jane and grin. "Let the negotiations begin."

"If you don't want another kick, you'd better stop staring at me!" Jane growls at the man.

You make a mental note never to piss Jane off as you push the 'talk' button on the side of the transmitter. "Yeah Jimmy can hear you."

"Who's that?"

"Never mind who this is," you say into the microphone. "We have Jimmy and we want our friend back."

"You kids have Jimmy? Don't make me laugh. Come on, tell me. How'd you steal his transmitter?"

"We took it off him when we captured him. Now listen, we want you to let Adam go or we're turning your friend into the authorities. Kidnapping is a serious offence."

"If you've got Jimmy, let me speak to him."

"He's a bit tied up at the moment," you say. "Do you want to deal or do I go to the cops?"

There is silence for a minute. You suspect the two men are deciding what to do.

"We'll do nothing until you let us speak to Jimmy."

You hold the microphone near Jimmy's mouth and nod to Jane.

Jane gives him another solid kick.

"Oomph! Oh for Christ's sake, the brats have got me, alright! Do what they say and get me out of here while I still have some unbroken ribs."

You pull the transmitter away from Jimmy and speak clearly into it. "Here's what you're going to do. Bring Adam to the waterfall in exactly half an hour. That's where we'll do the exchange. If you don't show up, or if you show up early, we go to the authorities. Got it?"

Once again there is a brief silence before the man on the other end of the walkie-talkie comes back on. "Right. Half an hour."

"And Adam better be unhurt or the deals off!" you snarl before clicking off.

"Why the waterfall?" Jane asks.

You motion her out of Jimmy's earshot. "I have a cunning plan."

"How cunning?" Jane asks.

"Cunning as a fox." Then you explain.

As you talk, Jane's grin gets broader. "You are evil … but I like it."

"It should work, but we'll need to get moving to get in place before the men arrive. First we'll need to get Jimmy to his feet and make it so he can walk."

Jimmy isn't a lightweight. By the time you roll him onto his back, cut some net away so he has limited movement and maneuver him to his feet, you and Jane are both sweating in the sticky jungle heat.

You give Jimmy a little shove along the path. "Right Mister Poacher, get waddling."

Watching him walk is funny. Netting encases him from head to calf and his arms are bound tightly to his sides. He reminds you of a woman in a tight skirt as he takes small, awkward steps.

Whenever he slows down you prod him with a stick.

"Stop poking me brat, I'm going as fast as I can!"

The steep path leading up towards the waterfall doesn't help Jimmy's speed.

You wink at Jane. "Just keep it moving Mister."

When the three of you arrive at the waterfall you stop, splash some cold water on your face and then pull out your map. You show Jane the path you spotted on it earlier.

"See just here." Your finger traces a line that runs from where you are standing, up and around the falls to the top of the cascade. "This is the path I was talking about. And here," you say, pointing to another line that leads from the top of the falls, around the far side of the volcano and back to the resort, "is our escape route."

"Perfect," Jane says.

You glance over at your captive. "Okay Jimmy time to do a little climbing."

Grabbing one of the vines tied around Jimmy's waist you lead him around the pond and up a narrow path. The track rises steeply. A couple of times Jimmy stumbles and you have to help him back to his feet.

After ten minutes or so the ground levels out and the trees and dense bush give way to flat slabs of rock. A rushing stream flows out of the jungle and thunders over the rocky ledge into the pond below.

Holding the vine around Jimmy's waist, you lead him to the edge of the rocky slab. Water rushes past beside you. When you peer over the edge, it is a straight drop to the water below, and because of the pools clarity, you can see all the way to its bottom. "Whoa. That looks further than I expected."

Stepping back from the edge, you maneuver Jimmy so that he is visible from the path below and then stand slightly behind him holding tightly onto the vine so he doesn't trip and fall.

"Jane," you whisper, "can you go find our escape route?"

Jane nods then heads off while you keep an eye out for the poachers.

A few minutes later Jane's back, she cups her hand to your ear. "Found it. The path looks in pretty good shape."

"Excellent."

"What now?" Jane asks.

"Now we get Adam back."

"My friends are going to make you brats pay," Jimmy snarls from his perch.

"You know, for a man standing on the edge of a waterfall with his hands tied behind his back you're not very bright are you?" You nudge Jimmy a little closer to the edge with the stick. "You sure you want to piss me off right now?"

Jimmy peers over the edge and swallows. "Sorry kid. Don't do anything crazy now."

"That's better," you say, pulling him back a bit. Now keep your trap shut."

It's Jane's keen sense of hearing that alerts you to the sound of approaching footsteps.

"That's far enough!" you yell to the men when they reach the edge of the pool."

The men shield their eyes from the glaring sun as they look up at you. They have tied Adam's wrists but he looks okay.

"Untie Adam and we'll let your guy go," you say. "Adam, when they untie you, run up the path to the right of the falls as quickly as possible."

You see a tiny smile pass between the two men. You can tell they've got something planned … but then so do you.

"Okay, we're untying him now."

As soon as Adam's wrists are free, he does as instructed and sprints off up the path.

"Okay, and here's your guy. You'd better get him before he drowns." And with that, you shove Jimmy over the edge. "Bye bye jerk."

"Noooooooooo!" Jimmy yells.

The splash sends a tower of water flying up.

"What the heck?" one of the men says as he dives into the water after Jimmy. The other man is about to run after Adam when his friend yells out. "Get in here. I can't hold him up on my own, moron!"

The second man dives into the water. When he surfaces the two of them are holding Jimmy's head above water and slowly dogpaddling back to a spot where they can get out of the water.

Jimmy is okay, but none too happy. "Just wait until I get my hands on those brats!" he splutters.

Moments later Adam arrives.

"Okay, time to get moving," you say.

"Hey thanks you two, good work," Adam says.

"Let's get out of here," Jane says. "We can congratulate ourselves once we're back at the resort."

Without any more mucking around the three of you scurry off into the jungle. You keep up a good pace but you're pretty sure your plan has worked and the poachers will try to leave the island quickly.

According to the map, the path you're on curves in a big arc around the slopes of the volcano. Being at a slightly higher altitude, this part of the mountain is covered in trees and broad-leafed shrubs, but every now and then you come across a patch of stunted growth trying to gain a foothold on top of an old lava flow.

At one such flow a pair of gray-brown birds with unusually large feet and orange legs are digging a burrow in the warm volcanic soil.

"Look, megapodes!" you say.

"Kwway-kwe-kerrr," the male bird sings.

"Kirrrr," the female replies.

"Funny looking things," Jane says. "What happened to the feathers on their throats?"

Below the bird's orange beaks is a sparse patch where the feathers look like they've been plucked.

"I think that's natural. I read these birds bury their eggs and then let the heat in the soil do the incubation."

"What? They just lay them and leave them?" Jane asks.

You nod. "I think so."

"Doesn't podes mean feet?" Adam asks.

"Yes," you say. "And mega mean really big."

"So we've discovered Big Foot?" Jane says, making a face of exaggerated astonishment.

Adam raises his eyes to the sky and sighs. "A big-footed chicken maybe."

You laugh at Adam's joke. "Hey you two, we've made good time. Let's take a minute and grab a bite and something to drink. It's important to keep hydrated in these hot climates."

You pull out your drink bottle and an energy bar and watch the birds as you eat, glancing occasionally back along the track in case the poachers appear.

When you've finished you re-shoulder your pack. "Okay break's over, we'd better get moving." You start along the track again. "I hate to think what Jimmy will do to us given the opportunity, especially after his belly flop off the cliff."

The twins don't need much convincing.

After crossing the old lava flow the three of you re-enter the forest and continue your loop around the mountain towards the resort. Small streams cut their way down the rocky slope and higher up the mountain, large birds soar as they pick up thermals near the volcano's summit.

You are just starting to cross a tricky part of the track, where heavy rain has washed some of it away, when you hear a low rumble from deep underground.

Just as Jane swings her head around looking for the source of the noise, the earth starts shaking and the rumbling gets louder.

"It's an eruption!" Adam yells. "The mountain's going to blow!"

And here you were thinking the volcano was safe. But then as quickly as the noise started, the rumbling stops.

You wipe the sweat off your forehead. "Phew! False alarm."

"Or prelude," Adam says.

You are about to move off, when you hear a strange clacking sound ... and it's getting louder. When you look up the slope in the direction of the noise you see rocks and boulders tumbling down the mountainside.

"Rock fall!" you shout. "Run for it!"

The three of you scramble over the wash-out and hit the track sprinting. Thankfully the track is reasonably clear and without too many tree roots to trip you up. When the rocks hit the bush line, you hear the cracking of branches in the jungle behind you. Then a tortured creaking as the trees struggle to hold back the weight of the larger rocks. Then, once again, there's an eerie silence.

"Oh boy, that was close," Jane says.

"Not wrong there," you say with hands on knees sucking in deep breaths of air.

"This island is a death trap," Adam says. "Poachers, volcanoes, boulders bouncing down the mountainside. What next?"

Having caught your breath you walk over and slap Adam on the back. "Don't worry," you say. "At least we haven't had a tsunami."

"Yet," Adam says, trying to smile. "You do know eruptions cause tsunamis, eh?"

"Oh stop being a worry wart," Jane says. "We're ninja spies on a great adventure. Nothing can harm us."

You like Jane's optimism, but you also know that it's foolish not to have a healthy respect for nature. "Let's just keep moving and watch out for potential hazards. Even ninja spies aren't boulder proof."

A few minutes later, when the ground starts shaking a second time, you suspect the volcano is only warming up. You grab the nearest tree and hang on. After a minute's vibration, the mountain once again goes silent.

"I think its practicing for the main show," Adam says. "Let's just hope it doesn't do a Krakatoa on us."

Jane's brow creases. "Krakatoa?"

"You know, the Indonesian volcano that blew up and wiped out over 30,000 people," Adam says. "That eruption caused a huge tsunami that wiped out whole towns."

Jane raises her eyebrows. "But were any ninjas hurt?"

Adam mutters under his breath and rolls his eyes skyward.

Jane makes a face at her brother. "I didn't think so!"

"Well I don't know much about volcanoes," you say, "except that I don't want to be on them when they go off." And with that said, you take off down the path again.

"I'm with you," Adam says falling in behind.

"Ninja spies, evacuate the mountain!" Jane says as she jogs past the two of you. "Last one to the resort is a monkey's bum."

"See what I have to put up with?" Adam says.

Adam may find his sister a pain at times, but he follows her lead and increases his pace.

It's only another half an hour before the track cuts through a forest of pandanus palms, with their narrow spiny leaves and their strange stilted roots that look like mini teepees holding the main trunk clear of the ground.

When you come to a junction you stop and pull out your map. Adam and Jane look over your shoulder.

You point to a spot where two tracks meet. "We're just here I reckon."

"This track along the beach looks longer," Jane says tracing her finger along the line that runs along the coast.

"Yes, it's longer to the resort that way, but it's further from the volcano," Adam says. "The further we are from the mountain, the better."

"But what if the poachers are following us?" Jane says. "They could take the shorter track around the volcano and cut us off before we get to the resort."

The twins look at you expecting a decision. Do you:

Take the beach track? **P184**

Or

Take the shorter jungle track? **P193**

Go back to the resort for help.

You can't see any other alternative other than going back to the resort to get help. What are two kids supposed to do against three criminals?

"They said they'd hurt Adam if we said anything," Jane says. "Do you think they're telling the truth?"

You look at Jane's worried expression. "They could be bluffing."

"But how do we know?" Jane asks. "And what if they're not?"

Adam's capture is certainly a dilemma. It will take time to get back to the resort, even if you jog the whole way. The men on the yacht could be long gone by the time you get help from the resort. You sit down, lean back against a coconut palm and think.

"Maybe you're right, Jane. What if they're not bluffing? They could dump Adam out at sea and deny ever having seen him. It would be their word against our. Could we even identify them properly? Remember if they've got Adam, they've got Adam's camera too."

Jane, normally so self assured, is looking shaky. "But what — what can we do?"

"I'm not sure but I think we need to try. Let's sneak back and see what they're up to eh? We might think of something."

Jane nods and then clenches her jaw in an attempt to look determined, but you see through her act. She's scared, and with good reason. Her brother is in danger and you may not be able to help him.

You step off the path and lead Jane into the jungle. "Hunters usually set their traps on paths."

"So that's why you're going off trail?" Jane asks.

"Yep. I'll lead us back to the cove cross-country, it may be harder going but we're less likely to run into trouble that way. You never know what booby traps the poachers have set up."

As the two of you work your way through the dense undergrowth, you hear the chatter of birds above you. You wonder if the birds are calling out a warning because you're in their territory, or just going about their normal business.

You figure you're about half way back to the cove when you see a thick length of black rubber stretching between two trees off to your left. The rubber is about eight inches wide and ten feet long. Interested, you veer towards it. As you get closer you see fine mesh hanging below the rubber. "It's a net."

The rubber is suspended just above head level with the net hanging to the ground below.

"Why rubber?" Jane asks. "How does that help them catch birds?"

You have a look at the set up. "I don't think it is for catching bird."

Jane goes pale "Wha—what do you mean? Is it for ca—catching people?"

"Wild pigs more likely," you say with a grin. "The rubber will give some flex and stop the net ripping when one runs into it. See over there." You point to a pile of husked coconuts, their fibrous outer covering removed, leaving only the brown hard nut."Whoever set this up has been collecting coconuts too. More likely locals than poachers."

"They sure got a lot of them," Jane says.

Then an idea hits you. "Of course! Coconuts!"

Jane gives you a funny look. "Huh?"

"What's the same size as a coconut and used to be fired by pirate ships?"

"What? Pirate ships?"

"Cannon balls!" you say. "Coconuts are like cannon balls!"

"But we don't have a cannon," Jane says.

"But we do have the makings of a slingshot."

"We do?" Jane says.

You point to the thick band of rubber stretched between the two trees. "Yes. A big one."

Jane's smile flashes onto her face as she sees where you're going. "So, your plan is to tie the rubber between two trees near the cove and fire coconuts at the yacht?"

You nod. "Exactly."

"But won't the poachers just pull up their anchor and sail off?"

"They might if they can get to the bow of their boat without getting knocked out. Our job will be to stop that happening."

"You are evil," Jane says. "I like it."

"Right, let's get this thing down."

You climb up one tree and get to work untying the rubber. Jane climbs up the other. Once back on the ground you stand on one end and try pulling the strip of rubber up with your arms. The band is incredibly strong. With you knife you cut a coconut-sized section of net to use as your slingshot's pouch and attach it to the rubber. Then you take off your day-pack and fill it with as many coconuts as it will carry. Jane does the same.

You shoulder your pack. "Right, bombardier, to the beach!"

Jane winks. "Aar me hearty. Let's sink these buccaneers."

The two of you make a cautious approach to the beach in case the poachers have posted a lookout.

"Look for two trees about six feet apart," you say as you scout around.

Jane spots a couple up ahead. "How about these two?"

You inspect the trees, and then walk in a straight line back from the beach to check the firing line. The angle seems good. And there's a bonus. The trees she's pointed out have a row of low shrubs between them and the water. These shrubs will give you cover while you set up and, with a bit of luck, hide your position for a time while the poachers figure out where the flying coconuts are coming from.

"Perfect," you say. "Let's get set up."

Setting up the slingshot is a simple matter. You take a double loop around each tree at about shoulder height and tie a knot. Then you clear a path so you can stretch the rubber back as far as possible before shooting.

"These guys are going to freak!" Jane says with a grin.

After a final check that all is right you look over at Jane. "Ready for action bombardier?"

"Aye aye Captain."

"Load coconut," you say as you slip the first coconut into the pouch.

"St—retch," Jane says as the two of you grab the pouch and pull back as hard as you can.

"Elevation," you say kneeling down and angling your shot upward so it will have some distance to it.

"Three, two, one, FIRE!" you yell in unison.

With a *twang!* the coconut flies in a parabolic arc towards the yacht.

"It's a hit!" Jane exclaims as the rock-hard nut crashes into the side of the boat, leaving a small dent in the fiberglass.

"Load!" you yell. You quickly repeat the process.

"FIRE!"

The next impact has the men scrambling up from below.

"Can you see Adam?" Jane says.

One of the men is standing on the cabin top, looking your way.

"Quick, let's get him! FIRE!"

The coconut lands in the cockpit only feet away.

"Someone's shooting at us," the man calls to his companion. "Let's get out of here."

A man comes up from below and moves towards the bow.

"Let's get him!" Jane calls. "Load!"

"FIRE!"

The coconut hits the deck a few feet from where the man is fiddling with the anchor rope. The shot's a miss, but it's close enough to give the man a fright and he scurries back to the relative safety of the cockpit.

"FIRE!"

This nut crashes through one of the yacht's side windows. There's more shouting from below.

Another man comes on deck with a pair of binoculars and scans the shore. The way he is sweeping back and forth means he hasn't spotted your position.

"Load," you whisper.

The two of you stretch back the slingshot. You take half a step to the right and aim at the man with the binoculars.

"Down a bit more," you say.

"Fire!"

The coconut screams out of the jungle. It is nearly upon him before he drops the binoculars and reacts. Unfortunately for him, he's too slow. The coconut doubles him over as it smacks into his pot belly. Then he staggers back and falls over the railing and splashes into the sea.

"Got him!" you say.

Jane points. "There's Adam."

The distraction you've created has allowed Adam time to open the front hatch and climb onto the bow. His hands are tied, but he steps over the railing and jumps into the water anyway.

"Give me your knife. I'm going to help," Jane says.

You reach in your pocket and hand it over.

"Cover me." And with that Jane streaks out of the jungle, runs down the beach and plunges into the water.

You load another coconut and pull back. Without Jane's help you really have to dig deep to pull the rubber back far enough, and you can't hold it long, or do much aiming before having to let go. But still you manage to fire three more nuts off in quick succession.

Thankfully, the men are too busy dodging coconuts and helping their friend get back on board to notice that Adam has jumped ship.

Adam floats on his back, slowly kicking his way to shore. As you fire another nut, you see Jane has nearly reached him.

She cuts the rope binding Adam's wrists.

Another nut hits the cabin top just as the men pull their friend aboard.

One of the men yells out. "The boy!"

"Fire!" you yell sending another nut flying through the air.

This one shatters a tray of food and drinks sitting in the cockpit. Glass goes flying.

"Let's get out of here," The injured man says as he drips on deck. "Get that anchor up!"

Jane and Adam are running up the beach. Soon you'll have a full crew of gunners again.

"Load!" Jane says as she grabs another coconut. "Let's teach these guys a lesson!"

With three of you the firing is much faster. Nuts zip though the air every fifteen seconds or so. Adam scouts around for more nuts, but after another five minutes you've exhausted your ammo.

"We'd better get out of here before they come ashore," you say.

"They'd better put the fire out before their boat burns you mean," Adam says.

You look at Adam. "What did you say?"

"Before I escaped I found a lighter and set the bunk in the front cabin on fire. It's polyurethane foam so it should burn like crazy."

"Holy moly!" Jane says with a grin. "My brother the arsonist."

Now that Adam's mentioned it, you can see a few wisps of smoke coming from the front hatch. The men have seen it too. One of them grabs a fire extinguisher from the cockpit and disappears below.

"Let's get out of here," Jane says. "I've had enough adventure for one day."

You look at the twins and smile. "There's always tomorrow me hearties."

Congratulations, this part of your story is over. You've saved Adam, and put a serious dent in the poachers operation. Maybe in another path you'll find some treasure.

It is time to make a decision. Do you:

Go back to the beginning of the story and try another path? **P121**

Or

Go to the list of choices and start reading from another part of the story? **P380**

You have decided to take the longer beach track.

"I think the volcano's going to blow," you say. "We'd better stick to the coast."

The twins follow as you veer left and head down the slope towards the sparkling water of the Pacific Ocean rather than carry on around the higher loop track.

Ten minutes later, when you feel another rumble beneath your feet, you're sure you've made the right decision.

Higher up the mountain, you hear rocks tumbling downhill and crashing into trees.

"I wouldn't want to be up there," Adam says, picking up the pace. "This mountain is angry about something."

As if to confirm Adam's point, a blast of ash and rock shoots out of the crater, peppering the upper slopes with rocks. The resulting tremor nearly knocks you off your feet.

"Crikey!" Jane cries out, in a poor imitation of an Australian accent. "Ground's jumping round like a kangaroo being chased by a pack of dingoes."

This time both you and Adam roll your eyes. But Jane's not wrong about the volcano. The mountain's definitely working up a head of steam.

The three of you keep up the pace, eager to get as far away from the eruption as possible and it isn't long before the track begins to level out. More ferns begin to appear and you can see the tops of the coconut palms in the distance. The ground under your feet is less rocky and the sound of waves breaking creates a gentle background to the chirping of the birds.

You're only half a mile from the coast, when you hear an explosion of some magnitude behind you.

"Holy moly," Jane exclaims. "The mountain's bleeding."

You look up through a gap in the trees. Near the top of the cone, blood-red lava flows out from vents in the volcano's flanks. Rivers of red run down the mountain, consuming everything in their path. Dense smoke billows into the air and with each explosion more rocks and debris are ejected high into the air.

A flock of lorikeets skim the treetops as they flee the upper slopes and you hear a loud crashing through the undergrowth that you suspect is a wild pig frightened by the rumbling.

"I wonder what's happening on the other side of the island," Adam says. "Do you think the lava will threaten the resort?"

You scratch your head. "It's possible. We'll find out soon enough I suppose."

When you come out of the bush onto the coast and look in the direction of the resort you see a curtain of smoke rising in front of you.

Jane grabs your arm. "What's that?"

"I hope I'm wrong, but I think one of the lava flows has made it all the way to the sea."

Jane frowns. "You mean we're cut off?"

You wave the twins forward. "I'm not sure. Let's check it out."

It takes about ten minutes to reach the lava flow. Its acidic smoke makes you cough. Thankfully a sea breeze is blowing most of the smoke is up the slope.

Only the lushness of the green tropical plants stops the fire spreading wildly across the island. Were it the dry season, heaven knows what sort of fires the lava flow would have started.

"It's wiped out the track," Adam says.

He's right. Although the lava is beginning to crust over, cracks show the fiery red, still fluid, lava running beneath.

You shake your head. "No way across that. We'd end up looking like overcooked marshmallows."

Adam looks nervous. "What now?" he asks.

"Goodness ... gracious ... great balls of fire," Jane sings in her best rock and roll voice.

Eyes roll.

While Jane tries to make light of your situation, you think hard about how to get out of this predicament. But then Jane surprises you with a suggestion.

"I've seen documentaries on TV. When lava flows into the ocean it makes lots of steam, but the water always wins in the end and cools the lava down. Couldn't we just swim around it?"

"I'm not that great a swimmer remember," Adam says.

But what Jane has said makes perfect sense.

"Let's go to the beach and check it out," you say. "We can always put some coconuts in our day packs for buoyancy."

"Okay," Adam says. "Anything's better than being captured."

"Or toasted," Jane says.

Where the lava meets the sea is a battleground. Hot lava flows forward and waves crashing on the shore put up a defense. Steam is everywhere. The lava crackles and pops as it is doused with cold seawater, but still it keeps coming.

"How wide is the flow do you think?" you ask the twins.

"Two hundred yards maybe," Adam replies.

"Easy-peasy," Jane says. "We can swim that no problem."

You put your pack on the ground and look around. "Okay let's gather some coconuts. And make it quick, this mountain isn't getting any friendlier."

If there is one thing this island isn't short of, it's coconuts. Within a couple minutes your packs are full to bursting.

"These are heavy. You sure they'll float?" Adam asks.

You raise your eyebrows at Adam. "Coconuts float all over the Pacific silly. Is your pack lighter than it would be if it was filled with water?"

Adam lifts his pack by its straps. "Yeah, I suppose…"

"Well anything lighter than water will float. There's lots of air trapped by the coconut's husk. Believe me, they'll float just fine.' You lift your pack and sling it over your shoulder. "Come on let's go."

There is no protective lagoon on this part of the coast. You'll have to enter the water from the rocks. You find an area where an old lava flow protrudes into the sea and walk out onto it.

"Time your leap so you get sucked out by a retreating wave," you say. "And don't lose hold of your pack."

Adam looks nervous.

"I'll go first," Jane says. "I'm the strongest swimmer. Once I'm in the water, I can help if one of you gets has problems."

Again Jane is making a lot of sense. You nod and watch as she shifts her pack onto her chest and puts her arms through the straps.

"Look guys, I'm the hunch stomach of Notre Dame."

Your eyes roll, "Enough with the jokes already," you say, but secretly you're pleased that Jane has a sense of humor. It will make things easier for Adam when it's his turn to jump.

Jane moves further out onto the rock and gets ready to leap. As a wave breaks, the white foam rushes up around her ankles, then as the water surges back, she takes two quick steps, leaps in, and is sucked out with the retreating wave.

She paddles out beyond the next wave and then turns back toward shore. Her day pack holds her upper body well above the water. "See, I told you. Easy-peasy."

You and Adam repeat the exercise without any drama and start swimming out around the lava flow. You're pleased you took your face mask out of your pack and put it in a side pouch. The sight below is spectacular.

Lava, red and burning, like an undersea river, flows out along the sea bed. Tiny bubbles rise from the boiling water where the lava touches the ocean. You can feel the heat radiating from the lava flow and are careful not to stray too close.

Then suddenly there is a silver flash beneath you. Then another. Your heart races, thinking that sharks have surrounded you, but then a dolphin jumps out of the water and twirls in the air before splashing down.

"Dolphins!" Jane yells. "Hundreds of them."

"I wonder if they're attracted by the heat of the lava?" Adam says.

More and more dolphins join in the fun as they leap over you, around you, and swim under you.

"So cute!" Jane squeals as a young dolphin comes up to investigate these new creatures that have invaded her territory.

Then after a series of gravity defying leaps, each more spectacular than the previous, the pod swims west and the dolphins disappear.

"Wow that was amazing," Jane says.

The dolphins have taken your mind off things and before you know it you have reached a spot where it's safe to come ashore. The place you've chosen isn't so much a beach as it is a channel in the rock between two old lava flows. Seaweed clogs the sides of the channel, but there looks to be a clear run up the center into shore.

You put your face down in the water, and kick your feet. Fish are everywhere. Sea urchins and hermit crabs crowd the bottom. It's like looking into an aquarium.

One type of coral looks like miniature red trees that have lost their leaves. Another resembles a pale blue brain. Anemones wave their tentacles and seaweeds of yellow and green sway gently in the tide. Electric-blue fish swim lazily by, while schools of red, white and orange striped fish move as one in shoals of a hundred or so. A bright yellow fish the size of a dinner plate nibbles at something on a lump of pale white coral and orange sea stars move slowly across the rocky bottom looking for shellfish to eat.

You're only twenty yards from shore when you see something sparkle. You stop kicking and float in place. Then you see it again.

You lift your face out of the water. "Stop, I see something on the bottom." You pass your sodden daypack to Jane. "Can you hold this please? I'm going to take a closer look."

After a deep breath you kick for the bottom. Once there you hold onto a piece of kelp to keep from floating up. Now where was that...

And then you see them. A trail of gold coins running along the eastern side of the channel.

In need of air you shoot to the surface. "Coins on the bottom," you tell the others when your head breaks the surface. "Heaps of them!"

"Holy moly," Jane says with a big toothy grin. "We're gonna be rich."

Jane passes Adam the two packs and you and she dive again. This time you manage to pick up half a dozen coins before having to resurface. With each dive, you find a few more coins, but it becomes obvious fairly quickly that this isn't the mother lode.

"How many coins have we got altogether?" you ask Adam who has been looking after the coins as you and Jane do the diving.

Adam does a quick count. "Twenty seven. What's the price of gold?"

You try to remember what you saw online before you left for your vacation. "About 1200 U.S. an ounce I think."

It's time for some quick calculations. You decide to multiply 30 times 1200 and then subtract 3 times 1200 to make it easy.

"Let see, 3 times 12 is 36. Put the three 0's back on and that's 36,000. Less 3 times 1200 which is 3600. That means we've got 36,000 less 3600. Or 32,400 dollars worth."

"Crikey!" Jane says. "That'll buy a few kangaroo burgers."

The three of you are congratulating each other when you hear a male voice nearby.

"There those brats are!"

You look towards land, but see nothing. Then you hear the low rumble of a diesel engine.

"The poachers aren't chasing us by foot," Jane says. "They've come by boat."

"They must be trying to beat us back to the resort," Adam says.

"No time to wait," you say, retrieving your pack from Adam and kicking towards shore. "Let's get out of here before they launch their dinghy."

Scrambling up the rocky beach, the three of you dump your coconuts and rejoin the coastal path. The men motor just off shore, watching you as you go.

"How are we going to shake them?" Jane asks.

"That's a good question Sis," Adam says before turning to you. "How are we going to shake them?"

"Let's just keep going. What can they do once we're back at the resort?" you say.

Your eyes follow the yacht as you walk quickly along the path. The volcano is still spewing ash and lava, and every now and then you feel the ground shaking.

Then a violent jolt knocks you off your feet.

"Holy moly," Jane says picking herself up. "That was the strongest one yet."

"Too big for comfort," you say. "I'm not liking this."

As you start moving again, you notice the sea receding. Where once there was water, now you can see fish flopping about. "That's odd," you say.

"Not odd," Adam says. "It's a tsunami!"

You look out to sea. A wall of white water is heading towards shore. "Run!"

The three of you drop your packs and move quickly away from the beach. "Keep running for high ground," Adam yells. "Who know how far it will come inland."

As you dodge trees and palms and head further inland the ground gradually rises. With the volcano still erupting you don't really want to climb too high, but then you don't want to get caught by the incoming wave either. Then you hit an old lava flow where the ground rises steeply. You take a narrow path up the side of the flow, pumping your legs for all they're worth.

By the time you get to the ridge, you figure you're far enough from the beach to be safe. You breathe hard and watch the wave approaching the yacht.

"They've seen it coming," Adam says. "They're trying to turn their bow into the wave."

The three of you watch, spellbound by the sight unfolding before you.

As the wave rushes in, the bow of the yacht rises, and rises. It looks as though it's going to make it over, but then the sheer force of the water forces the yacht back. When the bow drops, and the boat turns side on to the wave, you know the boat is doomed.

As the seabed shallows near the shore, the wave rises, and rises, and rises.

"Holy moly!" you say, stealing Jane's favorite expression. "Look at it go!"

The yacht is on its side, mast down in the water. You can see the men hanging on for dear life as the wave pushes the boat towards the land. The suddenly the yacht capsizes, the mast snaps and the men are tossed in the water.

"I don't like their chances," Adam says as the wave rushes to shore.

Soon after the yacht is smashed on the rocks, the wave retreats. This is a bad as its arrival. Everything and everyone is sucked back out to sea.

Once the wave has gone, the three of you walk down to the water, amazed at how the area has been stripped clean of vegetation, and anything else the wave could take with it. Much debris floats offshore.

"Our packs are gone," you say. "And the gold."

"And the poachers by the looks of it," Adam says. "Unless they managed to grab something to keep afloat."

You walk to the water's edge, searching for survivors. There is no sign of the men. Then as you're looking around, you see a glint of something in a tidal pool. You hop over a couple rocks and bend down to investigate.

It's a gold coin. Then you see another. "Hey look," you say, holding the coin up between your thumb and index finger. "Gold!"

"There's a couple over here too," Jane says, picking up a coin. Then she does a little dance and twirls. "There're all over the place!"

And she's right. The tsunami has picked up coins from the seabed and thrown them up onto the shore. The gold, being so heavy, got trapped in the cracks in the rocks and was left behind when the wave retreated.

As the three of you spend the next ten minutes searching, you wonder if this is the *Port-au-Prince's* treasure that the wave has picked up on its rush to shore.

"We could spend the rest of the day hunting for coins," you say, "but we should probably get back to the resort and see how things are. People could be hurt. If things are okay, we can come back tomorrow. Besides," you say, pulling a handful of coins from your pocket. "We've got plenty already."

So that's what you do. Half an hour later, as you round a protective headland you see that the resort survived the tsunami and everyone is fine. Even the volcano has gone back to sleep.

After reporting what happened to the yacht and answering a few questions over the phone with the police back in the capital, the three of you sit on the beach with a cold soda and watch the reds and oranges of the tropical sunset.

"Looks like we're coin collecting tomorrow," you say to the twins.

Adam gives you the thumbs up. "Meet by the pool after breakfast?"

"Sounds like a plan," you say.

"Crikey," Jane says as the last of the sun dips below the horizon. "We're gonna be rich!"

Congratulations you've reached the end of this part of the story. You've survived a volcanic eruption, tsunami and being chased by poachers. Well done!

Go back to the beginning of the story and try another path? **P121**
Or

Go to the list of choices and start reading from another part of the story? **P380**

You have decided to take the jungle track.

The mountain is quiet again so you decide to take the much shorter jungle track to the resort.

"I think speed is the critical factor here," you tell the twins. "The sooner we get back to the resort the better."

"I'm with you," Jane says.

As you proceed along the path, overhanging tree branches block out the sky and the jungle is eerily quiet.

"This place is spooky," Jane says, sticking close to you and Adam.

About a quarter of a mile along, you come to a fast-moving stream that has cut a deep chasm down the side of the mountain in its rush to get to the sea. From a rocky ledge at the chasm's lip, you look down. A narrow track zigs down, crosses the stream at the bottom, and then zags back up and out the other side.

"Watch your step, these rocks might be loose," you warn the twins as you carefully take your first step down the steep bank.

When you reach the bottom you wait for the others. Adam is first to arrive.

"That rock looks slippery," he says, pointing down at the smooth basalt on the bottom of the stream bed. "Maybe we should lock arms as we cross so we don't fall over."

The stream is only calf deep, but the water is rushing past at quite a pace. Below, in the darkness of the chasm you hear the sound of tumbling water, a waterfall perhaps, so keeping your footing is important.

The three of you link arms and take small tentative steps as you start across.

"You're right about the rock being slick," Jane says, tightening her grip on your arm.

The crossing is only ten or twelve steps, and you're nearly there when you and the twins are knocked off your feet by another big quake.

With a splash, you find yourself sitting in water up to your waist and sliding down the smooth rock deeper into the chasm.

"Hang on!" you yell. "Keep your feet below you for protection!"

The three of you, with arms still linked, are pushed at an ever increasing speed down the natural waterslide worn into the rock. There is nothing to grab onto and no place to get out. All you can do is go with the flow.

"Yikes!" Jane screams as the three of you go flying over an eight foot waterfall.

Thankfully the pool is deep enough so you don't hit bottom when you splash down, but you've barely had time to get over the shock of the drop and catch your breath before the power of the water whisks you downstream into the next half-pipe.

"Keep your arms linked," you tell the others, knowing you've got a better chance of survival if you stick together.

The deeper you slide into the chasm, the darker it gets.

When the gradient suddenly steepens to almost vertical and you see a tunnel entrance coming up. There is nothing you can do.

"We're going underground!" you yell.

Instantly it's so dark you can't even see the twins.

Adam's been quiet so far, apart from the odd grunt as he's struggled to keep his head above water, but now that you've gone underground you can hear him whimpering. Or is that you?

If this slide had been at a fun park, you'd be having the time of your life, but not knowing what is coming up next in the total darkness makes this the scariest thing you've ever experienced.

The slide seems to go on forever. It twists and turns, dips and dives. At times you hear a drop coming up, and at others you just fall into space not knowing how far you'll fall before you hit whatever's at the bottom.

Even though you're sliding quickly, time seems to move very slowly. It's like your brain has switched to survival mode. Adrenaline surges through you.

After what seems like ages you feel Jane's arm tighten on yours.

"Is that light I see?" she says.

You suddenly realize you've had your eyes screwed tight. Sure enough there is a faint light coming from cracks in the rocky roof of the tunnel.

Then there's another drop of about six feet and you're deposited into an underground pool almost as large as the swimming pool at the resort.

Soft light filters down from above, giving the cave an ghostly feel.

"The water tastes salty," Jane says. "This pool must join up to the ocean."

What Jane says makes sense. Water always runs downhill towards the ocean. You must have slid through an old volcanic vent worn smooth by hundreds if not hundreds of thousands of years of water running through it to the sea.

The cracks in the rock above must be the result of tremors and erosion.

"Now we just need to find a way out," Adam says, not sounding all that confident.

"I've got my waterproof flashlight," you say, rummaging in your backpack. You breathe a sigh of relief when it still works.

The narrow beam shows a low roof of hardened lava.

"If the sea is getting in," Adam says, "there must be an opening somewhere. We just need to find it."

"I'm the best swimmer," Jane says. "Give me the flashlight and I'll see if I can find one."

With flashlight in hand, Jane takes a deep breath and dives. You and Adam follow her progress as the light moves along the bottom of the pool, sweeping back and forth as Jane searches. About twenty yards away she comes up for air and then dives again.

It isn't until her third dive that she pops up with news. "I've found a passage!"

"Can we get through?" you ask.

"Fish are swimming in and out so we should be able to as well."

You and Adam dogpaddle over to where Jane is treading water. After taking a deep breath you dive down to check out the passage Jane has found. It's about fifteen yards long with faint light at the end of it. It looks plenty big enough to swim through.

You've just surfaced, when you feel a surge of water come pouring into the cave through the passage. The roof of the cave gets closer as all the extra water comes streaming in. Then as the water rushes out again, it's about all you can do to keep from getting sucked out with it.

"Man that tidal surge is strong," you say. "If we're going to get out of here we'll have to time our exit carefully."

Adam, being the weakest swimmer, looks petrified.

Jane sees her brother's nervousness. "Adam and I can link arms and go together."

The look of relief on Adam's face is immediate. "Yeah, that way we'll have twice the kicking power."

You could mention that they'll also have twice the bulk to move through the water, but there is no point in undermining his confidence. "Okay," you say. "That's a good idea. Do you want the flashlight?"

"Nah," Jane says shaking her head. There's plenty of light coming from the other end. We'll be fine." Jane looks at her brother. "You ready?"

Adam swallows loudly and nods.

"Okay, here comes the next wave," Jane says. "As soon as it starts going out, dive and kick like crazy."

The siblings link arms and tread water waiting for the water to start its outward journey.

"Three, two, one go!" says Jane taking a deep breath and diving.

You watch nervously as the twins disappear into the underwater tunnel especially as it's your turn next. You put your flashing back in the side pocket of your daypack and get ready to dive. You have time for three deep breaths before you feel the water in the cave begin to rise.

As the water starts to surge out, you take one last breath and dive. At first the pull of the water is slight, but as you enter the passage, and the volume of water is restricted, the pull is stronger and you barely need to kick. Most of your efforts are around trying not to scrape along the rough sides of the tunnel. The last thing you want is to end up in the sea with cuts bleeding into the water. Sharks might think you're lunch.

Your mind is taken off the thought of sharks as you pass an old anchor leaning against one wall of the tunnel. You wonder briefly if it might be from a pirate ship, but then before you know it, you see sunlight streaming down from above and you kick hard for the light.

When your head breaks the surface you look for Jane and Adam.

"Pssst!"

You look around for the noise.

"Pssst! Over here."

You turn to your right and see Jane and Adam hiding behind a rock. Then you see the poacher's yacht bobbing gently in the cove between you and the beach.

You can't believe your eyes. You've been washed down the mountain all the way back to Smugglers Cove!

"Get over here before they see you," Adam whispers, signaling you over.

Thankfully the men on deck have their backs to you.

You dive down and swim underwater towards the rock where Adam and Jane are hiding.

"We've ended up back where we started," you whisper. "This is one crazy island."

"And those horrible poachers are still here," Adam says softly, careful not to let the men hear him.

You look around for a solution, but the rock you're hiding behind is about twenty yards from any other cover. If you try to swim to shore, the poachers could see you.

"We might have to hang here until nightfall," you say.

Then you hear a loud voice drift over the water from the yacht. It's Jimmy berating his friends.

"Why don't you lazy sods give me a hand with the last couple of traps, then we can get out of here," he says. "I've had a hard day."

The two men laugh.

One of the men slaps Jimmy on the back. "Well at least if you decide to give up poaching, you can always take up cliff diving!"

"Shut up, you drongo!" Jimmy growls. "That fall almost killed me!"

The two men laugh again.

"Okay we'll help," the other man says once he's stopped laughing. "I don't want to be hanging around here when the authorities arrive."

The three men finish their drinks, climb down into the dinghy and start rowing away from you towards the shore.

You look at Adam and then at Jane. "Are you thinking what I'm thinking?"

Jane smiles. "A spot of piracy perhaps?"

"You got it."

"Those poachers will kill us," Adam says.

"Only if we get caught," Jane says. "And ninjas never get caught."

"It's worth the risk," you say. "If we hijack their boat, the only way they can get off the island is to come back to the resort. By then, we'll have the authorities waiting for them."

You look towards shore. The men are about half way to the beach.

"Once they've gone into the jungle we'll need to move fast. Who knows how long they'll be gone," you say.

It isn't long before Jimmy and the other two men drag the dinghy above the tide and march off into the jungle with their cages. As soon as they've disappeared, you and the twins start swimming towards the yacht.

"Ever driven a boat before?" Jane asks as she dogpaddles beside you.

You shake your head.

"I've done a bit," Adam says. "My friend's father has a boat, how different can it be?"

"About thirty feet, I reckon," Jane says.

The ladder at the back of the yacht comes right down to water level so it's easy for you and the twins to climb aboard. When you reach the cockpit, you're pleased to see the key is in the ignition.

Adam has a look around and takes the role of captain. "We need to get the motor running and motor over the anchor to unhook it from the bottom. Then once we pull the anchor up, off we go."

Never having done much boating you take Adams word for it. "Jane and I can pull up the anchor."

Adam puts the gear lever on 'N' for neutral and turns the key. There is an immediate puff of black smoke from the back of the boat and a satisfying rumble of the diesel motor as it comes to life. Water from the exhaust pours from a hole in the stern.

"Right," Adam says. "I'm going to ease us forward over the anchor so you two get hauling on that rope."

At first the rope refuses to budge, but then as the boat moves forward and the angle of the rope through the water changes, you feel movement.

"It's coming!" you yell back at Adam.

You and Jane coil the anchor rope on the deck as you pull. Just as the anchor comes out of the water you hear someone yelling from shore.

"Hey! What do you think you're doing?"

The men climb into the dinghy and one of them grabs the oars and frantically rows towards the yacht.

"Time to get out of Dodge, partner," Jane says in her best cowgirl accent. "Those pesky rustlers are back."

There is a surge of white water at the back of the boat as Adam pushes the throttle forward and the yacht picks up speed. For a brief moment Adam points the yacht out to sea but then he spins the wheel and brings the yacht back around.

"What are you doing?" you say. "Escape is the other way."

Adam pushes the throttle even further forward. The diesel engine is really racing now. The boat's speed increases.

You look at the indicator on the control panel. The yacht is doing nearly 11 knots.

You look at Adam. His face is wild. "I said, what are you doing?"

"Tidying up," Adam says, turning the wheel a bit to starboard and pointing the bow of the yacht directly at the men in the dinghy.

"Holy moly!" Jane says. "You're going to ram them!"

The men are quick to realize what Adam is up to as well. The rower has turned the dinghy around and is now frantically trying to get back to shore. Unfortunately for the poachers, panic and good rowing technique don't usually go together. Within ten seconds the men realize the yacht is going to collide with the much smaller dinghy and leap into the water.

Adam, showing skills you never expected, steers the boat until it is nearly upon the dinghy and then pulls back the throttle a little and spins the wheel hard to the left, swerving the yacht at the last moment.

"Take the wheel and point her out to sea," Adams says to you as he grabs a boathook and leans over the side. With a sweep of the hook, Adam snags the abandoned dinghy's painter and pulls the rope aboard. Then with a couple of loops and a half hitch around a cleat on deck, the dingy is secured and the three of you are heading back out to sea with the dingy in tow.

"Good skills Captain Hook," you say to Adam. "That was one slick maneuver."

By the time you're out of the cove, the bedraggled men are arguing with each other back on the beach.

A few hundred yards off shore, Adam turns the yacht to the southeast.

"Right, to the lagoon," Adam says pushing the throttle slowly forward until the rev counter hits 2200 rpm. "Now we just have to find the gap in the reef and we're home sweet home."

"Gap in the reef?" Jane asks.

"Yeah, when we get close, one of you will have to climb up in the rigging so you can guide me through the passage into the lagoon. You can't see the coral from deck level. The light's all wrong."

Adam picks up the radio in the wheelhouse and flips on the power. "*Moneymaker* calling maritime radio, *Moneymaker* calling maritime radio, please come in maritime radio this is urgent."

The radio crackles. "This is maritime radio *Moneymaker*, what is the nature of your emergency?"

Adam explains the situation and then hangs up the hand piece. "Well that should do the trick."

"What do we do with all the birds below? Should we release them?" Jane asks.

"Better keep them for the time being. The authorities will need them for evidence," Adam says. "They'll let them go once they've taken photos I'm sure."

An hour and a half later, as the yacht rounds the headland and the first resort buildings appear, Adam points to the southwest. "Nearly there. One of you'd better get up the mast as far as the first set of spreaders."

"Spreaders?" Jane says.

"Those metal cross-members sticking out from the mast that are holding the rigging in place," Adam says.

"Oh, okay," Jane says crossing the deck and putting her foot in the first of the aluminum steps attached to the mast. "Arrr, this should be fun me hearties." And with that she scampers up the mast like she's been at sea all her life.

"I'll cruise along the reef, you tell me when you see a gap big enough for the boat to fit though," Adam yells up to his sister.

Jane, throws one leg over the spreader like it's a horizontal bar in gym class, wraps her arm around the mast and concentrates on the reef. A few minutes later she calls out. "Gap ho!"

Jane points to a spot on the reef where the water is calmer.

"Okay," Adam says swinging the bow around towards the gap. "I see it. Yell out if I get off course."

"Aye aye, Captain Hook."

Within minutes the boat is inside the reef and you're dropping the anchor. Tourists watch from the beach. A float plane sits by the wooden jetty. You notice that two of the people on the beach are dressed in uniform.

When the anchor is on the bottom, Adam tells you to pay out a bit of extra rope and then tie off to the sturdy post near the boat's bow. Then he puts the motor in reverse and digs in the anchor before turning off the engine. "Welcome to paradise," he says with a smile. "The dinghy will be leaving for shore in exactly one minute."

"Aye aye," you and Jane say in unison.

"Hey," Jane says. "Before we go ashore, look what I found below." Jane shows you a small canvas bag filled with American dollars.

"Wow," you say with eyes agog. "Where did you find that?"

"In the main cabin, under some socks."

"So what do we do with it?" Adam asks. "Turn it in?"

You look at Adam and smile. "Why don't we discuss that as we row ashore?"

Congratulations, this part of your story is over. You've made it safely back to the lagoon, survived an eruption and foiled the plans of the lorikeet poachers. Well done!

Now it is time for another decision. Do you:

Go to the beginning of the book and try another path? **P121**

Or

Go to the list of choices and start reading from another part of the story? **P380**

Try to sink the poacher's boat.

Adam seems determined to sink the poacher's boat with or without your help. On his own he's bound to let emotion get the better of him and end up in trouble. You decide that it's better if you and Jane help. With three of you, at least there is a chance of success.

"Okay I'll help," you say. "But only if we make a plan and stick to it. No crazy stuff okay?"

"Glug, glug, glug," Jane says with a glint in her eye.

Adam gives his sister a smile then turns back to you. "What plan did you have in mind?"

Your left hand strokes your chin as you think. "Let's check in with our families and then meet up at the beach. We can plan our attack while we keep a lookout for the yacht."

The twins agree and head off towards their bungalow. As you walk through the compound you wonder what you've got yourself in to. Poachers are dangerous.

You think of all the things you'll need to do for the operation to be successful. You'll need to get onto their boat, release the birds, open a valve or drill some holes in the hull to let the water in and then get away unseen. And what happens if one or more of the men stay on board to guard the yacht?

After checking in with your family, you grab a couple more energy bars and head for the beach. Adam and Jane are already there when you arrive. Adam is fiddling with something under his beach towel.

"What have you got there?" you ask as you toss them each an energy bar.

Adam hefts the object. "When we were walking back to our room, I noticed one of the maintenance men working in one of the bungalows. His toolbox was on the verandah outside so I asked him if I could borrow a drill for a couple hours."

"To drill holes in coconuts," Jane adds, "for drinking the milk."

Adam lifts the corner of his towel and shows you a hand drill complete with a chunky half-inch wood bit. "A few holes with this bad boy should do the trick."

You run your finger over the edge of the drill bit. "Whoa that's sharp."

Adam gives you an evil looking grin. "I drilled a hole in a fence post outside our bungalow. Like hot steel through butter."

Jane giggles. She's enjoying the intrigue far more than she should be. "I can't wait to start."

"Let's not get ahead of ourselves," you say. "We have a few things to figure out first."

You sit in the sand next to the twins and start discussing possibilities. Nearly an hour has gone by when you see the yacht come around the headland in the distance.

"Here they come," you say. "The wind direction is coming off the beach so they'll need to drop their sail and turn on the motor before they can come into the lagoon."

As the yacht gets nearer they drop the mainsail.

"Why have they got a man up in the rigging?" you say.

"He'll be there to spot the gap in the reef and guide the boat through," Adam answers. "There will be too much reflection off the water to see the reef from deck level."

Ten minutes later the yacht is 100 yards off the beach and the men have dropped anchor. The yacht rocks gently in the light chop.

The men waste no time. One of them climbs down the stern ladder towards the dinghy floating at the end of its rope.

"Fingers crossed they all come ashore," you say.

Jane stands up. "I'll grab a surf board." Without waiting for comment, she runs over towards a collection of boards leaning against a tree for use by the resort's guests.

Unfortunately, only two of the men climb into the dinghy. The last of them unties the dinghy's painter from the cleat on the deck and tosses it to the men in the small boat. Then he passes them a set of oars.

"Get some pictures as they come ashore," you say to Adam. "We need all the evidence we can get."

Jane lays the surfboard down in the sand and sits back down. "You never know. It might come in handy eh?"

"So what now," Adam asks. "How are we going to do anything when they've still got a guy onboard?"

You shrug and go back to thinking.

A few minutes later it's Jane that speaks up. "What if I pretend to be drowning? Do you think he'd leave the boat to save me?"

Her idea is a good one and it makes you think. What sort of men are the poachers? Surely he wouldn't let a young girl drown. Even criminals protect their kids.

Adam looks doubtful. "But will that give us enough time?"

"It might if Jane gets him to bring her in to shore and not back to the yacht," you say.

Then you explain the rest of your plan.

"You are evil," Jane says . "I like it."

Adam still looks unsure. "Jane would have to be pretty convincing."

"Do ya'll doubt my acting ability?" Jane drawls in a mock Southern accent, her hands clenched to her chest, eyelids fluttering. "I'll have ya'll know I'm a fine actor."

"Swoon all you like Sis, we're talking about criminals here. Who knows what they'll do."

Trying not to laugh at Jane's performance, you give a brief nod towards Adam. "Your brother's right, Jane, we need a plan B in case plan A goes wrong. Think you guys. What do we do if the guy stays on the boat?"

By now, the two men from the yacht are dragging the dinghy up onto the sand. The one in charge tells the other to stay by the boat and marches up the sand towards the resort.

Adam watches as the man passes the surfboards and disappears into the resort. "He may not be gone very long. I don't think we have time for a plan B."

Having seen the man's urgency as he walked past, Adam may well be right. "Okay. Adam, grab the drill and let's go. Jane, give us a few minutes to get in to position before you hit the water."

"Ya'll come back now," Jane says, fluttering her eyelids once more.

You pick up the surf board and carry it to the water. It's one of those old long boards so both you and he have no problem fitting on it.

Paddling in a wide arc, you come at the yacht from the seaward side. The man on deck has his back to you as he watches the activity on the beach. Then you see Jane swimming towards the yacht, her strokes strong and steady.

About twenty yards short of the boat, she starts splashing and yelling. The man on the yacht stands up.

"Help!" Jane cries out. "My legs have got cramp."

To add effect, Jane sinks below the water briefly before clawing her way back to the surface and repeating her plea.

The man on deck is torn. You can almost see his mind working as he decides what to do. Your entire plan depends on the next few moments. He paces up and down the deck of the yacht. No doubt he's been told to stay on board by the boss man. But he's unsure.

When Jane goes under for a second time, the man takes off his shirt and shoes.

"He's going to save her," you whisper to Adam. "Come on mister dive in."

For a third time, Jane splutters and sinks below the waves and finally, the man steps over the railing and dives into the water.

When the man reaches Jane he flips her onto her back and starts side-stroking back to the boat.

Jane, realizing where he's taking her, starts to struggle."No, take me to my Dad."

For a moment the poacher hesitates, but then stops. Maybe he's just remembered he's got birds onboard.

Again Jane cries out to be taken to the beach. She becomes a dead weight, slides out of his grasp and sinks below the water.

The man gives up and does what she asks. Jane floats, allowing herself to be escorted to the beach. The 80 or so yards should take them a few minutes. You just hope it's enough.

"Go," you say.

You and Adam paddle flat out towards the yacht. When you reach the stern, you take the surfboard's leg strap and loop it around a rung of the ladder to keep it from floating away and scamper aboard.

The companionway hatch is open. Down four steps and you're in the saloon. On the floor sits two cages, each holding a twenty or so lorikeets.

"Let's get these cages on deck," you say.

The wire cages are awkward. The birds start making a racket when they see you.

Carrying an end each, you and Adam maneuver the cages up onto the deck. The birds are loud but thankfully the wind is blowing out to sea so most of the sound is carried away from the beach.

You take a quick look shoreward. Jane and the man are only thirty yards from the beach. "I'll let the birds out, you get drilling."

Adam heads below while you open the cages. The lorikeets waste no time in flying off.

After throwing the cages overboard, you stick you head through the companionway and look for Adam. You hear sounds coming from one of the cabins. "Drill quickly, because as soon as Jane hits the beach we're out of here."

Keeping low behind the cabin tops, you watch Jane's progress. As she and the man near the beach she starts struggling again. You can hear her cries of panic as she twists in the man's grasp. Finally, when the man can touch bottom, he picks Jane up, throws her over his shoulder and marches to where his companion is waiting beside the dinghy.

Jane pretends to be in distress, arm flapping, coughing and gasping for breath. Her rescuer moves Jane into the recovery position and hovers over her until one of the staff from the resort comes over to see what is going on.

"Okay time to go!" you yell down to Adam.

Adam appears from the depths of the boat. "The water's not coming in fast enough!"

"Well we can't stay here any longer!"

Then Adam sees something in the galley that attracts his attention. He grabs the bottle of mentholated spirits and starts pouring it all over the seat cushions.

"Hey," you yell, "this isn't part of the plan!"

"It's the new plan B," Adam says, striking a lighter he's found by the stove and setting fire to one of the seats in the saloon. "Let's hope these cushions are polypropylene. Burns like crazy that stuff."

Smoke begins to fill the cabin.

"Adam, we've got to go now!"

The two of you rush to the stern and leap into the water. You untie the leg rope, climb on the surfboard and start paddling like crazy, not towards the beach, but parallel to it away from the yacht.

"The poachers haven't seen the smoke yet," you say to Adam as you look over towards the beach. "Correction, they've just spotted it."

The two men are frantically dragging the dingy into the water. The larger of the two grabs the oars and starts rowing as fast as he can.

The men don't notice as you and Adam join another group of people mucking around on surfboards and wind surfers in the lagoon.

"I think we've done it," Adam says.

Adam was right about the polypropylene. Thick smoke billows from yacht. By the time the men in the dinghy row to the boat, the flames are too intense for them to get aboard. When a series of loud bangs start popping, you can only assume ammunition of some sort is going off inside the boat.

"It's a lost cause!" the man with the oars yells as he starts rowing back to shore.

By now there is a crowd on the beach. It includes the head poacher who is waving his arms and talking to a male staff member.

"See the guy on the beach with the poacher dude?" you say to Adam. "He must be their contact. We must get a picture of him when we get ashore."

"The boss man doesn't look too happy," Adam says.

You and Adam reach the beach at about the same time as the two men in the dinghy.

As you join the other tourists watching the burning boat, you edge closer to where the poachers are standing. The head poacher is cursing at his companions as if the fire were their fault.

Jane, now fully recovered, sees that the two of you are back on the beach and comes over to join you. "Good skills," she says. "Ninjas one, poachers nil."

Adam unzips a pocket in his shorts and pulls out three items about the size of small candy bars. "Wrong again, Sis. Ninjas three, poachers nil." And with that he drops a gold bar into each of your hands. "One each … just don't let the poachers see them."

"Where did you get these?" you say, turning your back to the poachers.

Jane's eyes are bulging, but she wastes no time slotting her bar into the pocket of her shorts.

"When I opened a floor panel to drill a hole, they were just lying there. I didn't see any point in leaving them behind."

You have a closer look at the ingot and read the small writing stamped into it. "One Ounce 99.9 per cent pure."

"What's that worth, I wonder?" Jane says

"Last I heard gold was over twelve hundred US dollars an ounce," you say.

"Wow," Jane says. "Being a ninja pays pretty good."

Adam puts his bar back in his pocket. "I'm going to donate mine to the Animal Rescue people."

You think for a moment at what you'll do with your share, but then realize you've got pretty much everything you need. You're on vacation on a beautiful island. You've got friends. Hey what else do you need?

You pass your ingot back to Adam. "Here, give them mine too. I'll just blow it otherwise. It may as well do some good."

Jane shakes her head. "But, I need shoes and dresses and—and… Just joking," she says, handing her ingot back to Adam. "I wouldn't feel right spending ill-gotten gold on myself anyway."

Adam tucks the gold away. "Thanks you two. This will make a big difference."

You shrug. "It's only money."

As the three of you watch the last of the boat disappear, you notice the sun is dipping below the horizon. Reds, fiery oranges and every color in between contrast the sparkling blue of the lagoon. The rocky point, shaped like the dolphin's nose at the far end of the lagoon is just a silhouette.

"So what adventure are we having tomorrow?" Jane asks.

"We've still got treasure to find remember?" you say. "Meet you here on the beach after breakfast?"

"Arrr me hearty," Jane says in her best pirate accent.

"Arrr," Adam says joining in the fun.

And with that the three of you head back to your families, excited at what tomorrow may bring.

Congratulations you've finished this part of your story. You have successfully stopped the poachers and found some gold which will go to a good cause. Well done!

Now it is time to make another decision. Do you:

Go back to the beginning and follow another path? **P121**

Or

Go to the list of choices and start reading from another part of the story? **P380**

You have decided to contact the authorities.

"Let's not do anything radical," you say. "Better we find a way to contact the authorities without anyone from the resort finding out and let them deal with the poachers. Using the resort's phones is out because of the calls having to go through reception, that's going to limit our options."

The three of you are silent a moment, as you each try to come up with a solution.

"I've got it," Jane says. "Boats have radios, right?"

"Yes…" you say hesitantly wondering where Jane is going with this.

"And the police have radios?"

"Yeah sure."

"Well there must be at least three boats in the lagoon. Surely one of them has a radio we can use." Jane looks like she's just eaten the last chocolate in the box.

"But the poachers have a boat too Sis," Adam says, countering her argument. "And if they hear our transmission they'll scarper. Then your whole plan goes down the gurgler."

Jane frowns. "Hmm … I didn't think of that."

"But what if they didn't hear the transmission?" Adam says."What if their radio antennae were out of order?"

You give Adam a questioning look. "And how do you plan on achieving that?"

"Well," Adam says. "I've done a fair bit of fishing with my friend and his dad. I can cast a lure pretty much wherever I want."

"Okay," you say. "But how's catching fish going to help?"

"Well," Adam continues, "if I cast a wire trace, with a big lure on it, over the yacht's antennae, and then start reeling in, I might be able to rip it off."

"You really think that will work?" you ask.

"I really think we should give it a go. What have we got to lose?"

"I'll admit, little bro's pretty good with a rod," Jane says. "Streuth, she's worth a crack!"

Two sets of eyes roll at the return of Jane's Aussie accent, but after some further discussion the three of you decide to try out Adam's plan.

"Right," Adam says. "Jane and I will rent one of the resort's small motor boats. Then we'll drop you off near one of the larger boats moored in the bay so you can get to their radio. Then, with Jane steering, I'll hook the antennae and then we'll motor off at top speed and do our best to rip the antennae off the poacher's mast."

"Sounds like something out of a movie," you say, wondering if the scheme will work.

"I'm not so sure. Fishing ninjas doesn't quite have the same ring to it." Jane says with a giggle.

After renting the strongest pole and tackle he can find. Adam rigs up a line. Then the three of you climb aboard the runabout you've rented.

"Which boat should we try?" Adam asks.

You look at your choices. "That marlin boat's pretty flash. It's bound to have reliable VHF."

Adam turns the key to start the runabout. "The marlin boat it is then."

Jane grabs your arm. "There they are, right on schedule!"

You and Adam turn your gaze towards the reef. Sure enough the poacher's boat is heading into the lagoon.

Your runabout starts first pop. Jane unties the bowline from the jetty and Adam pushes the throttle forward. As he points the bow towards the reef Adam yells over the roar of the 25hp outboard. "We'll do a loop and approach the marlin boat from behind so nobody from shore sees what we're up to. You'll have to jump overboard and swim the last 10 yards or so."

You swallow, and try to steady your nerves. "Just what I always wanted to do while on vacation, jump from a speeding boat."

Jane laughs. "Think of it as walking the plank. At least it's better than being keel-hauled."

You're getting close to the marlin boat.

"Okay, get ready to jump," Adam says. "I'll slow down the boat, but only for a moment. Oh and don't forget to use channel 16, that's the emergency channel."

Thirty seconds later, Adam throttles down and you leap over the side. Immediately he's back on the gas and bouncing away over the slight chop in the lagoon.

Thankfully the marlin boat has a ladder on its stern. You make your way into the wheelhouse and look for the switch to power up the radio.

After turning on the radio you look at the screen and see the radio is already set on the right channel. There is a crackle of static and you hear brief conversations come over the speaker. You lift the handset out of its cradle and get ready to transmit.

Meanwhile Adam has swung the runabout in a lazy arc and is heading to where the yacht is busy dropping anchor. Jane takes the controls as Adam lines up his cast.

The poachers antennae is a slim rod sticking up from a bracket near the top of the mast next to a wind speed indicator, radar reflector, and navigation light. You can't believe he really thinks he has a chance of snagging such a small target.

Adam stands in the back of the runabout, his backside pressed against the transom for stability. The long pole is upright. As you watch, Adam practices his casting by flicking the pole back and forth trying to get a feel for it.

As the runabout nears the yacht, one of the men is busy securing the anchor, while another is preparing the dinghy to come ashore. Then two of the men climb down into the dinghy and start to head towards shore.

Jane turns the runabout and goes around for another pass.

By the time Jane lines up for the next pass, the men and their dinghy are halfway to the beach. Jane throttles back just as Adam whips the pole forwards, sending the lure flying high in the air. The heavy lure passes clean over the bracket holding the antennae and Adam starts reeling for all he's worth. As Adam reels in, the lure stops midflight, drops and then hooks itself around the bracket. Adam fist pumps the air and then puts the pole into a special hole in the aluminum hull of the runabout designed to keep rods from falling overboard when fishing.

Jane lets out a rebel yell and steers the boat towards the yacht. When she's ten yards from colliding with the yacht she swings the runabout into a sharp turn and puts on more power.

As the runabout streaks away from the yacht the line tightens. At first the yacht's mast tilts towards the fleeing runabout and you're sure the line will break. But leverage is a wonderful thing and the line is stronger than you imagined. It holds as the yacht tilts further and further over.

The remaining man on deck trips and nearly falls over the side as the deck beneath his feet is suddenly no longer level. Then there is a wrenching sound as the bracket is ripped off the mast.

This time, as the deck tilts quickly back the opposite way, the man on deck is caught off balance again and goes flying over the rail.

You click the transmit button. "Maritime radio, maritime radio, maritime radio," you repeat three time as instructed by Adam. "Mayday. Come in maritime radio."

"This is maritime radio, what is the nature of your emergency?"

It takes you a few moments to explain the situation, but the operator agrees to call the police and pass on your message.

The man on the yacht is climbing up the ladder as Jane and Adam motor toward your boat. You give them the thumbs up, switch off the radio and dive overboard. A minute later Adam helps you out of the water and onto the runabout.

"Did you get through?" he asks.

"Ninjas one, poachers nil," you say. "The police are on their way."

"Yippee!" Jane yells.

You look over at the yacht and see the man looking around, still wondering what hit him and how he got tipped into the drink on a perfectly flat lagoon.

"Let's hope he doesn't notice the missing aerial before the police arrive," you say to the twins. "What did you do with the antennae you caught?"

Adam points to the middle of the lagoon. "It's now a dive feature over there at the bottom of the lagoon."

After dropping off the runabout, returning the fishing gear, minus some trace and a lure, and grabbing some cold drinks, the three of you go and sit on the beach to wait for the police to show up.

As you wait, the two poachers and a man from the resort walk down the beach and climb into the dinghy.

"They'll be off to do the deal for the birds no doubt," Adam says.

You cross your fingers. "I just hope the cops show up soon."

Jane takes a long sip of her soda. "Looks like we'll have to find the treasure tomorrow."

"We've got all week," you say. "The treasure's been here for 150 years. I don't think it's going anywhere this afternoon."

"Unlike our poacher friends," Adam says, pointing to the gray patrol boat entering the lagoon. "It's going to be interesting to see how they explain all the birds on board."

Congratulations this part of your story is over. You've done well. But have you tried all the possible path the story takes?

It is time to make another decision. Do you:

Go back to the beginning of the story and try another path? **P121**

Or

Go to the List of Choices and start reading from another part of the story? **P380**

Or

Go and check out some secret FAQs about Dolphin Island? **P127**

It's all about the math

"How did you do that so quickly in your head?" Jane asks.

By now Adam is listening too.

"Well it's not exact," you say, trying to think of an easy way to explain it. "But the yacht can go in pretty much any direction right?"

The twins nod.

"A knot is 1.15 miles. So 8 knots is a fraction over 9 miles. That means there will be a circular search area with a radius of 9 miles, minus a little bit of land, right? Imagine a big circle with a dot in its centre. The dot is the yacht and the rest of the circle is a place the yacht could be, apart from the small bit of land that makes up the island of course."

Jane and Adam seem to be following your explanation so you continue.

"To calculate the area of a circle you square the radius, squaring means multiplying the radius by itself and then we multiply that answer by pi or 3.14.

"What a radius?" Jane asks.

"It's the distance from the dot in the middle of the circle to the outer edge of the circle. Like the spoke of a bike wheel."

"So the radius squared is 9 times 9 which is 81 and then we multiply 81 times 3.14?" Jane asks.

"That's right," you say. "I made it easier by working out what 3 times 81 was first. 3 times 80 is 240 and 3 times 1 is 3.

Jane's got the hang of it now. "So that's 240 plus 3 which equals 243."

You nod. "Then I take .14 and multiply that times 81. This is a bit trickier but when you realize .14 is the same as 14 per cent, it's easy. To get 10 percent of 81 you move the decimal point one place to the left or 8.1 … let's call it 8 for simplicity. Then we take 4 percent of 81 which is a bit less than half of 10 percent … so let's just estimate it and call it 3.

"So we have 243 plus 8 plus 3 which is 254," Jane says.

You smile. "That's right. Then we just need to take off a bit for the land area. Like I said it's not exact but it's near enough."

"It like working out a puzzle," Jane says. "Kind of fun when you think of it that way."

"Yep," you say. "And the more you learn the better the puzzles get. Math is full of sneaky tricks. It's just a matter of knowing them."

Without any further explanation, you turn and start down the path back towards the resort. You hear the twin's footsteps behind you. Jane mumbles numbers as you half walk, half jog through the jungle.

[Back to the story **P154**]

Dolphin Island FAQs

Q. Is Dolphin Island a real place?

A. No, Dolphin Island is fictional island. However there are many islands in the South Pacific that have similarities to what has been described in this story. Polynesia means 'many islands'. If you are interested in the area where this story is set, try looking up and reading about Tonga or Samoa.

Q. Was the *Port-au-Prince* a real ship?

A. Yes. The *Port-au-Prince* was a tall ship of 500 tons that carried 24 cannon. The ship was built in France before being captured by the British. It then became a privateer (legal pirate by license from the British government) and was sent to raid Spanish ships off the South American coast. After some raiding the *Port-au-Prince* sailed to the South Pacific to hunt whales for their oil. Sometime in 1806, while in the Ha'apai island group in the Kingdom of Tonga she was attacked by the locals and is presumed to have sunk somewhere nearby. It was never discovered how successful the ship had been in her raiding as all her treasure is presumed to have gone down with the ship. Many experts believe remnants of *Port-au-Prince* was found in 2012 off Foa Island in Tonga.

Q. Are megapodes real?

A. Yes. Megapodes are real birds that bury their eggs in the warm volcanic soil to act as an incubator. There are many interesting birds in the South Pacific region.

Q. What happened at Krakatoa?

A. Krakatoa is a volcanic island between Java and Sumatra in Indonesia. It exploded in 1883 killing somewhere between 36,000 and 120,000 people (depending on how the statistics were calculated). The bangs from the huge explosions (4 in total) were heard over 3000 miles away in Australia. Some say the main explosion could have been the loudest in history. The volcano ejected over 6 cubic miles of rock, ash and lava and the tsunamis and pyroclastic flows of hot ash and steam, destroyed over 150 villages. The area is still very active.

What now? Do you:

Go back to the beginning of Danger on Dolphin Island? **P121**
Or
Go to the List of Choices and start reading from another place in the book? **P380**

SECRETS OF GLASS MOUNTAIN

In the beginning.

With the screech of diamonds on smooth black rock, a troop of Highland Sliders comes skidding to a stop ten yards from you and your schoolmates.

"That's what I want to do when I leave school," says Dagma. "Being a Highland Slider looks like so much fun."

Another classmate shakes his head. "Yeah, but my cousin went mining and struck it rich on his first trip out. Now he owns two hydro farms and his family live in luxury."

You look around the small settlement where you grew up. It's a beautiful place, high on the Black Slopes of Petron. Far below, past the sharp ridges and towering pinnacles, the multicolored fields of the Lowlands stretch off into the distance. At the horizon, a pink moon sits above a shimmering turquoise sea.

But the beauty of the place isn't enough to keep you here. You could never be a farmer or a merchant. You've always dreamed of travel and adventure.

Maybe your friend is right and mining is the thing to do.

You imagine heading off into the wild interior looking for diamonds and the many secrets these glass mountains contain. You imagine striking it rich and the ways you could use your new found wealth to help those you care for.

Or, do you become a slider like so many others from your family? What would happen to your home without the protection of the Highland Sliders? How would people move around the dangerous slopes from settlement to settlement without their expert guidance? And who would stop the Lowlanders from invading?

Your part in this story is about to begin. You will leave school at the end of the week and it's time for you to choose your future.

It is time to make your first decision. Do you:

Start cadet training to become a slider? **P221**

Or

Go to mining school so you can prospect for diamonds? **P275**

Start cadet training to become a slider.

"Eyes front, cadets!" the uniformed officer yells. "If you are going to become sliders you'd better listen like your life depends on it, because believe me, it does." The officer stamps a heavy boot for effect and scans your group "You've all made it through basic training, now it's time to see if you have what it takes to become true Highland sliders."

You knew this part of cadet training was going to be tough, but this officer looks like he eats black glass for breakfast. His dome shaped skull is covered in scars and half his right ear is missing.

You squirm on the hard stone bench and give the girl next to you a weak smile. The room is full of young cadets and like you, they all look a little scared.

Your stomach feels like it is full of moon moths. You cross your fingers and hope you won't let your family down.

"Right, you lot, I want to see you all at the top of the training slope in ten minutes. Anyone who's not there when the bell goes may as well slide right over and enroll in mining school. Now let's go cadets, move it!"

You stand up and quick march out of the room with the others. You've seen the training area from below with its shadowed gullies, crevasses, and sharp ridges, but you are about to look down upon its glistening black slopes for the first time.

You are third to arrive. You check the strap leading from your tow clamp to the belt of your harness and make sure everything is connected properly. As you line up for the tow, more moths have come to join their friends fluttering in your belly.

You point your front foot forward, and engage the metal rod that locks your boots together to form a stable platform for you to slide on. Then you bend your knees in readiness for a high-speed, uphill ride.

The towpath looks slightly damp and you know the black rock will be slipperier than the smoothest ice. The towline whirls around a big, motorized wheel downhill from where you are standing before it extends up the mountainside and disappears into a purple fog. You know there is another wheel at the top that takes the cable and sends it back down the hill again, but you won't be able to see that one until you've gained some altitude.

After flipping your tow clamp over the rapidly moving cable you gradually squeeze its handles together and slowly increase the pressure. Before you know it you are accelerating. The cable hums and vibrates as it drags you uphill. Wind whistles across your visor and around your helmet. You taste the dampness of the mist.

The two cadets on the towline ahead of you stand with knees slightly bent, their front feet pointed forward, their back feet angled slightly to one side. Lock-rods hold their boots just the right distance apart for maximum control. But despite months of training on the simulator, their knees still wobble a little.

You are a little unsteady on your feet too, but you figure this is caused as much by nervous anticipation as anything. When you relax a little, you find you do better. Fighting the tow just makes your leg muscles ache. You remember what the instructors have said about letting the cable do the work. You lean back into your harness and let it take your weight. As you do, you feel your legs relax.

You feel every bump and irregularity through the soles of your boots as you slide along, allowing you to make subtle corrections of balance. You must keep alert to remain upright.

The fog thins as you gain altitude. The top wheel comes into view and you know that in the next twenty seconds or so you will have to disengage your tow clamp and slide off the path onto the staging area. A clean dismount is all a matter of timing.

There are instructors at the top of the hill ready to grade your efforts. You disengage your tow clamp, hook it over a loop on your utility belt and spread your arms slightly to stay balanced.

You shoot off the tow a bit hot, but adjust your speed by lifting the toe of your leading foot a little, dragging the spike fitted to your heel into the rocky slope. A high-pitched squeal fills the air as the diamond digs into the surface and slows you down.

When you come to a stop, you release your back foot, kick the lock-rod back into the sole of your boot and stand to attention.

"Well done, cadet," an instructor says. "You've been listening to the lectures I see."

"Thank you sir," you say, snapping off a quick salute.

With a screech, the next cadet slides in and stands beside you. Others cadets arrive at the staging area every ten seconds or so until there are three rows of ten cadets standing shoulder to shoulder.

The cadet next to you is a tall boy with clear blue eyes. "Ready for the slide of your life?" he says with confidence.

You nod to the boy. "I think so. Bit late now if I'm not."

You are as ready as you will ever be. After all, you have been training for this day for the last year with classes during the day and practice on the simulator every night. You've had guide stick training, terrain training, balance training, combat training. You've studied geometry, navigation and communications. Now it's time to put everything into practice and have your first run under real conditions.

"Right cadets, it is time to show us what you're made of," the training officer says. He takes a step forward and points to the scars on his head. "I got these on my first run when I missed a turn and ended up crashing into the lip of an overhanging ridge. If you think my head looks bad, you should have seen the helmet I was wearing. I suggest you concentrate so you don't make a similar mistake." The officer looks along the line. "First one to the bottom will be promoted to troop leader. Are you ready?"

"Yes sir!" the cadets yell in unison.

"Right, line up and get ready to slide."

Shuffling forward, you stand near the edge, ready to leap off the narrow shelf onto the much steeper slope below. You look left, then right.

You've gotten to know the strengths and weaknesses of each cadet over the months of basic training. Your strongest competition is a stocky girl named Dagma from a neighboring community. Dagma doesn't like to finish second.

Gagnon, a tall boy with short spiky hair and pale green eyes nods in your direction. "Good luck," he says.

"Luck's got nothing to do with it." Dagma snarls. "Sliding is about skill. If you're going to rely on luck you should take up mining."

You look at Gagnon, and roll your eyes. Dagma can be such a grunter at times.

"Lock boots!" the instructor orders.

You release the lock-bar from the sole of your left boot and attach it to a fitting near the instep of your right. You hear a satisfying click as it snaps into place. You now have a rigid platform to slide on.

The instructor hands each of you a guide stick. "These are worth more than you are, so don't lose them."

The guide stick is almost as tall as you are. Its shaft is made from a flexible and incredibly strong wood obtained by trading crystals with the border tribes. Mounted on one end of the shaft is a sturdy blue-diamond hook. On the stick's opposite end is a thick pad of tyranium needle crystals.

The ultra-fine tyranium crystals create friction when dragged on the ground. This friction is used to control a slider's direction and speed when moving down the slope.

You rest the pad end on the ground and immediately feel how the crystals grip the glossy black surface. It's no wonder they are only fractionally less prized than blue diamonds. Without them it would be virtually impossible to travel, harvest eggs from the red-beaked pango colonies, drill mines and reservoirs, or build sleeping and hydro growing pods.

The instructor stands tall and barks out orders. "Are you ready cadets?"

You lower your visor and work your front foot as close to the edge as possible. Gripping the guide stick tightly in both hands, you rest it on the ground behind you. Now, the slightest push will send you plunging down the hill. The other cadets crowd together, bumping shoulders, hoping to achieve the most favorable slide path down the centre of the course.

You look down the run. There are gullies and ridges, knobs and small pillars. Some parts are near vertical, others flatten out only to drop steeply again when you least expect it.

The most popular line runs down the side of a steep ridge and then sweeps into a broad valley on the right hand side of the course. At the bottom of the valley it angles back towards the centre, cuts below two small pinnacles and then straightens towards the finish line. All the cadets have studied the course map and know the relative advantages and dangers of the various ways down.

The instructor raises his arm. "On my mark! Ready to drop in five, four, three, two, one..." His arm falls. "Slide!"

With a firm push you are over the edge and sliding. You squat low to create less wind resistance and tap the needle end of your stick to make subtle course corrections.

Dagma's strong push has her leading the pack, sliding smoothly to your right. The other cadets are sticking to her tail, trying to gain advantage by using her bulk as a wind shield.

Gagnon is near the front as well, sliding effortlessly, but unless Dagma makes a mistake it will be hard to pass her. It looks as though the other cadets have chosen to take the conventional and less risky route down the mountain.

You've seen the times posted on the classroom wall and know the winner of this race for the last three years has taken this route. But you also know that crowded slopes are dangerous. Each year at least one cadet has been badly injured after being bumped off course.

During your study of the map, you've seen an untried route that runs between the two small pinnacles in the centre of the main face. It's risky, but if you can turn sharply enough, you just might be able to enter the narrow chute at a point above the two small pillars, and take a straighter, faster line to the finish.

However, if you misjudge your timing, and miss the turn into the top of the chute, you could end up in a gulley of dangerous ripples. If that happens and you lose your footing, these ripples will slice you to ribbons.

You are sliding fast. If you are going to try to make the turn you will have to do it now. You've practiced this move plenty of times on the simulator, but in real life conditions, nothing is guaranteed. You look right, then left. It's now or never.

It is time to make a quick decision. Hurry! Do you:

Go for it and try to turn into the chute despite the danger? **P227**

Or

Follow Dagma and the others and try to win the race using the normal route? **P230**

You have decided to go for the chute despite the danger.

Making sharp turns on a slope of black glass isn't easy. Luckily you've had plenty of practice on the simulator.

You stand up tall and spread your arms. Special pockets of fabric, where your arms meet your torso, catch the wind and slow you down a little. Then you swivel your hips and drop your diamond hook. A three-second drag slows you down even more. Once you've lost enough momentum, you flip your guide stick around and repeatedly stab the ground with the needle crystal end. Each time the crystals hit the surface, you move a little to your left.

Looking ahead, you try to spot the entrance of the narrow chute leading down between the two pinnacles. On the shiny black surface it's difficult to see the contours. It should be coming up about...

You spot it, but you're too far left! More jabs of your stick move you back to the right. As you stare ahead, sweat drips down your forehead into your visor. You are on the correct line now. You crouch to regain speed. Your arms and guide stick are tucked tight to your body.

Flying over the lip at the top of the chute the ground falls away and you lose contact with the slope. As you drop into the steeply angled half-pipe, you rise slightly from your crouch and hold the guide stick out in front of you, using it to help keep your balance. If you are going to win the race, you must stay on your feet.

When your boots touch the ground you drop into a tuck and streamline your body. Momentum takes you up one side of the half-pipe and then gravity brings you back to the bottom.

You are really moving now, going faster than you've ever experienced on the simulator. Wow, what a feeling! You look down the slope. It's a straight run to the bottom.

Moments later, you flash across the finish line and drop your hook. But are you the first to arrive?

"What are you smiling about cadet?" the instructor at the bottom of the course says as you screech to a stop. "You think this is supposed to be fun?"

"Yes sir!"

The instructor scowls at you.

"I mean no sir!"

You hear the sound of diamond hooks above you. When you glance up, you see Dagma in a low crouch, leading the other cadets down the hill.

You've won!

"Congratulations cadet," the instructor says, giving you a mock salute. "Seems you've just earned yourself a promotion."

You can't wait to tell your family. They will be so proud. But you also realize this is only the beginning. You've only made it through basic training. Now the real work begins.

Seconds later, the other cadets are beside you. Some have their hands on their knees panting from exertion.

"Okay cadets, line up," the instructor says. "I'm pleased you've all made it down without incident. I want you to meet your new troop leader."

The instructor waves you forward. You move off the line and come to stand by his side.

"Leaders are only as good as their troop," the instructor says to the assembled cadets. "If you don't work as a team out there on the slopes, none of you will survive a season. You all have strengths and weaknesses. The strongest of you isn't the fastest. The best in navigation isn't the best in communications. You all have a vital part to play in the Slider Corps. Our communities depend on you working together to keep them safe."

The instructor turns to you. It is time to dismiss your troop.

"Right you lot," you say. "Head back to the pod and get ready for our first patrol tomorrow morning at dawn."

As you are about to move off, the instructor places his hand on your shoulder. "Wait," he says. "We have some things to discuss."

As the other cadets enter a narrow portal cut into the black rock, you wonder what the instructor has to tell you.

Once the last cadet has disappeared he turns and gives you a serious look. "You know they look up to you," he says.

Do they really? You know Dagma doesn't. She just sees you as competition, as an obstacle to her rising through the ranks. How is she going to react to your promotion? Will she follow you when the going gets tough, or will she undermine your every move?

"Not all of them sir," you reply.

The instructor raises one eyebrow and scowls. "I know you and Dagma have had your differences, but she's got a lot of skill and determination. You'd do well to give her some respect and see if you can utilize her strengths."

"Yes sir."

"Now it's your choice, but you need to select one of the cadets to be second in charge. Do you know who you'd like?"

It is time for you to make an important decision. Do you:

Choose Dagma to be your second in charge because of her strength? **P234**

Or

Choose Gagnon as your second in charge because you like him better and he is a good navigator? **P237**

You have decided to follow Dagma and the others.

You see the pinnacles ahead, but realize you are moving too fast to make the turn into the chute. You have no option but to join the other cadets in their crazy slide down the main route.

Dagma is out in the lead due to her strong start, but her size is also creating more wind resistance and you know that if you optimize your stance you can gain some ground on her.

You bend your knees a little more and twist your torso so that you are as thin to the wind as possible. Your elbows are tucked tight to your sides and your guide stick trails behind you, just a fraction off the ground, ready to hook when you need to slow down.

A cadet to your right is trying to snag Dagma's harness with his stick and pull past her, but every time he reaches forward, either the wind catches him and slows him down, or Dagma bats his stick away with her own.

The slope is faster than you'd imagined. You've picked up so much speed you wonder if you'll be able to keep your feet once you hit the more uneven terrain below.

Some of the cadets have already started dragging their hooks, trying to slow themselves down before they sweep around a banked turn and enter a section of the course known as "the jumps".

Although this part of the mountain is not as steep as the slope higher up, it has a series of rounded humps to negotiate. Hit a hump too fast and you lose your balance. Get your timing wrong and you land on the uphill slope of the next hump and twist a knee or an ankle.

Everyone is moving too fast. The first jump is coming up sooner than expected. All around you the screech of hooks is deafening as the other cadets desperately try to slow down. Even Dagma is leaning hard on her hook, trying to reduce speed, before hitting the first jump.

This is your chance.

Rather than dropping your hook, you twist your lower body so that both feet are side by side and the lock-bar between your boots is side-on to the slope, rather than the traditional stance of one foot in front of the other. You bend your knees and get ready to spring up. Now it's just a matter of timing.

Your knees are forced to your chest when you hit the front of the hump. A split second later, as you near its crest, you spring up with all your strength.

The ground falls away as you soar through the air. "Woot, woot!" you yell. "I'm flying!

While holding your guide stick at arm's length in front of your chest, you swivel your lower body back around so your front foot is pointing straight down the hill again. Then you bend your knees a little and get ready for impact.

You've done it! When you make contact with the ground, it is on the downward side of the third jump, having cleared the second one altogether. You force you legs upwards and spring off the crest of the fourth jump and land on the downward side of the last jump with a satisfying swish of boots on rock. You tuck back into your arrow stance and gain even more speed as you race to the finish.

You can't believe how fast you are moving. This is so much faster than on the simulator. The wind is howling. Wow, what a feeling!

You see the finishing flag less than a quarter of a mile ahead. A quick glance back up the hill and you know you've won. The others are well back. One cadet has fallen and is sliding on his backside trying to regain his feet. Dagma is the best of the others, with Gagnon close behind.

You flash across the finish, rise from your crouch and drop your hook, forcing it down hard onto the shiny black surface. You screech to a halt next to an instructor.

"What are you smiling about cadet?" the instructor says. "You think this is supposed to be fun?"

"Yes sir!"

The instructor scowls.

"Well it is sir!"

The instructor's eyes soften as he suppresses a grin. "If you say so, cadet."

You hear the screech of hooks behind you as the others finish. Dagma bangs the ground with her stick in frustration.

"Congratulations," the instructor says, giving you a mock salute. "It seems you've just earned yourself a promotion."

You can't wait to tell your family. They will be so proud. But you also realize this is only the beginning. You've only made it through basic training. Now the real challenge begins.

"Okay line up cadets," the instructor says.

They shuffle into line, breathing hard.

"I'm please you've all made it down without incident. I want you to meet your new troop leader."

The instructor waves you forward. You push your shoulders back and stand by his side.

"Leaders are only as good as the troops they lead," the instructor says. "If you cadets don't work as a team out there on the slopes, none of you will survive a season.

The instructor taps his guide stick on the ground. "Right, head back to your pod and get ready for your first patrol tomorrow morning at dawn."

As you are about to move off, the instructor places his hand on your shoulder. "Wait," he says. "We have a few things to discuss."

You watch as the other cadets enter a portal that has been cut into the sheer black wall and head back towards their accommodation area. You wonder what the instructor has to tell you.

Once the others have gone, the instructor turns and looks into your eyes. "They look up to you," he says.

"Not all of them, sir," you reply.

The instructor raises one eyebrow. "I know you and Dagma have had your differences, but she's got a lot of skill and determination. You'd do well to give her some respect and see if you can utilize her strengths rather than concentrating on her weaknesses."

"Yes sir."

"Now it's your choice, but you need to select one of the cadets to be second in charge. Do you know who you'd like that to be?"

It is time for you to make an important decision. Do you:

Choose Dagma to be your second in charge because of her strength and skills? **P230**

Or

Choose Gagnon as your second in charge because you like him better and he is a better navigator? **P237**

You have chosen Dagma to be second in charge.

After thinking over what your instructor has said, you realize that you need to find a way to work with Dagma if your troop is going to become a cohesive unit. The sooner you can forget your differences, the better off everyone will be.

"Well?" the instructor says. "Who's it to be?"

You straighten your shoulders. "Dagma will make a good second, sir. The others will follow her without question if I am injured."

"Dagma it is then," the instructor says. "Now get back to your troop. You leave for the Pillars of Haramon at first light."

As you walk through the portal and down the corridor towards the accommodation pods, you take in the significance of what the instructor has just said. The Pillars of Haramon are an advanced base an 80-mile slide from the training ground. You've heard stories and seen pictures of these towering, fortified columns of black glass ever since you were a child. You remember the history lessons you've had about the brave miners who first discovered these diamond-packed volcanic pipes that rise nearly a thousand feet from the shining slopes below, and of the legendary sliders who have protected the outpost over the years.

These days the twin towers of rock are honeycombed with tunnels and chambers and form one of the Highland's strongest and most beautiful fortified positions. Mining still takes place deep beneath the pinnacles, but the above-ground pipes were cleaned out many years ago and now form sleeping, hydro, and defense pods.

As you walk along the corridor, you look up at the ceiling. Circular shafts have been bored to bring light down from the surface. Halfway along the first corridor a junction splits four ways. You turn right and follow the eastern access towards pod 6.

You still can't believe you're going to the Pillars of Haramon. You remember hearing stories about the battles fought against the Lowlanders who have tried to capture them and the rich source of blue diamonds they contain. But generations of Lowlanders have been repelled by the Highland Slider Corps. Many songs have been written about their bravery.

For years now the Lowlanders have been quiet, building up their forces and growing stronger. Everyone knows it is only a matter of time before they attempt another invasion. When that happens, it will be up to you, your troop, and others of the Highland Slider Corps to make sure they don't succeed.

The thought of war does not thrill you. Nobody really wins a war. Even the winning side loses people that can never be replaced. After a few more twists down the tunnels you reach Pod 6E.

The pod has curved walls with a series of notches cut into it. Each notch contains a cubicle complete with bunk and storage space for the cadet's personal effects. In the center there is a seating area with a table, large enough to accommodate the 30 person troop.

"Congratulations," Gagnon says as you enter. "That was a brave move you pulled out there."

"Lucky," Dagma says from the end of the table. "You could have been sliced and diced trying a stunt like that. Was it really worth the risk?"

You turn towards Dagma. "Luck's got nothing to do with it. It was a calculated risk I'll admit, but I've been practicing the move on the simulator."

"So who have you chosen for your second?" Dagma says. "Your friend Gagnon, I suppose."

The troop looks at you expectantly. Twenty-nine sets of eyes are upon you. This is your first act of command. Will they understand?

"I've chosen you, Dagma. You're the strongest across a range of skills. If we can work together I'm sure our troop will be the best to graduate this year. Gagnon will be our advanced scout, because he is our best navigator."

When you look around, you see heads nodding. Gagnon seems happy with his role. The tight muscles in Dagma's face have relaxed a little. You hope it is a sign of her becoming more cooperative.

"Now, hit your bunks," you say. "We leave for the Pillars of Haramon at first light."

This last statement has the troop buzzing. Whispers and comments pass between its members. They too have heard the legends.

"Dagma and Gagnon, would you please come into my cubicle. We need to plan for tomorrow."

Gagnon grabs a map from a drawer in the table and follows Dagma. Once inside, he unfolds the map and sticks it to the wall of your cubicle.

"There are two possible routes to the Pillars," Gagnon says. "Do you want fast or safe?"

After a quick look at the routes, you turn to Dagma. "What do you think?"

"If it was just us three I'd say fast," she says. "But there is always a chance of rain and with a troop of newbies I think we should go for safe. The last thing we need is an accident on our first day out."

Both options have advantages. Fast means you'll spend less time exposed to the elements, which is a good thing, but the safe route will be easier for those with less skill.

It is time for you to make your next decision. Do you:

Choose the slower, easier route to the Pillars of Haramon? **P241**

Or

Choose the fast route and spend less time on the slopes in case of rain? **P248**

You have chosen Gagnon to be second in charge.

You've decided to choose Gagnon to be your second in command because you know he won't undermine your authority. He is also the troop's best navigator which is one of the most important jobs a slider can have.

Many sliders have come to grief because of a simple mistake in navigation. Take the wrong valley and you can end up going over a bluff or into a crevasse, especially in flat light, when the ground's contours are hard to see and cracks in the surface are hidden in shadow.

Sliders navigate by triangulation. The navigator takes sightings from at least three prominent features with a handheld compass. Mountaintops, bluffs, or pinnacles work best. The navigator then transfers these bearings onto the map. Somewhere on the map, these three lines will intersect to form a triangle. Your location will be somewhere inside that triangle.

The more accurate a cadet is when they map out the compass bearings, the smaller that triangle will be. Some cadets are sloppy and always end up with large triangles, while others, like Gagnon, have tiny triangles that show a high level of accuracy.

"Well," the instructor says. "Who's it to be?"

You straighten your shoulders. "Gagnon will make a good second, sir," you say, hoping you've made the right choice. "I think even Dagma will follow his orders without question if I am injured."

"Gagnon it is then," he says. "Now get back to your troop. You leave for the Pillars of Haramon at first light."

As you walk through the portal towards the accommodation pods, you take in the significance of what the instructor has just said.

The Pillars of Haramon is an advanced lookout some eighty miles from the training ground. You've heard stories and seen pictures of these towering pinnacles ever since you were a child. You remember the history lessons you learned at school about the miners who first discovered these diamond packed volcanic pipes rising a thousand feet from the shimmering slopes below and of the legendary sliders who have protected them.

They are honeycombed with tunnels and chambers. These form one of the Highlands strongest and most unusual outposts. Mining still takes place deep underground beneath the Pillars, and many diamonds are still being uncovered, but above-ground the diamonds were cleared out years ago.

Your footsteps echo. Initially the tunnel is lit by light penetrating in from the portal by reflecting off the mirror black surface of the walls. Deeper inside, circular shafts bored into the roof, bring light down from the surface. Your unit's pod is 6-East. Halfway along the first corridor a junction splits four ways. You turn right and follow the eastern access.

You remember hearing stories about the battles fought against the Lowlanders who tried to capture the Pillars and the rich source of blue diamonds they contain. Generations of Lowlanders have been repelled by the Highland Slider Corps and many songs have been written about their bravery.

For years now the Lowlanders have been quiet, building up their forces and growing stronger. It is only a matter of time before they invade again. When that happens, it will be up to you, your troop, and others of the Highland Slider Corps to make sure they don't succeed.

Pod 6E has curved walls. A series of notches are cut into the rock. Each recess contains a bunk and a shelf for storing personal effects. In the center of the pod a table, long enough to accommodate the whole troop takes pride of place.

"Congratulations," Gagnon says as you enter. "That was a brave move you pulled out there."

"Lucky," Dagma says from the end of the table. "You could have been sliced and diced trying a stunt like that. Was it really worth the risk?"

You turn towards Dagma. "It was a calculated risk I'll admit, but

I've been practicing on the simulator more than most. The odds were in my favor."

"So who have you chosen for your second?" Dagma says. "Your friend Gagnon, I suppose."

The troop looks at you expectantly. There is a hum of voices.

"Yes, I've chosen Gagnon. You might be the strongest across a range of skills but with your attitude I'm not sure we can work together."

"But..." Dagma is stunned. It is obvious that she thought she'd win the downhill race, and now she's not even going to be second.

"But I want you to prove me wrong, so I'm going to make you advance scout. Your strength and sliding talent will give us a real advantage if we met Lowlanders. I'm sure if we work together, our troop can be the best to graduate this year."

When you look around, you see heads nodding. Gagnon seems happy with his role. Even the normally strained muscles in Dagma's face have relaxed a little. You've helped her save face by giving her an important role. Perhaps this new responsibility will make her more cooperative.

"Now, get some sleep," you say. "We leave for the Pillars of Haramon at first light."

This last statement has the troop buzzing. Whispers and comments pass between cadets. They too have heard the legends.

"Dagma, Gagnon, come into my cubicle, we need to plan for tomorrow."

Gagnon grabs a map and brings it with him. Dagma follows you and once inside, leans casually against the wall of your cubicle.

"There are two possible routes to the Pillars," Gagnon says, pointing to the map. "Do you want fast or safe? We'll be exposed for a shorter length of time if we take the quicker route."

After studying the map, you look at Dagma. "What do you think?"

"If it was just us three I'd say fast," she says. "But with 30 newbies, I think we should take the slower route. The last thing we need is an accident on our first patrol."

It is time for you to make your next important decision. Do you:

Choose the slower and easier route to the Pillars of Haramon? **P241**
Or

Choose the faster route and spend less time on the slopes in case of rain? **P248**

Choose the slower, easier route to the Pillars of Haramon.

While the cadets sleep, you've been up studying the map. On it Gagnon has marked his suggested route to the Pillars of Haramon. For most of the trip you will traverse the upper slopes on one of the wider, main tracks. But you also want to become familiar with alternative routes in case a change of plan is required.

It's just as well you decided to take the slow route to the Pillars. Moments ago you received orders from Slider Command to take a class of mining students with you.

This seems unusual. You're only cadets yourselves. Why would your superiors give you such a responsibility? Traversing the high tracks will be dangerous enough without having to babysit a bunch of miners on your first patrol.

Even though all Highland children are given needle-boots as soon as they are old enough to toddle, and quickly become familiar with moving about on slippery ground, no sane Highlander would venture far from home without slider guides.

Escorting a group of mining students is a big job, especially when there's a possibility of rain. Even the best quality needle boots will lose over fifty percent of their grip on black glass if the surface becomes damp.

Because of their high cost, only members of the Slider Corps are issued with guide sticks, fitted with best-quality diamond hooks and premium tyranium crystals.

Mining students, traders and ordinary citizens are dependent on guides to move on even the simplest of routes between the communities, mines and hydroponic chambers dotted around the Black Slopes.

Your instructors have taught you all about guiding. They've taught you that having a plan-B is advisable. Now that your troop is escorting miners, you want a plan-C as well.

When the wake-up buzzer sounds, the peace and quiet is broken.

The cadets bound out of their bunks and dress quickly. They sort their equipment, pack their backpacks and sit at the breakfast table with a bubbling nervousness.

You feel a few moon moths fluttering in your stomach too, but you are determined to keep your nervousness in check for the sake of your troop.

Gagnon looks over your shoulder at the map. "Check, check and double check, aye?"

You see the hint of a smile on his face. He seems as calm as ever.

"I like the route you've planned," you tell him, "but it never hurts to have options."

"The higher we stay, the more options we have. There is nothing worse than being caught on low ground."

"Slider rule number one," the two of you say in unison. "Altitude is advantage."

As every slider knows, it's hard to slide when you're already at the bottom.

Gagnon points to the map. "Once we get past Mount Tyron we can follow Long Gully all the way to the Pillars. It's only a 1 in 30 gradient so it should provide a gentle ride for our passengers."

After making a few more notes, you join the other cadets. Most are eating their hydro with gusto, knowing that this will be the last fresh food they see for a while.

You help yourself to a large plate of the succulent greens and pour yourself a cup of steaming broth. When Dagma comes to sit beside you, you secretly smile. Maybe your plan to include her is working.

"A lovely day for babysitting miners," she grumps.

You can understand why Dagma isn't thrilled, but you want the trip to start on a positive note. Negativity can easily ruin morale. "I can't wait to see the Pillars," you say loudly. Around you, other members of your troop smile and nod. Your tactic worked.

Dagma shrugs and shovels another large spoonful of hydro into her mouth. She's a big unit, and it takes a bit of feeding to keep her energy levels up. Then she looks up from her plate. "Couldn't the miners use their whizzo anchor bolt launchers and zippers to make their own way?"

"No," you say. "They're only students. Besides, it's way too dangerous with overloaded sledges. None of them would make it."

Dagma grunts and shovels more hydro.

Once you've finished eating, you stand and tap your cup on the table. The rest of the cadets stop talking and look at you expectantly.

"You've all probably heard by now that we're escorting mining students today. We'll be leaving soon, so let's get this pod ready for departure. I'll see you at the bottom of the tow in fifteen minutes. Remember, we're professionals so act like it. Let's make the Slider Corps proud and the miners welcome."

The sound of scraping boots and excited voices echo off the pod's walls as cadets finish packing and tidy up their cubicles.

You put on your utility belt and adjust the strap on your backpack. Then you grab your newly acquired guide stick and make your way along the corridor back towards the portal. The walls of the corridor are as dark as your mood. Responsibility is a burden, but you know once you get used to it, it will be rewarding.

Outside the air is crisp and still. The sky is without any hint of cloud.

An instructor is waiting for you at the bottom of the first tow. Beside him stands a group of ten mining students, each with their own sledge loaded high with equipment. Once your troop has assembled, the instructor clears his throat and everyone goes silent.

"I know some of you are wondering why Slider Command has decided to give a group of cadets the responsibility of getting these mining students to the Pillars of Haramon," the instructor says as he looks out over those gathered before him. "It's certainly not something we planned on. But yesterday, one of our advanced units spotted a large number of Lowlanders camped in the northern foothills. It's estimated they outnumber the Highland Slider Corps by three to one. They also have some unusual equipment hidden under tarpaulins."

The cadet standing next to you gulps in the deathly silence.

"The Highland Slider Corps are now on high alert. All available personnel are moving into defensive positions. All leave has been cancelled and any further cadet training has been suspended."

The officer's expression is serious. "We all knew this day was coming."

The instructor sweeps his arm, indicating everyone before him. "Some of you standing here are sliders and some of you are miners, but remember first and foremost, you are Highlanders."

You look along your troop. Dagma's face is tight, her lips pressed together. One or two cadets look about ready to pee themselves.

"The Pillars of Haramon give us control of the upper slopes," the officer continues. "If the Lowlanders can't get up the mountain, they are below us and will remain vulnerable. We need your help if we are to keep the Highlands safe for our families. So, are you with me Highlanders?"

"Yes sir!" both the sliders and miners shout.

You step forward and salute the instructor. "Slider Troop 6E is ready for departure sir."

"Off you go then. Be careful, we need this equipment delivered safely."

You feel a wave of nervousness wash over you, but you are determined to do your family and the Slider Corps proud. "Yes sir," you say, straightening your back. "We'll get there or die trying sir."

"Just get there cadet. You are not allowed to die today. That is an order."

"Yes sir," you say. "No dying today, sir."

You look over your troop. "Right, three cadets per sledge, two front, and one back. Miners, double-check that your loads are secure and climb aboard."

The sliders form themselves into groups and attach their harnesses to the sledges. After checking their loads, the miners climb up and strap themselves on.

Pulling the sledges, the sliders shuffle towards the towline. The two front sliders stand opposite each other, one on either side of the humming cable. The slider at the back gets ready to act as brake if required.

The front sliders hook their tow clamps over the whirling cable and squeeze. As the clamps grip onto the cable, everyone accelerates up the hill.

You lead the last group. Dagma, because of her superior strength, is at the back of your sledge, ready to put on the brakes should your group become separated from the tow somehow.

When you reach the top of the first tow, you repeat the exercise up the next, and the next. Before you know it, the training ground is a faint speck in the distance.

At the top of the last tow, you stop briefly to enjoy the view. A range of glistening black peaks stretch off in the distance. You feel the cool wind that has blown in from the north and notice that faint wisps of cloud have appeared on the horizon.

You turn to your troop. "Right, Gagnon is our navigator, his group will take the lead. We've chosen the safest route to the Pillars of Haramon for a reason, so keep your speed down. Stay in control of your sledges at all times, and stay alert ... Gagnon?"

Gagnon raises his arm and points to a tooth-shaped peak in the distance. "Our first waypoint is sixteen miles to the west, just beneath Mount Transor."

The cadets turn to look at the towering peak. Mount Transor is one of the many unclimbed mountains on Petron. Light reflects off its near-vertical face. The tops of even higher mountains can be seen through the haze further inland.

"Now that we're traversing," you tell your troop, "we'll travel with one cadet in front of the sledge to steer, and two behind for braking. I want the strongest sliders at the back and, if in doubt, slow down.

Unlike our competition yesterday, this is not a race."

As the slider troop rearrange their order and refasten their harnesses, you do the same in preparation to leading your sledge. Once everyone is ready you wave your arm. "Okay move out!"

Gagnon leads. The track is about two sledge widths wide and slants ever so slightly downhill, which lets gravity do the work of moving the heavy sledges.

The sledge's metal runners slide easily over the ground. A fine coating of diamond dust on their outside edges keep the runners tracking in a straight line.

You look at the clouds and hope they stay away. Conditions can change rapidly in the mountains. Squalls often race in after picking up moisture from the lowlands. Troops have been surprised by rapidly moving fronts before. Your hand moves over your utility belt and checks that your tether and anchor bolt gun are in their usual places. One of the first things you learned as a cadet was how to fire an anchor into the rock and tether a sledge. The troop record for this procedure is six seconds, held by Gagnon.

After checking that your boots are firmly locked together, you point your front foot down the path and push with the needle end of your guide stick. Before long you are moving at a quick, walking pace, except you're not expending any energy. Gravity is doing all the work.

Those ahead of you are making easy work of the gentle terrain and everyone is starting to relax. The miners seem to be enjoying the ride. Dagma brings up the rear.

Just as you are thinking all is well, the lead slider in the group ahead of you takes a fall and loses grip on the surface. As soon as she hits the ground, the sledge behind her slews off course and slips perilously towards the edge of the track.

There is a screech of diamond hooks as the two cadets at the rear of the sledge lean down hard on their guide sticks. But one of the front runners has veered off the path onto steeper terrain. As much as the cadets try to hold it, the weight of mining equipment is slowly pulling the sledge off the track.

"Get ready to brake, Dagma," you yell, giving a big push in an attempt get close enough to hook one of the brakemen on the sledge in front of you, in order to give them some extra stopping power. You just hope that Dagma is as strong as you think she is, and that her technique will be enough to slow the runaway sledge.

Another big push and you've caught up to the group in front. You reach out with your stick and hook on to the backpack of a cadet in front of you.

"Brake, Dagma!" you yell.

As Dagma and the other cadet drop their hooks and dig them in, you feel the straps of your harness tighten. Will this added pressure pull the guide stick from your hand? How could you lead your troop without it?

If you get tangled, both sledges could be in danger. As Dagma digs deeper, you hang on as tight as you can. Your sweaty hands are beginning to slip. You are not sure if you can hold on.

It is time to make a quick decision. Do you:

Hang on to your guide stick and try to save the runaway sledge?
P254

Or

Unhook your stick from the group in front and save your own group? **P260**

You have chosen the faster route to the Pillars of Haramon.

You're up well before the alarm buzzer to check the fast route that Gagnon has marked on the map. It is the most direct route way to the Pillars of Haramon but has some switchbacks and tricky sections to negotiate. One part you're particularly concern with is known as "Zigzag Drop".

As you pore over the map, a courier enters and hands you a bright green envelope.

The envelope contains orders to escort ten mining students to the Pillars, all the more reason to get there as quickly as possible.

The chance of rain is low, but you are convinced that moving quickly and exposing your troop and the miners to the elements for the least amount of time is the right thing to do.

Miners, traders and common people are reliant on linked transport — where sliders escort travelers on specially designed sledges — to get around the various tracks. There are many stories about unaccompanied travelers "going to the bottom".

You are thinking about the best way to organize your caravan when the silence is broken by the wake-up buzzer. Cadets bound out of their bunks and dress quickly. They sort their equipment, pack their backpacks and eat breakfast with a bubbling nervousness of quick sentences and subdued giggles.

Gagnon looks over your shoulder at the map "Fast is good, eh?

"I like the route you've planned," you tell him. "There are a few tricky sections, but we should be okay."

After making a few more notes, you join the others at the breakfast table. Most are eating like hungry morph rats, knowing it will be a while before they'll have a chance to eat something other than travel rations and the occasional cup of broth.

You fill a large plate and pour yourself some steaming broth. You're pleased when Dagma comes and sits beside you. Maybe your plan to include her is working.

"I hear we've got miners to escort," Dagma says.

"At least it will give us a chance to show off our skills."

Dagma shrugs and shovels a large spoonful of stringy hydro into her mouth. Green strands hang down to her chin. She noisily slurps them up. You turn your head in disgust.

You stand up and tap your cup on the table. The rest of the cadets stop talking and raise their eyes.

"You all probably know by now that we're escorting a group of mining students to the Pillars of Haramon. We'll be leaving soon, so let's get this pod squared away for departure. I'll see you at the bottom of the towline with your gear in fifteen minutes.

The sound of scraping boots and mumbled voices fill the pod as the cadets move to their cubicles and finish packing.

You put on your utility belt and adjust the straps of your backpack. Then you grab your guide stick. It is your prize possession. You turn it up and check the tyranium crystal pad on its foot by running your thumb over the tightly compacted ultra-fine needles. They seem in good condition. At the other end of the six-foot-long handle is a two inch hook of pure blue. This diamond is the hardest material on the planet, it will dig into anything. It will slow you down when sliding on the slopes, and also act as a weapon if required.

Happy with your equipment, you make your way out of the pod and along the corridor back to the portal. Outside you find an instructor and ten mining students. One of the mining students is laughing and joking around. His high pitched squeal rings out over the assembly.

Unfortunately, the instructor is not in a mood for jokes. "If you're finished playing around, Piver, it's time to listen up."

Suddenly, it is so quiet that you can hear the distinctive screech of a red-beaked pango miles down the valley.

The instructor clears his throat. "Yesterday one of our scouts spotted a large number of Lowlanders gathered in the northern foothills. It's estimated they outnumber the Highland Slider Corps by three to one."

"Geebus!" you hear the funny little miner say as his face goes pale.

The instructor gives him a sharp look and continues. "The Highland Slider Corps are now on high alert. All leave has been cancelled."

Groups of miners and sliders are a buzz of conversation at this news.

The instructor holds up his hand, requesting silence. "Controlling the Pillars of Haramon gives us control of the Black Slopes. As long as we control the base and Haramon Pass at the head of Long Gully, the Lowlanders can't gain access to the pathways and reservoirs we have developed over the centuries. We need your help if we are to keep the Highlands free and safe for our families. Are you with me?"

"Yes sir!" the sliders and miners shout in unison.

You step forward and salute the instructor. "Slider Corps 6E is ready for departure sir."

"Off you go then. We need these miners and their equipment at the Pillars as quickly as possible."

A wave of nervousness floods over you, but you are determined to do your family and the Corps proud. You straighten your back. "Yes sir."

"Don't allow the Lowlanders to cut you off."

"Yes sir. We're going to take the fast route. With luck we'll avoid contact with any Lowland patrols that way."

"Luck's got nothing to do with it cadet. Just remember your training and everything will be fine."

You salute once more and then look over at your group. The miners' sledges are loaded to the max with equipment.

"Right sliders," you call out. "Two per sledge, one front and one back. The rest of you, keep an eye out for Lowlanders. Miners, climb aboard and strap in tight, this is going to be a quick trip."

As you watch, twenty cadets harness themselves up to the heavy sledges leaving ten cadets free for quick deployment should

Lowlanders be spotted along the route. A mining student jumps aboard each sledge.

"Ready to tow," the front cadet on the first sledge says.

You nod and lift your arm. "On my mark, three, two, one… go!"

The leading cadet hooks the tow clamp attached to the front of his harness, over the whirling cable and squeezes its handles. As the clamp grips the cable, the slack is taken up in the cadet's harness and the sledge begins to move up the hill.

Your group brings up the rear. Once you reach the top of the first tow, everyone repeats the exercise up the next tow, and the next. Soon the training ground is a speck far below and you can see the curvature of the planet off in the distance.

At the top of the last tow you stop briefly to enjoy the view. Peak after shining black peak stretch off into the distance.

Pleased at the lack of cloud in sight, you turn to your troops. "Right, Gagnon is our navigator. He will take the lead for now. We've chosen the quick route for a reason, so keep moving. Our first waypoint is sixteen miles to the west near Mt Tyron."

You look towards the towering peak in the distance. Light glints off its reflective face as the sun tracks around to the west.

Once everyone is ready you wave your arm. "Okay, move out!"

Gagnon, unencumbered by a sledge, shoves off with a push of his stick. The line of sledges follow.

Most of the sledges are overloaded with extra gear from Command. This equipment is needed at the Pillars to defend against the impending Lowland attack. The cadets at the back of the sledges are constantly dragging their hooks to keep them from gaining too much momentum as they make their way along the narrow track traversing the across the slope.

You feel every bump and irregularity as you slide along. Occasionally you need to correct your balance. A quick tap of your stick on the ground is usually all that is required. But you must keep alert. Things on the upper slopes can change in an instant.

When you hear a series of high-pitched screeches, you look up and see a flock of pangos heading out to feed. Their formation creates a massive V in the sky. The bird's wings barely move as they soar on the thermals created by the hot air rising from the dark, heat-absorbing slopes below

Above the pangos, Petron's smallest moon glows a faint pink. A fuzzy ring around it circumference shows that there is moisture in the upper atmosphere.

Instinctively you pat your utility belt and feel the row of anchor bolts every slider carries in case of emergency. If you are caught in a sudden downpour you'll only have seconds to fire a charge into the slope and clip yourself on. If you are too slow, you'll be swept down the slope without any chance of stopping.

You point your front foot ever so slightly downhill and push with your guide stick. It doesn't take much to get moving on the slick rock. Before long, the troop is moving along at a running pace, except you're not expending any energy. Gravity is doing all the work.

This track is steeper than the usual transport tracks. Still, everyone seems to be coping with the gradient so far. The troop is making good speed and you start to relax.

Just as you are thinking all is well, you hear a shout. The cadet leading the front sledge has fallen.

You can see the brakeman struggling to stop.

When a steering runner slips off the main track onto the steeper slope below, the front of the sledge lurches and skews sharply downhill. Its speed increases in an instant.

"Abandon sledge!" the brakeman yells. "I can't hold it!"

The fallen cadet unclips her harness and kicks herself out of the heavy sledge's path. Then she spins onto her back and digs in her heel spurs. The miner hits the quick release on his waist strap, jumps off the sledge, and rolls onto his belly, digging the tip of his pick into the slope to stop his slide.

The brakeman unclips his harness and, pressing hard on his guide stick, comes screeching to a halt.

As the runaway sledge rockets down the hill, you hear gasps from your group. Thankfully its crew, although shaken, seems to be okay. The slider who first fell is up and has made her way to the miner who is hanging onto his pick for dear life. With a *pop* an anchor bolt is fired into the rock and the miner is secured. Another cadet throws down a cable and those below clip on and start working their way back up to the track where the rest of you wait anxiously.

"Geebus!" a familiar voice exclaims. "That was close!"

You realize how right the funny little miner is. It's time to reassess things. Maybe taking the fast route with a troop of untested cadets wasn't such a good idea after all. But then the extra time you've taken after the accident means you are behind schedule.

What do you do now? It is time to make an important decision. Do you:

Slow down and put more safety precautions in place? **P282**

Or

Carry on down to the Pillars and make best speed? **P295**

Hang on to your guide stick and try to save the runaway sledge.

At first the strain is so great you think your arms will be pulled from their sockets. Your muscles burn, but you grit your teeth and hang on. Then after a few seconds, the pressure eases. Dagma and her fellow cadet have managed to bring the uncontrolled slide to a halt.

Once you come to a complete stop, you unhook your stick from the harness of the cadet in front of you and exhale with relief. "Are you all alright?"

The cadet who had been steering the sledge is back on her feet and looking over the pile of equipment at you. "Thanks. I've got it now."

The two cadets at the rear of the runaway sledge are red-faced and panting from exertion.

"Thanks for that," one says.

The other cadet tries to put on a brave face. "Yeah thanks. We nearly went to the bottom that time."

Everyone knows exactly what he means when he says "the bottom". The bottom is not a place people come back from ... well, not often, anyway.

You shake your head and try to get the ugly thought out of your head. "Okay, let's heave this sledge back onto the track and try it again."

As the cadets get to work, you can see they are still a little shaken from their close call ... and so they should be.

Once the sledge is safely up and its load secured, it's time to move off again.

"Let's take it a little slower this time," you say.

Thankfully, for the rest of the morning your group slides on without incident. Gradually your nerves settle down and you relax once more.

For lunch you stop on a small plateau which provides enough flat ground for everyone to anchor their sledges. It is the junction where the west and eastbound tracks cross.

The cadets remove their harnesses and sit on the ground. It's been a long morning. Tired legs and backs need a break. Ration packs are broken open and burners are lit to heat broth.

Gagnon informs you that the troop has traveled just over seventeen miles and lost 3000 feet of altitude.

You do a quick mental calculation. That equates to thirty feet of forward progress for every foot of lost altitude, pretty good going for a group of rookies. "At this rate we'll reach our camp well before dewfall," you say to Gagnon.

Since the accident you've been moving slower, but you know that once you get to smoother slopes your troop will be able to make up some time.

Lunch lasts half an hour. You make a few adjustments to the teams, and give Gagnon a break from leading now that you've come off the face and have reached a wide valley that is almost impossible to get lost in.

Dagma is keen to lead so you put Gagnon with her team at the rear and send Dagma forward to lead the next section.

"Just remember, Dagma, we're not all as strong as you, so keep your speed down."

Dagma gives you a curt nod and steps into the lead sledge's harness. "Don't worry, I know what I'm doing," she says. "Remember, I've done just as many hours as you have on the simulators."

You're still not sure about Dagma's attitude. She seems determined to prove to everyone how good she is despite what is best for the team. You suspect she still hasn't forgiven you for beating her in the race to become troop leader.

Before you have a chance to say "move out", Dagma is off, pushing with big strokes to get her sledge up to speed.

"Let's go," you say to the others. "Go at your own pace and don't worry if Dagma gets a bit of a lead on you. This is not a race."

The valley is nearly half a mile wide, mainly smooth and at the perfect angle for sliding. It stretches far into the distance. Steep hills crowd in on both sides. Occasionally a vertical pillar of black rock will rise up from the otherwise featureless landscape. These dormant volcanic pipes are a constant reminder of Petron's volcanic past.

The young miner on your sledge makes a comment about the possibility of blue diamonds being present in the pipes as you pass. His voice is filled with excitement and nervousness at the same time. You are happy to chat. It helps pass the time on this less demanding part of the journey, but after a while you start getting a sore throat from having to shout over the sound of the wind whistling around your visor as you whiz down the slope.

The planned stopping point for the night is a fortified tow-base near the bottom of this valley, almost ten miles away. Then tomorrow, you'll tow up to the top of a ridge where you'll find the track that will take you to Long Gully and then on to the Pillars of Haramon.

The tow-base has a maintenance crew of ten and a number of accommodation, defense and hydro pods bored into the solid rock. It will be a crowded night with the miners and their cargo, but even crowded accommodation is better than being out on the slopes after dewfall.

When you look down the valley you see that Dagma has pulled away from the rest of the troop. You shake your head and grumble under your breath. Why does she always need to prove herself like this?

You are about to send Gagnon off after her to tell her to slow down when your eyes are distracted by movement below and off to your left.

It takes a second to realize that what you've seen is a group of Lowlanders working their way up the left hand edge of the valley about half a mile away. The Lowlanders' dark uniforms are nearly invisible against the shimmering black rock.

Dagma has missed them. Unfortunately she is too far away for you to yell out a warning. You grab your scope and watch as the Lowland scouts raise their bows and prepare to fire at Dagma's group.

Luckily you've noticed the Lowlanders while you are still well above them. Your troop's camouflage is even better than the Lowlanders'. Even the sledges are almost invisible with their shiny black covers.

The Lowlanders haven't seen you. They must think that Dagma's group is travelling solo. You have the advantage.

You raise your fist with one finger extended, the signal for a silent stop. The cadets slow the sledges by turning them side on to the slope rather than dragging their noisy hooks.

"Lead cadets prepare for attack," you whisper once you've pulled to a halt.

You unhook your harness and spin your backpack around so it rests against your chest to act as a shield. Then you unlock your boots so you have a full range of movement.

"V-formation," you order. "We'll send them to the bottom before they know what's hit them."

You and nine other sliders group together, sitting on your utility belts with packs to the front. Your guide sticks are tucked tight under your arms with the hook end forward and the crystal end resting on the ground ready to steer you one way or the other in an instant.

"On my count," you say quietly. "Three, two, one, push…"

Within seconds, your formation is sliding down the slope, each cadet tucked close, protecting the cadet beside them.

"Time to increase our speed and show these Lowlanders who owns the slopes," you shout over the whistling wind.

On the front of your pack, behind a thin protective plate, is a small reservoir. You pull a lever and a fine stream of water shoots out onto the slope in front of you. After sliding through the damp patch, you feel the friction lessen and your troop accelerate like someone has fired a rocket launcher.

"Hard left, on my mark. Three, two, one, now!"

The cadets follow your order instinctively, forcing their guide sticks hard against the smooth rock and pushing your tightly-packed group to the left. You are bearing down on the Lowland scouts, sliding faster and faster.

A Lowlander looks up and sees you coming. He warns the others. They stop firing at Dagma and turn to face your group racing towards them.

"Sticks up!" you yell.

"Woot, woot!" your cadets yell.

The Lowlanders reload and fire. But your group is still accelerating and they misjudge their aim. Only one arrow strikes a member of your group and it is deflected by the cadet's armored backpack.

Your group is close now. The diamond spurs imbedded in the heel of your boots sparkle in the sunlight, ready to strike like fangs at the legs of the invaders.

When you collide with the Lowlanders, it is with such force that despite their protective armor, they fly off their feet and are propelled down the slope.

The impact has had the reverse affect on you and your cadets. It's brought you nearly to a halt.

"Hooks down!" you command.

The piercing screech of diamond digging into the black rock reminds you of the call of the wild pango as your cadets come to a stop. Their grim expressions have turned to elated smiles at having survived their first encounter with Lowlanders.

Down the valley to your right, Dagma has brought her sledge to a stop and is tending a cadet with an arrow sticking out of her leg.

The Lowlanders are off their feet and free sliding out of control. You watch their desperate attempts to stop before they run into something nasty. Then, as the terrain flattens out a little, the Lowlanders manage to bring their slide to a halt. Despite being bruised and battered they've survived, but they don't hang around. They quickly organize themselves and retreat further down the slope. Before long they are nothing but dots in the distance, scurrying home in defeat.

"Sliders one, Lowlanders nil," you say to your troop. "Well done.

Now, I suppose we'd better slide over and see if we can help Dagma."

You signal the cadets who remained with the sledges further up the hill, to proceed with caution down the slope and then stand up, lock your boots together and start pushing your way towards Dagma.

The cadet hit by the arrow is in pain, but at least the arrow missed all the major arteries, nor has it hit bone. After disinfecting the wound and wrapping a bandage around the cadet's thigh, she has no problem standing. The wounded cadet is given a couple of yellow capsules, a combination pain killer and antibiotic, and helped to her feet.

"Let's get you on one of the sledges," you say. "You'll be fine in a day or two if you take it easy."

"It's only a scratch. I can slide," she says gritting her teeth. "The pain killers should kick in soon."

You shake your head. "You may be able to slide, but for now there's no need. Just rest until we get to the tow-base."

Finding Lowlanders along your intended route was unexpected. It also means you need to make a decision. Do you:

Carry on down the slope towards the tow base in your current formation? **P295**

Or

Send some advanced scouts to test the route first? **P302**

Unhook from the sledge in front and save your own group.

You can feel the guide stick being pulled from your grasp. You know that if you don't unhook from the group ahead you will lose it, or even worse, send the sledge you are leading tumbling down the steep hillside as well.

With a twist of your wrist you free yourself from the group in front. Will they be able to stop without your help?

You aren't sure, but it's up to them now. Both of the brakemen are desperately trying to stop the runaway sledge but seem to be fighting a losing battle. The miner on the sledge is panicking and looks ready to jump.

"Stay on the sledge!" you yell. But has he heard you? If he jumps now, you know he'll end up sliding out of control. You doubt his pick will be enough to stop him from slipping all the way to the bottom. At least on the sledge he's got a chance.

Then miraculously, the lead slider regains her feet and with a desperate drive of her guide stick manages to turn the nose of her sledge side-on to the slope. The sledge is still moving fast, but without gravity trying to drag it down the mountain, the momentum is reduced. The two cadets at the back renew their efforts and gradually the sledge slows.

You exhale loudly and wipe the sweat off your forehead.

"Phew, that was close," you mumble as you slip out of your harness and slide closer to where the runaway sledge has come to a stop. They are slightly below you and off the main track, but at least they are all in one piece. The miner is white-faced and trembling.

With some ropes and extra pulling power you and your cadets manage to get the runaway sledge back onto the main track. After 30 minutes your troop is back in formation and ready once again to move off.

You've had a lucky escape. Thankfully, for the rest of the morning everyone slides on without incident.

For lunch you stop on a small patch of flat ground which provides enough space for everyone to remove their harnesses and anchor their sledges. Most of the sliders sit to give their sore legs and backs a break. Ration packs are broken open and a small burner is fired up to heat broth.

Gagnon informs you that the troop has traveled just over seventeen miles. "And we've only lost 3000 feet of altitude. That's thirty feet of forward progress for every foot of lost altitude, pretty good going for a group of rookies."

"And despite the accident, we're making good time," you say to Gagnon, acknowledging his navigational and route planning skills. "At this rate we'll reach the tow-base an hour before dewfall."

After lunch, you decide to take the lead and give Gagnon a break. There isn't much navigation to do in this section because you'll be travelling down a broad valley.

The terrain on the right-hand side of the valley is undulating but smooth. The other side is a different matter. A major fault line has created a chaotic jumble of crevasses and ridges. Not the sort of place to want to take sledges anywhere near.

"Remember to keep well to the right," you tell the cadets as you push off with your stick. "We've still got a fair way to go. Let's try to keep things unexciting."

For the first fifteen miles everything goes without a hitch, but when you see movement up on the slope to your right, you order everyone to come to a halt.

You take out your scope and focus. It is a group of fifteen Lowland scouts, climbing up towards the ridge. How did they get past the lookouts at the tow-base? How are they managing to get a grip on the steep slope? Have the Lowlanders developed some new technology that allows them to move on the slick black glass? Maybe they've found a source of needle crystals.

"Can your catapult reach that far?" you ask Dagma.

Dagma pulls out her scope and points it at the group of

Lowlanders. After making a few adjustments she lowers the instrument and looks at its dial. "It's reading just over half a mile. We'll need to get closer to have a chance of reaching them."

With the Lowlanders holding the high ground, their arrows will reach your group before your catapults can knock them off their perch. Sending your cadets any closer would be suicidal.

As you discuss the problem with Dagma, the miner riding on your sledge coughs. "Can I make a suggestion?" he says.

You nod. "As long as you do it quickly."

"I've got a cable launcher on my sledge," he says before pointing up the slope towards a small pinnacle on a rise behind you. "If we fire a line up to that outcrop, you can use my heavy-duty zipper to gain some altitude."

You think about what the miner has said. "How many cadets will it hold?"

The miner thinks a bit. "Six or seven I would think. Will that be enough?"

"It should be."

Sliders always try to attack from above. All their tactics are based on having the advantage of altitude. Trying to dislodge the Lowlanders from below will almost certainly mean the loss of some of your cadets.

After a brief discussion with Dagma you turn to the miner. "Okay, break it out. Let's get it set up before the Lowlanders realize what we're up to."

The miner removes the cover off his sledge and grabs a long tubular piece of equipment. This is attached to a sturdy tripod.

After setting the launcher up, the miner looks through a scope on the top of the firing tube and adjusts dials and levers. Then he attaches a spool of ultrafine cable to the back of a sleek projectile with fins on its tail and fits it into the back of the tube.

"Ready to fire," the miner says.

You've decide to lead the attack yourself so you grab the miner's heavy-duty zipper and attach it to the front of your harness ready to clamp onto the towline as soon as it is secure. Five other cadets link up to you, one behind the other. You look at the miner. "On my count. Three, two, one, fire!"

The miner pulls the trigger and the projectile hisses towards the pillar. The reel of cable whirls out after it.

A puff of dust erupts from the pinnacle as the projectile buries itself deep into the rock.

"Ready to zip on my mark. Three, two, one!"

You squeeze the grip on the battery-powered zipper and next thing you know you and five cadets are rocketing up the side of the valley.

As you slide, you wonder if the Lowlanders have spotted you. Surely they've heard the launcher or have seen you, despite your uniforms blending into the dark rock of the slope.

When you reach the top of the tow the zipper cuts out. The six of you look towards the Lowlanders. They are below you now, but not by much.

"Okay, get ready to traverse," you tell your cadets. "We need to get closer before they have time to get any higher. Dagma, let us know when you're within catapult range."

The other cadets follow as you push off with your stick. The swish of your boots sliding across the smooth rock sounds like compressed air escaping from a hydro growing chamber. You try to keep as high as possible as you traverse across the hillside.

It isn't long before Dagma signals a halt. "I think I can reach them from here."

She removes a Y-shaped piece of metal and strong synthetic tube from the top of her backpack along with a handful of water bullets. Each bullet is about the size of a pango egg and has a rigid shell designed to break on impact.

"Aim well above them," you say to Dagma.

Dagma slips a water bullet into the catapult's pouch and stretches the tubing back with all her strength. With a *zing* the bullet arcs off into the sky and splats on the uphill side of the Lowlanders.

The water, now released from its container, has nowhere to go but down.

You notice the first of the Lowlanders slip slightly as the first trickle runs under his feet. When Dagma's second bomb hits the slope they are all scrambling for anchor points.

Now that the Lowlanders' attentions are fully focused on staying attached to the slope, you can move closer. There is no way any of them are going to let go of their anchor points long enough to fire an arrow.

"Forward," you order.

You push off and slide closer to the Lowlanders' position. When you feel all the cadets will be able to reach the Lowlanders with their catapults, you motion them to stop.

"Load up hard shot," you say, grabbing your catapult and some lumps of stone from a side pouch of your backpack. "Let send these invaders to the bottom."

The Lowlanders are in trouble now. If they let go of their anchor points they will plummet down the hillside. If they don't, they will be pounded by hard-shot.

The Lowlanders' only choice is to rappel down on whatever cables they have and retreat with all haste. Even then it is unlikely that all of them will get away without injury. You see one of their scouts frantically untangling a cable and attaching it to an anchor point he's quickly fixed to the rock.

Just as he's about to clip on, he's knocked off his feet. He lurches for the cable as he falls, but misses it by a hand's width.

"That's one off," Dagma cries with glee. "Now let's get the rest of them!"

The cadets are all firing now. Hard shot is peppering the remaining Lowlanders. Desperately they push each other aside in their attempt to be first down the cable.

When another Lowlander slips and starts sliding towards the bottom, a cheer goes up.

Dagma fires more water bullets to keep the slope as slick as possible. The remaining cadets keep the hard shot flying. The Lowlanders are taking a beating.

Finally, the remaining Lowlanders manage to clip on and abseil down the cable at breakneck speed.

A mile or so down the valley the two Lowlanders who were knocked off have managed to stop and are regrouping. You peer through your scope and see them tending to their scrapes and bruises. Once the remaining Lowlanders have made it to the valley floor, two of them pull out their bows.

"After them," you say. "V-formation on my mark!"

Your cadets stow their catapults and unlock their boots. They reverse their backpacks, so they cover their chest and act as a shield, and point the hook end of their guide sticks to the front. The cadets sit on their utility belts in a V formation and lock arms, ready for a super-fast downhill slide.

"On my mark … three, two, one, go!" you yell.

When the Lowlanders see your flying wedge coming down the hill at them, they realize the hopelessness of their situation, drop their bows and flee.

"Hard right on my mark!"

You and your cadets push right with your sticks.

"Again!" you yell.

As one, your cadets stab the ground with the needle end of their sticks, aiming themselves at the Lowlanders.

"Line formation! Boots up!"

In seconds, what was a V-formation is a line spread across the slopes. Cadets have their sticks up like lances and their diamond studded heels raised, ready to knock the Lowlanders off the mountain.

The Lowlanders' eyes are huge. They have seen all they need to. With a yelp of panic they fling themselves down the hillside. By the time your troops hit the valley floor they are scurrying off toward their unlucky comrades further down the mountain.

"Hooks down!" you order.

You swivel your stick around and dig its hook into the slope behind you. You don't need your eyes to tell the other cadets are following suit. The screech of diamond on black glass is unmistakable.

Your cadets have all stopped within a few yards of each other.

"Well they won't be back for a while," Dagma says with a grin.

You stand and signal the cadets further up the valley to bring the sledges down. Then you look at the young Highlanders around you.

"Stop grinning, cadets! Do you think this is supposed to be fun?"

Your cadets hesitate a moment.

Then you burst out laughing. "Of course it is! Now let's give those Lowlanders a slider farewell!"

"Woot, Woot!" the cadets yell. "Woot, Woot, Woot!"

By the time your caravan is reorganized, the Lowlanders have disappeared and you have the valley to yourselves again. It's time to proceed towards your destination. You cross your fingers and hope for an uneventful afternoon.

But after sliding for less than an hour a miner, who's been looking through his scope, yells "Stop! There's something strange going on."

Once again you order the troop to a halt and pull out your scope.

Then you see what the miner is pointing at. There is an eerie light coming from a split in the side of a small rocky outcrop about 200 yards up the slope to your left.

"What's that glow?" you ask the miner. "Is it light reflecting off blue diamonds, do you think?"

At the mention of diamonds, everyone is scrabbling for their scopes.

The miner shakes his head. "I don't think so. It could be tyranium crystals, but it would have to be a pretty big deposit to glow so brightly."

Whatever it is, it isn't normal. Could it be a Lowland trap? You look up at the sky and calculate the time left before dewfall. There is just enough time to investigate, but you will be cutting it fine.

It is time to make a decision. Do you:

Go investigate what is causing the blue light? **P268**

Or

Keep going and forget about the blue light? **P272**

Go investigate what is causing the blue light.

"Get a cable launcher set up," you tell a couple of miners. "Dagma, you and I will investigate. Gagnon, stay here with the rest of the troop."

"Shall we get our catapults ready?" Gagnon asks. "Just in case?"

"Good idea. But be ready to take off in a hurry if something happens or Dagma and I get captured."

There is a buzz of voices as you and Dagma adjust your harnesses in preparation for a quick ride up to the outcrop.

Within minutes the two of you are zipping towards the eerie glow. As you climb, you see moon moths flitting about.

"Those moths are acting strangely," Dagma says.

The higher you climb the more moths you see. They are congregating around the crack in the rock.

"Moths are always attracted to the light," you say.

Dagma shakes her head. "But look at the patterns they are forming. They're like mini tornadoes."

Dagma is right. The moths are swirling funnels of iridescent blue, the bottom tip of which points down into the crack.

The zipper cuts out when you and Dagma reach the end of the cable. You unclip and slide your way over to the hole in the rock. As usual, Dagma rushes ahead.

Never have you seen so many moon moths in one place.

"I can squeeze through," Dagma says.

Before you can say "wait" she's disappeared into the opening.

Then you hear her laughing.

Of all the cadets in your troop, Dagma is the least jovial. Normally to get her laughing, someone has to break a leg or step in pango poo.

It's hard to believe it's actually her cackling away.

At the opening, you push your head through the swarm of swirling moths and look in. As soon as you do, you realize the crack is actually the opening to a large cave that extends quite some distance into the hillside. Due to the many moon moths, it is almost as bright inside as it is outside.

You hear laughter again. This time it's above you. You look up and see Dagma and a hundred or more moon moths. They have picked her up and are swooping around the cave with her dangling in mid air. Others are fluttering around, tickling her under the chin and spraying a fine mist into her face.

Dagma is laughing and woot-wooting like she's been drinking fermented fruit broth.

"Isn't this great?" Dagma yells. "Look I'm flying!"

Dagma is flying all right. What are those moths spraying into her face?

It isn't long before you find out. You were so busy watching Dagma swooping around that you didn't feel a bunch of moths grab onto the fabric of your uniform and lift you off your feet.

When you open your mouth in surprise, moths spray a slightly sweet mist into your mouth.

Instantly you relax. It's as if flying is the most natural thing in the world.

The moon moths are taking you deeper and deeper into the cave.

"Where are we going?" you ask Dagma.

"I don't know, but I don't care. This is so much fun!"

It isn't until you hear a familiar scurrying, and the gnashing of teeth that you start to worry.

"I hear morph rats," you tell Dagma.

"Me too. Woot woot! Here ratty, ratty."

Is this the Dagma you know? What has got into her? Here ratty ratty? Is she nuts?

Then you see where the moon moths are taking you. This is their breeding chamber. Hundreds of slender transparent tubes hang from the roof of the cave. Inside each tube you can see a dozen or so moth larva. On the floor of the cave below the tubes, morph rats are piling up on top of each other in an attempt to reach the baby moths.

"I think they want us to save their babies," Dagma says. "Look!"

You turn to where Dagma is pointing and see fifty or so moon moths picking up morph rats and dropping them into a pit at one side of the cave, but more rats are entering the cave than the moths can't deal with.

"Have you got a screecher?" you ask Dagma.

She reaches for her utility belt. "Just the one."

"Let it rip," you say. "We'll just have to plug our ears."

You pull two plugs from your utility belt and stuff one in each ear, then nod to Dagma.

Even with the earplugs, the screecher is loud. But loud for you is unbearable for the morph rats. It's only seconds before they start rushing from the chamber like their lives depend on it.

As you hover above, it's like watching water run down a plughole as the rats swirl around and dive into the pit to escape the sound of the screecher. In less than a minute, all that remains is the smell of fart.

A swarm of moths flutter about your face, ticking you under the chin and around your ears. Both you and Dagma are laughing now.

"We'd better get going," you tell Dagma. Dewfall isn't far away.

Dagma gives you a big smile. "These moths will hatch out in the next day or two. It would be a pity if the rats came back and ate them all. Maybe I should stay and protect them?"

You think about what Dagma has said. It must be the mist, Dagma usually only worries about herself. A couple days with the moths would probably do her good.

"Maybe I could train them to fly me places?" Dagma says. "Wouldn't that be good for the Slider Corps?"

She's right. Trained moths would be an amazing advantage. Imagine swooping over the slippery slopes without being reliant on needle boots and guide sticks.

"Okay, come back down to the sledges and get what you need. I'm sure there are a few extra screechers around somewhere. While you're here, try to find the spot where the rats are getting in and plug up the hole. Then the moths will be okay next year."

Dagma nods enthusiastically. "I think I saw some tyranium crystals when the moths were flying me around too. I'll try to collect them and bring them down when I come back to the Pillars of Haramon."

Ten minutes later, Dagma is heading back up to the chamber, armed with four screechers and a pack full of supplies. She still has a big smile on her face, possibly from the moth mist, or maybe it's just that for the first time in her life she's actually let herself have some fun.

[some years later]

"And did Dagma get back to the Pillars of Haramon okay Grandee?"

You adjust your grandchild on your knee and ruffle their hair.

"She sure did. Not only did she come back, she brought some pet moths with her. She was always happy after that and used to tell the funniest jokes ever. She's the reason Highlanders say, "What a dag", when something's funny.

"Geebus! Really? They named a word after her?"

"They sure did. Maybe one day we'll slide over and pay her a visit."

Well done. You've reached the end of this part of the story, but have you tried all the different endings? You now have another decision to make. Do you:

Go back to the beginning and try a different path? **P219**

Or

Go to the list of choices and start reading from another part of the story? **P381**

Keep going and forget about the blue light.

As interesting as the light is, getting to the Pillars of Haramon before dewfall is more important. You can always come back when you've got more time and less responsibility.

After getting everyone lined up and ready to move out again, you have a feeling in your gut that there might be more Lowlanders about.

"Dagma," you say. "It might be a good idea if you to take the lead for a while. I'd rather we have our best and strongest cadets at the front.

Dagma loves being out in front. She moves forward.

"On my mark, two, one..." Dagma yells, wasting no time in pushing off.

The only thing Dagma loves more than being in front is going fast. Everyone in the troop is fully concentrating on the sledge in front just to keep up with her breakneck pace.

It's not until you notice your shadow is in front of you, rather than on your left where it should be, that you realize Dagma, in her haste, has taken a wrong turn and led you down a side valley.

"Stop!" you yell out. "You're going the wrong way!"

You pull out a map, and spread it out on top of the sledge's cover.

Gagnon slides over to have a look too.

You point to an area on the map that is littered with crevasses. It is directly between you and your destination.

"Pango poo!" Gagnon says, "I should have been paying more attention. Now we've got to climb all the way back up to where we missed the turn, or find a way through the crevasse field."

You pull out your scope and focus on the crevasses.

"They don't look too bad," you say to Gagnon. "Maybe we should try to cut across rather than go all the way back up. We'll never make it to safety before dewfall if we do that."

"The field isn't properly mapped," Gagnon say. "But, if we take it slow..."

You look at the sun sinking towards the horizon. It's either that or camp in the open.

"Let's do it," you say. "Single file, Gagnon take the lead."

For twenty minutes Gagnon leads your troop in a weaving course through the jumbled field of crevasses and ridges. At times the sledges are perfectly safe with lots of room for maneuvering, at others you're right on the edge looking straight down hundreds of feet.

It's one of these scary times, when you're squeezing between two deep fissures, with little room to spare, that you see a glint of something down in the crevasse. You give the signal to stop and carefully work your way nearer the edge.

It looks like something made of metal, but you need to get closer to see it properly.

Taking an anchor bolt, you fire into the rock and clip yourself on. Very slowly, you lean out over the edge and peer down into the yawning crack.

A first you can't quite tell what you're seeing. Then as your eyes adjust to the light, you realize you're seeing the back half of a spaceship. The front must be embedded in the rock, or missing altogether. The ships skin is covered in metallic scales that remind you of pango feathers. A series of portholes run down the ship's side. Near the rear, just in front of a large thruster, is an open portal.

You've seen drawings of ships like this in the story books your family use to read you when you were a child. But you always thought that the tales of the first Petronians arriving in spaceships were just myths.

This could be a great historical discovery.

"Grab me that cable launcher," you say to the nearest cadet. "We need to investigate this."

It doesn't take long before you've rigged up a sling so you can safely make your way across the cable to the ship.

The ship is much larger that it looks from the small portion sticking out of the rock. Rows of cryogenic sleep chambers line the walls and stretch off into the gloom.

You hear a scraping on the metal floor behind you. It's a wide-eyed Gagnon looking around.

"Wow this thing is amazing," he says.

You nod in agreement. "We'll make camp here tonight. Let's get the troop to tether the sledges and come across to the ship."

Gagnon looks around at all the empty sleep chambers. "Good idea. There's certainly no shortage of beds."

Once everyone is safely across, some of the cadets set up a burner and heat broth. Others wander around the ship gawking at all the controls and pipes and wires and other equipment.

"Geebus," Piver says. "So, all the stories are true. Petronians did come from another planet."

You look at the funny little miner and smile. "It certainly looks that way."

Piver scratches his head and wander over to a row of symbols on the wall. He stares a moment and then turns to you. "I wonder what this says and why they came all this way?"

You walk over and trace the unfamiliar symbols with your finger. *Victoria* LIFERAFT ELEVEN - PLANET EARTH 2108. "Yeah I wonder."

Congratulations, you have reached the end of this part of the story. You have made an historical discovery that could change the history of your people.

It is time to make another decision. Do you:

Go back to the beginning of the story and try another path? **P219**

Or

Go to the list of choices and start reading from another part of the story? **P381**

You have decided to go to mining school.

Members of your family have joined the Highland Slider Corps for generations, but you have always wanted to become a miner and go prospecting. It's not that you don't respect your family's traditions. It's just that the idea of hunting for blue diamonds fills you with excitement. Ever since your first science class at school, geology has fascinated you. You even dream of finding blue diamonds. Besides, miners get to play with all the best equipment.

Maybe you'll go prospecting around an active volcanic vent and look for tyranium needle crystals. Although risky, the rewards can be great. After all, where would the Highlanders be without crystals to provide grip on the slopes?

Maybe you'll dig for diamonds. How would a slider's guide stick work without a diamond hook for stopping? How would the communities bore tunnels in the nearly impregnable black rock to create hydroponic growing chambers and secure sleeping and defense pods?

You've always felt mining technology has been responsible for keeping the Highlands free. Sure, the Slider Corps protect the communities and keep them safe from attack by the Lowlanders, but without the blue diamonds and needle crystals, the Highland communities could never have been built in the first place. Were it not for miners, the only inhabitants of the Black Slopes would be colonies of red-beaked pangos, cave-dwelling moon moths, and feral packs of egg-eating morph rats.

For the first year at mining school, you've studied mineralogy, mine construction and planning, mechanical engineering, and safety procedures. You've learned how to operate the diamond bores needed to grind through the layers of dense black glass to get at the diamonds hidden in the rock below. You've learned about cable launchers, exploration methods, volcanism and geology as well as mathematics and mining history. Every possible technique has been drilled into you.

Soon you'll be going on your first field trip to test your newfound knowledge. On this trip you'll receive practical instruction on how to distinguish between areas that contain diamonds from those that don't, as well as learn how to get at them.

You've been packing you sledge all morning next to a boy named Piver who keeps cracking jokes. He is the only other person at mining school that comes from a slider family and because of that, the two of you have become friends.

Your sledges will carry a boring machine, lubricant, drills, blasters, rock screws, diamond picks as well as food, personal gear and other equipment.

"Where do you find a morph rat with no legs?" Piver asks you as he throws a cover over his load.

"I don't know. Where?"

"Exactly where you left it."

You shoot a look in Piver's direction and shake your head and groan. "That was so bad."

Piver chuckles anyway.

As the two of you finish securing your loads, you hear Piver giggling at something under his breath. He's a strange one, but you'd far rather be around someone who's laughing than a grump any day. And you must admit his silliness makes the time pass.

Each sledge weighs over two hundred pounds by the time it is fully packed and takes a crew of two or three sliders to maneuver it safely around the Black Slopes.

Linked transport, using slider guides, is really the only way to get around safely. Mining expeditions have tried going solo, but accidents are common and many end up crashing to the bottom. It is far safer with an escort.

Your group is heading off to the volcanic rim of Glass Mountain, an area rich in tyranium needle crystals, not far from the Pillars of Haramon.

"OK students, listen up," one of your instructors says. "You'll be leaving in an hour so make sure you've got everything on your checklist packed and tied down securely."

You look at the long list in your hand. There are so many things.

The instructor looks sternly at the group, making sure everyone is listening. "Now I have an announcement to make. Every mining expedition needs a leader so we are going to appoint one of you to be in charge of your group."

There is a hum of voices as the students speculate on who it will be.

The instructor walks over and looks you in the eyes. "Are you up for it?"

This has come as a big surprise. "I think so, sir," you reply.

"Good. You've been our top student this term so trust your instincts and work with your slider escort. I'm sure you'll do fine. The rest of you, follow your leader's instruction."

Piver comes over and slaps you on the back. "Congrats."

But the instructor hasn't finished. "Make sure you keep your picks and anchor guns close at hand. Not only is rain a possibility, there have been sightings of Lowland scouts in the last few weeks. You'll need to be ready to help your escort if required."

The thought of coming across Lowlanders while prospecting takes some of the fun out of the expedition and being the leader increases your responsibility even more.

Fifteen minutes later, a group of thirty sliders arrive. You are introduced to the lead slider and the two of you discuss the trip. You do a quick tour of the sledges and make sure each of the miners has packed properly and then return to double check your own.

Three sliders come over to your sledge. Two of them attach their harnesses to the front and one attaches to the back. The slider at the back introduces herself as Shoola. She's a strong looking girl in her late teens. You can see the muscles in her legs and arms through her close fitting uniform.

"You can climb aboard now," Shoola tells you. "We're about to head up the first tow."

You climb on top of the sledge and hook your boots under a strap, another you clip around your waist like a belt. These will keep you from falling off as the sledge is dragged up the steep towpath.

The sliders lock their boots into a stable sliding platform with a short metal bar that slides out the sole of their left boot and attaches to a notch near the instep of their right. Shoola, at the back of your sledge, will act as the team's brake.

As the front sliders get ready to clamp onto the tow, they stand with knees slightly bent. One positioned on either side of the quickly moving cable.

You look up the towline. A faint purple mist shrouds your view to the top. The low sun creates a light show as its rays reflect off the shiny, black rock.

"On my mark," the head slider calls out. "Three, two, one, go!"

The two front sliders throw their cable-clamps over the towline and squeeze down on its handle. As the clamps grip, the slack goes out of the strap running between the clamp and the sliders' harnesses. There is a short jerk, and the sledge starts moving.

The acceleration up the slope is exhilarating. You feel your abdominal muscles tighten in an attempt to keep yourself sitting upright. When you look back down the hillside, past Shoola, you see the other sledges racing up the towpath behind you.

"Yippee!" you yell. "What a ride!"

Up and up you climb until you enter the mist. The view disappears and the temperature drops. You reach for your flask and take a few gulps of hot broth. You secure the flask and grab a couple hard-boiled pango eggs to munch on. Turning around, you show an egg to Shoola. She nods and rubs her stomach. Tossing an egg in her direction, she deftly catches it one handed while easily keeping her balance and takes a bite.

Finally, your group emerges from the mist and you see a large motorized wheel whirling the cable around its belly and sending it back down the mountain.

The two sliders at the front of your sledge prepare to release their tow clamps and dismount. Shoola gets her guide stick into position, ready to drag its diamond hook to slow you all down.

You come to a screeching stop on a flat platform cut into the side of the mountain. Before the next group arrives, your group uses their sticks to push the sledge along a short path towards the bottom of the next tow.

While you wait for the sliders to clamp on to the next cable, you look around at the scenery. Now that you are above the mist the air is clear. You can see a long way. To the west and east, a towering range of mountains extend as far as you can see. To the north a braided river delta protrudes into a turquoise sea. On the flatlands, crops create a patchwork of green, yellow, orange and red, and wisps of smoke from cooking fires drift on the light breeze. Behind you, to the south, the slope keeps rising up towards the jagged skyline.

You are brought back to the present when you hear a slider start the countdown as they get ready to head up the next tow. Moments later you're off in a blur, rocketing higher up the mountain.

After repeating this process three times on three different tows, the training center has disappeared far below.

From the top of the last tow, your group turns to the west and takes a narrow path along the ridge. This will lead you to a slightly wider traverse path across an exposed face into the head of the next valley.

Once in this new valley, it should be a simple slide down to the next series of tows some seventeen miles away.

As you slide along, you dream of diamonds, sparkling, blue and translucent. You wonder if you'll be a success or if you'll go broke and end up back in your home community growing hydro. After all, if diamonds were that easy to find, everyone would be out looking.

By the time you reach the next tow, your backside is sore from sitting on the sledge. You are looking forward to getting off, stretching your legs, and having some food.

Off to your left, on the far side of the valley, is a sheer cliff dotted with bore holes. Specks of light flicker and flit about in the various openings.

You point. "Look, moon moths!"

"Wow, there must be a lot of them for us to see them from way over here." Shoola says.

You pull out your scope and take a closer look, but even through the high-power lens you can't make out much detail being so far away. It's at night that the moon moths really shine. Their wings absorb sunlight and then at night their wings give off a shimmering blue glow.

Miners often capture moon moths and put them in little cages to use as a light source when their battery supplies run low. But you hate the idea of caging these beautiful creatures. It seems cruel somehow.

"Meal break," the lead slider says as the sledges pull up at the bottom of the next tow. "We leave in half an hour, so get some broth in you while you have a chance."

"And don't forget to tether your sledges," you say to the other miners, as you unbuckle yourself, climb down, and hook on to an anchor. "This ground may look flat but the slightest slope and anything not securely tethered will be off and away before you can say "Woosho.""

Once you're happy with your tether, you test out your needle boots. Unlike the sliders who are used to moving around the slopes, and have diamond spurs permanently fitted to their heels, your boots have far less grip so you need to be careful.

You eat some dried hydro and drink a cup of broth, and then start doing a few squats to stretch out your tight muscles.

Piver comes over and starts stretching next to you. As you exercise, you watch the humming cable disappear up the slope.

"This one looks even steeper than the last," you say.

Piver gives an excited jiggle. "I was talking to one of the sliders. He reckoned it's the longest tow in all of Petron. One thousand nine hundred vertical feet gained in less than fifteen minutes. Nearly a one in one gradient, no platforms, just straight up!" Piver's enthusiasm is contagious.

"Wow, that is steep," you say.

"See you at the top," Piver says. "It's all downhill from there."

You give him a thumbs-up and then start checking the straps on your sledge just in case something's come loose during the morning's run.

As you finish cinching the last belt, the lead slider clears his throat. "OK, everyone, mount up. We've still got some miles to cover before dark."

Just as you are about to climb onto your sledge a voice yells out.

"Take cover! Lowlanders!"

You and Piver duck down behind your sledges just as a small group of Lowlanders carrying a white flag come into view.

Off to your right the lead slider is forming his troop into an attacking formation.

Piver looks at you. "They're carrying a white flag. Why are the sliders getting ready to attack? As leader, aren't you going to say something?"

It is time to make a quick decision. Do you:

Encourage the sliders to attack the Lowlanders? **P324**

Or

Yell out for the sliders not to attack so you can find out what the Lowlanders have to say? **P331**

Put extra safety precautions in place after the accident.

Hindsight is a wonderful thing, but anyone can look back. Sliders are supposed to plan ahead so accidents don't happen in the first place. You should have known that one cadet on the back of a heavy sledge wouldn't be enough to control its speed.

Dagma stays silent, but by the scowl on her face you can tell she has a poor opinion of your leadership. Not that you can blame her.

"New formation," you say. "Two cadets at the back of each sledge. We need more braking power."

Why didn't you do this from the beginning? If you had, you wouldn't have lost a full sledge of valuable supplies.

"I take full responsibility," you say. "But we can't let this get in the way of completing our mission."

Dagma can't help herself. "So we're going to go slow now are we? How is getting caught in the rain going to help our safety record?"

"Better to arrive a bit late than not at all," you say. "Besides, there's no sign of rain at the moment."

"At the moment…" Dagma mumbles while kicking her sledge with the toe of her boot.

Yes, choosing the fast route was a mistake. But learning from your mistakes is how one gains experience. You're not too proud to admit you were wrong and change your methods.

"Everyone is going to have to keep an eye out for Lowlanders now that we're all harnessed up," you tell the cadets. "It's a setback, but we have to keep positive."

Dagma starts to comment. "Knowing our luck we'll…"

"Enough, Dagma!" you snap.

Dagma looks at the ground and grinds her teeth, but she stays quiet.

You look back to the other cadets. "Get ready to move out. We need to keep going if we're going to make the Pillars of Haramon by dewfall."

Even the bright and usually cheerful Gagnon looks a little shaken.

"Gagnon, you'd better stay out in front. We can't afford to have our navigator in harness."

Gagnon nods.

"In fact, why don't you extend out a bit. Signal with your guide stick if you hit a tricky section, then the rest of us will be ready for it."

You tell the miner whose sledge was lost to climb aboard yours then give the signal to slide. "Remember, eyes front and hooks ready."

Gagnon takes off down the track. The rest of the group follows. The other miners sit nervously, eyes wide, watching the track, but helpless to do anything.

You know that before long you will come to the most technical part of the journey, a series of steep switchbacks, known as Zigzag Drop.

The new combinations are working well. At least now, if one of the lead sliders slip, there are two others to stop the sledge and allow their fallen comrade time to regain their feet.

As you crest the broad ridge that leads onto the steep face of Mt Transor, and the start of Zigzag Drop, you call a brief halt.

The slope in front of you is dark and foreboding. Its black surface gives it the appearance of being smooth … if only that were the case.

A well worn track, cut into the rock, and used by Highlanders over the centuries, runs like a ribbon back and forth down the hill. You can't believe how narrow it looks from the top.

On a plateau far below, a jumble of sharp ridges and crevasses, the results of a backwash of superheated black glass when the mountains were first formed, look dangerous enough to weaken the knees of even the most experienced Highland slider.

Going over the edge here would be fatal.

"Cadets, let's take this real easy," you say. "Scrape the mountainside with your loads if need be, the further you are from the edge the better. If a single runner goes over here, you'll be heading towards the bottom before you have time to correct. Believe me, if there was ever a time you don't want to be free sliding, this is it."

You are about to wave your arm for everyone to move out when you remember the wise words of one of your instructors. He spoke of leading by example. Now might be a time to do just that.

After unclipping your harness, you move forward, past the other sledges, until you reach the first in line. You put your hand on the front cadet's shoulder. "I'll take the lead sledge down. You go and take my spot at the rear."

The cadet breathes a sigh of relief and wastes no time unclipping his harness.

You connect to the steering runners on the front sledge and wave your arm. "Okay, let's move. Steady as we go. Cadets at the back, keep your hooks down. I don't want to be moving at anything more than walking pace until we get to the bottom."

You can feel the sledge wanting to take off, but whenever the speed builds, you turn the runners inward and let the overhanging bundle of mining equipment scrape the slope. This, and the heavy braking from the cadets at the rear, seems to be keeping the load under control … so far anyway.

The screech of diamond hooks on rock sounds like a flock of angry pangos fighting for scraps.

Before long you've traversed across the width of the face. The first switchback is coming up. You lift the toe of your front boot and dig a heel spur into the rock. The front of the sledge presses against your backside. You can hear hooks digging deep behind you as the sledge slows even more.

Just before you reach the apex of the turn, you stab the needle end of your guide stick into the slope and kick both heels, pushing firmly to your left. The nose of the sledge responds, its runners grip, and the cumbersome load slowly swings around the hairpin. Once safely past the corner you realize you've been holding your breath and suck gulps of fresh cool air.

"One down and thirteen to go," you mumble to no one in

particular.

The second turn has been cut deeper into the rock leaving a knee-high barrier between you and the edge, but as soon as you are around the corner, the edge and the void beyond reappear. One hundred feet down the steep face, you see the track coming back the other way.

Sweat trickles down your forehead. A quick glance over your shoulder reveals the clenched jaws and wide eyes of the cadets behind you. You try to control your breathing. In through your nose and out through your mouth, slow and easy.

You were hoping the switchbacks would get easier as you went along, but that isn't the case. If anything they get harder. Your nerves jangle even more as you approach each new switchback. Your knees tremble. Some of the tremors are a result of the physical strain of sliding downhill, of holding back the weight of the sledge, but mostly your knees tremble in fear.

An instructor once told you that bravery isn't about not being afraid, it's about doing something despite your fear. Now that you're half way down the face … brave or not you've got no option but to continue.

When you finally round the last switchback you breathe a sigh of relief and raise your arm, signaling everyone to stop. "Once we get around these crevasses we'll have a proper break."

After a brief rest, Gagnon leads off once more. Ten minutes later you come to a halt on a flattish area beyond the crevasse field.

You give the order for the miners to tether their sledges. "Well done everyone. Let's break out the hydro and light the burners. I don't know about you, but I could do with a cup of hot broth."

Gagnon and Dagma fill their cups and come to sit beside you as you drink.

"I'm pleased that's over," you say. "That was tough."

Gagnon smiles. Color has returned to his face. "Now it's just the run down Long Gully and we'll be at the Pillars."

"We should go back to one brakeman per sledge," Dagma says. "If we're going to run across Lowlanders, Long Gully is where it's most likely to happen. Having all the cadets in harness will make us too slow to react. We should send a scouting party ahead of the main group as a precaution."

Gagnon shakes his head. "The sledges are too heavy. Why don't we double-sledge? With two sledges linked together we could get by with three cadets at the back. That way we can move fast but still have 50 percent extra braking power when we need it."

Dagma's head is nodding in agreement. "And we'll still have some spare cadets to scout ahead for trouble," she says.

You like Gagnon's idea. "Sounds like a good compromise. You're the strongest Dagma, would you like to choose another three cadets and lead the advanced team?"

Dagma seems surprised at your display of confidence. "What should we do if we come across Lowlanders?"

"Assess their numbers. If there's only a couple, try to capture them. That way Command can question them once we reach the Pillars of Haramon. If there are more than two, wait for the rest of us to arrive. No point in taking unnecessary chances."

Dagma calls out the names of the cadets she wants for her advanced team.

"Don't get too far in front, Dagma. Remember our goal is getting everyone to the Pillars in one piece. Let's not make any more mistakes, okay?"

Dagma gives you a funny look. "Have I made any mistakes today?"

She's right … you're the one who's made mistakes. A good leader has to trust their team members. You'll never gain her respect if you don't trust her.

"No, and that's why you're in charge of the scouting party. You're one of the best scouts we've got."

Dagma stands a little taller with the compliment. The hint of a smile crosses her face for the first time today.

"Okay everyone, listen up. Dagma and her team are going to scout

out front. Let's get these sledges reorganized. We've got to get to the Pillars before dewfall, and that means we need to get moving. Gagnon you act as guide for the rear group."

"Let's go," Dagma says, turning to her scouts.

Within a few minutes, Dagma's group are little more than charcoal dots on a black landscape.

The rest of the cadets are quick to reconfigure the sledges into pairs, a short cable linking them, one behind the other. One cadet clips on to the front of the front sledge and three cadets clip on to the back of the second sledge.

Long Gully is a slightly twisted half-pipe a quarter of a mile wide and sixty miles long. The idea is for the sledges to swoop back and forth down the valley in big sweeping S-turns using the natural contours of the gully to change direction and keep the sledges from gaining too much speed.

This part of the trip, assuming no Lowlanders are spotted, should be high-speed fun with little risk.

But things in the Highlands, are rarely simple, and never without an element of danger. To the south clouds are forming, pushing their way up the mountains from the interior. As the warm air rises, much of the moisture it contains fall as rain on the southern side of the divide but, unknown to you, some of the rain has crept over to the north and has begun to fall on the slopes high above you.

The first hint of danger is a trickle of water streaking the black rock on the far side of Long Gully. The water reflects silver in the afternoon light and is only a few yards wide, but there is no way you could run sledges through it without losing control.

Luckily one side of Long Gully is slightly lower than the other. By sticking to the high side your group can continue to travel. But, depending on how much rain falls on the upper slopes, you know this harmless looking trickle could spread and become a deadly torrent in a short space of time. Once that happens, wherever you are, you'll have no option but to find a place to anchor yourself and ride it out until it's safe to move off again.

You wonder if Dagma and her scouts have seen the danger. If so, they should have stopped by now, but there is no sign of them. Where could they be?

You signal the troop to a halt. "We need to find a safe place to anchor," you say raising your arm and pointing towards the rapidly widening stream. "That water is spreading."

The other cadets are chattering nervously between themselves.

Gagnon slides over to your position. "According to the map, there are some abandoned mine shafts about a mile down the valley. If we keep left we should be able to make it to them before the water spreads to this side."

There is no time to wait. You must make up your mind quickly.

"Everyone follow Gagnon. We need to get to shelter right now," you order.

Gagnon pushes off and does a series of shallow turns, keeping to the left-hand side of the valley. The rest of you follow. The water is spreading as new rivulets form. The water isn't that deep, but it doesn't have to be deep to be dangerous on the Black Slopes of Petron.

"There they are!" a cadet yells out. "I see the portals!"

Gagnon has seen them too. With a stab of his stick, he pushes towards a pair of narrow entrances cut into the slope of the half-pipe.

Some old scaffolding, once used by miners prospecting for tyranium needle crystals, is bolted onto the rock nearby, but there is no sign of current habitation.

"Hurry!" you shout to Gagnon. The water is nearly here."

Gagnon points his front foot at the portal and pushes harder with his stick. You look behind and see that new streams are forming across the slope. It is going to be a close call.

When Gagnon disappears into the hillside, you breathe a sigh of relief. The rest of you are right behind him. As long as there are no surprises in the tunnel, your troop will be fine.

"Tether your sledges everyone, we could be in for a long wait."

Once you've secured your sledge, you have time to look around. When you look up, it's like looking at the night sky. Moon moths have taken over. After admiring their beauty, you turn to look back outside.

The clouds have rolled in from higher up the mountain. Now, misty rain is falling and the far side of the gully has disappeared altogether. Water rushes downhill, following the contours of the ground. Small rivulets join together to form torrents.

Where is Dagma? Are she and her group of cadets still out in this weather?

They must have anchored themselves to the hill somewhere further down. If they haven't found shelter somewhere, they will be in for an unpleasant night out in the open.

Then you hear a hollow sounding voice echoing from further along the tunnel.

"What kept you?" It's Dagma and her scouts. "Didn't you see the water coming?"

Typical of Dagma to boast.

"You did have a head start remember. I thought I told you not to get too far in front."

"We've been investigating," Dagma says, changing the subject. "There's a side tunnel that runs downhill. It could lead towards the Pillars. Maybe we should go that way?"

Gagnon pulls out his map. "It's an old tunnel that comes out a mile above the Pillars, but it's miles long and over a hundred years old. Who knows what condition it's in."

"I think we should try it out," Dagma says. "Otherwise we're stuck here doing nothing until the slopes dry. Boring!"

You're not a big fan of sitting around either. It would be great to get closer to the Pillars. Then your troop won't have so far to go once the rain lets up. Command did say the equipment was urgent.

But old tunnels can deteriorate over time, and they get colonized by morph rats. How do you know if it is safe? You also know that earthquakes still rumble from time to time as the molten core tries to force its way to the surface.

It is time to make a decision. Do you:

Try to get closer to the Pillars by going down the tunnel? **P291**

Or

Stay put and wait for the slopes to dry before proceeding to the Pillars? **P293**

You have decided to go down the tunnel.

Moon moths light your way down the tunnel for the first mile or so, but as you and your troop get further into the tunnel, the moon moths become less frequent.

Before long you are forced to strap on headlamps so you can see where you're going. Slender veins of tyranium crystals streak through the black rock and make patterns along the walls as you slide.

Gagnon is back in the lead, with Dagma and her scouts close behind. The rest of your troop is sliding in formation behind them. In parts of the tunnel the slope is steep, requiring the dragging of hooks. Screeches fill your ears as they echo down the tunnel.

At first, you don't notice the trickle of water as it creeps down the tunnel behind you.

With every drop the rock you are sliding on becomes slicker. You need to put in an anchor bolt, and quickly. But to do that, you need to be stopped. All you can do at the moment is lean down on your hook and hope the ground levels out.

The rear sledges, caught by the water, are sliding faster than those in front. You hear a yell behind you. With moisture underfoot, nobody can slow down. You hear the sound of sledges colliding. Another cadet yells as she is knocked from her feet.

Will Gagnon and Dagma realize what is going on in time and be able to put in an anchor to stop the rest of you from sliding uncontrolled to the bottom of the tunnel in a jumble of bodies and equipment?

"Emergency anchors!" you yell at the top of your voice.

But it is too late. Water is rushing down the tunnel.

The sledge behind you smacks into your back and knocks you off your feet. You've made a huge mistake. Now your entire troop is heading towards the bottom of the tunnel in an uncontrolled slide.

Unfortunately, this part of your story is over. It was a poor decision to take your group down the old tunnel without checking it first. If you had, you would have discovered the tunnel had been damaged by earthquakes and that water would leak into it from the surface.

With luck some of your cadet might survive the pile-up at the bottom, but for you this part of your story has come to an end. Would you choose differently next time?

It is now time for you to make another decision. Do you:

Go back to the beginning of the story and try another path? **P219**

Or

Go back to your last decision and make the other choice? **P293**

Wait for the slopes to dry rather than go down the tunnel.

"We may as well light a burner and have some broth," you say to the cadets. "Who knows how long it will be before we can head out."

The others waste no time in getting a makeshift kitchen organized. A thin boy with blond hair comes to where you are sitting and hands you a steaming cup.

"Thanks," you say, leaning back against your pack and looking up as you sip. Hundreds of glowing moon moths hang from the ceiling

After finishing your broth you close your eyes and try to sleep.

The rain continues for the rest of the afternoon and most of the night. When you wake up and look outside it is just getting light. As the temperature rises, and the sun sneaks over the ridge, vapor rises from the black rock.

Thankfully, the sky is clear with no further sign of cloud.

"Okay everyone, the slopes are drying fast. We should be able to move out in less than an hour. Get some food into you and then get these sledges turned around and ready to go."

Everyone is keen to get moving again, especially Dagma, who helps light the burner and gives the other cadets a hand passing out broth and dried hydro.

"There might be a few damp patches on the slope, so let's hook up with two brakes per sledge," you say. "We don't want any accidents so close to the Pillars."

"But what about scouts?" Dagma says, disappointed to be back in harness.

You shake your head. "I doubt any Lowlanders will be left on the slope after that downpour. Better we play it safe."

Dagma shrugs and finds a spot at the back on one of the sledges.

When you feel the slopes have dried enough, you turn to Gagnon. "Shall we get out of here?"

The morning air is cool and clear, but already you can feel the warmth of the rock beneath you. Whatever dust was in the air has been washed away by the rain. You can see so far it's amazing.

The braided river delta far below sparkles like a diamond necklace. The ocean and horizon beyond seem closer somehow. Twenty miles further down Long Gully, you can just see the tops of the Pillars of Haramon poking above the surrounding terrain.

Gagnon pushes off and leads the group on a swooping path that takes you up one side of the valley and then across to the other.

You smile as you slide, the wind in your face, whipping at your hair. This is what you like best about being a Highland slider. It's the feeling you get as you race down a mountainside, the whole world spread out before you. It's being part of a group that will do anything to keep you safe and knowing you will do the same in return. It's the way a slider can use gravity to move with grace and speed with so little effort. It's the closest thing to soaring you've ever felt.

Before you know it, your troop is screeching to a stop outside the main portal of the northernmost pillar.

An officer is there to greet you. "Well done, cadets," he says. "Welcome to the Pillars of Haramon."

Congratulations, you have made it to the Pillars of Haramon. You've brought much needed supplies and equipment that will help keep your communities safe from the Lowlanders. This part of your mission is complete. But have you tried all the different paths the story can take? Have you gone mining? Fought off morph rats? Discovered the moon moths' secret?

It is time to make another decision. Do you:

Go back to the beginning of the story and try another path? **P219**

Or

Go to the List of Choices and start reading from another part of the story? **P381**

You have decided to make best speed.

"Keep an extra sharp lookout everyone," you say, before giving the order to move out.

You look over your shoulder. Back up the valley, clouds are beginning to boil over the upper slopes from the south. Scouting ahead takes time. Getting down the slope quickly makes more sense. At the tow base you will find shelter from both the elements and any Lowlanders that might be lurking.

The base you're heading towards is built deep within the rock face. Its defensive positions overlook the slopes, making approach from below by any attacking force difficult.

You've seen pictures of Tow-Base 9's defenses in the cadet training manuals. Once the sun's rays shine into the valley, the base is almost unassailable. Mounted in strategic positions are a number of dish-shaped lenses that can focus the burning rays of the sun onto any intruder foolish enough to attack. Like a magnifying glass, this concentrated beam will fry anything it touches faster than pango egg on a burner's plate.

After dewfall in the early evening and until the slopes dry the next day, moisture makes movement almost impossible for the Lowlanders, who lack high quality needle crystals, and the other hardware needed to traverse the slope in anything but the best possible conditions.

The tow's rotating wheel is protected by huge blocks of black glass on its three exposed sides, leaving only a narrow slit, on the uphill side, open to allow the towline an unobstructed run up the towpath to the ridge above.

The Highland Slider Corps have placed this base with precision. Any attack would have to be late enough in the day for the dew to have evaporated, but be staged prior to the sun shining into the valley when the Highlanders can focus their burning disks, a window of less than an hour each day.

As you slide, you wonder what the Lowlanders had been planning.

You suspect they were trying to circle around and get above the base. That way they could mount a surprise attack from above. It's just as well your troop showed up. Lowlanders in control of the tow would have been a disaster for the Slider Corps.

Now is not the time to think about your success, you tell yourself. You need to keep your mind on your current task. But with the amazing views off to the north, it's hard to focus. You try to imagine the awesome forces that formed this place — the rumbling earthquakes, and massive lava flows. Despite the seriousness of the situation, you can't help but smile. After all, your love of nature was the main reason you became a slider.

As you travel down, you notice the terrain on both sides of the valley is getting steeper. On one part of the slope, a number of slender volcanic columns thrust up from the slope to tower above the surrounding terrain. You can tell that these pinnacles have been here a long time because wind and rain have eroded them. Fissures and holes are dotted about their pitted surface.

In these cracks and crannies, hundreds of wild pangos have made their nests. You can see the bird's light grey bodies and shiny red beaks contrasting the dark rock as they crowd together, screeching and squabbling for the limited nesting spaces. At the base of one of the columns is a crude shelter used by egg hunters during the laying season.

During the breeding season female pangos sit on their eggs while the males fly many miles to the lowlands where they fill up with grain and fish before making the return journey to empty their gullets to feed the sitting females.

Once the clutch of pango eggs hatch, both parents make the journey each day, bringing back food for their babies until the young are able to fly and hunt for themselves.

Your attention is distracted from the pango colony by Gagnon waving and pointing down the slope to the right. It's Tow-Base 9. You can see the sun glinting off the tow's cable as it runs up the hillside.

You lower your guide stick and turn the sledge you are leading a little more to the right. A hand signal tells the cadets on the back to get ready to drag their hooks. Within minutes, your group is pulling up at the tow-base.

Some crew members have spotted you coming down the valley and have opened a portal. Pushing right once more, you allow the last of your momentum to carry the sledge neatly through the opening and into the parking bay bored deep into the rock.

Two members of the tow-base's crew are there to greet you.

Once your cadets are inside, a door glides shut with barely a sound. Thin slits in the outer wall provide just enough light for you to see a three-way junction about ten paces further on.

In typical Slider Corps fashion, single letters indicate where each tunnel goes. A indicates accommodation, H for hydro chambers, and D for the base's defensive positions. The Slider Corps have always been ones for simplicity.

"Okay everyone get your harnesses off and await instructions." You turn to the tow's crew and salute. "Troop 6-E reporting as instructed."

"Nice to see you made it, cadets," the older of the two crew members says. "We've had reports of Lowlanders in the valley."

As you tell them about your trip, one walks to a series of small holes bored in the smooth black wall. She shouts into one of them and then listens closely for the reply. You've heard about these communication pipes, but this is the first time you've seen them.

"Your troop is in accommodation pod 2," the crew member says. "I'll call ahead and let them know you're coming."

You are impressed with the base's method of communication. These holes must lead all over the base.

"Let's get you lot settled. Your gear can stay where it is."

You and your team follow the tunnel marked "A" deeper into the hillside. Holes bored in the roof provide just enough light to see where you are going. Although long and dingy, the corridor eventually leads to pod 2. The pod is circular and has sleeping notches cut into the wall like those at the slider training base. But unlike the training base, the notches here are stacked three-high and there is not much extra space to store personal stuff. Not that you expected luxuries at an advanced base like this one.

The crew member waiting to assist your group to settle in is surprising in more ways than one. Firstly, she is taller than any of your group and secondly her flame-red hair makes you look twice. It has to be the brightest hair you've ever seen.

When Gagnon sees her, he can't help staring.

"Is there anything else I can get you?" the redhead asks.

You shake your head. "I think we can find our way around. This pod is laid out similar to our last one."

"I hear the Lowlanders are gathering," she says. "Sometimes they dip their arrows in pango poo you know. Boy, does that cause infection."

"Thankfully we carry antibiotics for that," you say.

"Just as well. Now, if you'll excuse me, I'd better get back to work."

Just as she is leaving, another crew member comes in with a trolley loaded with hydro and broth. The cadets and mining students are starving and descend on the cart like a pack of scavengers.

Just as you're finishing the last of your broth, a slightly distorted voice echoes through a communication hole in the wall.

"Cadet Leader 6-E, please report to Defense One."

You're not exactly sure where Defense One is, but you know it will be down the "D" corridor somewhere.

When the message is repeated, you figure it must be urgent and waste no time in leaving the sleeping pod. When you reach the junction you turn into the D corridor. Not far along, the tunnel splits into four. Each is marked with a number. You take the first and start up a narrow set of steps cut into the pure black rock.

The staircase spirals around in a tight circle. You start counting each step as you go without even realizing it.

Defense One has a curved window of black glass, ground so thin it is almost clear. "Nice view," you say to a pair of officers sitting around a small table in the middle of the pod.

The window overlooks the entire valley. Wisps of smoke rise from the foothills far below where the Lowlanders have made their camp.

"It will be until I see those 20,000 Lowlanders marching up the valley," an officer says.

You gulp when you hear the number.

The officer does not look happy. "We've heard they've got some new machine that moves up the slope by drilling holes that allow a rotating sprocket on the front to grip the slope. Our scouts have seen them from a distance but that's about all we know. The machine our scouts saw was towing a hundred Lowlanders at a time. The Lowlanders must have found a new source of diamonds somewhere."

You start to say something, but then stop. This is a time to listen to those with more experience.

The officer has worry lines across his forehead. "We'll need more information if we're to send these machines to the bottom."

"So what is Troop 6-E to do, sir?"

"Tomorrow morning you will continue on to the Pillars of Haramon, as planned. If you see one of these machines along the way, your orders are to stop, watch, and in the event you spot a weakness, attack. We can't let the Lowlanders get above us. All our defensive positions are based on them coming at us from below. If one of these machines transports enough of their men up onto one of our main trails we could be in real trouble. Think your troop is up for that?"

You swallow hard. "Of course sir!"

"Okay. Best you get back to your cadets and get a good night's sleep. Tomorrow could be a long day."

That night you dream of shiny black pillars, and all the possible ways tomorrow might go. When the wake-up buzzer goes off, you bounce to your feet, keen to get going.

After a quick meal and toilet stop, you lead your troop back to the sledges and sort out the teams. This tow is steeper and longer than the others you've been on and there are no stops on the way up. It's just one long run to the ridgeline.

You check your harness and get ready to clamp on. The cable is a blur as it whirls up the slope. "On my mark…"

As your clamp grips, you and your sledge start moving up the slope. You've been warned by the base's crew that the offloading platform at the top is narrow. Hopefully everyone will be alert. The last thing you want is for a team to overshoot the ridge and go plummeting down the other side.

The intensive cadet training has paid off and everyone arrives at the top in one piece. An officer is waiting.

"Now keep your eyes open," he says. "Remember, we know almost nothing about this new machine, so obtaining information is vital. Don't risk yourselves unless you see a weakness you can exploit. Good luck."

You salute and order your troop move off along the ridge. This narrow track will lead you to a traverse that runs towards the top of Long Gully. Then it's down Long Gully to the Pillars of Haramon, some fifty-two miles from where you are standing.

Once again Gagnon takes the lead. Everyone handles the traverse track well, but when you turn into Long Gully proper, you spot something you've not seen before.

A series of angled holes have been bored into the rock. As you inspect the holes you can just imagine how a machine, fitted with a large rotating sprocket, could move up and down these holes without any problem. Each tooth on a sprocket would have a corresponding hole for it to lock in to. The machine could climb as fast as the wheel could rotate and a drill could drill.

You fit your guide stick into one of the holes and the toe of your boot in another and take a step up. At least you and your cadets can use this track to gain altitude as well.

But that doesn't change the disturbing fact that one of these Lowland machines is above you. This is exactly what the officer at the tow base was afraid of. Should you follow the track and try to gain vital information? Or is the equipment you're transporting more important? You can see merit in both courses of action.

It is time to make one of the most important decisions of your command. Do you:

Go up the mountain and scout out the Lowlanders' new machine? **P311**

Or

Take the vital equipment to the Pillars of Haramon? **P321**

Send some advanced scouts to test the route first.

Sending advanced scouts to check the route makes sense. Advanced scouts will enable you to see any Lowlanders that may have infiltrated the area before they see you, and more importantly, while you are still above them. Altitude is a critical advantage when on the Black Slopes of Petron.

Rather than sending Dagma out, you choose to lead a small group yourself. Now that you know Lowlanders are daring to come up the mountains, you want to be in a position to make quick decisions.

"Gagnon, come with me. Dagma, you hang back with the others and wait for my signal."

Dagma frowns. You can tell she hates being left at the rear. "So we all need babysitting now do we?" she mumbles.

It annoys you that Dagma isn't a team player. Why does she have to make snide comments under her breath? What good will that do the troop?

"Shut it, Dagma," you say. "One more word and I'll put you on report."

"You wouldn't…"

"… just try me!"

Dagma, so often the dominant personality in the troop, isn't used to being told what to do. Her mouth begins to open, but no words come out. Instead, she looks down at her feet in silence.

The other cadets snicker.

"Right, Gagnon, let's get going. The rest of you wait for my signal before sliding down to our position."

You relock your boots, put your front foot forward and push off with you guide stick. Gagnon follows. The soft hiss of boots on rock is all you can hear.

You aim towards the far right-hand side of the gully where you'll get a clear view down the slope. Once there you sweep left in a gentle arc towards the center again.

It's amazing how quickly you progress down the slope. Within a few minutes the cadets look like toys in the distance.

You drag your hook and come to a stop. Then you pull out your scope and look down the slope.

"All clear," you say to Gagnon.

You know Dagma will be impatiently studying you through her scope. You wave an arm and signal her and the other cadets to slide down and join you.

At first, the vibration under you feet is barely noticeable. You attribute your slight loss of balance to a gust of wind. But when the second tremor shakes you off your feet, you realize it's an earthquake.

You pull the anchor gun from your belt and fire a bolt into the rock. Both you and Gagnon clip on as quickly as possible. There may be more to come.

As suspected, the first jolts were pre-shocks to the main event.

A low rumbling is approaching, getting louder and louder as it does so. When the wave of energy reaches the surface a huge crack appears in the slope above you, ripping the gulley in half from one side to the other and creating a gaping crevasse between you and the cadets sliding down the slope towards you.

The shaking goes on for over a minute. The crack widens. How deep it goes is hard to tell from your position, but you have no doubt it will be deep enough to severely injure, if not kill, anyone falling into it.

You get your scope out of its pouch and focus on the cadets above. Some have fallen. There is nothing you can do apart from shout a warning and hope they manage to stop in time.

Another aftershock hits you, nearly as big at the first jolt. The dots above are getting bigger. You hear screeching. When the shaking stops and you manage to focus your scope again, you see that many cadets are still off their feet desperately trying to get up.

Standard procedure in these situations is to turn your sledge side-on to the slope to stop its downward momentum, but to do that, the cadet steering the sledge needs to be in control. That is impossible when you are on your backside free sliding down the hill. Sledges are skewed. One sledge is on its side dragging its crew down the hill behind it.

Before long those above are close enough for you to pick out individual faces. Dagma is nearest. Her large frame stands out from the crowd. She is still on her feet with her hook hard down. Her sledge has nearly stopped. For once Dagma rushing off in front is an advantage. Thankfully the others sliding behind her are still much further up the slope.

You hear the pop of an anchor gun as Dagma fires a bolt into the rock. In a flash her sledge is tethered and she is looking back over her shoulder figuring out how to stop the others.

A couple of the sledges are slowing due to good work by their crew, but two are out of control and gaining speed. They are now within a quarter of a mile of the yawning chasm angling across the slope below them.

Another rumble passes up from below. The edge of the huge crevasse cracks and sends sharks of black glass plummeting down into it.

Your eyes are riveted on the drama above. You hear another two pops in quick succession, as more cadets manage to anchor their sledges.

Dagma quickly shrugs off her harness and slides across the slope, pulling a cable behind her. She crosses the path of the two out of control sledges sliding down towards her. Once she's gone far enough she fires another anchor bolt into the ground and wraps the cable around it.

"She's trying to snag the runners of those two runaway sledges," you say to Gagnon.

"Will it be strong enough?" Gagnon asks.

"We'll know in a couple of seconds." You cross your fingers and hope Dagma's plan works.

When the runners of the first sledge slide under the cable you can see the line begin to stretch. The sledge's momentum slows, but in the process the sledge skews sideways.

Dagma fires another anchor bolt into the slope and wraps the excess cable around it.

The cable seems to be holding, but the sledge is now side-on to the slope and starting to tip over.

"It's going to roll!" Gagnon yells.

Just as the sledge reaches tipping point, the second sledge hits the cable.

The extra stretch its impact provides drops the first sledge back onto its runners long enough for the cadets harnessed up to it to get their own anchors in. Thankfully the second sledge is going slower than the first. Its runner slides under the cable and it comes to an abrupt, but satisfying halt.

"Wow that was close," you say.

"You're telling me," Gagnon says. "But what now?"

You look up at the tangle of sledges and their shaken passengers. A huge crack lies between you and the rest of your troop. To your right the crack runs slightly downhill, across the slope and all the way to the cliffs beyond.

To your left the crevasse runs to the far side and up the opposite slope for nearly fifty yards terminating in a steep bluff. There is no detour around the crevasse that way. You have no option but to find a way across.

You and Gagnon start working your way back up the slope towards the newly formed crevasse. Dagma has clipped on to a line and is abseiling down to check out the obstacle from above.

The crevasse is deep. The gap between you and your troop is about five yards.

"What now?" Dagma yells out across the void.

That is a very good question. You could sling a cable and get your cadets across the gap, but the heavy and cumbersome sledges are a different proposition altogether.

You would fail in your mission if you left all this valuable equipment on the slope when it is so desperately needed at the Pillars of Haramon.

One of the miners has abseiled down to where Dagma is standing.

She secures herself and then looks at you across the empty space. "Can I make a suggestion?" the miner says.

"Sure," you say, happy to have some ideas come your way.

"If we put a series of anchor bolts on both sides of the crevasse, we can use mineshaft props to build a makeshift bridge."

"Would it hold the weight of a sledge?"

"No problem," the miner says.

You look at Gagnon. He nods.

"Okay," you say. "Let's do it."

It takes about an hour for the miners to get the metal bridge bolted together. It looks like a big ladder made from pipe. Then you've got the tricky job of maneuvering the bridge across the crevasse and anchoring it securely to both sides.

Once it's secure, the runners of a sledge should be able to slide across the ladder without falling through the gaps … in theory at least.

Each sledge has a steering lever that can be controlled from onboard so the crew can climb aboard and ride across. The sledges speed can be slowed by a cable attached to a belay point on the uphill side.

The first trip across the bridge is a nervous affair.

"Geebus that's a long way down!" Piver says once the sledge he's riding is safely across.

Once all the sledges have crossed, a miner comes over to you. "I'm pretty sure I saw a vein of diamonds in that crevasse as I was crossing."

"Really? You've got good eyes."

"Light reflects differently off diamonds. It's just a matter of knowing what to look out for."

You look at the miner and wonder if he knows what he is talking about. But then if anyone is to know about diamonds, it makes sense that it would be a miner. Why would he make this up? In fact, why would he tell you about the diamonds all? He could just come back at some time in the future and keep them all for himself.

"So why are you telling me?"

"You sliders saved my life. I was on that sledge heading for the crevasse."

Of course, one of the sledges Dagma saved.

The miner continues. "I think we should take some samples and stake a claim. We can all share it. Imagine how rich we'll be."

He has a point. Finding a vein of blue diamond would be big news and big profits. Few of the cadets come from wealthy families. Nobody joins the Slider Corps for the money.

"Can we do that?" you ask.

The miner shows you a sparkling row of teeth. "Yep. We sure can. I'll get my climbing gear and some survey pegs, okay?"

"Sounds like a plan," you say, eager to find out if what the miner says about the diamonds is true.

It only takes ten minutes to rig up a harness so the miner can safely abseil down into the crevasse. Attached to his belt are a hand pick, collection bag, impact drill, and pry rod.

"Dewfall isn't that far away," you tell the miner before he goes over the edge. "You've got fifteen minutes to get what you need. After that, we're pulling you up."

The miner nods, leans out over the void and walks backwards down the sheer wall of stone, letting out cable as he goes. When he gets to the layer he spotted earlier he stops and starts chipping away.

You lie on your belly and look over the edge. "Are they diamonds?"

"Sure are. Number 1s by the looks of them," he yells back.

Number 1s are top grade, used for making the hooks on guide sticks and drills for boring holes in the tough black glass.

After a few more minutes you yell down again. "Okay time's up.

We need to get going."

Half a dozen cadets start hauling on the cable. Before long, the miner and his collection bag are back on the surface.

"Have a look," the miner says.

You hold out your hand and he pours a number of sparkling blue stones into your palm.

"They don't look much in their raw state," he says. "But once they've been polished, you'll barely be able to look at them without some sort of eye protection.

You are lost for words. They are beautiful, alive with light, glowing softly in your hand.

"Wow," you finally get out.

It takes some discipline to take your eyes away from the mesmerizing sight, but you know you need to get your troop down to the tow-base ... and soon. Dewfall is fast approaching.

"Are you just going to leave the ladder here?" Dagma asks.

"Yes," you say. "If we need to get back across in a hurry, it will come in handy."

Dagma grunts and attaches her harness to the back of a sledge.

"Oh and well done Dagma, you did a great job saving those runaway sledges. I'm going to recommend you for an award when we get to the Pillars of Haramon. You deserve one."

The others overhear your comments and congratulate her too. For the first time during the trip, you see her smile.

You give Dagma her moment in the sun, but when you look back up the slope you can see wispy clouds forming near the tops. "Okay, let's get moving. We've still got a few miles to go and it's starting to look like rain."

The aftershocks have stopped. After sliding for another hour or so without incident, Gagnon yells and points down the slope to the right. It's your destination.

As the last of the sun reflects off the oiled cable from Tow-Base 9, you lower your guide stick and turn your sledge a little more to the right. Then you signal the cadets at the back to begin dragging their hooks.

Someone has spotted you coming down the valley and has opened a portal. Pushing right once more, you allow your remaining momentum to ease the sledge neatly through the entry and into the parking bay bored into the rock. The others are right behind you.

Two members of the tow-base's crew are there to greet you. They guide the troop to its sleeping pod where a meal has been prepared.

The next morning your troops make their way up a long tow, along the ridge and then into the head of Long Gully. Sixty miles down this picturesque valley are the Pillars of Haramon and your final destination.

You imagine turning up with your troop, a bag of number 1s and a $1/40^{th}$ share in what could be one of the biggest finds of diamonds in recent times.

The miner who spotted the vein of diamonds in the crevasse has transferred to your sledge, and he's been giving you a crash course in prospecting and mine management while you travel. It's amazing how finding diamonds has sparked an interest you never realized you had.

By mid afternoon the next day, your troop is pulling up outside one of the Pillars.

An officer greets you with a salute and directs you and your cadets to their accommodation pod. The miners get busy unpacking the much needed equipment for improving defensive positions and creating more magnifying disks to fight off invasion.

You climb up a narrow set of stairs to the top observation pod where you are debriefed by Command. While you are there you register the mining claim you've pegged out on behalf of your cadets and the student miners.

"Looks like everyone's hit the jackpot," the officer says. "Once tax is taken out, you should be left with a tidy profit."

You think about the officer's words and realize you *have* hit the jackpot. You're doing something you love. The profit you make from your share of the diamonds means you can help your family out, and you're standing a thousand feet above one of the most beautiful landscapes on the planet. What's not to like about that?

From high up in the observation pod you can see a patchwork of fields on the Lowlands below. Bright purples, greens, pinks and oranges create a mosaic of color across the flats towards the delta where braided rivers shimmer like necklaces as they meander back and forth. Beyond the delta, the ocean stretches off into the horizon.

You've heard stories about the ocean and wonder what it's like to swim in so much water. You wonder what it's like to be a Lowlander, to walk around on flat ground, where there isn't any danger of slipping and sliding to the bottom. Then you look back towards the towering Black Slopes of home and you realize you're happy where you are. Like generations before you, you are a Highlander, and proud of it.

Congratulations, you have reached the end of this part of your story. You have made it successfully to the Pillars of Haramon with your precious cargo and you have a share in a diamond mine. Well done!

But have you followed all the possible story lines? Have you gone mining, found tunnels, heard the cry of the wild pango, been attacked by morph rats? Discovered the secrets of the moon moth?

It's time for another decision. Do you.

Go back to the beginning of the story and try another path? **P219** Or

Go to the list of choices and start reading from another part of the story? **P381**

Go up and scout out the new Lowland machine.

The track is nothing more than a series of fist-sized holes drilled into the slope. It runs straight up the mountain. Each hole is a perfect fit for the toe of your boot so it should be no problem following the track uphill.

The sledges are another matter. There is no way you can take them with you. Nor do you want to leave them unattended where another Lowland patrol might find them.

You'll have to split your troop up. But how many cadets should you leave behind to guard the sledges? Maybe rather than having them wait, you should send the sledges on down to the Pillars of Haramon with the mining students while a smaller group chases this machine.

You decide that three heads are better than one when it comes to making decisions.

"Dagma, Gagnon, we need to talk."

The two cadets unclip from their sledges and slide over.

You look once more at the track running up the hill. Then you take your glove off and stick your hand in one of the holes. The rock is still slightly warm from the friction of being drilled. The machine can't be too far away.

"What do you think? Should we split up and get the miners down to the Pillars while the rest of us check this out?"

Gagnon's gaze follows the track up the slope. He shakes his head. "Weirdest thing I've ever seen. It must be quite a contraption to be able to cut into the rock like this."

"Let's go up and get them," Dagma growls. "I'm not afraid of Lowlanders and their stupid machine!"

Once again Dagma is overflowing with raw emotion. Is it clouding her judgment? You wonder if she will ever realize that being afraid is okay. Real bravery is about doing what you must, despite your fear, not rushing at things like a demented morph rat.

You wish you had more time to consider things, but the time is passing. Your troop must get to the Pillars of Haramon before dewfall makes the slopes impossible to travel.

"I'm thinking most of our group should keep sliding down the valley towards the Pillars. A small scouting party will be less visible from above. If we can find out what the Lowlanders are up to, we might even come up with a plan to stop them."

Gagnon nods. "Sounds like a good idea. You have to walk softly to catch a pango."

"What?" Dagma snarls at Gagnon. "Why are you talking about pangos?"

Gagnon shakes his head and shrugs.

You turn to Dagma. "He means we need to move slowly and cautiously."

"Well why didn't he just say that?"

You ponder things a moment. "I agree with Gagnon. If we're going to get any useful information there's no point in rushing blindly up the hill just to get captured and end our days picking grain on some Lowland penal farm."

Your mind is whirling with options. Do you want Dagma on this expedition or should you send her down to the Pillars with the miners? What if she loses control and does something stupid?

"Okay. Listen up everyone," you say, "I'm sending the majority of you on to the Pillars of Haramon. Gagnon you'll be in charge."

Most of the miners seem relieved to be heading towards safety. You have little doubt the level headed Gagnon will get them there in one piece.

"Dagma, myself and two other cadets, will scout up the hill and try to find out what the Lowlanders are up to. If they spot us, we'll free slide back down as quickly as possible and catch up with you." At least with Dagma by your side, you can keep an eye on her. "Gagnon get going. We want this equipment as far from the Lowlanders as we can get it."

After picking two of your fittest cadets, you prepare to start the chase. "I hope you all feel like climbing," you say to your small group, "because it's all uphill from here."

Over your shoulder you hear Gagnon give the order for the sledges to move out.

You look at your three cadets. "We'll take turns leading. One will climb then the others can zip up to conserve their strength. That way we won't have to stop for breaks. It's the only way we'll have any chance of catching up with this machine of theirs. I'll go first. Get ready to move."

Without waiting for comments from the others you grab a cable and climb rapidly up the line of holes provided by the Lowland machine. After a hundred quick steps, you stop and belay the others who clip their battery-powered zippers onto the light-weight cable. The tiny, but powerful rotor whirls and the cadets are quickly dragged up the hill.

"Dagma, you climb next," you say.

She takes hold of the cable and repeats the procedure, sprinting up the hill like it's a race. When Dagma reaches the end of the cable and has a secure belay in place, you and the other two cadets clip on and zip up to her.

By taking turns doing the hard uphill slog, it isn't long before the four of you have made considerable progress up the mountainside. When you reach the highest point on the ridge, the machine's tracks turn west.

You pull out your scope. In the distance you see the Lowland machine steaming along. A mechanism mounted on an extendable arm in front of the machine is drilling the track holes with quick precision. Behind the drill is a big sprocket with pointed teeth that fit neatly into the pre-drilled holes. As this sprocket rotates, it pulls the machine along the smooth rock on its long metal runners.

The machine has armored sides with viewing holes along its length and there is some sort of spring loaded mechanism on top and piles of cable. These must be the nets you've heard about.

Sitting on top of the machine are Lowlanders.

The machine is also towing a cable with at least thirty more Lowland troopers clipped on to it. How many Lowlanders are inside the machine is anyone's guess.

You and the other cadets lie on the ground and study the scene before you.

"Where do you think they're going?" Dagma asks.

You pull a map from a pouch in your utility belt and spread it out on the ground before you. "They must be heading toward the Haramon Reservoir," you say. "All the settlements north and west of here, not to mention the base at the Pillars, rely on that water."

"Do you think they are going to poison it?" Dagma asks.

"I don't know. But we need to find out."

Protecting the Haramon Reservoir has never been a priority. Lowlanders have never been able to get this high up the mountain before, so security is minimal.

"What are we going to do?" Dagma asks.

"We're going to think of a way stop to them," you say. You turn to the cadets crouched behind you. "I need you two to slide back down and let those at the Pillars of Haramon know what is going on, just in case Dagma and I get captured or injured. Can you do that?"

"Yes," they say in unison.

"Well get going. It's important that they know that their water supply might be compromised, so be safe and get there in one piece."

You would have liked to have kept one of the two cadets with you, but you know that traveling in a pair is always safer than going solo. The two cadets waste no time in locking their boots together and sliding off down the slope. You and Dagma resume your study of the Lowland machine through your scopes.

After a few minutes you put your scope down. "Any ideas, Dagma?"

"There are so many of them," she says. "We might be able to handle a few, but…"

For the first time Dagma's voice seems a little shaky. You lift your scope again, hoping you'll see something that Dagma has missed.

The machine is making steady progress along the ridge towards the next valley where the reservoir is located. As you follow the ridgeline with your scope, you notice there is one point where it narrows to little more than the width of the machine. A plan begins to form in your mind.

"How much do you reckon that machine weighs, Dagma?"

"I don't know. A ton and a half at least … plus the weight of the crew and those riding on top."

"So that's maybe four thousand pounds altogether. What do the thirty Lowlanders being towed behind it weigh?"

As you wait for Dagma's answer you do some calculations in your head. Thirty times an average weight of 150 pounds per Lowlander is 4500 pounds, a little more that the weight of the machine, its crew and passengers.

"If we can somehow push the troopers being towed over the edge just as the machine reaches that pinch-point on the ridge, do you think their combined weight will be enough to pull the machine over?"

Dagma considers what you've said a moment and then grins. "It's worth a crack. Once the first few are knocked off, it might start a chain reaction that takes them all."

"Stealth and timing will be everything. If they hear us coming, we'll be pin cushions before we even get close."

"You'd better follow me then," Dagma says with a grin. "I'll make a good shield."

As crazy as her comment sounds, it actually makes good sense. At least with Dagma in front, if you're spotted the mission still has a chance of success.

"You're crazy, Dagma. Brave, but crazy."

Once again you look through your scope and calculate the distance the machine has to travel to the narrowest part of the ridge. Then you estimate how far it is from your current position to the Lowlanders being towed.

At the current rate of progress the machine will be in position in about one and a half minutes. That gives you less than a minute to come up with a better plan or change your mind.

You look at Dagma. "We've got to decide now. Are you sure you want to do this?"

An evil grin crosses Dagma's face as she reverses her pack so that it protects her chest. "Does a morph rat stink? Let's send these pango-headed fools to the bottom."

You were afraid she'd say that. You've already started counting down in your head. After one last look through the scope you pack it away and get ready for the slide of your life.

"Tuck in behind, hands on my waist," Dagma says. "Let's go in low, fast and quiet."

"You have the lead, cadet," you say unhooking your boots and crouching down behind Dagma's bulk.

Dagma places her guide stick on the ground ready for a big push. "On my mark, three, two, one…"

Both of you push off as hard as you can and tuck into a low crouch. Only subtle adjustments are needed to keep you heading down the ridge towards the Lowlanders.

The wind is cool against the skin on your face as you peer over Dagma's shoulder. With every second, you gain speed.

When you are forty yards away, a Lowlander riding on top of the machine spots you and raises the alarm, but it is too late to save the last Lowlander from being slammed over the edge and down the steep slope. Before the next trooper has time to brace, he too is plucked off the ridge. The first two jerk the next one off his feet and over the edge, then another, and another.

You and Dagma drag your hooks to a stop and watch the perfect chain reaction unfold.

Now it's only a question of whether their combined weight will be enough to dislodge the machine.

You hold your breath as the last of the towed Lowlanders goes over. The weight on the rope has pulled the machine's rear end off line. Its rear runners are inching closer and closer to the edge.

Just as the machine starts to topple, the troops on top shift their weight to the opposite side from where the troopers have gone over. The machine teeters on the brink.

With a squeak, the back door of the machine flies open. You expect to see more troopers jumping out and attempt to stabilize the machine, but those fleeing the machine are too small to be troopers.

"The machine's full of children," you yell out to Dagma.

This is not at all what you expected. What are the Lowlanders doing with a bunch of children way up here?

"We've made a mistake Dagma. We've got to help."

Before you have time to stop her, Dagma has pushed off and is sliding towards the machine. She pulls a light-weight cable from her belt and forms it into a loop.

As she nears the back of the machine she throws the cable over a bracket and then turns and plummets over the opposite side of the ridge to where the Lowland troopers have fallen.

Seconds later you hear the familiar pop of an anchor gun.

The machine's runners edge closer to the sheer drop. Voices of struggling Lowlanders call out from below. You hold your breath as the cable Dagma has hooked onto the machine stretches tight.

You understand what she's done and why and slide down to help. You throw another cable around a handrail along the side of the machine and shoot a bolt into the rock.

Lowland children mill about wondering what to do. The machine has stabilized, but any false step could send one these youngsters down the steep face on either side of the ridge.

The right-hand side of the machine is almost at the edge, but at least the machine isn't moving now due to the anchors you and Dagma have put in on the other side.

Then you see Dagma's head appear above the ridgeline as she

climbs back up the cable. When she reaches flat ground she flops down and heaves a huge sigh.

"Phew, that was exciting," she says, wiping the sweat off her forehead.

As you move towards Dagma, the adult Lowlanders work frantically to get their machine stabilized. A few Lowlanders look in your direction, but you are no longer a threat. Besides they are too busy securing the machine and keeping the children safe to worry about you.

"Should we take off?" Dagma whispers, her inherent distrust of Lowlanders coming to the surface once more.

"I want to find out why they have children up here. Something strange is going on. But if you want to make a run for it, feel free."

Dagma shrugs and stays where she is. "Best we stick together, don't you think?"

A few minutes later a Lowlander comes over to where the two of you are sitting. "I suppose you want to know what's going on," he says.

"We thought you were going to poison our water supply," you say as you stand to face him. "But then we saw the children and realized we'd jumped to conclusions."

"Understandable I suppose," the Lowlander says. "We've not had the best of relationships with you Highlanders over recent years."

"So why are you up here?" Dagma asks. "We nearly sent you all to the bottom."

"We're refugees from the delta. We escaped by stealing one of the Lowland army's new machines. We found some old uniforms to put on to keep warm. We're not used to the chilly mountain air."

You look around and notice that many of the Lowlanders are women. Normally Lowland troops are male. Then you see the patched elbows and frayed cuffs.

This ragtag bunch is made up of family units. It's not a troop of fighters at all.

"The Lowlanders are trying to force our men to fight. But we have no quarrel with the Highlanders. We are all the same blood after all. We just want a peaceful life, shelter, food and happiness for our children."

"Sounds fair enough, but where do you plan to go?" you ask.

"We are going to resettle on the far side of the mountains. We hear there are good pastures in the interior."

You nod. "Yes, I've heard that too. Still, that's quite a dangerous slide, especially with children and without trained people to escort you."

"What other choice do we have?"

You can understand his position. Lowlanders that refuse to fight are put into penal farms and used as forced labor. Nobody in their right mind would want that as a life.

"I have an idea," you say to the man.

The Lowlander seems interested. "I'm willing to listen if you can suggest something that will keep my family safe."

"We Highlanders are in much the same position as your family. We just want a peaceful life without interference from the Lowland Council. But unless we can come up with a way to defeat these new machines of theirs, we will have no option but to cave in to their demands."

"They are formidable machines," the Lowlander says. "They move uphill very fast and fling nets to entangle anyone who gets too close. Your Slider Corps will struggle to defeat them."

This is exactly what you were thinking.

"What if I guaranteed you safe passage and a slider escort down the mountain to the interior, in exchange for this machine? Both of us would gain. Yes?"

You can see the Lowlander thinking. His eyes close a little and his head bobs up and down. You hope he goes for the deal. For Slider Command, having one of these new machines to study would be a great advantage in the conflict that is sure to come.

A few seconds later he looks you in the eye. "You are very clever for one so young."

You smile at his compliment but remain silent.

"I like this plan of yours," he continues. "A strong Highland force will act as a buffer between our settlement and the Lowlanders. We would be able to trade too, our crops for your minerals and hydro."

"It sounds like we're in agreement then?" you say.

"Yes, I think we are," the man says.

"Okay, I think the first thing to do is to get your people settled. You can stay at the reservoir while I go back and organize some sledges and sliders to take you and your people down the mountain. There is a small base by the reservoir that has a spare accommodation pod. It might be crowded but at least you'll be safe."

The Lowlander nods his understanding.

"Some of your men can help us get this machine down to the Pillars of Haramon. Then within a few days, I'll send enough sliders and sledges back to get you all safely down the other side."

You hold out your hand to the Lowlander. "It will be nice to have some Lowland friends for a change."

"I agree," the Lowlander says. "We all bleed green, do we not?"

"Indeed we do," you say, "greener than the yolk of a pango's egg."

Congratulations, you have reached the end of this part of the story. You successfully obtained a Lowland machine for Slider Command to study, and made allies of a group of Lowlanders that will enrich your community. Well done! But have you tried all the possible paths yet? Have you gone mining or found of the secret of the moon moths?

It is time to make another decision. Do you:

Go back to the beginning of the story and try another path? **P219**
Or

Go to the List of Choices and start reading from another part of the story? **P381**

Take the equipment to the Pillars and don't follow the machine.

You have decided to carry on to rather than go investigate the track the Lowland machine has made.

The officer told you that if you came across the machine you were to investigate, but this isn't the machine, it is just the machine's track. Why risk your troop? You can't take the sledges up the mountain, and for you to follow the track you'd have to split your troop into two sections which would only make each group weaker.

After unclipping your harness, you take out your scope and scan the upper slopes for any sign of the Lowlanders, but the track disappears over a ridge and there is no sign of the machine.

"Are we going after them?" Dagma asks. "We've got to do something."

"But how far up are they? They could be miles ahead. And if their machine climbs as quickly as we think, how do we know we'll even be able to catch them?"

Gagnon has heard your discussion and has pushed his way back to your position. "We can't let them get above us. Advantage comes with altitude, you know that. They could slide right down on us."

You bang your stick on the ground. "Our job is to get this mining equipment to the Pillars, not go chasing machines. I've made my decision."

Dagma looks at Gagnon and shakes her head. You hear the hiss of air as she inhales through her teeth.

"You're making a mistake," Gagnon says. "Please reconsider."

You glance up the slope once more. Maybe by rotating climbers, and using zippers to drag you up the mountain you could catch the machine, but you hesitate. What if you waste precious time climbing up and the real danger is coming from below? How are you to know?

"Let's take a vote," Gagnon says.

"Yeah." Dagma looks at the other cadets in the hope that a stare will make them agree with her.

"This is not a democracy," you say. "I'm in charge and my decisions are final."

The cadets don't seem happy with your last statement — Highland communities value consensus above all else. Having their opinion ignored is a pet hate of all Highlanders.

"Yes, let's vote." You hear a few other cadets say.

"Seems the others want a say in this too," Dagma grunts.

"No. Get ready to move off."

Before you manage to clip on, Dagma sees her chance. With a sweep of her stick, she knocks you off your feet. Then she pushes you down the slopes with all her strength.

Before you know it you are free sliding down the hill, gaining speed as you go.

You try to regain your feet where you might have some control, but the ground is uneven and whenever you try to stand, a bump in the ground knocks you flat once more.

Spinning around you sit up with your feet out in front of you. Leaning down on your hook you try to slow your speed, but before you can come to a complete stop you hit a steeper patch and take off again. Further ahead you see a series of knife-edged ridges. If you hit one of those it will cut you to ribbons.

You have two choices. Try to stop, or use your stick to steer and avoid the danger below.

You dig in your heel spurs and jab your stick, pushing yourself further into the centre of the gully away from the dangers on its left. You are moving too fast for your equipment to slow you down. None the less, you lean down hard on your hook. After the steep patch the ground levels out and you manage to stop, but by then the rest of your troop is well out of sight.

Being isolated on the slope is not a good thing. You've got no one to belay you, no one to help with the climbing. You're limited in what you can do.

In this situation you've got little option but to carefully traverse back and forth across the slope and try to get down to the Pillars of Haramon without breaking your neck.

What a disaster. Your first patrol and your cadets have rebelled, pushed you down the hill, and left you on your own, just because you didn't listen to them.

As you sit and ponder what to do, you remember what the officer said when you first started this trip, "you all have a vital part to play in the Slider Corps, and you need to listen to each other."

But you didn't listen. You thought you knew better. Your ego made you lose the respect of your troop. You didn't work as a team.

You hang your head as you traverse back and forth across the slope on your way down. What will you say when you arrive alone? How will you explain?

You can only hope that you get another chance some day to make up for your mistake. That you get a chance to regain respect and become a valued member of the Highland Slider Corps.

This part of your story is over. Unfortunately you failed in your mission to get your troop to the Pillars of Haramon. However, you do have another chance. You can go back and try another path. Next time, listen to your fellow cadets.

It is time to make a decision. Do you want to:

Go back to the beginning of the story and try another path? **P219**

Or

Go to the list of choices and start reading from another part of the story? **P381**

Encourage the sliders to attack the Lowlanders.

You've heard stories about Lowland treachery all your life. You've never actually met a Lowlander, but you believe what your family says.

"Miners, grab your picks and rope up," you yell to your team. "Get ready to fight."

As the sliders form themselves into a V-formation, ready to do a high-speed downhill attack, you and your fellow miners fit a light-weight cable drum to an anchor point in the rock ready to belay down and help. Once the cable is reeled out, each miner clips on to the line.

"We'll wait until the sliders attack, then we can reinforce where required," you tell the others.

The sliders are nearly ready to go. They sit on their utility belts with their feet forward, guide sticks tucked under their arms ready to steer. The Lowlanders know the effectiveness of this tactic and are retreating downhill around a small headland.

"On my mark!" the lead slider yells. "Three, two, one, go!"

You are amazed at how quickly the sliders gain speed as they rocket down the hillside. Each has their guide sticks pointing to the front ready to strike and their diamond studded boots up and ready to kick.

The sliders use the needle end of their guide sticks to make a sweeping turn to the right. Within moments they too will be out of view.

"We need to move further down the valley so we can see what's going on," you say to your group.

You push the release button on your zipper and slide down the cable past the protruding ridge to a point where you can see the sliders pursuing the retreating Lowlanders. The other miners follow your example.

Then you see a machine crawl out of a natural depression in the slope. It's an unusual contraption and surprisingly quick. It races up the valley towards the fleeing Lowlanders. When it reaches the retreating men, the machine stops and the Lowlanders climb in through a door in its armored side. Faces peer out tiny viewing holes along its side.

Mounted on the front of the machine is a high-speed drill which pecks holes in the ground. Behind the drill is a huge sprocket with pointed teeth. The turning sprocket is powered by a chain that runs to a gear at the back where a vent releases steam and the thumping sound of an engine can be heard coming from within. As the sprocket turns, its teeth fit perfectly into the holes made by the drill, and pull it rapidly up the slope.

"I don't like this," you say to Piver. "What *is* that thing?"

For the first time ever, Piver looks serious. His cheeky grin is gone and his face is slack. "I don't know, but I doubt it's here to make our lives any easier."

The sliders have seen the machine too. They are doing their best to stop before they get too close. The high-pitched screech of dragging hooks echoes around the valley.

But the Lowlanders have planned their ambush well. The sliders are out in the open and have nowhere to hide. The machine blocks their downhill path.

With a *twang,* a series of spring-loaded catapults, mounted on top of the machine, fling nets towards the now motionless sliders and because of their tight formation, the nets entangle many at once.

"This is not going well," Piver says

"We've got to go and help, but what can we do?" you say.

Before you and Piver have time to discuss the matter further, an amplified voice booms up the valley.

"Surrender now and you will be spared. This is your one and only warning."

Piver and the other miners look at you for instructions, their young faces showing their concern at the situation.

You never have liked ultimatums. "Quick, back to the sledges!" you yell. "Get aboard and cut them loose, we'll have to take our chances free sliding down the mountain."

Despite the look of fear on their faces, the other miners are quick to follow your lead. They zip back up the cable and rush to their respective sledges. Anchor lines are released and they jump aboard.

"Keep as high as you can, and head for the far side of the valley. We need to get out of here before the Lowlanders net us."

Each sledge has a simple steering system. Normally it is controlled by a slider at the front, but it can also be operated by a lever mounted on the side that is linked to the front runners. The diamond dust on the sledge's runners will give you some control, but any grip is reduced the faster you go.

"See those steep cliffs on the opposite side of the valley?" You say. "Aim for those. We can use the slope below them to bank our turn and direct us back down the valley below the Lowlanders."

"Are you sure this is a good idea?" Piver asks. "It's going to be a pretty wild ride."

"Fancy life on a Lowland prison farm?" you reply.

Piver shakes his head.

"I didn't think so."

Having reeled in the sliders, the Lowland machine is grinding up the hill again. White steam belches and gears clunk.

"Let's go, we're running out of time!" You wave your arm for the other miners to follow and push off.

Your needle boots give you a little grip as you give the sledge a big shove and leap aboard. Before you know it you are gliding across the slope.

You lie on your stomach and grab the steering lever with your right hand while holding tightly onto a strap with your left. Your sledge cuts across the slope above the Lowlanders' machine and rockets towards the far cliffs.

The sledges runners click and clatter as they skitter across tiny ridges in the glassy black rock.

You hear the twang of nets being fired and the dull thud as they hit the slope behind you. A high-pitched whine starts.

The speed of the free-running sledge is exhilarating and scary at the same time. You look back and see that the last sledge in your group has been snagged by a net and is being reeled in like a big fish. A day that had held such promise is quickly turning into a nightmare. Now there are only nine of you.

Normally, speed on the slopes is your enemy. Today however, it is your only chance to escape. How the Lowlanders got past the fortified Pillars of Haramon without being detected, you're not sure. What you do know is getting down the valley to the fortified base is your best chance. You certainly can't hang around on the slopes with this many Lowlanders around.

Your sledge slows as it begins to climb the slope on the far side of the valley. The cliffs are close now.

You pull the lever hard back to turn right and use the natural contour of the hill to bank your turn. The sledge swings around and you head back towards the opposite side of the valley at an angle that will take you well below the Lowlanders' position.

The valley has become a gigantic half-pipe as the sledges race down toward the Pillars. You swoop from one side to the other, using the natural banking to help you change direction and control your speed. A cool breeze whistles around your visor.

The machine is obviously better going uphill than down, because you've left it and the Lowlanders far behind.

After just over an hour of high-speed and at time crazy, on-the-edge sledging, you see two towering black columns rising from the valley floor. A distance that would have taken you and your slider escort a whole day to cover has been completed in hardly any time at all.

The massive Pillars of Haramon rise straight up from the valley floor for over a thousand feet. They glisten in the afternoon light. At 100 yards wide, and perfectly smooth, apart from the numerous tunnels that pockmark their surface, the Pillars are one of the natural wonders of Petron.

Between the two monoliths are strung a number of sturdy cables with gondolas hanging beneath them so people and equipment can travel from one pillar to the other. Magnifying disks sit in some of the tunnel openings ready for use in case of attack.

A colony of pangos has made its home near the top of one of the pillars. These tasty but rather stupid birds provide a plentiful supply of fresh eggs and protein for the fort's occupants.

Although you can't see them from down below, you also know that some of the old mining tunnels are now used as hydro growing chambers and sleep pods for the three hundred or so Highlanders that make this isolated outpost their home.

As you steer onto the loading platform near the base of one of the pillars, a strong safety net catches your sledge and brings it to a halt. The rest of your group soon slides in to join you.

"Welcome to the Pillars of Haramon," says an officer that has come out of a portal to join you. "Where is your escort?"

After describing how your escort was captured by the Lowland machine and detailing your wild ride down the valley, the officer gets your group to park their sledges in a large chamber where cable drums, drills, grinders and other tools are stored.

"You must be exhausted after your ordeal," the office says, "but I'll need you to report this new information to Command right away. This is a serious development."

After your troop is directed to a visitor's pod where they can eat and rest, you follow the officer through a narrow portal and up a series of steps cut into the smooth black rock. Moon moths hang from the ceiling, lighting the way.

You crane your neck up so you can look at them as you walk.

"We encourage them to breed here. Saves us a lot of effort lighting all the tunnels," the officer says when he sees you studying the bright-winged creatures. "The Pillars have one of the biggest moth colonies on Petron."

You've never seen so many moon moth this close before. You are amazed by how their iridescent wings glow softly in the dark.

"They're beautiful," you say. "I'm surprised they aren't disturbed by your movement through the tunnels."

"Occasionally they'll get spooked and fly off all at once, but that's rare. I think they realize we mean them no harm."

Your leg muscles start to burn as you climb. Your breath is coming in gasps by the time you enter the command pod.

There are six officers in the pod. All but one gives you a quick once-over and then turn back to their work. The other comes over and directs you into a side chamber.

After repeating what you told the first officer about the capture of your escort and the Lowland machine, the officer leans towards you. "So you've seen it. Do you think we can defeat this machine?"

You haven't really had much time to think about it. You and your fellow miners have been far too busy trying to stay alive on your crazy slide down the valley to have time to think about defeating the Lowland machine.

"Well?" the officer says.

"I … I'm not sure, sir. I'm a miner, not a slider."

"But you and your troop learned about engineering and mechanics in mining school. What is your honest opinion?"

You remember how easily the machine captured the sliders. How the drill on its front-end cut a track in the tough black rock allowing it to move quickly up the slope and how the machine's armor plating protected the Lowlanders within.

But then you remember the openings along the machine's side that allowed those within to see out, it's slower speed when moving downhill, and its reliance on an engine. You try to imagine how you would go about attacking such a contraption.

"Well…" You close your eyes and try to picture the machine. "If we can jam the drive gears the machine won't be able to move uphill," you say. "But can your sliders get close enough without being captured in their nets?"

The officer thinks hard for a moment and then nods slightly "Would you be willing to come with us? Sliders aren't trained mechanics. We aren't used to dealing with machinery. If you could come and tell us what we need to do to disable this thing, we'll find a way to get close enough somehow."

You want to help but you've not been trained for this sort of thing. You're a miner, not a tactician ... or a fighter for that matter. You know about drills and crystals and props and shafts. Maybe talking peace is the answer?

It seems to you that there are two possible solutions. Fight or talk.

There is a chance the Highlanders might be able to send the Lowland machine crashing back down the mountain. But do you want to be responsible if your plan doesn't work and it results in injury and death? Maybe talking peace with the Lowlanders is the best idea. Everyone loses something when it comes to war, even the victor.

It is time to make a decision. Do you:

Tell the office you think they should talk peace with the Lowlanders? **P334**

Or

Volunteer to go with the sliders and attack the Lowland machine? **P336**

You have decided to yell out for the slider not to attack.

You stand up and move towards the head slider. "Hang on a minute! Aren't you going to find out what they want?"

The head slider looks at you and scowls. "They're Lowlanders. You expect me to trust them?"

"Do you see them carrying any weapons?" you say.

Squinting into the glare, the slider looks down at the Lowlanders again. He grumbles something under his breath, and then turns back to you. "Well I suppose we could hear what they have to say. But any tricky business and my troop will send them straight to the bottom!"

Piver gets up from behind his sledge and comes to stand beside you. He turns and whispers, "I'll come with you. Two heads are better than one, even if they are pango heads."

"You're crazy Piver, but I like your logic."

You take a step towards the head slider. "Piver and I will speak to them. I think it's better if your troop stays here. They'll feel less threatened that way."

The Lowlanders have stopped. They look up at you, their white flag fluttering.

"Well if you want to risk your lives, who am I to stop you?" the slider says.

You wonder if you really are risking your life. Maybe the head slider is right. Even though the Lowlanders are waving a white flag, have they really come in peace?

"Looks like the j—job is ours," Piver says nervously. "Do you want to do the talking or should I?"

"When we want to make them laugh, I'll let you know. In the mean time let me do the talking, okay?"

"We'd better throw down a line and go see what they want then." Piver takes a light-weight cable from his utility belt and ties one end onto an anchor bolt. Once it's attached, you both clip on and start working your way down the slope towards the Lowlanders.

When you and Piver are about five paces from the group you stop.

A couple of the Lowlanders look a little nervous. Not surprising considering there are thirty armed and highly trained sliders, arranged in attack formation, just waiting for an excuse to send them to the bottom.

"What are you doing way up here?" you ask, trying to keep your voice from wavering. "You're a long way from home, don't you think?"

One of the Lowlanders takes a step forward and pulls out a small tablet. He unfolds its protective cover and starts to read. "I come as a representative of the Lowland Council. My council wishes to meet with your Highland leaders to see if we can find a way to end the bloodshed that has plagued our two peoples for so many years. In exchange for peace, all the Lowland Council requires is a small act of good faith on behalf of the Highlanders."

"Act of good faith?"

"A small tax, to cover the cost of administration, health and education," he continues. You will gain many benefits from becoming part of the Federation of Lowland States."

"What do you consider small?"

"A mere ten percent of any minerals mined from the Black Slopes. A very reasonable request, don't you think? You pay nearly that much to the border traders already in commission, not to mention what it must cost you to defend the Highlands."

You shrug. His proposal doesn't sound unreasonable. Some education you already get, but there are only limited health facilities in the Highlands.

You look briefly at Piver, shrug, and then turn back to the Lowland leader. "I'm happy to pass your message on to my superiors. How do we contact you with our answer?"

"We have troops gathered in the foothills below the Pillars of Haramon. Tell your leaders to send an envoy to us there with your answer no later than the last day of the full moon. If we don't hear from you by then…"

You wait for him to finish his sentence but he remains silent.

"Then what?" you ask.

"Let's just say if I were in your position, I'd do my best to persuade my leaders to do as we suggest. Believe me when I say your Highland sliders are no match for our recently developed technology. The Highland communities can either choose to be a small part of our federation or we will send you all to the bottom. It's your choice."

With that, the Lowlanders turn and move off down the hill.

You press the trigger on the handle of your zipper, its battery whirs and pulls you up the cable where the others have been waiting.

The head slider shuffles over. "Well, what did they say?"

You give him the main points of the discussion.

"Those … those Lowland scum," the lead slider says. "We should send them back to their leaders in pieces. How dare they demand such a thing!"

"Wait," Piver says. "The Highland Council should be the ones to decide."

You nod your head. "Piver's right. It's not our place to start a war. Besides, their offer could be of some benefit."

The head slider is almost growling in disgust. "I think we should attack while we have the numerical advantage. Then there will be less Lowlanders to fight later. But seeing you miners are paying for our escort to the Pillars…"

You understand the slider's position. Hatred of Lowlanders runs deep in the Slider Corps, but you also know that war is a costly exercise, even for the winner.

The situation is tense. It is time for you to make a decision. Do you:

Join the sliders and attack the Lowlanders? **P324**

Or

Carry on to the Pillars of Haramon with the Lowlanders' message?
P336

Tell the officer they should talk peace with the Lowlanders.

"Look," you say to the slider officer, "I don't know how to disable the Lowlanders' machine. What if my ideas fail? Surely talking peace is a better option, especially when the opposition has a technological advantage."

The officer sneers at you like you're a pango dropping he needs to scrape off his boot. "If you won't help, I'm sure one of the other miners will come up with a plan."

"But…"

The officer's face is turning red. "Sliders do not surrender. We attack!" he yells. "I should have known better than to ask a miner for help."

You can't understand the officer's reaction. When did you say anything about surrender? Talking and compromising isn't surrender, it's saving lives.

"Wait, I didn't say surrender…"

But the officer isn't listening. He has stomped away and is talking with a stern-faced officer on the far side of the pod. You can tell you'd be wasting your breath trying to reason with him anymore. He stopped listening the moment you said "peace".

After being ignored for a few minutes, you realize you may as well head back to the other miners. Besides, you're not a slider, and therefore not under slider control. You and your fellow miners can make up your own minds about the situation.

When you re-enter the pod, the miners look at you expectantly.

"What's going on?" one of them says.

"Yeah," says Piver. "Has war been declared?"

"It's certainly looking that way," you say. "These sliders aren't keen on talking."

"What should we do?" Piver asks.

"We need to make a decision. We either help Slider Command or leave the Pillars and make our way back up the mountain to home. If there is going to be an invasion I know where I want to be and that's with my family."

You look at the worried faces all around you.

"But how will we get home?" one of the miners says.

Piver is looking increasingly agitated, but he comes and stands by your side.

You glance around, trying to gauge the mood of the others. "We can leave the mining equipment here and make our way back home by using the tows and the safe routes."

Miners are shaking their heads and mumbling under their breath. Most come from a long line of mining families. The idea of striking out across the slopes without a slider escort is unthinkable. They are far less informed about travel on the slopes. Understandably it frightens them.

You may not be a trained slider, but you've heard slider stories and discussions on tactics and tricks for maneuvering on black glass ever since you were a baby. Mining school taught you a few trick about getting around as well. With a bit of gear from your sledge, you're confident you can get back home without an escort.

From the body language, and mumblings of the miners, you can tell they want to stay where they are, safe under the protection of the base commander here at the Pillars of Haramon.

But you're not sure about that man. He seems a little too eager to fight. You were always taught to think for yourself rather than blindly follow orders that don't seem right. On the other hand, you can't deny that travelling the slopes can be dangerous, and you don't like the idea of leaving your classmates behind.

It is time to choose. Do you:

Help Slider Command disable the Lowland machine? **P336**

Or

Leave the Pillars of Haramon and strike out for home on your own? **P344**

Volunteer to go with the sliders and attack the machine.

You can't bring yourself to leave your comrades, so helping Slider Command seems your only option. The Lowlanders and their strange machine will create havoc amongst the Highland communities if something isn't done quickly. You'll most likely end up fighting anyway, so you may as well do it before the Lowlanders are any higher up the mountain. Your family would be disappointed if they found out you hadn't volunteered. If things go wrong, at least you would have tried to make a difference. You let your fellow miners know what you intend and go back to the stairs and start climbing.

"The miners will help," you tell the officer in the command pod. "We all have mechanical knowledge, but only myself and Piver come from slider families and know how to move safely around the slopes. The others should stay here to help fortify the Pillars."

"That makes sense," the office says with a curt nod. "The last thing I want is a bunch of miners slowing us down." The officer holds out his hand. "Welcome to the mission. Glad you've decided to come along."

As you shake the officer's hand, you wonder if you've made the right decision. You've been on a few trips around the Highlands with your family and they've taught you a few basics about travelling around the slopes, but your experience is limited. You might know more than the other miners in your group, but compared to these sliders, you're only a beginner.

"Go get your equipment. Make sure you and Piver are at the main portal in twenty minutes," the officer says. "Pack as light as you can. We'll be moving fast."

You start back down the steps towards the accommodation pod, but before you get far, a faint voice echoes down the staircase. You stop to listen.

"You really think those two miners are going to make any difference? They're not much more than kids."

"What other option do we have?" the officer says. "Their mechanical knowledge is our last hope. How many people did we lose trying to stop that machine from skirting around our defenses?"

The unfamiliar voice does not reply. The conversation fades as it moves to another part of the command pod and all you can hear are mumbles. Maybe the outspoken Highlander was right. Maybe you won't be much use stopping the machine. All that you know is that you have to try. When you get back to the others, you pull Piver aside and tell him the plan.

"We're going with the sliders?" Piver asks, making sure he's heard right. "Geebus! Thanks for asking me!"

You give Piver a little grin. "The sliders seemed a bit glum. I thought you could cheer them up a little."

"Funny ha ha," Piver says. "I doubt there will be much to joke about when we're all free sliding towards the bottom."

You head down to your sledges. "I think tangling their machine in cables somehow, is our only chance to stop it," you say to Piver as you work. "It shouldn't take much to jam up all those gears and chains."

"Assuming they don't net us before we get close enough."

Piver is right. Your slider escort didn't do too well. Why should this lot fare any better?

Between the two of you, you sort out what you need from the sledges. It isn't much because you have to carry whatever you take. You pack a launcher with some spare charges, an impact drill, and an assortment of hand tools, cables, zippers and clips.

Piver grabs a spool of high-temp cutting cord as well. "I've always wanted to use this stuff!" he says. "I hear it cuts through rock at over a foot a second."

"Just don't drop it. I've also heard it's not that stable."

You hear movement behind you as a troop of sliders make their way down one of the tunnels towards the portal. The sliders tower over you and the even smaller Piver. Their uniforms show off their muscular legs and arms. Each has a pack on their backs and a utility belt around their waists.

The officer from earlier is among them. "You miners ready?"

You swallow and nod.

He throws you each a pair of diamond spurs. "Better put these on. Should keep you from slipping."

The diamonds on the spurs are tiny, but each is cut in such a way that a sharp point digs into the rock every time you dig in your heel.

Once strapped onto your boots, you try them out. The grip they provide is remarkable. Then to your amazement he hands you a guide stick.

"You'll need one of these too," the office says. "Look after it, they're expensive to replace."

You look at the stick in your hand. "Wow, thanks. I never thought I'd get to use one of these."

"Pretty hard to travel with the Highland Slider Corps without one," the office says. "Just remember it's a lot more sensitive than the cheap commercial models so don't over correct on your turns."

Without further ceremony, the officer pulls a lever just inside the portal and a section of the wall rolls back to reveal a steeply angled tunnel disappearing down into the ground.

One of the Highland sliders sits on the ground next to the hole and lowers his feet into it. Then without warning he pushes off and disappears with a *whoosh*.

"Where's he going?" you ask the officer.

"This shaft takes us below ground to a secret chamber," the officer says. "When the miners first started excavating here at the Pillars of Haramon, they had to figure out a way to get rid of all the excess rock. To solve the problem, they drilled a tunnel from under the Pillars, up through the hillside to the ridge above. Inside this tunnel, they built a high-speed conveyor that took the rubble up and dumped it into the valley on the other side where it slid down the hill and into a crevasse."

"Sounds like a lot of work," you say.

"It was, but the rich pickings made it all worthwhile. Fifty years ago, when the main mining operation ceased, the Slider Corps began using the conveyor as a lift to get troops up the mountain where we have the advantage of altitude over any invaders. Sure beats climbing or using tows. Besides, a conventional tow would be vulnerable to attack. This one is totally hidden."

"Why haven't I heard about this?" you ask the officer.

"It's ultra-top-secret."

"Great." Piver said with a grin. "Now that we know their secret, they'll have to kill us."

The officer looks down at Piver, shakes his head and chuckles. "Only if the Lowlanders don't get you first."

The two of you watch slider after slider drop feet first into the tunnel. When it is your turn you sit on the ground and scoot nervously towards the edge. All you can see is the first fifteen feet of smooth black rock angling steeply down into the darkness. You hesitate…

"Happy landing," the officer says pushing you towards the edge with the toe of his boot. "Don't forget to bend your knees."

"Wait I'm not… Whoa!" You feel your stomach lurch for a second or so, but then the tunnel gently angles you down into the core of the mountain. It feels strange sliding in complete darkness. The turns and twist are so frequent, at times it's hard to tell up from down.

When a faint light reflects off the stone in the distance, you know you'd better relax and get ready for impact. With a *swish* you pop out of the tunnel into a wide chamber. Moon moths cluster together on the ceiling, giving you enough light to see sliders standing around waiting for the rest of you to arrive.

You skid across the floor and come to rest in a fine net stretched across the chamber. Strong hands pull you to your feet.

"Wow, that was strange," you say. "Sliding in the darkness is really disorientating."

"You get used to it," a slider says.

You hear a delighted squeal as Piver pops out of the tunnel. "Geebus that was fun! Forget this mining lark. I want to be a slider!"

Piver throws his head back and laughs with his mouth open so wide you could drop a pango egg down his throat without even touching the sides. You've never seen him so animated.

"Pleased you enjoyed it," the officer says. "Now will you stop giggling like an idiot and get ready to move out."

Piver snaps his mouth shut, turns bright red and adjusts his pack.

While you sort your gear, the officer walks across the chamber towards a wide belt whirring up another tunnel. Every ten feet or so, a metal lip runs across the width of the belt. These barriers would have stopped the crushed rock from sliding back down the belt as it travelled to the surface for disposal.

"This next part is tricky," the office says. "You've got to time your jump so you end up on a flat part of the conveyor. Those metal shutters are hard and the belt is moving at pace so be careful. If you keep low and lean forward, you'll be fine."

You watch the sliders time their jump as you move towards the front of the line. The large drum that is rotating the belt beneath your feet makes the floor of the chamber vibrate.

"I'll count you in," the officer says.

You move to the edge of the conveyor and prepare to jump.

"On my mark. Three, two, one, now."

You hit the belt and immediately drop to all fours. The belt is really moving. Before long you are in total darkness once again.

"Don't worry," the slider behind you says. "Getting off is the easy part."

When you get to the top you see why. The belt dives around another drum, and deposits you into a narrow chute that slopes down towards a drop-off some twenty yards away. All you can see at the end of the chute is … nothing!

"Whoa!" you yell, as you scrabble for something to hold on to. But there is nothing but smooth black glass.

You only see the ultra-fine netting strung up across the chute, as it brings you to a sudden stop a yard from the edge of the cliff.

"Phew." You say as you regain your feet. "You should warn people about that. I thought I was heading to the bottom."

You see the sliders trying to suppress their laughter. It's obviously a trick they play on everyone who takes the conveyor for the first time.

When you hear a squeal of abject terror behind you, you know Piver has arrived.

"Geebus!" Piver says as he wobbles over to join you. "I nearly pooped myself."

A few of the sliders hear Piver's comments and laugh.

"Tell me about it!" you say to Piver. "Seems you're not the only comedian on this trip."

The officer taps his guide stick on the ground. "Okay, listen up people. We've got an important mission to accomplish. We need to figure out how to stop this new weapon the Lowlanders have developed. We've brought two miners with us for their mechanical expertise. Look after them. We need them in one piece."

"I like being in one piece," Piver whispers.

You tap him in the shin with the toe of your boot. "Shush."

The officer continues. "We're going to traverse along this ridge as far as we can. Hopefully the Lowlanders are still in the valley. Once we find them, we'll assess the situation and then decide what to do."

"You miners will be linked to a slider front and back. If you feel yourself beginning to fall, yell out immediately so my men have time to put in an emergency belay. Got it?"

The two of you nod. This is all beginning to sound rather serious.

"Parts of this ridge have been overrun by morph rats, so watch out for burrows," the officer says. "We don't want anyone breaking a leg."

"Just what we need, morph rats," Piver says. "Those things give me the creeps."

You're not a big fan of morph rats either. They eat everything in their path and they leave burrows in the most unexpected places. You also hate the sticky slime that covers their hairless bodies, and the sucking sound their feet make as they move around the slopes.

You've heard they're edible, but by the time all the slime and stench is boiled off them, and their tough hide is removed, the small amount of stringy meat you'd get seems hardly worth the effort.

The officer is speaking again. "... okay, let's get our boots locked and get ready to move out. We need to take advantage of what light we have left."

Everyone clips their boots together and shuffles into a line. The officer is out front and will lead the troop himself.

"On my count. Three, two, one..."

He pushes off and starts traversing across the slope along a narrow path worn into its surface. The path runs ever so slightly downhill, but because the ridge is high above the valley floor, you are still able to travel up towards its head. By the time you reach the valley floor, your group is already three or four miles above the Pillars.

"We'll have to use zip lines from here," the office says.

You pull your scope from your pocket and scan the upper slopes. Everything is dark and in shadow. There is no sign of the Lowlanders or their machine.

The officer turns to you and Piver. "Can you fire an anchor bolt into that pinnacle up there?" He points up the slope to where an old volcanic pipe rises out of the slope near the ridgeline. "We could zip up and continue traversing that way. Save our legs for when we find the Lowlanders."

You waste no time in setting up the launcher. Climbing has never been your strong point.

When the launcher is ready to go, Piver sets off the charge. The anchor bolt streaks off towards its target, and the fine cable whirls off the drum beside you. With a cloud of dust, the bolt smacks into the rock at the base of the pinnacle.

"Nice shot," the officer says. "Okay. Let's get up there and get sliding."

Once you're on the ridge, having gained some valuable altitude, you pull out your scope again. The machine is hard to spot in the shadows of the upper slope, but its tiny puffs of steam give its position away.

"I see them," you say. "They're at twenty-eight degrees, south by southeast."

The officer pulls out his scope and checks the coordinates. "Good spotting. Looks like they're getting their camp sorted before dewfall. We need to get above them if we're to have any chance of sending them to the bottom."

You go back to your scope and watch the Lowlanders' preparations. You can just barely make out the track their machine has made as it drilled its way up the hillside. The Lowlanders have anchored it on a semi-flat spur near a side gully.

Some of the Lowlanders are rigging up covers in case it rains, while others are tending cooking pots.

You can see Lowland guards stationed on the upper side of the machine. If an attack is to come, they know the Highlanders are most likely to strike from above.

Meanwhile the sliders are talking about climbing around the Lowlanders so they can attack from above in typical slider style. This makes you think.

You zoom in on the track and see the regular series of holes the machine has drilled into the slope. This track runs all the way up the valley like a staircase.

If the Lowlanders are expecting an attack from above, why not use the track made by their own machine to climb up and attack at night after dewfall when the Lowlanders least expect it?

But what happens if the Lowlanders spot you coming? You will be below them and they will have the advantage of altitude. Your suggestion could be responsible for a terrible defeat.

It is time to make a decision. Do you?

Suggest an attack from below? **P355**

Or

Stay quiet and let the sliders plan and attack from above? **P360**

You have decided to leave the Pillars and strike out for home.

You put your hands on your hips and look at the other miners. "Well I don't know about you lot, but I'm not going to get involved in a war without at least trying to find a peaceful solution. If you want to follow some blood-crazed slider, be my guest!"

As you start packing up your gear, everyone mills about not knowing what to do.

"In fact, you probably should stay here," you say, as you shoulder your pack. "I don't need a bunch of inexperienced miners slowing me down."

You leave the pod and head towards the sledges to get the extra gear you'll need to make the long trip back to your home community.

After untying the cover on your sledge you grab a spool of light-weight cable, an extra zipper, some anchors and a cable launcher and stow them in your pack along with some travel rations and broth. Then you sit to strap on the pair of diamond spurs your family gave you as a going away present. "In case you ever need grip in a hurry," they'd said.

Just as you are tightening the last strap, you hear footsteps coming down the corridor. It's Piver.

"Didn't think I'd let you go on your own did you?"

You give him a big smile and slap him affectionately on the back. "I was hoping you'd decide to come," you say as he starts packing. "It's a lot safer moving around the slopes with two. That's for sure."

After ten minutes or so, you've both got everything sorted. Then Piver starts strapping on some spurs.

"I see you got a going away present too," you say.

"Slider parents are like that," Piver says. "Just as well, eh?"

"Yup, just as well."

"Should we tell the sliders we're leaving?" Piver asks.

"Don't worry, they'll see us. Let's just hope that crazy slider in charge doesn't go completely mental and try to fry us with one of their big magnifying lens."

Piver's eyes widen. "Would he do that?"

"Don't worry, it will only hurt for a minute,"

Piver's face goes white.

"Got you!"

Piver exhales with a rush of air. "That wasn't funny."

You chuckle and lift your pack onto your shoulders and tighten the waist strap. "Shall we start climbing?"

Without looking at Piver, you head towards the portal. You're pleased when you hear the distinctive click of diamond spurs behind you.

It's just as well you've studied this area. There are a number of routes you can take, but because dewfall isn't that far away, you and Piver will need to find a safe place to camp for the night within a couple hours.

"Let's launch a cable up to the ridge and gain some altitude," you tell Piver. "We need to get sliding if we're to make any distance."

The two of you put a charge in the launcher's tube and fire a light cable up to a rocky outcrop on the hillside above you. There is a puff of black dust as the anchor bolt buries itself into the rock.

"Up we go," you say as you clip your zipper onto the cable. "See you at the top."

The charge in the zipper is good for three thousand vertical feet. After that, you'll have to do your climbing the hard way.

Once the two of you reach the top, you look back at the Pillars below. "Beautiful, aren't they?"

Piver is deep in thought and doesn't reply.

Far below, low cloud is banking up against the foothills. The Borderlands are disappearing into the mist, which make the Black Slopes look like an island set in a violent sea of purple foam and crashing waves.

Over the next two hours, you and Piver make good distance by zipping up and then traversing. You are pleased you paid attention in navigation class when the entrance of an abandoned mine appears right where you calculated it would be.

"Looks like we've got shelter for the night," Piver says.

"As long as the morph rats haven't taken over." The thought of the slimy creatures gives you the shivers.

"Should I toss a screecher in?" Piver asks "That'll flush them out."

"Good thinking, but I didn't bring any."

"Just as well I did then." Piver unclips a round object from his belt and pushes a button on one end. A high-pitched ear-splitting screech starts to blast out.

"Quick toss it!" you yell, clamping your hands to the side of your head.

Piver throws the sphere into the opening of the mine shaft and steps to one side. You do the same. If there are morph rats in the hole, it won't be long before they scurry out.

As the two of you stand with your backs to the stone wall on either side of the shaft's entrance, you hear the screecher rolling further down the tunnel.

At first the clicking is faint, but before long its volume increases. Morph rats are coming. Within a minute it sounds like a thousand pebbles are bouncing along the tunnel towards you. The first morph rat scuttles past and throws itself out of the opening and slurps and slimes its way down the slope. More follow in a slithering mass of hairless bodies.

The rats don't notice the two of you in their headlong rush to get away from the brain piercing sound that is amplified by their extremely good sense of hearing and the hollowness of the tunnel. It smells like the tunnel has farted as the rats pass.

"Geebus that's horrible!" Piver says holding his nose.

You look over at him and can't help but laugh at his expression. "You should have stood on the upwind side of the opening."

'Piver clutches his throat and screws up his face, playing it up for all he's worth. By the time the last morph rat has disappeared, the two of you are on your hands and knees laughing.

You give the stench a moment to clear and then enter the tunnel, careful to walk on the high side of the tunnel, away from the puddles of slime left behind by the departing rats.

While you set up a small burner to heat some broth, Piver rummages in his pack for some hydro bars. Once camp is sorted you sit down around the burner and eat.

Piver takes a sip of broth and then looks up. "So what are you going to do when you get home?"

"I'm not really sure. Try to talk the communities into making peace with the Lowlanders I think. It's time we try to work things out between us. Surely we have more in common than differences. Who benefits from war?"

Piver takes another sip and nods his head. "Makes sense."

Then you hear the sound of footsteps at the mine's opening. Who could that be?

You and Piver look up from your food.

"Hello traitors!" a gruff voice says. "We thought you might stay here for the night."

You recognize one of the men from the command pod. It's the slider the officer was talking to after you told him you thought they should talk peace with the Lowlanders.

"What are you doing here?" you ask. "And what do you mean, traitors?"

"You didn't think Slider Command was going to let you walk away did you? Stupid miners!"

You don't like the sound of this. What is he inferring? Are they going to take you back to the Pillars?

"Yeah, stupid miners," the other slider says. "Time you had an accident and went for a slide."

The two sliders look at you and Piver. It sounds like they're planning to throw you down the slope.

"But it's after dewfall." you say. "We'll go all the way to the bottom."

"Not our problem," the officer says. "We've been listening to your conversation and know you're off to spread discontent amongst the communities. That doesn't suit Slider Command."

"Peace doesn't suit Slider Command?" you ask the officer. "Are you afraid you'll lose all your power and influence?"

"So naïve," the officer grunts.

The two sliders turn and have a brief conversation. While they do, you catch Piver's eye and nod towards the slime trail running down one side of the tunnel where the morph rats ran out.

It's a slippery mess, but it might be your only chance.

"Time for a slide all right," you say to the men as you snag your pack and launch yourself, belly first, onto the trail of slime heading down into the depths of the tunnel.

You hear a grunt as Piver hits the slope behind you.

You spin around onto your back and place your feet below you, hoping they will protect you if you run into anything unexpected.

"Whoaaaa!" you hear Piver say behind you. "Where does this go?"

His voice sounds frightened, and so he should be. But at least this way, you are sure the sliders won't follow you.

"Stay loose and get ready for a sudden stop," you yell back to Piver. "If I remember the map correctly, there's a side tunnel coming up that leads to an exit further down."

Your speed is increasing as you slide through the darkness. The slime smells of rat and feels both sticky and slippery at the same time.

"I feel I'm sliding through liquid fart," Piver yells. "Death might be better than this!"

No way are you opening your mouth to reply.

Your momentum is slowed as you splash into the pool of slime at the bottom of the tunnel. Before you know it, you are sitting waist-deep in the awful stuff.

Faint moonlight reaches you from a tunnel opening to your right.

"Ewwww!" Piver say, lifting his arms above the slimy mess. "This stuff is worse than pango poo!"

"Better than going to the bottom though don't you think?"

"Only just," Piver says as he stands up and struggles out of the sticky muck.

Using your hands, you sweep the slime off your torso and legs. Thankfully your uniforms are made from a tightly woven water repellant fabric that comes clean relatively easily.

"I don't hear anything from above," Piver says, tilting his head. "What now?"

"Don't worry, I have a plan."

"I hope it's better than diving into a stinking pool of slime," Piver says.

"If only it were that simple," you say with a smile. "Did your family ever tell you the story of the back-to-back slide made by two slider cadets when the Black Slopes were first being settled?"

"They got caught in a storm, didn't they?"

"That's right. They had no option but to abandon their camp after six days and take their chances free sliding. They sat on their packs and linked arms back to back. Then, using only spurs to steer, they took off down the mountain."

"I remember," Piver said. "But…"

"Remember how the rear cadet dragged his spurs like an anchor to slow them down, and the front cadet used his to steer?"

"So that's your plan? A suicide slide back to the Pillars?"

"Not to the Pillars, to the Lowlands!"

"All the way to the bottom? Geebus, are you crazy?"

You shrug and give Piver a smile.

Piver's eyes search your face. "You're serious, aren't you?"

"We have to talk to the Lowlanders and get them to hold off any invasion until we have time to speak to the elders in the communities. We need to end the conflict once and for all."

You can see Piver's mind working. He shakes his head and mumbles something under his breath. Then he looks up at you and smiles. "You always said I was crazy. Now it looks like I get a chance to prove you right."

You slap Piver on the back. "Good. Now try to get some sleep. We'll take off at first light."

The next morning, after a quick bite, you move over to the exit and pull a map out of the pouch on your belt. Unfolding it, you lay the map out on the floor in the dim light and study the contours of the terrain you will be sliding over.

"It will be plain sliding until we reach the Pillars. If we stay in the shadow, on the left of Long Gully, we should slip right past without anyone noticing."

"But not too far left," Piver says, jabbing his finger at the map. "Or we'll end up in the crevasse field."

You nod in agreement. "It's the ridges below the Pillars that scare me." You point out an area of rough ground that looks extremely dangerous.

"The words slice and dice come to mind," Piver says. "I've seen pictures of what happens to people who hit riffle ridges at speed. It's not pretty."

Your finger traces a narrow valley that branches off Long Gulley just below the Pillars. "That's why we need to take this route. It's the only safe way to the bottom."

Piver's eyebrows crease as he studies the map. "You think we'll find it sliding at speed?"

"We'd better."

You sit at the tunnel's exit, your feet dangling over the edge. You realize there is every chance that this could be the last sunrise you ever see.

For some reason, as the sun peeks over the mountains in the distances, this thought makes the scene even more beautiful.

When the light reaches the slopes below you, you turn to Piver. "We'd better get going."

Piver nods and follows your lead by creating a seat from his backpack. He tightens the arm straps around his legs to hold it firmly in place.

It may not be much, but at least the packs will give you some protection from the friction and bumps as the two of you slide down the hillside.

"Now make sure you keep even pressure on both of your spurs unless I yell left or right. If I do, just drag that spur until I say release. Got it?"

Piver gulps. "I think so."

After some final adjustment to your straps, you both scoot towards the edge. With Piver's back against yours, the two of you lock your arms together and stretch out your legs testing the bite of your spurs.

"Ready Piver?"

"It's all downhill from here," he replies, giving a shove that sends you both over the edge and onto the steep slope below.

Before you know it, you are moving with pace towards the valley floor. Piver's heels screech like a pair of demented pangos behind you, sending a shiver down your spine. A quarter mile down the valley you make a sweeping turn. Up to your right, you see the two sliders standing on the ridge. They are shaking their heads.

"Yippee!" Piver yells at the top of his voice. "Try to catch us now, morph heads!"

You admire Piver's spirit, but you also know the sliders have no intention of following. Why would they? They think you're sliding to the bottom, and not in a good way. And maybe they're right. They certainly will be if you miss the entrance to the side valley you hope to take.

"Left!" you yell when you see a small crevasse in the slope below you. "Left!"

The screech of Piver's spur increases as he digs it in. You kick your right boot into the slope at the same time, shunting the two of you further to the left. You skid past the crack with barely a yard to spare.

"Whoa, that was close," Piver says looking back up the slope.

"Release!"

Piver goes back to dragging both heels equally.

You see the Pillars looming up in the distance. "Left!" you yell again. "Pillars coming up. "

Surely guards at the Pillars will hear your spurs as you slide past. Thankfully the sun isn't high enough for Slider Command to be able to use their burning lens yet. Otherwise the two of you would be toast.

Despite Piver dragging his spurs for all he's worth, the remaining dampness on the glassy black rock means you are sliding fast. The speed makes you wonder if you'll have enough control to enter the narrow valley.

"Hard left!" you yell. "I see the entrance!"

Both of you use your heels desperately trying to move left on the slope. You stab your right heel down in repeated motions. With each kick you move a yard to the left.

"Harder!" you yell to Piver.

You kick your heel into the slope, bang, bang, bang as fast as you can. Then you're in.

"Release!" You let out a breath. "Phew, that was scary."

"Imagine what it's like when you're sliding backwards." Piver says, with a slight tremor in his voice.

The sun is up over the ridge now and is starting to reach the valley floor. Within a few miles, your progress slows a little as you hit drier slopes. You feel your control growing.

"I think we're actually going to make it," you say with relief.

The slopes begin to flatten out and within another ten minutes you are barely moving.

"I can see the Lowland camp," you tell Piver.

"Let's just hope they're as pleased to see us as we are to see them."

You dig your heels in and slide to a stop just as the last of the black rock disappears under a slope covered in pale green moss. The two of you stand and stretch your backs and shoulders.

As you stretch, you look around. It seems strange to see so much flat land in front of you. "It's so lush," you say.

Piver studies the scene. "Yeah ... weird isn't it. But it's pretty in a funny sort of way."

You can't help but agree. You adjust your pack and look towards the Lowlanders' camp. "I suppose we'd better go talk to them."

"Can I do the greeting?" Piver asks. "I've got a phrase in mind that I've always wanted the opportunity to use."

"Oh yeah? And what's that?"

"Take me to your leader," Piver says with a chuckle.

You shake your head. "You really are nuts you know."

"For once I'm pleased to say I'm not the only one."

As the two of you walk towards the Lowland camp, you wonder if you'll be okay. Will the Lowlanders be friendly?

You're apprehension doesn't last long. Before you get to the cluster of Lowland huts a group of children run out to greet you. As they crowd around, one holds out a crackle berry, the legendary fruit of the Lowlands.

You've heard stories about this celebrated fruit. You've even seen a picture of it in one of your school books. But no one from the Highlands has seen one up close, let alone tasted one, for over 300 years since the fighting began.

While you're thinking about this offering, Piver snatches the crackle berry and sinks his teeth into its succulent blue flesh.

You watch and wait, wondering if he'll like it.

As Piver chews, and without even realizing it, he rises up onto his toes and does a little jiggle with his hips. Then he sinks back down, wipes his lips with the back of his hand and says, "Geebus! That's the best thing I've ever tasted!"

Congratulations, you made it down the mountain in one piece and are about to start talks that might bring about peace between the Highlanders and the Lowlanders. Well done! But have you tried all the different paths the story takes?

You now have one more decision to make. Do you:

Go back to the beginning of the story and try another path? **P219**
Or

Go to the List of Choices and start reading from another part of the story? **P381**

You have decided to suggest an attack from below.

You put down your scope and take a step towards the officer. "I think we might have a better chance if we sneak up from below."

The officer gives you a funny look. "What? Are you mad?"

You know your suggestion goes against every slider principle. All your life you've heard about the advantage of altitude, but maybe new times need new solutions.

"Look," you say, pointing towards the series of holes running up the valley. "The Lowlanders have provided us with a staircase that leads right to their camp. We can climb at night after dewfall. They'll never expect us."

You can see the cogs in the officer's mind working. His brow scrunches together and he scratches the side of his face. He pulls out his scope and looks again at the track. Then he calls one of his men over and has a chat.

After a moment, he turns back to you. "Okay so let's say we go along with your pango-brained scheme. What do we do once we're in the camp?"

"We mount a winch further down the mountain. Once we get to the Lowlanders' camp, we hook a cable onto their machine, cut its anchors, and winch the thing off the mountain. Once the machine is dislodged from its track, it will only have one way to go."

"Can you guarantee your equipment can pull that machine out of its track?"

You nod. "We can if you and your sliders can keep the Lowlanders off our back long enough."

Piver nods his agreement. "That machine will go all the way to the bottom and believe me, it won't be in very good order once it gets there."

"May our ancestors have mercy on us," the officer says. "If this fails, we'll go down in history as the sliders who attacked from below. I hope you're prepared to become a laughing stock."

"Or heroes," you say.

With the decision made to climb the machine's track after dark, your group moves to a safe spot to wait for dewfall. Then once it's dark, the long climb up to the Lowlanders' camp can begin.

The spot the sliders have chosen to wait is tucked into a shallow depression about a mile below the Lowlanders' camp. With all the shadow in the valley, the dark colors of your uniforms will blend in with the slope.

Everyone moves carefully. Noises travel a long way in the still evening air and you don't want to alert the Lowlanders of your presence. Only the distant screech of pangos and the sound of activity in the Lowland camp break the silence.

The waiting sliders are all clipped onto a strong cable. Some eat dried hydro while they await the order to climb.

About an hour after dark the officer whispers for everyone to prepare to move out. It will be a slow climb due to the need for quiet and the dampness of the rock. Anything that can clunk or clang is secured into pockets. Your pack is heavy and awkward.

"Move out," the officer signals with his hand.

You slot your toes and fists into the holes bored by the machine and take a step up. Shifting you hands to the next set of holes, you repeat the motion until you and the sliders have established a rhythm. The weight of your gear wants to pull you back so you make sure to keep your weight forward on the steep slope.

When your group is about 100 yards below the Lowland camp, you and Piver use a couple of expansion bolts to lock the winch into the track holes. Piver attaches a heavy-duty cable to the winch's drum and hands the spool to one of the sliders to carry the rest of the way up.

Leaving Piver below, you and the sliders start to climb again. It will be your responsibility to connect the cable to the Lowland machine in such a way that it does not snap when the winch is activated. The sliders will cut the machine's tethers and keep the Lowlanders busy.

Despite the cold night, sweat drips from your forehead. You're not used to this sort of exercise.

The leading sliders have reached the camp. You can see their shadowy figures moving around just below the machine. Through a series of hand signals, you are instructed to move forward. A slider hands you the end of the cable and you start looking for the best possible place to attach it to the machine.

It's important that the cable twists the machine sideway so it dislodges the sprocket from the holes in the track. If it only pulls straight down, the winch may not have enough power.

You look at the sides of the machine, but they are smooth. There is no obvious protrusion for the cable to hook on to. Then you see a bracket that forms part of the catapult mechanism. It looks a perfect place to attach the cable, but it's above your reach along the top edge of the machine.

You signal the slider beside you and point to the bracket. He nods, understanding your problem. Interlacing his fingers he creates a place to put your foot and hoists you up so that you can hook the shackle onto the bracket.

You've just finished securing the shackle when there is a shout from the camp.

The Lowland guards have spotted someone and raised the alarm.

"Down the cable!" you yell to the Highlanders.

The Highlander lowers you to the ground and the two of you clip on to the cable.

"Quickly."

Going down is a lot easier than going up. All you have to do is pull a trigger on your zipper and you slide freely down the cable. Release the trigger and the zipper clamps onto the cable and brings you to a halt.

Before you know it you and the Highlanders are back beside Piver.

"Now, Piver. Let's rip that scab off the mountain!"

Piver wastes no time in throwing the winch into gear. It splutters and coughs, then starts to wind the excess cable around the drum. By the time all the slack cable is wound up the drum is spinning at quite a good speed.

You hold your breath. Will it be strong enough to jerk the machine off the hillside?

When the last of the slack has been taken up, the cable rises off the ground and starts to stretch.

Any moment now.

"I don't know if it's going to be strong enough," Piver says as the winch groans in protest.

Then you hear yelling from up the mountainside. Lowlanders are shouting warnings to their comrades. All their gear is on the machine. They'll be stranded if they lose it.

Suddenly the cable goes slack and you hear a scraping noise from above.

"It's off," you yell. "Cut the cable!"

Piver grabs a pair of cutters from his belt and bears down on the cable. With a *ping* it separates from the drum.

The scraping is getting louder.

"Geebus, I hope it doesn't take us out on its way past," Piver squeaks, nervously.

So do you, but there is nothing you can do about that now.

Whoosh! The machine slides by before you even see it coming.

"Whoa that was close," Piver says.

Piver's teeth sparkle in the dark.

"Well done, miners. I'm proud of you," the officer says. "That's one machine that won't be roaming the Highlands any time soon."

You must admit you're a little proud of yourself too. Sliders will sing songs of this encounter for many years to come. You and Piver have etched a place in slider history, even though you're only miners.

"Okay troops, the sun will be up in less than an hour. Let's get out of here."

"What will happen to the Lowlanders?" you ask.

"We'll send some sliders for them in a day or two. They'll be very happy to surrender after a couple of cold nights on the slopes.

The climb back down is easier. With a series of belays, you and the sliders make your way down to the Pillars. By the time you are standing outside the main portal, the sun is climbing over the ridge.

It's another beautiful day on the Black Slopes.

"Hey," Piver says. "Where do you find a group of Lowlanders when they've lost one of their fancy machines?"

It's a bit early in the morning for jokes, but you're in a good mood. "I don't know. Where?"

"Exactly where you left them!"

Congratulations, you and Piver have saved the day. Later that month you were both awarded the Highland Medal of Bravery and made honorary members of the Slider Corps. The sliders even let you keep your guide sticks.

But have you followed all the possible paths this book has to offer? Have you encountered morph rats? Found the secret of the moon moths?

It's time for you to make another decision. Do you:

Go back to the beginning of the story and try another path? **P219**

Or

Go to the list of choices and start reading from another part of the story? **P381**

Stay quiet and let the sliders plan their attack from above

You are hesitant to tell the sliders how to do their job, even though you think that sneaking up from below might be the right thing to do.

The slider officer has gathered his troop together to discuss strategy. You move a little closer so you can hear what they are saying.

"We'll have to wait until morning," the officer says. "Trying to get above the Lowlanders at night would be too dangerous with a couple miners in tow."

You watch the Lowlanders through your scope as you listen in on the sliders' conversation.

"But if we wait till morning, we may never catch them in time," another slider grumps.

You think a moment. "Wait, I have an idea."

"And what might that be?" the officer growls, angry at having his thinking interrupted.

"What if Piver and I climbed up the machine's track to the Lowland camp, while you and your troop go up and around? If you distract the Lowlanders from above, it will give us time to hook a cable onto to their machine and pull them off."

"You think you two can handle that on your own?" the officer asks, a little surprised.

"Climbing the track will be easy. The holes will give us all the hand and footholds we need. The winch we need to pull them off is heavy, but we won't have as far to go as you sliders so we can take a few breaks during the climb."

The officer looks at his team. Many of the sliders are nodding their heads.

"Okay, that's the plan then. You two will have one hour after dewfall to get your equipment in place. When we attack, you'll need to move right away. There is always a chance the Lowlanders will retreat behind their machine. If that happens they will see you for sure."

"Just go easy on them for the first few minutes of your attack.

That's all it will take for me to hook a cable on that steaming contraption of theirs," you say. "After that, you can do whatever you like."

Everyone seems happy with the strategy. The Highland sliders adjust their gear and get a few extra anchor bolts out of their packs.

"Good luck," the office says. "Remember, exactly one hour after dewfall."

You wave as the sliders head off. It will be hard climb time for them. Still, that is what they've trained for.

Unlike the sliders who are climbing the long way around, you and Piver waste no time getting ready to take a gentle slide across the valley to the point where you will intersect the track made by the Lowland machine.

The winch is broken down into two parts, with Piver taking the drum of heavy cable while you take the motor and mounting.

The valley is in shadow. Dewfall is less than an hour away by the time the two of you point your boots slightly downhill and get ready to push off towards the other side of the valley.

"Let's keep as quiet as we can," you say to Piver. "We don't want the Lowlanders to know we're below them."

Piver grins. "Not wrong there. It could get tricky if they start throwing rocks."

With a grim determination, the two of you start your slide. The wind in your face is cooler now that the sun has disappeared behind the ridge. Everywhere you look it is a duller shade of black now that there is no light reflecting off the surface of the slope. Were it not for the flickering lights of the Lowlanders' camp, you would never have known they were there.

You are almost upon the track when you see the series of holes running along the slope. "Here it is," you say to Piver. "Let's get an anchor in and a sling rigged before dewfall. Once it's fully dark, we can start climbing."

You and Piver only get half an hour's rest before the light is gone completely. The night is still, and the only sounds are the odd rattle and voices from the Lowland camp.

"Steady as we go," you say to Piver. "This rock is slipperier than the slime on a morph rat's back."

Standing with your toes jammed into holes, the two of you tighten your packs and rope yourselves together.

"Only one of us moves at a time," you say. "A brief tug on the rope will signal that I'm ready for you to move up."

Piver chuckles nervously, jams his guide stick firmly into a hole and braces himself, ready to hang on should you fall. "Well you'd better get going then," he says.

You sling your stick over your shoulder, stretch forward, and place a fist in each hole. Once your hands are secure you take a few steps. You repeat this process until you're fifteen or so yards further up the slope before jamming your stick in a hole to belay Piver. Giving the cable a light tug, you signal him to climb up to join you.

The two of you repeat this procedure until you are only twenty yards at most below the Lowland camp.

"Quiet," you whisper.

Setting up the winch in absolute silence, in the dark, is even trickier than you thought it would be. Luckily there aren't many moving parts, and most of the assembly can be done by feel. Attaching the winch firmly to the slope with expansion bolts is the hardest part. Thankfully the holes in the track save you from having to drill your own. By the time the job is finished, both you and Piver are sweating.

"When the sliders attack, I'm going to drag that cable up the last few yards and shackle it onto their machine as fast as I can," you say.

Piver smiles. "Then I start the winch and drag the morph-heads off," Piver whispers, his teeth gleaming in the dark.

"Exactly," you say. "Just make sure you give me time to get out of the way before you turn it on. Oh and don't forget to cut the cable once they're off. Otherwise it will swing the machine in your direction and…"

"Squish, splat. I get it."

You tap Piver on the arm and throw the cable over your shoulder. "I'm going to get a little closer," you whisper. "The sliders" attack should start any moment now."

With your belly close to the ground, you slowly work your way up the track until you are lying only yards away from the platform where the Lowlanders are camped. You are so close to the camp, you can hear the Lowlanders farting around their burners as they eat their beans and mash.

All is black around you until a slice of moon pokes its head above the western ridge of a mountain in the distance. You're please to have a little more light, but hope the diversion the sliders are going to create happens soon, otherwise you might get spotted.

When you look down the mountain you can just make out Piver's silhouette against the slope. Moonlight reflects off his teeth, and you wish for once the plucky fellow would stop smiling.

Time moves slowly. Your heart pounds. Thump thump — thump thump — thump thump. It sounds so loud. "Hurry up," you whisper. "They're going to hear me."

When you hear a yell from above, you are relieved. Within a few moments the entire hillside is alive. Moon shadows stretch across the mountain as the Lowlanders respond to the Highland attack.

You stand in a half crouch and move up the track. Before you know it you are on flattish ground and reaching to steady yourself against the rear of the machine. You need to move forward so you can attach the cable at the front where the winch will have a chance of pulling the machine's sprocket wheel out of its holes and send it tumbling down the mountainside.

The Lowland voices seem further away. The sliders must be drawing them up the slope, as they pretend to retreat.

You work your way forward, feeling for protrusions to grip on to as you go. Then you see a bracket sticking out of the side of the machine near its front left corner. It is a perfect place to attach the cable.

The shackle only takes a moment to attach. Once done, you clip on to the cable and start back down towards Piver, sliding fast. The sound of fighting above is getting closer. The Highlanders must be on the charge again.

You know that if your plan doesn't work, the sliders will fight to the death to defeat this machine.

"Winch!" you yell out to Piver. "Quickly!"

You hear the familiar whine of the motor as it takes up the slack in the cable. The winch strains at its mountings. There is a torturous scrape of metal on stone from above as the machine's front end is dragged around side-on to the slope.

Then the cable goes slack.

"It's off." you say to Piver. "Quick, cut the cable."

Piver grabs a pair of cutters from his belt and bears down on the cable. With a *ping* it separates from the drum.

The scraping and clanking is getting closer.

"I hope it doesn't take us out on its way past," Piver squeaks.

So do you, but there is nothing you can do about that now.

Whoosh! A dark shadow skids by within feet of where you and Piver are standing.

"Geebus! That was close," Piver says.

The fighting rages on for another ten minutes or so, but without their machine the Lowlanders are no match for the Highland Slider Corps. A couple of times you hear someone yell as they plummet down the slope past you in the darkness. You can't tell if they are Highlanders or Lowlanders. Regardless, mothers will weep and families will grieve.

Suddenly, it's like someone's turned off a switch and everything goes silent.

"I wonder who won?" Piver says.

It doesn't take long for you to find out.

"Hey, you miners still alive down there?" a familiar voice calls out.

"Yes." Piver replies.

The two of you climb up the path to the small plateau where the sliders have the Lowlanders sitting in a group with their hands tied together.

This is the first time you've seen Lowlanders up close. They look remarkably like members of your own family.

"Well done, you two," the officer says. "As soon as their machine was off, they gave up reasonably easily."

"So what now?" you ask.

"We'll wait until morning and then take them down to the Pillars. They'll get to go home again once their relatives have paid the ransom."

You're pleased that the Lowlanders won't be locked up forever. They don't look much older than you.

"Oh and by the way," the officer says to you and Piver. "I'm going to recommend that you and funny boy here are made honorary sliders."

"Geebus!" Piver says. "Real sliders?"

"Yes," the officer says, "real Highland sliders. Assuming you don't trip and go to the bottom on the way home that is."

For once, your grin is as wide as Piver's. Your family will be so pleased. Now you can follow your dream to be a miner, while being a slider too.

Congratulation, you have finished this part of the story. But have you tried all the different paths? Have you found the moon moth's secret chamber and fought the morph rats? Have you explored the old mine shaft and discovered the reservoir? It is time for you to make another decision. Do you:

Go back to the beginning of the story and try another path? **P219**
Or
Go to the list of choices and start reading from another part of the story? **P381**

Carry on to the Pillars with the Lowlanders' message.

You are pleased the sliders have left the decision up to you and are ready to continue on to the Pillars of Haramon with the Lowlanders' message. To start a war without the Highland Council discussing the matter would be irresponsible and put many lives at risk.

What if the Lowlanders really do have some new technology that would make fighting them pointless? Maybe joining their federation would bring benefits to your community. Whichever the case, the Highland Council will have to decide which course of action to take.

"Well if we're not fighting, we'd better get sliding," the head slider says. "We've still got a lot of rock to cover if we're going to get to the Pillars before dewfall."

You tell the miners to check their loads and climb aboard their sledges.

"Any objection if we take the fast route to the Pillars?" the slider officer asks. "I'm assuming this message is urgent."

"Do what you need to, as long as we get there in one piece," you say.

The officer reorganizes his troop for fast travel, one slider steering and two braking on each sledge.

You cinch your waist strap tight and get ready for a speedy ride.

"This should be fun," Piver yells over to you. "I've always wanted to be on a sledge with a bunch of crazy sliders going at top speed down the mountainside. NOT!"

You know how he feels, but you also know that the council will need time to discuss the Lowlanders' offer. The more time they have, the better decision they are likely to make.

"On my mark!" the officer yells.

And with a jerk of the sledge you're off.

The fast route zigzags down a steep face then cuts across a ridge into Long Gully. Further down Long Gully are the Pillars of Haramon, one of the Highland's most secure outposts.

As your slider escorts guide you down the mountain track, you look around at the scenery. Far below is a wonderful mosaic of color. To the west, dark brooding mountains march off into the haze.

"Here comes the tricky part," Shoola calls as your sledge screeches around a hairpin bend.

You look off to the side of your sledge and see only air.

"Geebus that's steep!" you hear Piver shout from the sledge behind you.

He's not wrong. You swallow hard and hold on a little tighter. Looking down makes you feel a little queasy. You look out over the ranges and pretend you're on a simulator. Only unlike the simulators at mining school, this one has a stiff breeze blowing in your face and the screech of sliders straining on their hooks to slow the sledge down for the corners.

When your group finally gets to the bottom, you breathe a sigh of relief. Once they've skirted a small crevasse field, the sliders turn the sledges onto a small plateau and stop.

"You have ten minutes," the leader says.

While most of the sliders sit to rest their legs, the miners are off their sledges a quickly as possible to attach tethers and then stretch. Hydro bars are unwrapped as some have a quick snack.

The bone rattling ride down the mountain has made you need to pee, so you move away from the group and duck behind a small rocky outcrop about twenty yards from the main group.

Just as you start to loosen your uniform, you hear the slurping feet and gnashing teeth of morph rats. Apart from an unexpected cloud burst, this is the most dreaded sound in all the Highlands.

"Morph rats!" you yell, forgetting all about your need to pee.

You look up the slope and can't believe you eyes. There must be a thousand of the horrible creatures, and they are heading in your direction. Their slimy bodies are a light green and the suckers on their feet slurp with every step they take on the slippery black rock.

As they get closer, the clattering of their teeth gets louder. These teeth can strip a full-grown pango to nothing but bone in less than a minute.

Feral packs eat anything in their path. Thankfully, their sense of smell and eyesight are really bad. You can fight them or hide from them.

You need to make a decision quickly. Do you:

Climb up on top of the rocky outcrop and hope the morph rats go around you? **P369**

Or

Run back over to the others and fight the morph rats as a group? **P371**

You have decided to climb on top of the rocky outcrop.

You're not sure that you have time to get to the others before the morph rats are upon you, so you start climbing up the rock. With a bit of luck, the pack of morph rats will stream around you and continue blindly on down the slope.

Their slurping footsteps are getting closer, their teeth chattering like pebbles tumbling down the mountainside.

"Sliders! Uphill V formation now! Miners, get in behind!" you hear a slider yell.

From your vantage point on the rock, you see the sliders bunch together, each has turned their pack around to the front to protect their chest. Their guide sticks, with diamond hooks to the front, are tucked firmly under their armpits, while both hands hold firmly onto the shaft.

The miners are behind the sliders' formation, hand picks up and at the ready.

The pack of morph rats move like a writhing wave of teeth and slime down the hillside.

When the wave hits, those at the point of the V-formation will sweep the rats to the side using their sticks.

"Try to flip the rats onto their backs so they lose their grip on the slope," the head slider says. "That way, by the time they regain their feet they'll be too far down the mountain to be of any danger."

The clicking and slurping sends a chill down your spine. One slip and everyone is rat food.

You don't have your pick with you. You left it leaning against your sledge when you headed for the rock. That was a big mistake.

Without your pick, all you can do is hope the rats go around the rock rather than over it. If any rats do decide to climb towards your position you just hope you'll be able to kick them away.

You watch with a morbid fascination as the wave of slimy flesh and pointed teeth surges towards your rock. Anyone that ends up in this seething mass of animals won't last long.

The sliders stand with sticks at the ready.

All you can do is watch and wait.

When the mass of rat flesh reaches your position, the sheer weight of rats behind the front of the wave, pushes rats up the rock you are standing on. The first few you manage to kick off, but before long your boots are covered in slime and standing on the rock is becoming more difficult.

You chance a quick glance at the others and see that the sliders' technique is working. The wave of rats is parting around the sliders and miners on the slope.

You feel teeth dig into your shin and try to kick the rats at your feet away, but slime is all over your rock now. You try another kick, but lose your balance. You are falling into the swarm.

Unfortunately this part of your adventure is over. You made the mistake of thinking you could escape the morph rats by climbing the rock. You should have gone back and joined forces with the others. There is always safety in numbers when it comes to fighting off morph rats.

It is now time for you to make another decision. Do you:

Go back to the beginning of the story and try another path? **P219**
Or
Go back to your last choice and make a different decision? **P371**

Run back and fight the morph rats off as a group.

"Sliders, uphill-V-formation, quickly! You miners tuck in behind," the head slider yells.

You move as fast as you can to where the sliders are forming into a defensive position to take on the advancing wave of morph rats.

The rat's slurping footsteps are getting closer. Their teeth clatter and click as they move.

The sliders bunch together. Each has turned their pack around to protect their chest from the rat's razor-sharp teeth, should one of them break through. Their guide sticks, with diamond hooks pointing to the front, are tucked under their armpits. They clutch the shaft firmly in both hands. Grim determination is set in their eyes.

You and the other miners squeeze in behind the sliders' formation, hand picks at the ready.

The pack of morph rats moves like a writhing wave of teeth and slime down the hillside towards you. It isn't a pretty sight, and smells even worse.

When the wave of rats reaches the V-formation, the sliders at the front furiously sweep the rats to each side using their sticks like brooms. The sliders near the rear of the group then try to flip the rats onto their backs so they lose their grip on the slope and slide too far down the mountain to be of any danger.

"Geebus, look at them!" Piver shivers in disgust, his pick at the ready. "They have got to be the ugliest creatures alive."

Snap, click, snap go thousands of teeth.

"Ugh, I can smell their breath from here," Piver says. "It's like rotten eggs."

The sliders are struggling to sweep aside the writhing mass as it slurps past.

"Yeow!" a miner yelps as a morph rat chomps onto his leg. He swings his pick knocking the rat out and then kicks the hideous creature down the slope. "That hurt!"

And then, as suddenly as they came, the rats have passed, slithering further down the slope in search of plump pangos.

"Well done sliders," the officer says. "Never get isolated by morph rats, if you do, you're better off free sliding. Being swarmed by morph rats is not the way you want to go, believe me."

You see Piver close his eyes and shudder. Sometimes his overactive imagination leads to funny situations, at other times it can be a curse.

"You okay Piver?" you ask. He looks a little pale.

"Yeah, it's just that…" He shakes his head. "Never mind, I don't want to think about it."

"Right, load up," the head slider says. "We've got to get to the Pillars before dewfall."

Remembering you needed to pee, you rush back over behind the rock and relieve yourself. The rock is covered in rat slime. If you'd stayed there you wouldn't have survived.

After everyone is ready your little caravan sets off again, moving at top speed towards the Pillars of Haramon.

"Cute little critters those rats, eh?" Shoola says as she slides down the mountain behind you.

"Yeah right," you say. "Ever eaten one?"

"Just once. My troop was trapped high up the mountain in a storm. All we could do for six days was anchor ourselves on the mountain and hang on. By the time it was safe to move around, we hadn't eaten in three days."

"Three days?"

"We were just about to slide off, when a small pack of rats came by. Let's just say it was messy. By the time we'd skinned a couple, there was slime everywhere. I can still smell it in my uniform some days."

You can't imagine not eating for three days. But even then, you don't know if you'd ever get hungry enough to eat a morph rat. "Yuck. Sounds horrible."

Shoola smiles. "Let's just say I've taken dumps that smelled better and leave it at that."

You laugh and look out over the valley. The sun is getting low in the sky. Soon it will disappear behind the ridge and the temperature will drop six or seven degrees. An hour after that, dewfall will start. You just hope you've arrived at the Pillars by then.

About forty minutes later, you see two towering monoliths rising high above the valley floor in the distance. The black stone pillars are the most beautiful sight you have ever seen. Smooth and shining, they dwarf everything around them. Sunshine still illuminates their tops.

You want to make some comment to Shoola about how amazing they look, but your mouth is hanging open in awe and any words you come up with seem inadequate.

"Not far now," she says.

Within ten minutes your caravan is outside one of the Pillar's main portals. A door slides open at its base and the sliders maneuver the sledges inside a cavern hollowed out of the solid rock.

With a hiss of air, the massive doors close again and you unbuckle your straps.

"Welcome to the Pillars of Haramon," a crew member says. "Cutting it a bit fine for dewfall weren't you?"

The head slider steps forward. "Considering we ran into Lowlanders and a huge swarm of morph rats, I think we've done well just to make it here in one piece."

You and the other miners mumble your agreement.

"I need to get a message to the Highland Council," you say. "The Lowlanders have given us an ultimatum."

"You'd better go up to the command pod and tell the officer in charge. Ultimatums are above my pay grade."

The crew member points you towards a spiral staircase cut into the rock. "They're on the top floor."

"You mean I've got to climb a thousand feet to the top of the Pillars?" This is not what you had in mind.

"No, silly. There's a cable-lift two flights up."

You breathe a sigh of relief and start up the first flight. You wonder how big each flight is and start counting. The first flight is 39 steps. By the time you reach the landing you are sweating. "I must do more exercise," you tell yourself.

At the top of the second flight, you come to a place where a vertical shaft has been bored into the rock. A motorized cable runs up the tunnel. Every five seconds or so, a sturdy platform appears. You watch as a slider steps onto a platform and is whisked up the tunnel. Now it's just a matter of timing your step. After counting and watching for a minute, you feel you've got it worked out and prepare to step aboard.

"Five, four, three, two, one, step," you count.

For a split second you think you've made a mistake, but then you feel something solid beneath your feet. Your knees bend slightly and you are plunged into darkness as you rise up the shaft.

"But how do I get off?" you mumble to yourself. "I should have asked someone."

Your hand tightens around the cable. You can feel it vibrating as you climb. Every fifty feet or so, you move past an opening and can see out of the shaft into what must have been mine workings many years ago. Now they are just empty chambers, with ventilation holes overlooking the valley below.

You hear voices from above. The top can't be far away. Light is starting to penetrate down the shaft from above and the sound of a drum whirling the cable back down is getting louder.

An opening appears. You jump.

Your landing in the command pod isn't graceful, but at least you've made it. You hear chuckling and see three slider officers looking at you.

"Welcome miner," one of the men says. "You have a message for us I believe."

"Yes, for the Highland Council."

"Well spit it out."

You look at the slider officer. "Are you on the council?"

The officer looks down at the three cut diamonds pinned to his chest. "See those stars?"

You nod.

"Know what they mean?"

You shake your head.

"It means I'm chief of the Highland Council. Don't they teach that at mining school these days?"

"Sorry, no," you say, a little embarrassed.

"Well come on. What's the message?"

You give him the message about joining the Lowland Federation. You tell him about the offer of education and healthcare ... and the tax. You also tell him about the Lowlanders' threat, and how the one you spoke to seemed extremely confident in their new technology.

The council chief's face takes on a stony appearance as he considers what you've said. "Our spies have seen these machines. But I can't imagine the members of the council agreeing to the Lowlanders' terms. Highlanders have been fiercely independent for generations and we don't take kindly to threats."

"But what about the healthcare, education and other benefits they offer?" you ask. "Aren't they worth considering?"

"We have education."

"Not a very good education it seems."

The chief scowls at you. "I'm not sure I like your tone."

"Why can't we talk peace?" you say. "Do we have to keep this hatred going just out of pride?" You look up into the chief's brooding face. "How many will die in this war? All of us?"

The chief isn't used to people standing up to him. He stomps his foot and snarls like he's about to bite his tongue off and spit it at you. "How dare you!"

You take a step back as spittle flies in your direction. The man is grinding his teeth and growling like a wild animal. "Sliders never surrender!"

"And in my family we never enter a fight unless we know we can win!"

This makes the chief pause. He harrumphs and walks to the far side of the pod and looks out the window at the shadowed slopes below. It seems an age before he turns around and faces you.

"Do you really think we could lose everything?"

"I don't know," you say. "But even if there is the slightest chance of that happening, is it worth the risk? And if by some stroke of luck we do come out on top, how many of your friends will die in the process?"

Once again the chief's face turns to stone. You can almost see him thinking. "You're pretty plucky for a miner," he says a minute or so later.

"I come from generations of sliders, remember."

Finally you get a little smile from the chief. "Okay, get back to your pod. I'll speak to the council and see what they say."

When you arrive back at the accommodation pod, the others are eating. You grab some broth and take it over to sit with Piver and Shoola.

"So what's up?" Piver asks.

You fill them in on your meeting with the council chief.

"You think they'll talk peace?" Piver asks. "It would be the first time in three generations."

"I don't know. I just hope that the council can see the bigger picture. Life is tough enough on the slopes without having to fight all the time."

"I have a cousin who is a Lowlander," Shoola says.

"Really?" Piver asks. "How did that happen?"

"He just slid off one day and disappeared. Seems he'd met a girl from one of the border tribes during a trade meeting and fell in love."

Piver's eyes grew wide. "And he never came back?"

"He did some years later. Tried to tell everyone that the Lowlanders were just like us, but the people in the communities wouldn't listen."

"So what happened?" you ask.

"He had no choice but to go back down the mountain. It broke his family's heart."

The three of you sit in silence for a while, sipping your broth, lost in your own thoughts.

"Just like us?" Piver finally said.

Shoola nodded.

Piver looked confused. "Then why are we fighting them?"

Shoola shrugged her shoulders. "I think it's been so long, everyone has forgotten why we started."

Later, you think about what Shoola has said as you fall asleep on your bunk.

The next morning you are awoken by someone shaking your shoulder.

"What?"

"Come with me," a slider says. "Chief wants a word."

You get up and dress quickly. The slider leads you towards the cable-lift.

When the two of you reach the command pod there are twelve people sitting around a large table.

The chief waves you to a seat near one end. "Please sit."

You wonder what is going on. Everyone is looking at you.

The chief clears his throat. "This is the young miner I told you about." Eleven faces swivel towards you. "We've sent a delegation to talk peace with the Lowlanders. They left at first light this morning."

You can't help but think they've done the right thing.

An older woman stands up and walks towards your seat. She places her withered hands on your shoulders. "I am an old woman, but I know a clever mind and a good heart when I see one."

You look up into her clear green eyes.

"I want you to take my seat on the council young miner. We need new blood. Blood untarnished by years of conflict."

Is she talking about you joining the council? Surely not. What experience do you have?

"But…"

"Quiet," the old woman says. "It's time the council heard the truth. And you, young as you are, are the first person to give it to them."

"If the Highlands are to prosper, we need to stop putting so many of our resources into fighting the Lowlanders. Joining The Federation of Lowland States might be just the opportunity we are looking for."

Heads around the table are nodding in agreement.

"So do you accept the appointment?" the chief says to you.

"I ... I'm a bit..."

"Surprised?" the chief says

"Geebus!" you say, using Piver's favorite exclamation. "Now there's the understatement of the century."

A light chuckle runs around the table.

"So what do you say?" the old woman asks. "Will you help us steer the Highlands towards peace?"

You think for a moment and search the faces before you.

"Well ?" the chief says. "Are you up to the job?"

You think about your family and how proud they would be if you were to become a member of the council. How their disappointment at you deciding to become a miner rather than a slider would wash away like pango droppings in a heavy rain.

"Of course I'm up for it. I come from good slider stock remember?"

Congratulations, this part of your story is over. You successfully helped start the peace process on your planet and became a member of the Highland Council, a great honor to you and your family. Well done! But have you followed all the possible paths? Have you gone to slider school? Gone down into a scary cave? Been caught in a storm?

It is now time to make another decision. Do you:

Go back to the beginning of the story and try a different path? **P219**

Or

Go to the List of Choices? **P380**

More 'You Say Which Way' Adventures .

Between The Stars

Pirate Island

Lost in Lion Country

Once Upon An Island

In the Magician's House

Secrets of Glass Mountain

Danger on Dolphin Island

Volcano of Fire

The Sorcerer's Maze Adventure Quiz

The Sorcerer's Maze Jungle Trek

The Creepy House

Dragons Realm

Dinosaur Canyon

YouSayWhichWay.com

List of Choices

SECRETS OF GLASS MOUNTAIN

(continued next page)

Please Review This Book at Amazon

If you had fun reading this book, please take a few moments to review it on Amazon.

These reviews help others decide if the book is right for them and give the authors valuable feedback.

Thanks from the You Say Which Way team here at the Fairytale Factory.

YouSayWhichWay.com

Printed in Great Britain
by Amazon